Sullivan's Evidence

Also by Nancy Taylor Rosenberg

Mitigating Circumstances

Interest of Justice

First Offense

Trial by Fire

California Angel

Abuse of Power

Buried Evidence

Conflict of Interest

Sullivan's Law

Sullivan's Justice

NANCY TAYLOR ROSENBERG

Sullivan's Evidence

KENSINGTON BOOKS
http://www.kensingtonbooks.com

KENSINGTON BOOKS are published by

Kensington Publishing Corp.
850 Third Avenue
New York, NY 10022

ISBN 0-7582-1506-1

First Trade Printing: May 2006
10 9 8 7 6 5 4 3 2 1

Printed in the United States of America

To Forrest Blake and Christian Gabriel Nesci

CHAPTER 1

St. Louis, Missouri

As the sun disappeared and darkness fell, death lurked in the shadows. Outside the winds were howling, causing the shutters in the cramped living room to rattle. Eleanor Beckworth headed to the bedroom to change into her nightclothes. Even when she wore her slippers, the cold hardwood floors chafed her feet. She was a petite woman. Her weight had never risen over one twenty. When she was younger, she stood almost five four, but now she was barely five feet. Age had not only shriveled her skin, it had compressed her spine.

Eleanor stopped walking, sensing something. The atmosphere in the room felt different. Was it a change in the barometric pressure? Maybe the storm they were predicting for tomorrow was moving in early. She hoped not, as her roof was badly in need of repair and the boiler was acting up again. Reluctantly, she had called her handyman, Mitch, today. She had space heaters, but she knew they weren't always safe, and she was terrified of fire. Maybe Mitch could patch the roof as he'd done the year before.

Eleanor tried to live on the money she received from social security, which was barely enough to pay the mortgage and buy groceries. She had twenty thousand in her savings account and a modest amount of equity in her house. She had pulled out most of the money over the years, but she wanted to leave something for her granddaughter when she died.

Glancing at Elizabeth's pictures lined up on the walls in the hall, she touched her finger to her lip, and then pressed it against her granddaughter's face. She'd raised the girl from the age of three after her daughter, Anna, had died of leukemia. Since Anna hadn't married the child's father, the young man had left town, never to be heard from again. Eleanor gladly served as Elizabeth's mother.

Elizabeth was such a darling girl, Eleanor thought, but terribly unlucky when it came to men. Her granddaughter had dated one young man for five years, letting him live with her in her apartment. The man had never contributed a dime, worked only a day or two a week, and refused to commit to a permanent relationship. Elizabeth had finally had no choice but to toss the freeloader out. Her little heart had been shattered.

Men living off women! Eleanor thought in disgust. She remembered the days when a man opened your car door, took you out for a nice dinner, treated you like a lady. They didn't swoop down like vultures on lonely women, use them like prostitutes, then take off as soon as they got bored or decided there was nothing more they could take.

"Oh, well," she said, entering the bathroom. She hung her clothes on a hook so she could wear them the next day and stepped into her blue flannel nightgown. Once she had removed her dentures and was bundled up in her bathrobe, she performed her nightly rituals: checking to make certain all the doors and windows were locked, watering the plants on a ledge above the kitchen sink, then selecting the pills she took every night and placing them inside a plastic lid.

Eleanor had always thought her granddaughter would live close by. She glanced at the clock and wondered why Elizabeth hadn't called yet. They spoke on the phone once a week, and Sunday was her night to call. Eleanor rarely phoned Elizabeth, as the girl sometimes talked for hours, and Eleanor couldn't afford to run up her bill calling California. Elizabeth must have lost track of time. She was a computer technician who worked out of her home.

When the phone rang, Eleanor rushed over and grabbed it. "Is that you, darling?" she said. "I was worried I wasn't going to hear from you tonight."

"I'm sorry I didn't call you earlier, Mom," her granddaughter said.

Since childhood, she had called Eleanor "Mom." "Matt and I had a terrible fight."

"Oh my," Eleanor said, "I thought your marriage was working out wonderfully."

"So did I," Elizabeth said, her voice cracking with emotion. "Matt's not the man I thought I married, though."

"Dear, dear," Eleanor said, taking a seat on a stool beside the phone, saddened by what she was hearing. "Maybe you've been on your computer too much and not paying him enough attention. A man needs to be doted on, honey. I'm sure you'll work things out. Where's Matt now?"

"I don't know. He got so angry, Mom. I've never seen him that mad. He's been stomping around all day. About an hour ago, he left without telling me where he was going."

"It might make him even angrier if he hears us talking, honey. What goes on in a marriage should remain between a husband and wife. No man wants people poking around in his private affairs."

"You're right," her granddaughter said, sighing. "I'm sorry I said anything." She paused, then whispered, "I think I hear Matt now. I'll call you next week."

"I love you," Eleanor told her, hating to end the call so abruptly.

"I love you, too, Mom."

Eleanor was asleep when she heard a noise. Glancing at the clock on the table by the bed, she saw that it was a few minutes past five in the morning. She was certain the noise she heard was the garbage truck, but she decided to check. Putting on her robe and slippers, she made it halfway down the hall when she saw a large, dark figure standing in front of her. "Get out of here!" she shrieked, her hand over her chest. "I have a gun. If you don't leave, I'll shoot you."

As she turned to run back to the bedroom to call the police, the intruder grabbed her around the neck, then released her. She fell face first onto the wood floor. The man was on top of her, his hot breath in her ear. "My purse is in the kitchen," she panted, pain shooting through her left hip. "There's cash . . . take it . . . you can buy drugs with it."

"Drugs, huh?" the man said, wrenching her arms behind her. "I don't need drugs. Killing is a natural high. Are you afraid to die? You should be."

He rolled off and yanked her to her feet. She sank against his arm, unable to stand. "I think my hip is broken," Eleanor said, moaning. Breaking a hip at her age was worse than a heart attack. If she couldn't care for herself, she would have to go into a nursing home. "I'll never walk again, you evil man," she spat at him. "God is going to strike you dead."

"Really?" he said, grabbing a handful of her hair and pulling her along behind him. "If there was a God, he would have struck me dead already. The things I've done, the things I've gotten away with. Shit, killing an old woman like you is like swatting a fly."

When they reached the bedroom, he picked her up and tossed her on the bed. Eleanor made a frantic move to grab the phone, but the man ripped it from the wall. The phone tumbled to the floor with a loud thud. She saw the awful man wrapping the phone cord around his wrist, and scooted up close to the headboard to get away from him. "Oh, no, please!" she pleaded. "Help me! Please have mercy on me!"

He squared his shoulders and faced her. The seconds ticked off inside her head. Through a crack in the blinds, a beam of light from a passing car struck his face. "You!" Eleanor shouted, her body shaking in terror and outrage. "For the love of heaven, it can't be you!"

The man circled to the side of the bed, leaping on top of the mattress behind her and planting his feet on either side. "Your eyesight is pretty good," he said, bending over and wrapping the cord around her neck. "Too good."

He twisted the cord in his hands, watching as it cut into the crinkly skin on Eleanor's neck. Placing his foot on her collarbone, he extended his leg, pushing her toward the foot of the bed until she began to struggle. "Sorry you're not happy to see me," he said. "I'm the last person you'll ever see. Don't blame yourself. I was going to kill you even if you didn't recognize me."

Eleanor tried to scream but couldn't. There was no air. Her body buckled, her eyes felt as if they were going to burst out of their sockets.

"Just relax, old girl. It'll be over in a few minutes. All you're going to do is take a long nap." The attacker stood, the muscles in his leg shaking from exertion until Eleanor's body became limp and lifeless. He stared down at her, wiping his mouth with the back of his hand. Once he was certain she was dead, he wrapped the cord around the bedpost and tied it into a knot. His victim's head dangled several inches off the pillow.

Jumping off the bed, he tossed the electric blanket over the body, turned on the bedside lamp, and began rummaging through Eleanor Beckworth's drawers and closets.

CHAPTER 2

Ventura County Corrections Services Agency
Ventura, California
Thursday, September 14—2:10 P.M.

"Have you heard anything about the DA's office cutting a deal with Robert Abernathy?" Carolyn Sullivan asked her supervisor. As usual, she had walked into his office unannounced. Anyone else would have been tossed out. Most people knew Carolyn had been a close contender for Brad Preston's job and that the two of them almost ran the unit in concert.

"What happened to your hair?" he said, moving a stack of file folders to clear a spot on his desk. Outside his open door, phones jangled and voices rang out, mixing with the brushing sound of shoes moving rapidly across carpet.

Carolyn ran her fingers through her new short haircut, causing several curls to stand up on top of her head. She would turn forty next year. From someone who'd never given much thought to her appearance, she'd changed into one who tried on three or four outfits each morning before deciding what to wear. Her once slender hips and waist had expanded, and her clothes were not only snug, they seemed as if they belonged to a much younger woman. She wasn't sure what a woman approaching forty was supposed to wear, and she was convinced that she'd suddenly become hideously ugly. Today she was wearing a cream-colored dress that was a hand-me-down from her mother. "I went to Supercuts on my way home yesterday, okay?" she told him. "I wanted to look like Meg Ryan."

Preston flashed a smile. "I kind of like it. It makes you look cute and innocent, something we both know you're not. I'm sure you'll be a big hit at the jail. From the way you're dressed today, I gather you've given up trying to get criminals to talk by dressing seductively."

"I've given up a lot of things," Carolyn said.

"Abernathy's got you down, huh?" he said. "Take a seat."

Brad Preston was an exceptionally handsome man. His blond hair was fashionably cut, his eyes a vibrant blue, his skin bronze and unlined. He was a natural athlete, but more than anything, Brad was a thrill seeker. The walls were lined with photographs of him standing in front of high-powered race cars.

Carolyn walked over and flopped down in one of the two blue chairs facing his desk, inhaling the scent of freshly brewed coffee. Brad's assistant, Rachel, made him a pot every morning, using the gourmet blends he brought from home. His favorite was vanilla mocha. He offered her a cup, but she declined. "One of the DA's investigators said they were going to let Abernathy plead guilty to two counts of tampering with evidence if he agreed to spend thirty days in a mental hospital," she told him, swinging her leg back and forth. "What happened to the perjury counts? Every case Abernathy processed evidence in is up on appeal. Jesus, he even handled the DNA testing on the Tracy Anderson homicide. The next thing I expect to hear is that Carl Holden is back on the streets."

"I'm sorry, Carolyn," Preston said, avoiding her eyes. "Holden's conviction was overturned almost two years ago. The DA's office decided not to try him again because they felt certain they couldn't obtain a conviction without the DNA evidence. After what's come to light regarding Abernathy's lab work, of course, it's been ruled inadmissible. If you recall, none of the surviving rape victims were able to positively identify him. The entire case hinged on the DNA."

Carolyn closed her eyes, appalled at what she was hearing. She had known it was bad, but she hadn't known it was this bad.

A fresh-faced woman in her mid-twenties walked into the room. "Harry's back from court," Rachel told Brad, referring to the agency's superior court officer, who represented other officers' recommendations on routine felonies, thus saving them the time of juggling scores of court appearances. "Do you want his report now, or do you want him to come back later? He said everything went pretty good. Walker's recommendation was the only one that didn't fly." She saw Carolyn in the chair behind her. "I'm sorry. I didn't realize you were in a conference, Brad. Should I close the door?"

"Please," her boss said, taking a swallow of his coffee.

Carolyn straightened up in her seat, her face frozen into hard lines. "Why didn't someone notify me about Holden?"

"I only found out myself a few months ago," Brad said, cracking his knuckles. "I knew how much it would upset you, so I decided there was no reason to tell you. Holden is only one in God knows how many cases that were affected. As far as Abernathy is concerned, it's taken the county years to unravel what he did and put together accurate accounts as to which cases were compromised. The man was the chief forensic officer for the county. The poor guy had a nervous breakdown. The cops and prosecutors put tremendous pressure on these people, and the amount of evidence they process is enormous. They aren't miracle workers. Abernathy decided to give them what they wanted, probably just to get them off his back." He cleared his throat. "The DA didn't have much choice but to cut a deal with him. They want to keep as tight a lid on this thing as they possibly can. The only person willing to testify was Warner Chen, and Abernathy's attorneys have painted him as a disgruntled employee who intentionally set out to discredit the boss so he could inherit his job."

"Why would they give Abernathy's job to Chen?" Carolyn asked him. "He went and blabbed everything to the press. They ran an article in the paper just last week. If the cat's already out of the bag, why let Abernathy skate?"

"They fired Warner Chen last week," Preston said. "That's when he got pissed and went to the press."

"Abernathy's not crazy, Brad. He's a lazy, incompetent moron. They say he didn't run tests on half the evidence that came into the lab. He simply fabricated reports, or he used the DNA samples collected from the suspects after their arrests, and then claimed they matched whatever was found at the crime scene. The man had a God complex. He probably got off on the fact that he could control who went to prison and who walked. Sure, he was influenced by the investigating officers, but there's no excuse for what he did. He should have received the same treatment as any other criminal. With his position and the opportunity it presented to destroy lives, if it were up to me, he would have received twice as long a sentence as the average offender." She slumped back in her chair, disgusted with the whole situation. "This is a disaster. Now even I don't have faith in the system."

Preston tapped his pen against his teeth. "We cut deals with murderers all the time. Why not one of our own? I'm not saying I agree, just that I understand why the DA's office felt they should run damage control. The more this is played out in the media, the more cases will come up on appeal. The courts are already swamped. How can we come up with the resources and manpower to retry half the crimes committed during the eleven years Abernathy ran the lab?"

Carolyn didn't answer. Discounting Robert Abernathy's gross misconduct, forensic evidence was not always accurate for a variety of reasons. Samples could be corrupted, or too small for the necessary tests to be conducted. Evidence could be contaminated at the scene or during processing at the lab. Sometimes equipment malfunctioned. Bias was another problem, as demonstrated by Abernathy's desire to please the police and prosecutors. Courts and juries had learned to rely so heavily on forensic evidence, particularly DNA, which was presented as irrefutable, that eyewitness testimony, logic, and material facts were no longer sufficient to bring in a conviction.

Preston stared up at the ceiling, then slowly met her gaze. "I have more bad news. Holden's been convicted of a new crime. I want you to handle the report. The offense is destruction of private property. Judge Reiss placed him on summary probation, so no one's asking you to supervise him."

"Summary probation!" Carolyn exclaimed, bolting to her feet. "Carl Holden is a serial rapist and murderer. And you're telling me Reiss didn't think someone should actively supervise him? We've got a violent criminal on the street and no way to keep tabs on him. He's not even on parole. Christ, how irresponsible can we get?"

"I assigned the case to you for two reasons," Brad said, forging ahead despite her outburst. "Since you handled the original investigation eight years ago, you know Holden better than anyone else. A little intelligence gathering might come in handy if he commits another act of violence in the future."

"I don't want to gather intelligence on him," Carolyn said, crossing her arms over her chest. "Let Judge Reiss gather intelligence on him." Realizing she was being unreasonable, she added, "Fine, give me his file. I'll do the best I can." Her thoughts turned to the murder victim's husband. "Has anyone told Troy Anderson?"

"I assume the DA did," Preston said, entering the case assignment into his computer.

Carolyn walked over to his desk and picked up a framed picture of him with a young blonde, standing next to a race car. "New trophy?" she asked, showing it to him before she placed it back on his desk.

"Not recently," he said, answering without looking. When he finally saw what she'd been referring to, he laughed. "That's my mechanic, Trixie. Want to see one of the girls I've been dating?"

"I'll pass," Carolyn answered. The fact that he'd referred to her as a girl was enough.

The Carl Holden case had been one of the first major crimes Carolyn had handled as an investigative probation officer. The woman he'd murdered, Tracy Anderson, had been a thirty-six-year-old housewife. Carolyn had recommended that Holden be sentenced to thirty-two years for the combined total of the four rape convictions, plus the indeterminate term of twelve years to life on the homicide. The judge had imposed her recommendation, which totaled forty-four years. Holden had served eight.

"What's the destruction of property about?"

"Some guy jumped him in a bar," Brad said, placing his arms behind his neck. "In the ruckus he pushed Holden into a plate-glass window. The culprit skipped before the cops got there, so the owner of the bar filed a complaint against Holden."

Carolyn snorted. "He made a scene in the courtroom when he was sentenced on the original crimes, in case you've forgotten. He claimed I betrayed his trust, that I twisted the statements he made during the interview to convince the judge into imposing a longer sentence. Just so you know, Holden hates me. I doubt if he's going to tell me any secrets." She was about to walk out when he called out to her.

"I scheduled Holden for four-thirty tomorrow."

"Damn," Carolyn said, "now I'll have to stay late on Friday night. The least you could have done is let me decide when I wanted to see him. Thanks, Brad, thanks a lot. You're a real sweetheart." He had that stupid grin on his face that she despised. He tried to look serious, but the corners of his mouth and the glint in his eyes gave him away. Brad saw life as a series of adventures. In the right context, it made him seem boyish and appealing. At the moment, she felt like slugging him.

"Just trying to make things easier for you."

"Don't do me any more favors, okay?" Carolyn said, disappearing through the doorway.

She was sitting at her desk, about to open Carl Holden's file, when Veronica Campbell stepped up behind her and said, "What's going on?" ruffling her hair.

Carolyn spun her chair around, relating what she'd just heard about Robert Abernathy, as well as the fact that she would be seeing Carl Holden the next day. "Norton at the DA's office told me victims have been calling them nonstop since the story broke last week," she continued. "They're trying to figure out if Abernathy was involved in their cases. I don't know why the D.A.'s office thinks they're covering up anything since it's been in all the papers."

"There's plenty of people in prison who won't hear about it," Veronica told her, taking a seat in the chair beside Carolyn's desk inside the cramped space. "Not if they squash it now. Most of them are probably guilty anyway. Didn't you handle cases other than Holden where Abernathy processed the evidence? I had a ton of them."

"Of course. Holden is the first murderer to be set free, though. What about you?"

An outspoken woman in her late thirties, Veronica had a daughter almost the same age as Carolyn's son, John, as well as three other children, aged eight, five and two. She wore her frizzy blond hair short, had a round, friendly face, and was about twenty pounds overweight, most of it left over from her last pregnancy. The two women had known each other since grade school. They didn't always agree on everything, but they were best friends. "Remember that child mutilation I handled last year?"

"The eight-year-old boy, right?"

"Billy Bell," Veronica said, pulling a tissue out of her sweater and blowing her nose. "This is the umpteenth cold I've had this year. Drew has it too, and the baby's been up three nights with the croup."

Not wanting to listen to her ramble on about her husband and children, Carolyn prompted her, "The case . . ."

"It's on appeal right now. Davidson at the DA's thinks we may lose the conviction on Lester McAllen. Billy's mother committed suicide after the . . ." Veronica's eyes glazed over, and the area around her mouth grew pale. "Well, you know . . . losing a child that way. I mean, not many women could withstand that kind of pain."

"This one got to you, didn't it?" Carolyn said. "Why didn't you go to Brad and ask him to reassign it?"

"This is the job, you know," she said, rubbing her finger across her eyelid. "The father owned a painting business. They struggled for years to have a baby. The wife took fertility drugs. When the doctor told them it was going to be a multiple birth, they opted to abort all but one fetus. After Billy was killed, I'm sure they had regrets about that. They were a nice, middle-class family. The mother worked for a bank, and the father owned a painting business. They worshiped that kid. When I called to tell him about Abernathy, he said he'd had to file bankruptcy. He wasn't even sure he could keep his house."

Carolyn's eyes expanded. "You called him?"

"I call all the victims on the cases I handle as soon as I verify they were involved," Veronica said, leaning her chair back against the partitioned wall. "The victims have a right to know. Even the ones who read the articles in the paper may not fully understand the implications. I mean, a forensic scientist falsifying and tampering with evidence doesn't say much to people outside the system. Tyler Bell didn't think it had anything to do with him because the man who killed Billy was already in prison."

Veronica leaned forward and opened one of the drawers in Carolyn's desk, rummaging around to see if she had any food, then closing it when she saw it was empty. Carolyn was always munching on something—raisins, nuts, granola bars. Recently, she'd become a die-hard chocoholic. She usually had two or three candy bars stashed away, and Veronica would occasionally sneak in and steal one.

"I'm sorry I don't have any comfort food," Carolyn told her. "I ate the last Hershey bar yesterday and forgot to go to the store to pick up some more."

"It's all right," Veronica said, standing. "A candy bar isn't going to fix things. I need something that will make me feel better for longer than two minutes. I'm trying to dig up some old charges or something to slap McAllen with if he gets out. With guys like that, you know there's always something left hanging when they get shipped off to prison."

After Veronica walked off, Carolyn stared out the window at the parking lot. A desk with a window was highly coveted, and she'd earned hers by seniority. Veronica used to work in the cubicle next to hers. She'd lost her spot after taking two years off to stay home with the baby. Beyond the parking lot, Carolyn could see the Ventura foothills. If the building had faced the other direction, she would have had a partial view of the ocean.

She thumbed through Holden's file. When she reached the autopsy photos of Tracy Anderson, she started to set them aside, then forced herself to look at them. When the job became overwhelming, the lifeless bodies of victims reached out from the photographs and spoke to her. She reminded herself that this was the last stop on the train. By the time a case reached her desk, the police had concluded their investigation, the DA had successfully brought in a conviction, yet the most important part of the process was still to come—determining the extent of the punishment. And it was here that she had the chance to make a difference.

Carolyn was certain Holden had killed other women, burying their bodies where no one would find them. How could such a vicious criminal be back on the street? She placed her palm on her forehead, contemplating what Abernathy had inflicted on those no longer alive to protest. She felt great compassion for the families, but the victims were her boss. When she went to deposit her paycheck, she didn't see the numbers or the county insignia. Unlike others, she never complained about her salary. The modest salary she made seemed more than adequate. Far too many of the victims had paid with their lives.

The system had failed Tracy Anderson, just as it had failed Billy Bell. Carolyn was a part of the system. Eight years for snuffing out the life of a vibrant young woman was not justice, nor was it the forty-four-year sentence the court had ordered Carl Holden to serve at her recommendation. Now a job she'd thought was done had been undone. She had a lot more work to do for Tracy Anderson.

To clear her head, Carolyn headed to the break room for a cup of coffee. She heard a phone ring two or three times, then abruptly stop, not followed by the sound of someone speaking. People were letting their voice mail pick up. In most instances, probation officers answered calls when they came in so they wouldn't have to track down callers later.

A cloak of silence seemed to have fallen over the entire agency. No one seemed to be making calls, either—calls to set up appointments with defendants or victims, to talk over cases with police officers and prosecutors, even to check to see if their kids got home from school safely. She glanced inside the cubicles as she passed, seeing her fellow probation officers either intently reading or staring at their computer screens. Her coworkers were probably searching for old warrants, probation violations, other jurisdictions that might have charges still pending against an offender. They were all trying to right the overturned ship, or maybe come to turns with their anger.

CHAPTER 3

Thursday, September 14—3:45 P.M.

Robert Abernathy shuffled to his bronze Acura in the parking lot of the Ventura County government center. He had thirty days to get his affairs in order before he surrendered to Bollinger's Psychiatric Hospital in San Francisco. At fifty-eight, he was a heavyset man with a round, jowly face and thinning gray hair. His deeply set eyes were obscured behind dark glasses. The inexpensive brown suit he was wearing was wrinkled, its underarms stained with perspiration. Today's meeting at the DA's office had lasted four agonizing hours.

The past two years of his life had been a nightmare. He was partly responsible that it had gone on this long. He'd steadfastly refused to admit any wrongdoing. Experts from all over the country had been brought in to dismantle his lab and review every piece of evidence he and his technicians had ever processed. He had only falsified or tampered with a few cases. Even one would have been enough, however, to make his entire body of work unreliable.

When Abernathy reached his car, a deep voice called his name, and he turned around. A large, dark man wearing what appeared to be a white baseball cap stood in the middle of the road about ten feet away. Abernathy quickly ducked inside his car and sped out of the parking lot, thinking the man was another newshound.

As he traveled down Victoria Boulevard toward his home in Oxnard, he noticed a pickup in his rearview mirror that appeared to be following him. He tried to see if the driver was the man he'd seen earlier, but all he could make out was a shadowy stick figure behind the wheel. His *Retinitis pigmentosa* was rapidly stealing his eyesight. First his peripheral vision had gone. Then, in the last five years, it was as if he were looking at the world through a straw. He'd tried to hide the problem, desperate to keep his job. Now he would travel the one-way road to blindness in disgrace, locked inside Bollinger's with a bunch of lunatics.

He turned down Clover Street and headed toward Orange Avenue, driving slowly as he hugged the steering wheel so he could see where he was going. He seldom varied his route, as when he did, he sometimes got lost and panicked.

Divorced for fifteen years, Abernathy lived alone in a modest, three-bedroom house. His adult daughter, Janie, resided in Irvine and spent Saturdays with him, taking him out to dinner since he could no longer drive at night. They still spoke on the phone, but she hadn't come to see him for over a month, mad about what he'd done. He'd consistently lied to her, telling her he no longer processed evidence and merely served as an administrator.

When he stopped at the light, Abernathy thought he saw the pickup again, but he couldn't be certain. His fingers trembled as he fired up a Marlboro. After a few puffs, he began coughing. He stubbed the cigarette out in the ashtray and rolled down the windows.

Fear that someone might try to harm him was one of the reasons his attorneys had argued in the plea agreement that he should be allowed to serve his time in a facility outside the local area. Although he dreaded being confined, at least he wouldn't have to constantly be looking over his shoulder.

Abernathy had refused to admit what his problem was to the prosecutors and county supervisors during the various negotiation conferences, much to the dismay of his attorneys. He decided it was better for them to think he'd suffered some type of breakdown than to tell them the truth, that it had gotten to the point where he could see very little, even through his microscope. He should have quit years ago when he first realized something was wrong with his vision. He was a stubborn man, though, and he loved his work.

He'd tried to assign most of the work to his senior technicians, but in the serious cases, the prosecutors and police would push to have him process the evidence personally, so he could appear in court and represent his findings as an expert witness.

How could he give up his work when everyone had suddenly developed a fascination with it? He'd gone from being an unknown guy in a lab coat to a celebrity, consulting on TV shows, giving speeches, writing articles for newspapers and magazines.

Warner Chen had been his right hand, and his right hand had turned against him. Chen had known what was going on, unlike some of the other lab technicians. Overnight he had suddenly grown a conscience. Then, after he'd blown the lid off Abernathy's life's work, he'd conveniently gotten himself a cushy deal where all he had to do was cooperate with the investigation. Now truckloads of criminals would have to be retried, and many cases would end up in acquittal. The county had done everything possible to keep the situation under wraps, but Chen had decided to spill his guts to the media. Abernathy hoped Chen enjoyed his sixty seconds of fame.

Abernathy carefully steered his car into his driveway. It was quiet when he opened the car door and stepped out. The street was lined on both sides with mature trees, and dense foliage encircled his house. He liked his privacy.

Most of the people on his block weren't home from work yet. Their yards were full of tricycles, jungle gyms, and other kid stuff, but the children themselves were all in day care. No one in his neighborhood had money for nannies, although the houses had steadily risen in value over the years. Even a house like his now sold for over five hundred thousand. He'd planned to sell when he retired and live off the profits. But the equity in his house was almost gone now. After he paid his attorneys, the small amount that would be left would go toward the twenty thousand in fines the state had assessed him as part of the plea agreement.

Fear coursed through Abernathy's body when he heard the same deep voice shout his name again. Through the tunnel of his vision, he saw a pickup parked across the street. Opening his gate, he scurried up the walkway. Footsteps. He turned around, seeing a dark figure looming over him.

"Are you Robert Abernathy?"

"What do you want?" Abernathy said, his voice shaking. "Get off my property."

"Just answer the damn question. Are you Robert Abernathy?"

"No," he said, turning and rushing toward his house. It must be a reporter. What did these idiots want from him?

The man remained on the sidewalk as Abernathy fumbled for his house keys. "Go away," he yelled, turning around and shaking his fist at the stranger. "You have the wrong person. If you don't leave now, I'll call the police. I don't know anyone named Abernathy."

"Oh, you know," the man said, pulling out a large black gun from inside his windbreaker.

"No! Please!" Abernathy pleaded just before the man pulled the trigger.

The force of the gunshot slammed him against the door. His body slid to the ground, his legs splayed out in front of him. His head fell forward onto his chest. Blood dripped onto his pants, forming a spreading pool on the concrete porch beneath him.

Abernathy would no longer have to worry about his mistakes, his finances, his failing eyesight, or the time he was scheduled to serve in the mental hospital. As he had wrongfully decided so many people's fate, someone had taken it upon himself to decide Robert Abernathy's.

Carolyn decided to leave early as she knew she would have to work late the following day. Her briefcase was packed with case files. She took work home almost every night. It was the only way she could stay on top of the constant influx of crimes and still spend time with her children. The traffic was surprisingly light, and she arrived at St. John's Catholic Church at five-fifteen. Parking her white Infiniti, she made her way to the side entrance of the building.

St. John's was a small parish and didn't have an evening mass during the week. Now and then Carolyn would go to the service at St. Bernadette's a few miles away. Her time was limited, though, and although she tried to partake of the sacraments as often as possible, she derived the greatest benefit from the quiet, solitary reflection she found inside an empty sanctuary.

Walking down the center aisle toward the first row, she genu-
flected, then entered and knelt to pray. Occasionally she would see
another man or a woman, and she always wondered if they were
praying for a sick family member, had recently lost a loved one, or,
like her, had come to atone for their sins.

Carolyn had taken a life. The shooting had been ruled self-
defense, and she was certain she wouldn't be alive today if she hadn't
acted as she had. The man she had killed had been a hardened criminal, a murderer, employed by an international arms dealer. Nonetheless, he'd been a human being, and she had ended his life in what
seemed like the blink of an eye. She didn't even remember making a
conscious decision to fire. That's the way it always went down, her
friends in the police department told her. In situations like the one
she'd been in, instinct took over.

People perceived her as a strong, even relentless woman, but underneath the fragile and idealistic child was still present, hiding deep
in her psyche. She longed to live in a beautiful, peaceful world, where
people were kind and respectful, and where guns, war, and violence
didn't exist.

The stress of the day began to melt away. Inside this place there
seemed to be a modicum of hope, something to keep her going at
least one more day.

But when Carolyn walked outside fifteen minutes later, reality
smacked her squarely in the face. A man across the street was washing what looked like a late-model black BMW, and a tow-haired little
boy was using a large, soapy sponge to help Daddy scrub the wheels.
She heard a string of profanity, then saw the man yank the child by
the arm. "I told you not to get water on my pants, you little shit!" he
shouted. "Get back down there and get those wheels clean, you hear
me?" He let go of the child's arm, causing the youngster to tumble to
the pavement on his side. The little boy scrambled back to his feet
and began scrubbing harder on the chrome-plated wheels his father
seemed to value more than he did his son.

Carolyn reached into her handbag and pulled out a small notepad,
jotting down the address and license plate of the BMW to give to social services to investigate for child abuse. Just then the little boy

turned around and smiled brightly at her, as if nothing whatsoever had happened.

The calm she'd experienced inside the church evaporated. If she were God, she decided, she would take the world down and start over.

CHAPTER 4

Carolyn had spent the day reading trial transcripts, making calls to schedule appointments, and organizing her calendar. Now that her desk was fairly clean, she pulled out Carl Holden's file again to prepare for their four-thirty meeting.

One of her old ID cards slid out. She had no idea what it was doing there. Looking at her picture, she recalled how young and naive she'd been. She winced, seeing how her lovely chestnut hair had perfectly framed her oval face. At the time she'd interviewed Holden, she'd resembled a girl in her late teens or early twenties.

She thought about the young women she'd seen Brad squiring around town. Their skintight pants hung on protruding hipbones, and they pranced around with their midriffs exposed like belly dancers. Carolyn's stomach was marred with stretch marks from giving birth to two nine-pound babies.

She studied the mug shot of Carl Holden from eight years ago. She remembered how, wanting to make an impression on her supervisor, she had decided to interview Holden face to face rather than behind the glass, where she'd be protected. The rooms inside the jail didn't resemble the interrogation rooms at the police department, or the spacious facilities depicted in TV and movies. Most of them were eight by ten, close enough that an officer could be seriously injured or even killed by a violent perpetrator.

Relaxing into her chair, Carolyn pulled out the original report she'd written on Holden. She came across a stack of her handwritten notes, which no one else would be able to decipher. Even back then she didn't use a tape recorder like most of her coworkers. Criminals knew not to talk when their words were being recorded. Of course, many probation officers, unlike Carolyn, didn't care what the offender had to say. Their only objective was to finish their report and move on to the next case.

Although she carried a yellow pad and a pen, she never used them during the actual interview. She was fortunate in possessing something close to total recall. As soon as she left, she would scribble down what the offender had said. She had her bag of tricks that she'd refined over the years to entice criminals into opening up and providing her with incriminating information, but she had never once cheated, claiming a criminal had confessed something he had not said. Over the years, she'd established a unique style, more along the lines of a conversation between two friends. The fact that offenders frequently mistook probation officers for social workers, ministers, or public defenders also worked in her favor.

She studied her notes. In one of the margins was what appeared to be an address. Closing her eyes, she drifted back eight years to the day she'd been locked inside that claustrophobic room with Carl Holden.

She could remember the feel of the cold chair underneath her dress. Holden had been her first murder case, and she'd been nervous. The man in front of her didn't look like a killer. He could have been a neighbor, teacher, or friend. Carl Holden was tall and slender, with brown hair parted on one side and intelligent light eyes. The records indicated he was forty-four, but he appeared at least five years younger. Was it possible he could be innocent?

With the first words out of his mouth, the murderer appeared.

"Fresh meat," he said, his speech slow and deliberate. "Why did they send someone like you over here?"

"To ask you some questions," Carolyn said, speaking low so he would have to strain to hear her. Most of his criminal activities had been limited to rape. Tracy Anderson had changed everything. This time he'd raped and killed.

"Oh, I know why they sent you . . ." he paused to see if Carolyn would fill in the blank. When she didn't, he took a deep breath and exhaled the words, "You're not my type, little girl. I like them older, riper. If I took you, you'd flop around like those fish I used to catch at the lake."

Carolyn refused to let him unnerve her. "You've been convicted of four counts of rape and one count of second-degree murder," she stated. "Why did you kill Tracy Anderson? You didn't kill the other women you raped."

Holden ignored her, his eyes focused on a spot over her head. "When the fish couldn't breathe anymore, the tail would stop twitching, but it wasn't the end. One last pulse and then there was nothing. Do you believe in the Almighty, Miss . . . ?"

"Sullivan."

"Miss Sullivan," he said, leaning forward in his seat, "what do you think will happen to you when you die?"

"I'll go to heaven." Carolyn felt foolish for uttering such a childish response to a killer. Even though her statement had been somewhat automatic, drilled into her during the years she'd attended Catholic school, her belief in God was unshakable. Where or what precisely heaven or hell was, she couldn't say. Doubting that evil existed, however, was absurd. She was staring it in the face.

"Lies, my sweet, innocent one," Holden told her, startling the probation officer out of her thoughts. "When I put my fingers around their necks, there was life. Face flushed, eyes wide in terror, blood pumping as their lives slowly slip away with the tightening of my hand. Then there is no breath, no screams. The eyes close. No bright light comes down from heaven to take their soul away. Just darkness, that's all, not heaven. The last memory will be my ugly face. Do I look like God to you?"

"I didn't come here to discuss theology with you," Carolyn said, knowing she had to turn things around. She shouldn't have confronted him so quickly. The fact that he was a murderer, coupled with her youthful appearance, had caused him to believe he had the upper hand. Now she had to backtrack, attempt to establish some kind of rapport with him. "Did you grow up here in Ventura?"

"Yeah," he said. "I went to Ventura High."

"So did I," she said, perking up as if she were excited. "Where did you live? We may have grown up in the same neighborhood."

He told her his mother's address, then added, "School was stupid. They didn't teach anything that mattered. Do you think I need to know algebra on the construction site? How to spell? It was a waste of my time."

"Why didn't you drop out?"

"Who says I didn't?"

"You seem to be an intelligent man, Carl," Carolyn told him, hoping flattery might open up the conversation. "I assumed you were a college graduate. Maybe you could have become something other than a construction worker if you'd taken your education seriously."

He became agitated. "The educational system is a form of governmental control. When I was fifteen, they gave me an IQ test. My score was in the top one percent in the nation. They said I was gifted. I agreed with them and stopped going to classes. From that day forward, I educated myself. My mother was very supportive."

"Your father wasn't around?"

"He took off when I was young," Holden said, a catch in his voice. "He didn't care about anything but himself."

"My husband's a teacher. I've always been interested in people who educate themselves." Carolyn had married Frank Polizzito as soon as she'd graduated from high school. They'd both enrolled in college, but she'd gotten pregnant three months after they married. After her son was born, she'd worked as a secretary so her husband could get his teaching certificate. At present, he was teaching high school English and working on his first novel, leaving little time for his wife and children. "What kind of books did you study?" she asked, tilting her head.

"Primarily ancient Greek and Roman philosophers," Holden said proudly. "You've heard of Titus . . . Titus Lucretius Carus? He argued, as I do, that there is no immortal soul and that people like yourself who accept traditional religious doctrines are being unacceptably superstitious. Are you superstitious, Ms. Sullivan?"

"I don't understand why a man as smart as you would rape and murder," Carolyn said. "What happened to you, Carl? What went wrong?"

"'He who is unable to live in society," he stated, "or who has no need because he is sufficient for himself, must be either a beast or a god.' We already know I'm not a god. It's my nature to be the beast."

"Plato?"

"Aristotle," he answered, a menacing look on his face. "I take pleasure in being the beast. It's almost second nature to me."

Carolyn's eyes darted around the room. She wanted insight, answers, details. "Have you ever heard of circumstances in aggravation and mitigation, Carl? Well, I'm the one who presents these to the court. Do you realize that you can be sentenced to serve your terms concurrently or consecutively? In my report, I determine these factors. Whether you realize it or not, I'm a very important person in what remains of your life. The more you cooperate with me, the more I might be willing to recommend a lenient sentence. Right now, I don't see any reason not to ask the count to stack the counts as high as they'll go. The number I came up with is forty-four years to life. How does that grab you?"

Holden fell silent, clearly stunned by her outburst.

"Tell me about your family," Carolyn said, hammering at him. "Were there problems at home that caused you to do these things? Do you really want me to write in my report that you take pleasure in being a beast? Statements like that indicate you have no remorse, that you committed these horrific acts for no reason whatsoever outside of self-gratification. Does such a person deserve mercy?"

"She was like my mother," he said, averting his eyes. "The side of her I wished I could forget."

Finally, she thought, she had broken through the wall. "Who was like your mother? Tracy Anderson?"

"Yes, but at a different time."

Carolyn listened to what he was saying. Every word had meaning. God, she thought, he'd killed more women than Anderson. Her mind replayed something he had said earlier that had failed to click. *When I put my fingers around their necks* . . . . He'd used the plural rather than singular form of the word *neck*. The only person that the police believed he had strangled was Anderson. His rape victims had injuries on their faces and torsos, but none had reported anything about Holden putting his fingers around their necks. She had to stay focused. He could be giving her valuable information, maybe even a clue as to where he'd buried his other victims.

"What about Tracy Anderson reminded you of your mother?"

"Her walk," he said. "The heavy purse she had strapped around her shoulder. There were hard things in there, things that could break bones. She would have hurt him. I had to strike before she did."

"Are you talking about Tracy Anderson's four-year-old son?"

"Sammy," he said, finding her eyes. "Is he okay?"

Carolyn decided to ignore his question. He had no right to ask about his victim's child. He must have been stalking her, though, as the boy was at his aunt's house at the time of the crime, yet Holden knew his name. "Is your mother still . . . alive?"

"I love my mother," he said with vigor. "I would never hurt my mother. She's my whole life."

"But she abused you as a child?"

"True," he mumbled. "It was for my own good. You know, to make me stronger. To stand up to the others."

"The others?"

"The kids at school made fun of me. I talked slow, and my back was arched, causing me to slouch over. They called me Turtle-boy. Mom was trying to help me. She hit me in the back all the time, sometimes with heavy objects. It hurt, but it was my fault. I was a pathetic wimp."

"You took your hatred out on these women because they reminded you of your mother?" Carolyn said, adjusting her position in the chair. "Is that a reason to rape and kill strangers? Don't you think your alcoholism played a role?"

"In every genius there's a madman." Holden told her, ignoring her question. "I can't explain what I did or what I'll do in the future. Aristotle said, 'All human actions have one or more of these seven causes . . . chance, nature, compulsions, habit, reason, passion, desire.' Which two do you think motivated me?"

"Compulsion and chance?" Carolyn said.

"Wrong," Holden said, his superior tone resurfacing. "Passion and habit."

Carolyn swallowed hard. Had he developed a habit of raping and murdering women? She'd never heard anyone express such vile acts as a habit. She recalled seeing something in the crime-scene photos that the police had written off as insignificant, and decided to question him about it. "Tell me about the golf glove. Did you leave it as a calling card?"

He smiled. "I'm afraid you'll have to figure that out for yourself."

Perverted bastard, Carolyn thought. "Did you rape or kill anyone other than Tracy Anderson?"

"That, too, you'll have to figure out," Holden told her. "Now run along now, little probation officer. Tell the court that I wanted to protect Sammy from his abusive mother, that my childhood was traumatic, that underneath I'm a person worth salvaging. That was our deal, wasn't it?"

"Sure," Carolyn lied, standing and pressing the button for the jailer. She would recommend they lock Holden up for as long as possible.

CHAPTER 5

Carl Holden appeared at the probation department fifteen minutes early. Carolyn told the receptionist to deposit him in an interview room. She intentionally made him wait, then walked toward the right side of the floor where a row of small rooms was located.

In addition to interviewing probationers, the officers used the rooms to dictate their reports to the word-processing pool. The rooms also served as a quiet place to collect their thoughts when the large, open room where they worked became too noisy.

Holden looked good, Carolyn thought, too good for a man who'd been behind bars for eight years. He'd been out for two years, though, so most of the jailhouse dust had blown away. He would be fifty-four now, but there was no gray in his brown hair and only a smattering of lines around his eyes and mouth.

She sat down in a chair at a small, round oak-veneer table. Holden wore a neatly pressed shirt and a pair of khaki pants. His appearance was so disarming, she momentarily forgot the horrendous crimes he'd committed. Then her gaze met his eyes, and her skin became clammy.

"You're all grown up, Carolyn," Holden said, grinning. One of his upper teeth protruded and reflected light from the overhead fixture. "Do you remember me? I remember you. I'm the guy you wanted to lock up and throw away the key. I know what you're all about. Such a pretty face, but underneath you're a spiteful, mean woman. You put an innocent man in prison."

"Look, Carl," Carolyn said, "I have no desire to play your games." She didn't give him time to reply. "Let's get something straight. Your sentence was overturned because of a stupid man. You and I both know you're not innocent, so cut the crap. The court placed you on twenty-four months' summary probation for this offense, with the added term that you must pay six hundred and fifty in restitution to the owner of Pete's Bar over the next six months. After today, you won't see me again unless you commit another crime. If you do, I'll make certain you're on the bus back to prison. Do you understand?"

Hatred shot from his eyes.

"Now," she continued, "where are you presently living?"

"I lost my job because I had to spend a day in the hospital after that guy shoved me through the window. Doc wanted to make sure I didn't have a concussion. My landlady evicted me when she found out I was a registered sex offender. My attorney was supposed to clear that up, but I'm still on the list."

Great, Carolyn thought. At least he was suffering some ramifications for his crimes. "Where are you sleeping? You don't look like you're living on the street."

"I stayed at the shelter last night," Holden said. "I knew I had to come see you, so I bought some new threads." He reached in his pocket and pulled out a stack of bills. "Count it," he said. "That's six hundred and fifty."

Carolyn picked up the bills, fanning them out like a deck of cards. "Where did you get this?"

"I didn't steal it, if that's what you're thinking," Holden told her, tipping his chair back on its hind legs. "I saved it from my job. The people where I worked are Koreans. I can always get another job pressing clothes. I plan to go back into the construction business. Just waiting for the right situation." He glanced at her left hand. "Where's your wedding ring? You ran him off, didn't you? No one likes to be married to a bitch, Carolyn. Didn't your mother teach you that?"

Her back stiffened. When Frank had failed to get his first novel published, he'd started sleeping with other women to bolster his confidence. A year later he became addicted to cocaine. He stopped seeing his children and never paid a dime of child support. "My personal life is none of your business."

"Oh, you're wrong there," Holden said, circling a finger around his mouth and licking it with his tongue.

His blatantly suggestive gesture made Carolyn sick to her stomach. She couldn't stand to be in the room with him a moment longer. The noise outside the door had died down. Some officers stayed until six, but most left around five. She shouldn't have made Holden wait. "Stay right here," she said, standing. "I need to give you a receipt. I didn't bring the right forms with me."

When she stepped outside the interview room, no one was around. Of course, she told herself, it was Friday night. No one worked late on Friday night. Now she was alone with a killer. She grabbed a cash-receipt book out of a steel cabinet in the supply room, banged the door shut, rushing back to the interview room to give Holden his receipt so she could send him on his way. When she yanked open the door, her mouth fell open.

Holden had disappeared.

Carolyn went to the lobby to see if he'd gone to the bathroom. Satisfied he'd left the premises, she returned to her desk to get her purse and briefcase. Her ears pricked when she heard faint footsteps on the carpet outside her partition.

Ducking underneath her desk, she opened her purse and removed her nine-millimeter, then pulled the chair back in place to conceal herself. Her fingers trembled on the safety. Releasing it, she pointed the gun through the legs of the chair. She'd already taken one life, and she knew Holden had more than earned a bullet.

The Ventura County government center complex was similar to a small city. The courts, district attorney's and public defender's offices, as well as the records' division, were all housed on the left side of a large, open space. A bubbling fountain stood in the center, surrounded by concrete benches. To the left were the probation department, the sheriff's department, and the women's and men's jails. The general public assumed that the two structures weren't connected, yet an underground tunnel was used to transport inmates back and forth.

The jail was actually a pretrial detention facility, and as a result of housing over one thousand inmates in a rated capacity of 412, the fairly new facility had the infrastructure of a thirty-year-old building. About eleven years ago the county had erected another detention center, the Todd Road Jail, in the city of Santa Paula. Todd Road was designed to hold over 750 sentenced male inmates.

Detective Hank Sawyer tapped a uniformed officer on the shoulder in the booking room at the main facility. A skinny black man, Alfonso Washington, was being photographed and fingerprinted. He'd robbed six liquor stores within a two-week period, and was a hard-core drug addict. A twenty-three-year-old officer, Danny Alden, had found him urinating in the bushes a few minutes after a new holdup was reported, an empty forty-five magnum in his pocket, along with the sixty-eight dollars the clerk had given him from the cash register. Since this was Alden's first major bust, Hank had met him at the jail to commend him. "I'm going to take off," Hank told the young officer. "Go back to the station and finish your report, then you can call it a night. Good work, ace."

Hank stepped outside into the brisk night air. He'd called the station earlier, and there wasn't much going on outside of the usual—domestic disturbances, traffic accidents, loud parties, drunk drivers—nothing of interest to a homicide detective. Of course, on Friday night, anything could happen. And there were many hours left before dawn.

Since his promotion to lieutenant over the crimes-against-persons division, Hank had shed thirty pounds. His once flabby stomach was now hard and flat. *Not quite a sixpack,* he thought, *but pretty damn good for forty-seven.* He lifted weights every morning and ran three times per week. Since none of his old clothes fit, he'd decided to splurge on a new wardrobe. When he'd been overweight, how he dressed didn't seem important. Now he enjoyed getting up every morning and stepping into a nice pair of slacks, a crisp, tailored shirt, and a tasteful tie. He glanced down at his shoes—real Italian leather. He'd also purchased several new sports jackets, one that had cost a bundle. The problem was he didn't have anywhere to wear his new clothes outside of work. He took a waitress named Betty out dancing now and then.

Reentering the building through another door, Hank climbed the stairs to the probation department on the second floor. Part of his fitness program was to park as far away as possible in a parking lot and always take the stairs instead of the elevator. Carolyn Sullivan was a workaholic, and there was a good chance she might still be in the office.

Hank remembered the first day he'd laid eyes on her. How long had it been? Eleven, maybe twelve years. He remembered seeing this fresh-faced girl walking across the courtyard, staring at her outside the window of the DA's office one day. Carolyn was a little thing, barely five four, and back then she'd worn spiked heels to appear taller. Her skin was pale and delicate. She didn't roast in the sun like most California women. The contrast against her chestnut hair was striking. But it was her big, soulful eyes that got him—that, and her smile, with those two adorable dimples. Getting them to appear, though, wasn't always easy.

The main door leading into the lobby was open. Generally the last person out locked it. Someone was still working. He stepped in and began making his way to Carolyn's partitioned cubicle. If she was here, she must be the only one. The place looked deserted. He saw her nameplate, but, glancing over the top of the partition, he didn't see her at her desk. As he started to leave, a voice shouted, "Stop or I'll shoot!"

Seeing the barrel of a gun poking out through the legs of a chair, Hank reached across his chest to remove his gun from his shoulder holster—and then he caught a glimpse of Carolyn's frightened eyes peering out at him. "Jesus, is that you?" he yelled. "It's Hank, for God's sake. What in the hell are you doing?"

Carolyn shoved the chair away and crawled out. Hank extended his hand to help her to her feet. "Is this the way you spend your Friday nights these days, cowering under your desk?"

She stood and smoothed out her cream-colored dress. She bent down again and retrieved her purse, dropping her gun inside. "What are you doing here? I could have shot you," she said.

"Oh, yeah?" Hank said, laughing. "I think it would have been the other way around. Who's the better shot, huh? How long has it been since you've fired that thing?" As soon as he said it, he regretted it. A little over a year ago, Carolyn had been in the car with him when he'd unknowingly driven into an ambush. A hardened criminal had taken aim on her while Hank was busy returning fire from other shooters. She'd had no choice but to defend herself. At point-blank range, the man had been killed instantly. This was the type of thing a person carried to their grave.

They both fell silent, Carolyn staring down at her desk. Hank spoke up. "Are you gonna tell me what went on just now, or do I have to beat it out of you?"

"Holden," she said, stuffing several files inside her briefcase. "Carl Holden's conviction was overturned because of the Abernathy fiasco, in case you haven't heard. He got busted on a minor offense, and Brad insisted I write the report."

"I remember Holden," Hank said, as he gazed at her inquisitively. He knew something was different about Carolyn, but he couldn't quite place what it was. At first he thought she had her hair tied up, and then he realized it was gone. "What happened to all your hair?"

"Don't ask," Carolyn said, scowling. She filled him in on how Holden had skipped out on the interview.

"At least you don't have to supervise him."

Carolyn looked at him distraughtly. "He belongs in prison, Hank."

The detective was no stranger to what she was experiencing. "So do thousands of others just like him, Carolyn. You can't let the job get to you this way. If you do, you'll go insane." He smiled and rubbed his hands together, hoping to lighten things up. "So, are you seeing anyone new?"

"No," she said, sighing. "I haven't had a date in nine months. It's okay, though. I've been able to spend more time with the kids."

"Tell you what," Hank said. "Why don't we grab some supper."

"Oh, Hank," she said, leaning forward and pecking him on the cheek. "You're such a great friend. I don't know what I'd do without you. Just give me a minute to call and get the kids squared away." She dialed her home number and left a message. Turning back to him she said, "Rebecca was supposed to go her friend's house after school, but she should be home by now. John's probably in his room with the door closed." She tried her daughter's cell phone but hung up when the recording came on. "What's the use of buying them a cell phone?" she exclaimed. "They never answer it when you call them. I'll check in later. If they haven't scrounged up something to eat, I'll stop and get them something on the way home."

She collected her briefcase, and they headed to the elevator. Now it was her turn to ask Hank, "How about your love life? Got a new lady to go with that new body?"

"Not really." Hank's heart was pounding against his chest. Once they were inside the elevator, Carolyn leaned against the back wall. As soon as he pushed the button for the ground floor, he positioned himself beside her. A delightful odor drifted past his nostrils. Was it perfume, or simply the scent of her skin? He stared at the graceful line of her neck, the way her dress hugged her shapely body. "I'm surprised you're not involved with anyone," he said, fishing for information. "You seem to always have a man on a string and another in the wings."

"You know that isn't true, Hank," she told him. "Most of the men in my age bracket are chasing girls in their twenties. Besides, I've got two kids, an awful job, and a mountain of debt. Who would want to step into that picture?"

They brushed up against each other when Carolyn stepped in front of him to exit the elevator. He wanted to say something, but he didn't think the timing was right. She looked weary and tense. Maybe it was because he'd reminded her of the man she'd killed. Or perhaps it was because of her confrontation with Holden.

As they stood outside the entrance to the building, she said, "Are you still dating that waitress? What's her name?"

"Betty," Hank said. "I parked behind the jail."

"Can't we take my car?" Carolyn protested. "You know how nervous is makes me to ride with you after what happened."

"Look, you have to put what happened last year behind you. It was a freak incident, Carolyn. It's never going to happen again. Even I don't get into shoot-outs on a regular basis. Some of the guys on the force have never fired their weapon. This is Ventura, for Christ's sake, not South Central."

"Fine," she said.

Once they were on the road, he asked her where she wanted to eat. "Marie Callender's, Islands, Mario's, what's it gonna be?"

"El Torito," Carolyn said.

"El Torito it is, then," Hank said, thinking he'd have to make certain he stayed away from the chips. He could go off the diet every once in while, but he didn't want to make it a habit. The dispatcher's voice sounded over the radio, advising him that a detective with the Oxnard PD was trying to contact him. He punched in the number on his cell phone and soon heard the high-pitched voice of Sergeant Arty McIntyre on the speaker phone.

"We just found the body of Robert Abernathy," McIntyre said. "Looks like he was shot in the head. His daughter came over and found him after she couldn't get him on the phone. It's our homicide, of course, but I thought you might want to know."

"Are you certain it wasn't a suicide?" Hank asked, glancing over at Carolyn. "You know who he is, don't you?"

"Yeah. But there's no chance of it being a suicide. Neighbors said they didn't see or hear a thing. Abernathy's house is set back from the street with a high fence and a lot of greenery. The ME is already here. He thinks the guy's been dead since sometime yesterday. The killer must have caught him just before he unlocked his front door."

"I'll stop by in about an hour," Hank said, not wanting to give up his dinner plans with Carolyn. He copied down the address of the crime scene on a pad mounted on his dashboard. Turning to Carolyn, he said, "Guess Abernathy got what he deserved, huh? Have any idea who killed him?"

Carolyn shook her head, trying to sort through her feelings about what she'd just learned. Maybe Abernathy had genuinely suffered from some type of mental illness. Hearing he had a daughter made him seem more human. She'd only met him on a few occasions in the past, and he'd appeared to be an affable character, a man who enjoyed what he did for a living. She'd held such overpowering animosity for him that she felt as if she'd been the one to pull the trigger. "Just drive me back to my car," she told the detective. "We'll catch dinner another time."

"Hey," Hank said, "you aren't going to use this as an excuse to not ride with me again, are you? I told McIntyre I wouldn't stop by until later. There's no official reason for me to respond to a crime that went down outside of our jurisdiction. We can still go to El Torito. You're the one who's been so up in arms about Abernathy. You should be elated that someone bumped the sucker off. The DA was going to let him slide with a stint in a mental hospital."

"Maybe I was wrong and they were right," Carolyn said. She leaned over and touched the detective's arm. "I'd rather we go to dinner another time, Hank. Seeing Holden today was unnerving. Regardless of who's responsible for him being back on the street, he's going to kill again. That is, if he hasn't already. Holden doesn't care if he gets caught and shipped back to prison. He lives for it, understand? Killing is his hobby."

Hank dropped her off at her car at the government center, waited until she was safely inside, then gunned the big engine on his unmarked Crown Victoria and steered it in the direction of Oxnard. Rolling the windows down, he inhaled the night air, now thick with excitement.

As much as he'd wanted to have dinner with Carolyn, his disappointment had already faded. His blood pumped faster as he grew closer to the scene. He was eager to be a part of the event unfolding—the urgency of the investigators and the CSI team, the emergency vehicles with their flashing lights disrupting the quiet of a residential street, onlookers and reporters straining against the yellow police tape, hoping for a morsel of information or a glimpse of the dead body.

Death had a strange way of making a person feel alive. And stepping in on another agency's crime was the best. He didn't have to worry about writing reports, barking orders, or getting pissed that his people weren't paying enough attention to the fine details that could make or break a case. He could poke around, ask questions, shoot the breeze, and then, when the flurry of activity died down, take off and get himself something to eat. The food would taste better, the air would smell fresher. Afterward, he would go home and relish a hot shower while he replayed the night's events in his mind. Later he would drift off to sleep in his warm bed, grateful that it wasn't him being zipped inside a body bag and shoved into a frigid drawer at the morgue.

Hank screeched to a stop behind a row of police cars, clipped his gold shield to his belt, and leaped out of his car to head into the action.

CHAPTER 6

Friday, September 15—7:00 P.M.

The killer was dressed in a long, dark trench coat, a cowboy hat pulled down low on his forehead. The flattened section of land was perched on top of a hill, and the city stretched out below him. On the left stood the framed shells of future houses. Not large homes, but expensive because of the view.

How long did he have?

A few months back, he'd called the sales office and inquired when they would be starting on the second phase of the development. Some silly woman had wasted ten minutes of his time trying to convince him he should buy now, as the homes in the new addition would be fifty thousand more.

Walking back to the unpaved road, he counted off the paces to the grave. Once he was standing on top of it, he reflected on the night he'd buried her. So much time had elapsed, it seemed like another lifetime. Everything had gone well, far better than he'd expected. No problem with the authorities whatsoever. He had made few, if any, mistakes. He couldn't really consider the location an error. At the time, the spot had been in the middle of nowhere, a hill covered in scrub brush. Houses were everywhere now, as well as condominium complexes, apartments, parks, and shopping centers. Because of the ocean, the city could only expand in one direction. He looked behind him, wondering when the next moving equipment would appear and flatten that area as well.

Squatting down, he scooped up a handful of dirt and let it sift out between his fingers. She'd been a pretty girl—common, but attractive. She was far from brilliant, but then again, not at all stupid. He could have thrown the dice and let her live, but that wasn't how he operated. She was fine where she was, in the ground, just not in this particular ground.

He suspected there wasn't much left of her. *Good,* he thought, as she'd been heavy. Not overweight, just dead, and a dead weight seemed far heavier. In addition, the human body was cumbersome, with so many protruding parts. Even on the darkest of nights, it was risky to walk around with a body slung over your shoulder.

He stood, a fragrant breeze from the ocean brushing past him. Soon the air around him would stink of humanity—car exhausts, cooking odors, dirty diapers, garbage. He didn't have long before he would have to move her. But first he had to find another location. And how could he be assured that the same thing wouldn't happen again? He couldn't risk driving long distances carrying human remains. Another solution was required, something that would put an end to the problem, allowing him to move forward without having to always look over his shoulder.

By now, outside of the digging, it wouldn't require a great deal of effort. Time and insects had minimized his task. All he would need was a plastic sack.

Carolyn headed home, rock music blasting from the speakers of her ten-year-old Infiniti. She'd purchased the car three years ago at an auto auction run by the Feds to dispose of confiscated vehicles. The car had served her well, but she needed to take it in and get the brake pads changed. When she stopped, she could hear them rubbing against the drum. She'd gotten such a good price because the Infiniti had over a hundred thousand miles on it. Part of the reason she'd picked it was the dynamite stereo system that some drug dealer had probably paid a fortune for. Like everything else she owned, though, the car would soon need major repairs.

Her taste in music was eclectic, ranging from groups like the Fine Young Cannibals to Prince, Peter Gabriel, and Sting. There was a group of nuns who sang like angels called the Daughters of St. Paul, who produced their own music. It was far from boring religious music. Some of it you could even dance to, and the joy in their voices never failed to lift her spirits. She also liked blues singers like Etta James and John Lee Hooker.

Tonight she needed something that might rock her out of her present funk. She settled on Prince. She couldn't listen to him with Rebecca in the car because of his suggestive lyrics and profanity, so this was her secret. But after her frightening confrontation with Carl Holden, even the music couldn't dispel her gloom.

Turning into her driveway, she saw the real estate sign on her front lawn. The agent had told her it wouldn't be long before the home she'd raised her children in would be sold. Most people would be happy with the amount of cash she'd receive at the close of escrow. It was her home, though, and the thought of giving it up was depressing. So much had happened within those walls. Certain memories would linger for a while, then be forgotten once the familiar rooms were no longer there as a reminder.

The house had to go, Carolyn told herself. Her eighteen-year-old son, John, had been accepted at MIT. He'd graduated from Ventura High last year and had worked as a busboy at a local Italian restaurant all summer, trying to earn money for his education. He was slated to start school in the spring if Carolyn could come up with the necessary funds.

John was a brilliant young man, over six feet tall, with thick, dark hair, clear skin, and a likable, easygoing way about him. Girls flocked to him, but he found intellectual pursuits more interesting, although she was fairly certain he wasn't a virgin, as if any eighteen-year-old boy was these days. He'd worked hard throughout junior high and high school—she couldn't ask him to go to a less expensive university. Attending MIT was his dream. Yet, even with student loans and scholarships, his four years of college would cost over a hundred and fifty thousand. And then there was graduate school to consider. She wanted John to go as far as his intellect could take him.

A few years back Carolyn had attended law school, hoping she would have her own law practice by now and could earn enough money to pay for both of her children's education. She'd been unable to stretch her income as a probation officer to cover her tuition, however, and going to school and working while raising two teenagers on her own had turned out to be too difficult.

Her younger brother, Neil, had offered to chip in, but Carolyn had refused. As an artist, his income was unpredictable. Besides, Neil obsessed constantly about running out of money.

As soon as she clicked the release on her seat belt, her cell phone rang. "Hey," Neil said, "you haven't called me in almost a week. Mom's complaining, too. I need my big sister. Since I broke up with Melody, I'm here all alone."

"You were all alone when you were with Melody," she said, having formed a great dislike for that materialistic young woman. Neil would say anything to get attention, which was why he'd mentioned Melody, but she knew he'd long ago reverted to his bachelor traits and was now juggling a dozen women. She was the one who should be complaining about being lonely, at least as far as companionship with the opposite sex went.

Neil and Carolyn had an uncanny ability to read each other's minds. John, already a die-hard skeptic, insisted such a thing was nonsense. Since childhood, though, whenever sister or brother thought of each other, or one of them was in trouble, the phone would invariably ring. "Can I talk to you tomorrow, Neil? I just got home, and the kids may not have eaten."

"They'll live," he quipped. "God, Carolyn, you're not going to cook, are you?"

"Shut up," she said, laughing. "I'm a good cook, and you know it."

"I've eaten your stuff, remember?" Neil took a deep breath. "Poor Mom. If you don't call her soon, she's going to call the elder abuse hotline. When I talked to her last night, she said she didn't have much longer to live. I cried myself to sleep."

"Mother has been saying that for the past fifteen years, and you know it. I talked to her on the phone for an hour Wednesday night. I'm going over there Sunday with the kids. You're coming, aren't you?"

"You know I want to, Carolyn," he said, dramatically, pretending to be devastated. "Unfortunately, I have a showing. You and Mom need to spend some quality time together. You know—talk about whatever women talk about. Female problems, hairstyles, Depends."

"You're incorrigible, Neil." She smiled, always a sucker for his brand of humor. Then, "Wait a minute. I didn't see anything in the paper about you having a show this Sunday. You're lying so you don't have to drive Mother to mass. It's your turn, damn it. I pay all of her bills and do most of her grocery shopping."

"So?" he said. "You've lied to me before."

"When?"

"That time you said you were going to the store for milk, and bought candy, then hoarded it all for yourself."

"Jesus, Neil, I was only twelve."

"Olga just walked in the door. She's the Swedish model I've been painting. Cheekbones to die for, and the longest legs I've ever seen. Doesn't speak a word of English. I love it."

Carolyn hit the END button on the phone. They never said goodbye. They both instinctively knew when a conversation was over. She opened the car door and stepped out, gazing at her house. It was in need of a fresh coat of paint. John hadn't had the time to mow the yard lately, as he generally worked the lunch shift. The grass was high, and her once beautiful flower beds were nothing but dirt. When things got to her, she went outside and furiously pulled weeds. *At least that part's done,* she thought. Tomorrow she would try to find time to go to the nursery and pick up some bedding plants before the Realtor started showing the house.

Unlocking the front door and stepping inside, Carolyn tried to look at her home as a stranger would. She noticed that the furnishings were worn, and in several places the carpet was threadbare. The neighborhood was decent, though, even today. Ventura College was only a few blocks away, as well as the high school and several hospitals. True, the street wasn't as lush as some of the more pricey areas, and the nearby strip centers and buildings needed a face-lift. Still, it had been a satisfactory place to raise her children.

She headed to Rebecca's room. When she opened the door, the girl was moving her head back and forth to the music on her iPod as she painted her toenails blue. Carolyn pulled the earphones off her head. "Have you eaten, sweetie?"

"Nope." Rebecca said, uninterested.

"I'd thought about cooking some steaks, but I'm beat. What do you want me to pick up for dinner?"

"Nothing," the girl said, standing, then flopping down on her unmade twin bed. Clothes, magazines, school books, plates with old food on them, and other unidentifiable items were strewn all over the floor. The fact that her daughter refused to keep her room in order annoyed Carolyn, but she considered both her children's rooms their private space. If Rebecca wanted to live like a slob, it was her decision. All her mother asked was that she keep the door closed. Now, however, with the house on the market, things would have to change.

Rebecca toyed with her hair. "I figure if I don't eat, you can save money, and then maybe we won't have to move into a stupid apartment. My friends all live in houses. Only people on welfare live in apartments. Am I going to have to buy my lunch with food stamps now?"

"You're exaggerating," Carolyn told her. "Living in an apartment isn't anything to be ashamed about. We're downsizing, that's all. People all over the world are less fortunate than us. You should appreciate that you're not living in a cardboard box in the rain, having to rummage through garbage cans for food."

The girl rolled her eyes. "Please, Mother, if you start lecturing me again, I'm going to throw up. All you have to do is tell John to go to another school. Why does he have to go MIT? No one I know has ever heard of it. It's a geek school, right? Why doesn't he go to UC Santa Barbara? That's where I'm going."

"You'll be going to beauty school if you don't take your schoolwork more seriously," Carolyn told her. "And clean up this pigsty. The real estate agent is going to start showing people the house."

Rebecca kicked her backpack off the edge of the bed onto the floor. "So I'm a dummy, huh? Just because I think physics is boring, you think I'm a loser. I'm going to be a fashion designer, or a famous painter like Uncle Neil. I showed him some of my drawings last month, and he said they were great. He thinks I'm ready to work in oils."

Her mother glanced over at the easel in the corner, draped with dirty clothes. "It doesn't look like you're working on your art to me."

"I need supplies, okay?" her daughter argued. "I didn't ask you because I know they're expensive. Uncle Neil said he would give me some, but he must have forgotten. I don't want to draw anymore, I want to paint."

Carolyn remembered how her mother had belittled her brother when he was Rebecca's age, insisting art was only a hobby and he would never be able to support a family if he didn't chose a more suitable career. With no encouragement from either of their parents, Neil had ended up studying at the finest art institutes in the world. He'd even restored priceless works of art in the Vatican. "Just write a list of what you need," she told Rebecca. "I'll speak to Neil for you. If he doesn't have some supplies he can give you, I'll stop by the art store one night next week and buy whatever you need." The girl's eyes moistened with tears. Carolyn leaned down and kissed her on the forehead, stroking her silky hair off her face. "I love you, honey. You know I'll support you in anything you want to do. I shouldn't have made that comment about going to beauty school. I had a bad day at the office." She placed her finger underneath the girl's chin. "Wanna make up and start over?"

"I guess," Rebecca said, a mischievous look returning to her eyes. "Do I have to clean my room tonight, Mom? I have really bad cramps."

Here we go again, Carolyn thought. "You had cramps last week. You're not having your period again, Rebecca! Please, just clean your room. That's all I'm asking of you."

When Carolyn walked out into the hallway, she heard the girl say something. "What did you say?"

"Chicken," Rebecca said, sitting on the floor in the midst of her clutter, looking overwhelmed.

Carolyn placed one hand on her hip. "Are you calling me names now?"

"El Pollo Loco," her daughter said, hurling her clothes into the open closet. "If you pick up Pollo Loco, I'll eat it, but only white meat. White meat has less fat."

"Try doing your laundry instead of hiding it."

"The people aren't going to look in my closet, Mom, so don't have another fit." When her mother didn't respond, Rebecca spun around. "Oh my God, they are, aren't they? You're going to let strangers come in here and sniff my underwear. I'm going to move in with

Hillary. Her mother said I could. Her room is almost as big as our entire house. She even has her own bathroom."

Carolyn closed her eyes, trying to maintain her composure. She didn't know which was more difficult, dealing with criminals or having to put up with a fifteen-year-old.

She gazed at her daughter's face, so reminiscent of the girl's father's. Frank was Italian, and Rebecca had inherited his looks as well as his temperament. Carolyn suspected that volatile temperament was why she had trouble getting along with her daughter. Rebecca's hair was so dark it bordered on black, and she wore it long, several inches below her shoulders. She had Frank's eyes and mouth. She was a beautiful girl, with large brown eyes fringed with thick lashes, perfectly straight teeth, and a winning smile. "I'm pleased that you're interested in art, honey. I just think it would be wise if you got a good education, so you'll have something to fall back on."

"Like what?"

"You could be a lawyer, something along those lines. Maybe you could major in journalism. You're a wonderful writer."

"I'm only fifteen, Mother," her daughter said. "Can't I just be a kid right now and worry about all that stuff later?"

"Of course you can, darling. But you could start thinking about it. You know, just in case fashion design or something in the art field doesn't work out for you."

"Fine," Rebecca said. "I'll think about it."

Carolyn knew she had sounded just like her mother, but apparently she couldn't help it. She changed the subject. "Where's John?"

"Where do you think? In his room."

She closed the bedroom door on the way out and headed toward the converted garage at the back of the house. After knocking, she said, "Can I come in?"

"Sure."

Her son was sitting at his desk, slouched over, writing.

"What's going on, guy?"

"Paperwork," he said. "I talked to Grandma today, and she told me about a scholarship that I could apply for. Fifty thousand. Also, I found at least thirty other ones on the Internet today. I'm going to apply to them all."

Carolyn's mother was a retired chemistry professor. She lived in an upscale retirement complex in Camarillo, a town about fifteen minutes from Ventura. Walking over to her son, Carolyn placed a hand on his shoulder. "Did I ever tell you you're a perfect son?"

"As a matter of fact, you did," John said, smiling, then falling serious again. "If I can get just get a few of the big scholarships, you might not have to sell the house."

"We don't need the house," his mother insisted. "Rebecca and I will be fine. The apartment complex I'm considering is really nice. Lots of trees, streams running through it, as well as three swimming pools. I'm staring down some major repairs on this place, honey. With the taxes and insurance, it just makes sense to cash out now while it's a seller's market. Don't pay any attention to your sister. Once we get settled, she'll meet lots of new friends and everything will be fine." She took a deep breath, and then slowly let it out. "I'm going out for food. What are you hungry for?"

"Whatever the demon child wants."

"After we eat," she said, "I'll see if I can help you with some of that paperwork."

Carolyn ordered their food at El Pollo Loco, then took a seat at one of the tables while she waited. A man and woman walked up to the counter. She didn't pay much attention to them, outside of noting that the heavyset woman was dressed like a streetwalker and the shirtless man had the type of tattoos on his upper and lower back that were common with men who'd spent time in prison. The woman erupted in profanities as she stomped over to the soda machine with a paper cup in her hand, shoving it under the dispenser and filling it. "I ain't gonna pay you, bitch," she yelled at the young Hispanic girl behind the counter.

"Yeah," the man said, filling his cup as well. "Fuck off, you lousy spick."

Carolyn reached into her purse for her gun, certain the restaurant was about to be robbed. The other customers froze in their seats. The man and woman brushed past her though, exiting the restaurant and jumping into a late-model green Sebring in the parking lot. She memorized the license plate and stood, planning to go after them, but a second later she lowered herself back into her seat. It wasn't worth risking her life for the price of a couple of soft drinks. From the looks of the car they were driving, lack of money wasn't their motive. She suspected they got their kicks by terrorizing people like the young girl behind the counter. The punks who'd talked to her like dirt, unlike the clerk, probably survived by criminal activity rather than holding down a job.

When Carolyn went to pick up her food, she handed the girl a few extra bills, leaning toward her and whispering, "So your drawer won't be light tonight." Then she added, "If those two come back again, call the police. Don't argue with them—they're more than likely dangerous. Understand?"

The girl nodded, her eyes glistening with tears. "Thank you," she said with a heavy Spanish accent, depositing the money in the cash register. "I just started here last week."

Once she and the children finished eating, Carolyn spent some time working with John on his scholarship applications. She tried to review some of the cases she'd brought home but was too frazzled to concentrate. After dressing for bed, she tried to sleep but finally got up and put on her bathrobe, knowing she couldn't. The empty flower beds, seen through the living room window, resembled fresh plots in a cemetery.

As a child, Carolyn had experienced a repetitive nightmare in which she was playing catch with Neil in the backyard when her ball ended up in a flower bed. There weren't any flowers, just dirt, and when she went to retrieve the ball, a hand reached out and pulled her under. She was certain it was the devil, and delayed going to bed at night for fear she would have the dream again. After months of the same nightmare, her mother had taken her to a child psychiatrist, a stern-looking fat man who asked her stupid questions and spent the rest of the time staring at her. If anyone was the devil, she decided, it was this guy. She became even more frightened than before. One night she dreamed that she surfaced from underneath the ground over by the tree stump in the neighbor's yard. After that, she never had the dream again.

It sure seemed as if the devil had been out and about the past few days, Carolyn thought, staring at the dirt-filled flower beds and wondering if a hand would reach out and pull her under like it had in the dream. Maybe the devil was celebrating the fact that Carl Holden was back on the street and Lester McAllen could be on the verge of getting away with butchering a child.

Returning to the house, Carolyn impulsively grabbed the large artificial floral arrangement from the vase on the dining room table that her mother had given her years ago. She then found her hand shovel in the shed in back of the house and carried it to the front yard.

John's window overlooked the front of the house. Seeing his mother outside, he went to check on her. "What are you doing, Mom?" he asked. "It's almost midnight."

"I'm planting," Carolyn told him, digging a hole and shoving in one of the artificial flowers, then propping it up with dirt. "There aren't any weeds left to pull."

John stretched his arms over his head and yawned. Spotting the bunch of flowers in a pile next to his mother, he picked one up and sniffed it before he realized it wasn't real. "Is this a joke or something?"

Carolyn rocked back on her haunches. "I'm afraid something will happen and I won't make it to the nursery tomorrow. I want the house to look nice."

"I never heard of anyone planting artificial flowers," John said, laughing. "Jeez, this one even has drops of dew on it." When he saw his mother was crying, he walked over and squatted down beside her. "It's okay, Mom," he said, stroking the curly wisps of hair away from her forehead. "Everyone has a bad day now and then. Tomorrow will be better. Besides, I think what you're doing is cool. At least we don't have to worry about the flowers dying if we forget to water them."

Carolyn smiled, wiping the tears away and leaving a muddy streak across her cheek. "How bad is my hair?" she asked, touching it with her fingers. "Be honest. It's awful, isn't it?"

"You look great," John said. "If your hair was blond, you'd look exactly like Meg Ryan. I bet she plants artificial flowers in her garden, too." He helped his mother to her feet, draping his arm around her shoulders. "The good news about your hair is that unlike these flowers, it'll grow. Let's go inside, melt down some candy bars in the microwave and drink them. Then we'll come back out and finish planting. Does that sound like a deal or what?"

"Deal," Carolyn said, following him into the house.

CHAPTER 7

Saturday, September 16—8:47 A.M.

Carolyn was in a deep sleep when the phone rang. "Carolyn, it's Margaret, Margaret Overton, with Harbor Realty."

"What time is it?" Carolyn asked, thinking it was still the night before. She must have been even more exhausted than she'd thought. She'd gone to sleep without taking her sleeping pill. After fighting insomnia for most of her life, a night of natural sleep was rare. She'd slept so long, her eyelids felt as if they were stuck together.

"I'm sorry to disturb you," the Realtor continued. "I spoke to your daughter yesterday and asked her to tell you to call me, but I guess she forgot to give you the message. I'm holding an open house today. That is, if it's okay."

"I don't think that's a good idea," Carolyn said, going over and looking out the backyard window through a crack in the blinds. To her surprise, the yard had been freshly mowed. John must have gotten up at dawn. She knew he had to be at work by noon, and the restaurant where he worked was in the San Fernando Valley, almost an hour's drive away.

"I have several people that want to see the house today. Holding it open may create a bidding war. Would eleven be too early?"

"I thought you were going to hold off showing it until I made some repairs."

"I must not have made myself clear," Margaret said in a placating voice. "The listing became active last week. I'm fairly certain the house will sell without your making any improvements. The new owners will probably remodel. The land is far more valuable than the structure."

Carolyn got up and began making the bed with one hand. "Okay, but please try not to come before eleven. I need to get the house in order."

"Thanks so much for your cooperation. Just remember, the most important thing is that we sell your house quickly, and for the highest possible price. That way, you'll have the least inconvenience."

"Sounds good," Carolyn said, not feeling good at all. Things were moving too fast. But the sooner she got it over with, the better. Although she wouldn't admit it to Rebecca, she also hated the thought of people traipsing through her home and being privy to her personal belongings.

"Oh," Margaret added, "it's always better that the owners aren't in the house when we hold it open. People like to wander around at their own leisure, discuss it with their spouses, take measurements. . . . Well, you know."

"Yeah, sure," Carolyn told her. "I have some work to do at the office, anyway."

As soon as she hung up, she threw on her robe and rushed out of the bedroom, yelling for the children. "John! Rebecca!"

"What's up?" John shouted from the kitchen. "I made some coffee for you."

"The Realtor is coming at eleven to show the house." Carolyn skidded into the kitchen, grabbed John's face and kissed him. "Thanks for doing the yard, sweetie. Is your room clean?"

"Yeah," he said without hesitation, walking over and pouring her a cup of coffee, then handing it to her. "Drink your coffee, Mom. Calm down. Everyone knows this isn't a model home. Rebecca left about thirty minutes ago. I didn't check out her room. She said you gave her permission to go to Knott's Berry Farm with Hillary today. She didn't just skip out, did she?"

"No, no," Carolyn said, having forgotten. She sloshed coffee onto the wood floor in the hallway en route to her daughter's bedroom. John trailed along behind her. When she opened the door, she gasped. Except for the clothes Rebecca had thrown in her closet, the room looked exactly the same as it had the night before. "I'm going to strangle her."

"Now that's a chore I'd love to handle," John said, taking the coffee from his mother before she spilled it on the carpet. "Don't ask me to clean up after her. I've got to shower and get to work. Saturdays are big tip days. I've been working in the yard since six, and I'm pulling a double shift today."

"What's that smell?"

John sniffed. "I don't smell anything."

Carolyn followed her nose to her daughter's unmade bed, then knelt down and felt around underneath, pulling out an ashtray with what looked like a partially smoked marijuana cigarette in it. "She's smoking dope now! What else don't I know about your sister?"

"Hey," John said, throwing his hands in the air. "Don't look at me. I don't touch the stuff. I'm not saying I haven't tried it a few times. Rebecca's fifteen, Mom. She's experimenting. Don't go psycho on her, or she'll do something even worse." He reached over and took the ashtray from her. "I'll get rid of it. Spray some room deodorizer. If I don't leave now, I'm going to be late for work."

Carolyn stood in the shower, the warm water soothing her tense muscles. She wasn't in the mood to go into the office, not after cleaning up Rebecca's filthy room. Maybe she'd take a walk on the beach. It was only a few miles away, and she was appalled at how little time she spent there. After yesterday's encounter with Holden, she decided, it would do her good to take in some fresh air.

After she towel-dried her hair, she wiggled into her peach-colored bathing suit and covered it up with a floral print sundress that extended a few inches below her knees. She pulled out her gym bag, and packed it with sunscreen and bottled water. Spending an afternoon by herself was something she hadn't done in years. What was she going to do about Rebecca?

She remembered when Rebecca was a rambunctious ten-year-old. Carolyn had left her and John with a baby-sitter so she could take care of some shopping. It had always been hard to take Rebecca to the store, as the child wanted everything she saw and would shriek until her mother either bought it or dragged her out. On this particular day, after the babysitter had arrived, the girl had chased her out of the house and halfway down the sidewalk, yelling, "Child abuser!" Carolyn had been humiliated, as well as fearful that the neighbors might take her seriously and call the police.

Avoiding the freeway, she decided to drive on Foothill Road, going toward the old section of Ventura, then cutting over to the beach. Her thoughts drifted to Holden. She had to find a way to get him back in prison before he raped and murdered another woman. Not an easy task, however, to stop a crime before it was committed.

Carolyn was jolted back to the present by the loud sound of a horn. Looking to her right, she flinched as a car crashed into the passenger-side door of her Infiniti. Glass shot across the car seat, and she instinctively threw her hands up to protect her face. She slammed on the brakes. The car skidded and came to a stop.

"Are you all right?" a male voice rang out a few moments later.

"Yes, I think so," Carolyn said, still dazed.

"Don't move," the man said, opening the driver's-side door and reaching over to unbuckle her seat belt.

Carolyn looked up, coming face to face with a stranger. Brushing the remaining glass off her sundress, she asked, "What happened?"

"You ran the stop sign," he said. "Don't worry, my car didn't suffer much damage. It's you I'm worried about. Try to move your head slowly from left to right."

She did as he asked. "I feel like an idiot, but I'm okay," she said, climbing out of the car. "I'm so sorry." She shielded her eyes from the sun. The man was driving a cream-colored Jaguar convertible. "What about you? Are you injured?"

"I'm fine," he said, smiling as he dusted off his clothing. "It's a good thing neither of us was speeding. Let's try to get the cars out of the road, then we can exchange information."

Most people would be furious, Carolyn thought, surprised at his pleasant demeanor. He was wearing a black turtleneck that looked as if it was made out of silk or some other kind of exotic material, pleated slacks, and a boxy, stylish jacket with a silver emblem on it, similar to the ones you saw on uniforms for pilots. Light reflected off his flashy gold watch. She was fascinated by the large, intricate watch face, having been unaware that Cartier even made watches for men.

It looked good against his tanned skin. His hair had a few strands of gray in it, but he didn't appear much over forty. "Shouldn't we wait until the police come before we move the cars?"

"Why?" he said, extending his hand. "I'm Marcus Wright. Not exactly the most favorable conditions, but it's nice to meet you, Ms. . . ."

"Sullivan," she said. "Carolyn Sullivan." Fortunately, the Infiniti's engine turned over, and she made it to the curb before it sputtered and died. The passenger door was dented and wouldn't open, and the glass in the window was shattered. He drove up and parked behind her. She wondered what he did for a living. He looked like a movie producer, or someone who worked in the entertainment industry. He certainly wasn't your average Joe.

Removing her insurance information from the glove compartment, Carolyn exited the car again and walked up beside him. He was talking on his cell phone, and agilely slipped out of his jacket and tossed it into the backseat. This was a handsome, charming man. He was probably married to a tall, willowy blonde, had two perfect children, and lived in a mansion in Beverly Hills. What was he doing in this part of Ventura? If he'd been near the marina, it might make sense. Then again, he didn't look like a boater.

"Listen, Carolyn," he said, placing a hand on her arm. She caught a scent of his cologne. It made her think of thoroughbred horses and leather saddles, with just a hint of something floral. "You don't have to report this to your insurance company," he went on. "All they'll do is raise your rates. The damage to my car is insignificant. I don't think we even have to report it to DMV."

Carolyn walked around his car, noticing a streak of white paint across the fender as well a clear indentation. With a car this expensive, the repairs could cost a fortune. The dealership would more than likely advise him to replace the entire bumper. For all she knew, he was acting nonchalant because he was planning to sue her. She took out one of her business cards, flipped it over, and started to copy down her driver's license number.

"You don't need to give me that," Marcus said, pushing the pen down and taking the card from her. "Is this you? Ventura County Corrections Services Agency. Wow, that's a mouthful"

Carolyn nodded, bedazzled, feeling as if her tongue were two inches thick.

"Interesting," he said, turning the card over in his fingers. "Are you a cop?"

"A probation officer," she said, thinking her job title might as well have read janitor. She suspected he was wearing more on his back than she made in a month. "I'm sorry about what happened. The sun was in my eyes, and I wasn't paying attention." She heard an approaching siren. A passerby must have called 911. Several fire department vehicles pulled up and stopped. A man jumped off the back of one vehicle and another from the passenger seat.

"Ma'am," the taller of the two firemen said to Carolyn, "we need to take a look at you. Please sit down here on the curb." He opened up a large metal box that contained medical supplies, then put her through some routine tests for head trauma. "Looks like you have a cut under your chin."

"Really?"

The fireman pulled out something to wipe the small amount of blood away. "You're looking pretty good. The only thing you need is this." He held up a Band-Aid. After applying antiseptic, he placed it over the cut. "Do you want us to call for someone to pick up your car and give you a ride home?"

"That won't be necessary," Marcus said, walking over to the fireman. "I've got a tow on the way. If you don't mind," he said, looking down at her, "I'd be happy to drive you home. That way, we can let these men get back to work."

"Thanks," Carolyn said, smiling.

"That settles it," Marcus replied, turning his attention to the firemen. "You guys are doing a great job. Responding to a call in less than ten minutes—amazing. Simply amazing."

Carolyn was thinking the same thing, but not about the fireman. She watched as Marcus walked alongside the men to the ambulance, saying a few more words to them before they left.

When the tow truck arrived, Marcus came over and interrupted the driver as he was asking Carolyn where she wanted the car towed. "I know a great place that isn't very far from here," he said. "The owner is fast, and his prices are competitive."

"Okay, then," Carolyn said, lifting her shoulders and then letting them drop. "I'll take your word for it."

CHAPTER 8

Saturday, September 16—12:47 P.M.

Marcus and Carolyn followed the tow truck to the garage. The shop was at the end of a dead-end street on the outskirts of Ventura, its lot filled with exotic cars of every make and model. She shouldn't have allowed Marcus to call these people. Their fees must be outrageous.

A friendly-looking Latin man with *EMILIO* embroidered on his shirt greeted them. He treated Marcus like a celebrity. Rushing to open the door to the office, he asked them both if they wanted a cup of coffee, a soda, or some bottled water. When they declined, he said, "Have a seat. I'll finish with this customer, take a look at the cars, and be with you in less than five minutes."

"Emilio will have you back on the road by Monday," Marcus told her, flashing a confident smile. "The guy works seven days a week. That's why he's the best. I respect a man who's willing to work for a living."

"Great," Carolyn said, impressed.

"Okay, we'll take care of it," Emilio said, returning and taking a seat behind his weathered oak desk. "Anything for my friend, Mr. Wright. Should be ready by Wednesday."

"Monday's better," Marcus said, glancing over at Carolyn. "She needs her car to drive to work. She has an important job."

"No problem," Emilio told him, looking flustered. "But that means I'll have to paint it today so it can dry."

"How much is it going to cost?" Carolyn interjected. "Can you give me a written estimate? You know, just so we don't have any misunderstandings."

Before Emilio responded, Marcus answered, "Since I brought you here, the repairs will be on me."

"No," Carolyn protested, turning sideways. "I caused the accident. If anything, I should pay for *your* repairs."

Marcus stood and took her hand, leading her out the door. He gave a firm glance to the owner of the shop. "Do a good job on her car, Emilio. This is a special lady. I always take care of you, don't I? Now you have a new customer."

"Yes sir, Mr. Wright," Emilio said, trailing behind him. "Don't you want us to repair the Jag? I can give you an excellent loaner. I have a Mercedes or a BMW. Whatever you want."

Marcus waved good-bye and ushered her out. Carolyn decided arguing with him over the repair bill was futile. He wouldn't be around when she picked up the car on Monday, and she was sure Emilio, no matter how accommodating, would be more than willing to take her money. She'd slipped one of his cards into her purse and would make a point to call him and get an estimate as soon as she got home.

"Let's forget about the accident," Marcus told her, guiding her through the crowded parking lot. "No reason to ruin such a beautiful day, right?"

"What about your car?" Carolyn asked. "Aren't you going to get it repaired?"

"Not now," he answered. "I'll drop it off when I get some free time. I have other cars I can drive. Where do you live?"

"Take the freeway to Victoria," she told him. "I live close to Ventura College." She thought about it, then changed her mind. "Maybe you should drop me off at the Barnes and Noble on Telephone Road. I'm selling my house, and my Realtor is showing it today. I'll call a friend to come and get me in an hour or so. If push comes to shove, I can always walk home."

"That sounds more like an opportunity than a problem," Marcus said, another broad smile on his face. "Can I interest you in lunch? I'm starving."

Carolyn didn't want to seem overeager. "Sure," she said, slowly meeting his gaze, "but under one condition."

"And what's that?"

"I pick up the tab."

Marcus laughed. "You drive a hard bargain."

"Don't worry," Carolyn tossed back. "I'm going to take you to the Olive Garden, not a five-star restaurant."

What a strange set of events, she thought, leaning back against the plush seats in the Jaguar, the wind blowing through her hair. If she hadn't left the house when she had, someone else might have crashed into her and she would never have met Marcus. She could also be dead. Or worse, her reckless driving could have cost someone else's life. From all appearances, Marcus Wright was a gracious, intriguing man. He didn't wear a ring, but that didn't mean anything. A lot of married men didn't wear wedding rings. Even if he wasn't married, he surely had his pick of women. She pulled down the visor and glanced at herself in the mirror. Wasn't this the way it always happened? She'd left her house to go to the beach. No makeup, her hair fresh from the shower, wearing a dress she should have discarded years ago. She started to pull out her lipstick, but it was too late for that now. He'd already seen the freckles on her nose, and had probably noticed that she didn't have much in the way of eyebrows. She slipped her hands under her hips. Her nails were chipped, and she chewed on her cuticles, a habit she'd had since childhood. Seeing him staring at her, she said, "Your car is beautiful."

"Thanks," Marcus said, his long fingers gripping the glossy wood steering wheel. "It has a fairly smooth ride. When I get out of it after a long day in traffic, I don't feel like I'm climbing out of a coffin." He peered out the window. "Am I going the right way? I know there's an Olive Garden around here somewhere."

"We just passed it," she said, pointing. "Turn into that alley."

Once they were seated and the waiter took their orders, Carolyn asked him, "Do you live in LA?"

"Not really," Marcus said, "I have a home about thirty minutes from here. I only stay in LA when I get jammed at work." He poured her a glass of red wine from the bottle he'd ordered. "I knew a guy once who was on probation. He had to report every month and be tested for drugs. Is that what you do?"

"Not very often," Carolyn told him, resting her head on her fist. She then folded her hands in her lap, remembering how her mother used to tell her to keep her elbows off the table. *Etiquette,* she thought, wondering if anyone even knew what the word meant these days. The people in her income bracket couldn't afford fine dining. They ate at places like the one they were at now, which offered casual dining at modest prices. "I work in a division of probation called court services. My job is to investigate cases prior to sentencing, interview the various parties, apply circumstances in aggravation and mitigation, and basically interpret the sentencing laws. When the judge imposes a sentence, he relies heavily on the investigating probation officer's recommendation."

"Fascinating," he remarked, listening intently. "Do you have a law degree?"

"No," she told him, taking a sip of her wine. "I completed my first year of law school, then I had to drop out. I wasn't spending enough time with my kids, and the tuition was too steep for my budget. I'll go back one day, maybe after I put my children through college."

"What about your husband?" Marcus asked. "What does he do for a living?"

"Oh," Carolyn said, her expression darkening, "I've been divorced for a long time. My ex doesn't help out with the kids. It's fine. He wasn't a very good role model. Ah, what about you? Do you have a wife and family?"

"Nope," he said, his knee brushing against hers under the table. "I've never been married. Not that I have anything against it." He shrugged. "Just haven't met the right woman, I guess. How about you? Are you seeing someone?"

Was her moon in Venus or something? Carolyn thought. Could this dream of a man, who'd seemingly come out of nowhere, actually be hitting on her? If she told him she hadn't had a date in nine months, he would think there was something wrong with her. No one wanted what everyone else had turned down. "I was involved with a race-car driver," she said, deciding to use her former relationship with Brad Preston. Why tell him they worked together and the affair had been over for years? It wasn't really lying, more a sin of omission. "We decided to end it. I have plenty to keep me busy, so dating isn't a big priority."

Marcus gave her a questioning look. Carolyn felt like an idiot. She hadn't been with a man in so long, she didn't know how to act. Just before she opened up her mouth and said something else moronic, the waiter brought their food. She kept her head down as she ate her veal, trying to take dainty bites and dabbing at her mouth with her napkin.

"Couldn't this be construed as a first date of sorts?" Marcus said, linking eyes with her.

Carolyn almost choked on her food. "Well," she said, gulping down the rest of her wine, "yes . . . I think it could." She waved her hand over the food. "We're having a meal and everything." She was trying to act sophisticated, but it was hard when she was so excited. She cupped her hand over her mouth and giggled. Marcus tossed his head back and laughed as well. The stress of the past few days was swallowed up by a wonderful sense of anticipation. She could tell when something was going to happen, and it was going to happen between her and this man. The chemistry was so strong, she wouldn't be surprised if the waiter had noticed it. "We're not kids," she said. "We should be able to say or do whatever we want." She saw his face light up, and quickly added, "I'm not talking about anything sexual, of course, just . . ."

"You're cute," he said, refilling their wineglasses. "Not only that, you're intelligent." He touched the tip of her nose. "I love the way your nose turns up on the end."

"I like you, too," Carolyn said, sucking in a deep breath. "I've never known a man with a dimple in his chin. How do you shave it?"

"Very carefully," Marcus joked.

"I'm glad I ran that stop sign today," she continued. "Of course, I'm sorry I damaged your car. And we're lucky neither of us got hurt."

"I'm glad you ran that stop sign, too," he told her. "Are you ready?"

"Oh . . . yes," Carolyn said, watching as he made a check mark with his hand and the waiter came running. She sat there with a giddy expression on her face while he tossed a handful of bills down on the table, then rushed around to pull out her chair.

A man had been watching her from an adjacent table. He looked vaguely familiar, but Carolyn couldn't place him. Seeing her stand, he got up and walked toward her with an angry look on his face. As he got closer, she recognized him and knew this was trouble.

CHAPTER 9

Saturday, September 16—1:47 P.M.

"Ms. Sullivan, I'm Troy Anderson," the man said. "My wife, Tracy, was murdered about eight years ago. I talked to you about the court report. The man who killed her was Carl Holden."

"Yes," Carolyn said, extending her hand. She saw a young boy sitting at the table where the man had been, his dark hair covering one eye, a surly expression on his face. "That's your son, Sammy, I presume. He resembles you. How are you doing?"

"Not very good," Anderson said, his eyes drifting over to Marcus, then back to Carolyn. A small man, he was at least a head shorter than Marcus. He wore a blue denim shirt, jeans, and his feet were clad in Nike tennis shoes. "I thought I saw Carl Holden on the street the other day, over by the courthouse. That couldn't be possible, could it? I get emotional when I come back here. I've been living in Arizona for the past three years. Sam and I came to visit my mother. She's in a nursing home."

Carolyn felt a hard ball of tension forming in her stomach. "Weren't you notified? Carl Holden was released two years ago."

He took a few steps back in shock. "No!" he exclaimed, his jaw locking. "They were supposed to let me know when he came up for parole. No one told me anything, and now he's been released. How is that possible?"

Carolyn started to tell Marcus to leave without her, but she couldn't afford to take her attention away from Anderson as the situation was too volatile. "Holden's conviction was overturned. When the DNA evidence was ruled inadmissible, the DA decided not to try him again. Did you let anyone at the DA's office know you'd moved?"

"How could the DNA be inadmissible?" Anderson said, attracting the attention of several diners. "They verified it was Holden's blood under Tracy's fingernails. That scientist guy testified. I think his name was Appleby or something."

Some other people were trying to leave the restaurant, but Anderson and Carolyn were blocking their way. Carolyn gestured for the man to step outside in the lobby. He told her he needed to check on his son first. "Don't leave," he said, leveling a trembling finger at her.

"You should go," Carolyn whispered to Marcus. "I'll catch a ride home. If I can't reach someone, I can always call a cab."

"As long as you don't mind," he told her, "I'd just as soon stay. This guy looks like he's about to come unglued and slug someone."

When Anderson returned, Carolyn picked up the conversation, speaking softly as she explained the situation with Robert Abernathy. "I can't tell you how sorry I am that this happened."

Anderson ran his hands through his hair, becoming even more agitated. "What about the other women, the ones he raped? DNA wasn't an issue in those cases."

"If you will recall," Carolyn said, "the women he raped failed to pick Holden out of a photo lineup. I know two of the victims identified him in the courtroom, but the defense destroyed them. He was cleared on those counts as well. If it's any consolation, Abernathy is dead. Someone went to his house and shot him in the head."

Anderson's hands closed into fists. "The courts stink, and all you people who work in them are shit. And Sam, for God's sake! What should I tell my son? He's in special education now, with all the idiots and troublemakers. Sam is a smart boy. He never got over losing his mother. Fuck you, fuck all of you." He turned and stomped back to the table, digging in his wallet for his credit card, then slapping it down on the table.

Marcus said, "Let's go, Carolyn."

"All right," she said. She wanted to explain to Anderson that Holden could be retried if new evidence surfaced in the future, but at this point, she realized, nothing anyone said would make the man feel better.

Back in the car, Carolyn sat quietly, lost in her thoughts. She finally gave Marcus directions to her house, hoping that the Realtor would be gone by the time she got there. As they were gliding over the roads in his Jaguar, she began talking and couldn't stop. It was similar to being in a shrink's office. When she would stop speaking, thinking Marcus had heard enough, he would present another question, and more would pour out of her. Before she knew it, she'd rattled off the various details of the crimes Holden had committed, told how he'd disguised himself as a FedEx man, and related the way he had alluded to killing other women when she'd first interviewed him. When she told Marcus that she'd seen Holden Friday for a new offense, and the court had failed to even place him on supervised probation, her companion's face showed his shock.

"But aren't you his parole agent?"

"No," Carolyn said, sighing in frustration. She sometimes thought her job was so insignificant to the general public that they should just do away with it. But presentence reports were mandated by the court on all felonies. "I'm not even Holden's probation officer, except in the sense that I collected his fine and spoke to him. A parole agent works for the state, and only supervises men and women who've been released from prison. We occasionally catch some of their overflow, but even in supervision most of our so-called clients are on probation, not parole."

"What's the difference?"

Marcus was smart, yet like everyone else, he just didn't get it. She'd read newspaper articles where they referred to a person as a parole agent, then two paragraphs later called him a probation officer. "A person is placed on probation after serving time in jail."

He shook his head. "But jail is prison, right?"

"No," Carolyn said, slightly louder than she intended. "A jail is supposed to be a presentence detention center—you know, the place you stay while your case is being processed. Technically, an offender isn't usually sentenced to serve more than a year in jail. Sometimes, though, a person is convicted of a number of minor crimes and ends up serving a longer period of time at the local level. Like DWIs, for instance. Even if a guy racks up four of them, unless he kills someone, he won't go to prison. When he's released, he's generally on formal probation for anywhere from three to five years. Offenders are sentenced to prison for felony offenses, most of them serious."

"Jesus," Marcus said. "This stuff is fascinating. Why don't they have a show about it on TV?"

"Because no one is interested," Carolyn told him, chewing on a piece of skin near her nail. "Either that, or it's too hard to explain." She hadn't told him about *wobblers,* crimes that gave the judge an option of choosing prison or jail, depending on the circumstances. The judicial ruling applied there was that the probation officer making the recommendation had to determine if the interests of justice would be served by sending the offender to prison. Talking about her work was helping her recover from the confrontation with Troy Anderson. "I'm sorry you had to be involved in that scene at the restaurant," she said. "Things like that happen occasionally. Generally they occur at the office, but every now and then, someone snags you when you're out in public."

"What you do is dangerous," Marcus remarked. "Not only that, it's complex. The way it sounds, you do most of the judge's work, then have to stand by helpless while he screws everything up."

"You summed it up about right," Carolyn said, forcing a smile. "You left out one major element, though. I get paid only a fraction of what a judge earns, and he doesn't have to get his hands dirty dealing with criminals."

"That's not right," Marcus told her.

"Haven't you heard?" Carolyn asked. "For some of us, life isn't fair."

Margaret was placing the Open House sign in the trunk of her Mercedes when they pulled up in front of the house, so at least Carolyn knew she could go inside. The real estate agent stared at the Jaguar, thinking Marcus was a potential buyer. Carolyn waved her away. Margaret placed her fingers near her mouth and ear, mouthing the words, "Call me."

"Are you staying in the area after you sell your house?"

"I have to because of my job," Carolyn told him. "And my family lives here. My son is going to college next year, and I have a fifteen-year-old daughter. Education is expensive these days, so I decided to cash in some of my equity."

"I can't believe you have a son old enough to go to college," he exclaimed. "You look too young."

"Flattery will get you everywhere," Carolyn said, reaching for the door handle. When he seemed to be losing interest in her, she asked, "Will I see you again?"

"Of course." Marcus rummaged around in his pockets, coming up empty-handed. "If you have a pen and something to write on, I'll give you my number. I don't have a card right now."

"That would be nice," Carolyn said, leaning over and pecking him on the cheek. She handed him a dry cleaner's receipt and a pen. She certainly didn't want to let this one get away. That is, if he was genuinely interested. She wasn't used to calling men, but that was the way things were today.

"You were wonderful this afternoon," she told him, accepting the paper with his number on it. "The accident, driving me to the repair shop, everything. Our lunch was an oasis in the middle of my otherwise chaotic life. Maybe if there's a next time, we won't be bothered by someone like Troy Anderson."

"I learned some things I didn't know," Marcus told her, getting out of the car and preparing to walk her to the door. "Seems like you're putting up a good fight, but the criminals are winning."

"Would you like to come in?" she asked when he appeared to be lingering at the door. She saw the artificial flowers lining the walkway and turned away, hoping not to draw his attention to them. He might be able to tell they weren't real. At least the house was clean.

"No, no," he said, looking at his watch. "I have to meet a business associate. I was driving around in circles while we were talking, so I need to run. Next time, maybe."

"Next time, then," Carolyn said, unlocking her front door and waiting until he'd jumped into his convertible and sped away.

Business associate, she thought, flopping down on the sofa, her legs sprawled out in front of her. Marcus probably had a date and she'd never see him again. Regardless, outside of the confrontation with Troy Anderson, it had been a pleasant day.

*   *   *

It was late, after eleven. A tall man dressed in a long, dark coat, wearing a cowboy hat and sunglasses, paid the cab driver and took off on foot, disappearing into the shadows.

After a brisk ten-minute walk, he unlocked the main gate to Eagle Self-Storage, continuing on until he reached his rental unit. Pulling a baseball bat from underneath his coat, he jumped up and smashed the spotlight near his stall, ducking so he wouldn't be struck by the shattered glass.

His storage unit was at the end of the street, so the area around him was bathed in darkness. Inside was everything he needed—a black Ford pickup and some assorted tools. Stretching out a blanket in the bed of the truck, he loaded a shovel, a hammer, a rake, two ice picks, and a box of heavy-duty garbage bags. Pulling on a pair of latex gloves, he went outside and filled a bucket with water from the spigot. After carrying it back into the storage unit, he squirted in some Lysol liquid soap, then spent the next thirty minutes scrubbing down the concrete floors and thinly coated white walls with a large sponge. The rent was paid for the next six months, but after tonight, he had no intention of returning.

Picking up another blanket, he spread it over the contents in the back of the truck. Before he left, he stood inside the shed with the door closed, his eyes searching the walls and floors to make certain he had removed everything and that the place was thoroughly clean.

He'd already sanded the VIN numbers off the truck several months ago. When he was finished with the tools, he would clean them, then dump them at a construction site. Everything else, including the cowboy hat he was wearing, his jeans, shirt, coat, underwear, and socks, would be packed inside the duffel bag and later deposited inside a locker at one of the 24 Hour Fitness Centers. He'd purchased a membership under a fictitious name, which offered unlimited access to every club in the chain.

With present technology, it was a snap to create a new identity. He was surprised there weren't more people like him. If a person paid attention to what he was doing, and possessed the ability to conceive and execute the right plan, the chances were good that he would never be apprehended.

Backing the truck out of the shed, he was pleased no one was around. He got out and put the padlock in place on the door before exiting the parking lot. The storage company was in a good location, a block from the freeway on-ramp. Traffic was light this time of day, which was good, as he had some manual labor ahead of him as well as a fairly long drive to reach his final destination.

Fifteen minutes later, he drove through the darkened streets where the first phase of the development was being constructed. The wind had picked up, and it made a strange high-pitched sound as it blew through the framed houses. Reaching into the car's glove compartment, he brought out some dark glasses and put them on, not wanting to get dirt in his eyes when he reached the area where the grave was located.

Sometimes the police made the rounds, probably for perks given to them by the developers. Occasionally they used unpopulated areas to park and take a nap, or to work on their reports. To make certain they didn't spot his truck and become curious, he parked it inside what would eventually become a garage in one of the unfinished houses. If the police spotted it, which was unlikely, they would assume it belonged to one of the workmen.

He walked briskly in the direction of the grave, carrying the shovel, an ice pick, and the hammer rolled up in one of the blankets. He had several garbage bags stuffed in his jacket pocket. He carefully counted off the paces, then stopped and began digging. The moon was out, providing light. A flashlight could draw attention, and he'd become accustomed to working in the dark. He hadn't buried the body that deep, as he'd wanted the heat and insects to speed up the decomposition process. The previous summer had been a scorcher. By then she had already been in the ground for a long time.

His calculations were accurate. He first thought it was another rock he'd hit, but when he reached down and picked it up, it turned out to be a skull. Sitting Indian style on the ground, he felt it with his fingers. A few strands of hair were still attached, so he plucked them out and let the wind carry them away.

The teeth were already gone, having fallen out once the flesh had either decayed or had been consumed by insects and other animals. The remaining teeth he picked up with his gloved fingers, dropping them in one of the garbage bags and sealing it to be discarded later.

It wasn't difficult to find the teeth as the body had been facedown and they were all only a few inches apart. He didn't count them; he didn't think it was necessary. A tooth or two would just get scooped up in the clumps of earth when the site was graded for the new housing tract. Even if the body was eventually identified, which he had taken measures to forestall as long as possible, no one would ever trace it back to the original burial site.

The rest of the bones he picked up one by one, depositing them in the second plastic bag. Rummaging through the dirt, he was finally satisfied that he'd gotten everything. Her clothes had been removed and burned before he'd buried her.

The sack containing the bones was surprisingly light. He knew this was due to their state of decay. In addition to the hot summer, they'd had heavy rains the year before, enough to cause mud slides and road closures. Even the weather had worked in his favor.

Instead of placing the sacks in the bed of the truck, he placed them in the cab on the floorboard. Having stored a bag of garbage the last time he'd visited his storage unit, he dumped the contents on top of the bones. If the police stopped him for some reason, one whiff of the stinking refuse would be enough to discourage them from wanting to sort through the rest of the contents. He would just tell them that he'd been meaning to take his trash to the Dumpster but had been too busy to get around to it. His face was smudged with dirt, and there were perspiration stains under the armpits of his shirt, so it wouldn't require much to make the police believe he was the kind of man who would do such a thing.

He removed the dark glasses so he could see to drive. The mustache and black hair color were long gone, having served their purpose. Once he'd decided to dispose of the woman, he'd intentionally guzzled beer, quickly developing an unsightly gut, which he made look even larger by wearing his pants a size too small. The extra weight was also gone. Like a snake shedding his skin, he'd discarded most of what linked him to the woman. Now all he had to do was dump his problems at the new location, and drive to a nearby town where there was a 24 Hour Fitness Center.

After he completed his workout, jumped in the shower, soaked in the Jacuzzi, then dried off in the sauna, he would put on a fresh set of clothes, leaving the clothes he was wearing behind in the duffel bag. His membership card would be tossed in the nearest trash can. He would remove the plates on the truck and park it on a street in an area not served by the same police agency where he intended to bury the bones. After a week, maybe a month, the police would tow the truck as an abandoned vehicle. When no one came to claim it and no stolen vehicle report was found on file, the city would auction the truck off to pay the storage fees.

Within a matter of hours, this particular problem would be solved. If everything worked as planned, the woman whose bones now sat in the bottom of a plastic bag would be nothing more than a fading memory. Even at this stage, it seemed as if she'd never existed. In time, the police could hook him up to a lie detector, show him a picture of her, and he could safely say he had never seen her before in his life.

His ability to believe his own lies was one of his finer traits. Killing someone and getting away with it was the ultimate game. Overall, however, murder was similar to marriage—nothing more than a convenience. Why spend a year in divorce court, or take a chance some psycho broad would end up on your doorstep and shoot you? As long as they pleased him, they lived. When they started complaining, arguing, or poking into his private affairs, his motto was simple.

Kill them, bury them, and walk away.

When he went to bed at night, he slept like a baby.

CHAPTER 10

Monday, September 18—11:15 A.M.

Death should be powerful enough to punch out the sun, Carolyn thought, but this was California. While people killed each other, the palm trees swayed in the breeze, waves washed up on the shore, and multicolored perennials bloomed along perfectly manicured parkways.

Carolyn drove west on Victoria Boulevard, where the government center was located, and steered John's Honda Civic onto the ramp for the 101 freeway. The city was building a new overpass at the Santa Rosa River, causing traffic to snarl during rush hours. When it was finished, the bridge would be illuminated with old-fashioned street lights that resembled lanterns, adding a touch of charm to an area that had formerly been unsightly. The crime rate was so high, large pieces of construction equipment were suspended in the air at night and on weekends to keep people from stealing them.

Exiting at Vista Del Mar, a short distance from the Pierpont Inn, Carolyn saw the sign for the Alessandro Lagoon and made a sharp right. She stopped when she saw the string of police cars, CSI units, unmarked detective units and the coroner's panel vans. Human remains had been discovered Sunday night in the lagoon that ran adjacent to the 101 freeway. In her rearview mirror, she could see the Ventura Pier and the Holiday Inn, both local landmarks. Beyond that was the shimmering blue of the Pacific Ocean.

Turning off the ignition, Carolyn opened the car door, removed her shoes, and exchanged them for a pair of old tennis shoes, wishing she'd brought a pair of rain boots. It was difficult to see much of anything from the narrow access road. Depending on rainfall, the lagoon consisted of shallow water, with dry patches in between. Reeds grew six or seven feet high, and there was a good deal of scrub brush. The area was protected with a six-foot-high chain-link fence, but several sections had either fallen down or had been forced open by trespassers.

Looking beyond the uniformed officers protecting the crime scene, she spotted Detective Mary Stevens, but she didn't see Hank Sawyer. Mary was usually easy to find. A striking black woman in her early thirties, she looked as if she belonged on the cover of a magazine rather than exhuming a body. She always wore a red shirt when performing that task, calling it her murder shirt. Even with the white overalls she was wearing today, the red shirt showed through.

One of the uniformed officers stopped her. "Lieutenant Sawyer asked me to meet him here," Carolyn said, showing him her ID before she attached it to her belt. "Do you know where he is?"

"The grave," Officer Wyman said, glancing behind him. "Over by those trees where everyone is standing. Sawyer was right next to Stevens a few minutes ago. I can't see him now."

Carolyn started to walk away when the officer stopped her again. "You'll have to suit up before you go out there, Sullivan," he said, glancing down at her tennis shoes. "The CSI van is open. There are some extra jumpsuits, caps, and gloves in there. The paper boots aren't working out that well with the water, but that's all we've got right now."

"Thanks," Carolyn said, walking to the van and digging out the smallest suit she could find. Once she put it on, she shoved what little hair she had inside the cap, and tucked her pants legs inside her paper-covered tennis shoes in an attempt to keep the water out. Finally, she made her way to the grave site.

Elbowing her way through the crowd of officers, Carolyn spotted Hank peering down into what appeared to be a three-by-four-foot hole. Metal supports had been placed against the soggy walls to keep them from collapsing, and the reeds and brush had been cleared to give the investigators space to work. Other officers' heads could be seen weaving in and out between the tall reeds.

Several tables had been set up on the side of the road, and large circular sieves were being used by the CSI team to sift through the mud and debris for evidence.

Charley Young, one of the top pathologists in the county, was dictating notes into his cell phone, which would be uploaded through his wireless connection directly to the word-processing pool. The notes would be typed and waiting for him by the time he returned to his lab. One of the reasons Charley was so efficient, Carolyn thought, was his knowledge and use of sophisticated technology. In that respect, Hank was a dinosaur.

A man Carolyn had never seen before was recording the proceedings on video for the person she assumed was his boss, Dr. Martha Ferguson. She'd never met Ferguson, but she'd read about her in newspaper articles and seen her once on television. Since the body was skeletonized, Ventura had brought in the renowned forensic anthropologist. Ferguson was a small forty-something redhead, her weather-worn skin speckled with freckles. Her eyes were partially obscured behind goggles, and she wore knee-high rubber boots.

Charley was a small Korean man, barely five six, who probably weighed less than one forty fully clothed. In all the years Carolyn had known him, she'd never seen him lose his temper. And with the police constantly pressuring him for autopsy reports, maintaining his composure couldn't have been easy. No one could push harder than a cop.

She'd read in the paper that Robert Abernathy's funeral was scheduled for tomorrow. She almost felt obligated to go, but she hardly knew the man. She wondered if they'd ever find out who had killed him. When Hank had called her that morning, he'd advised that Oxnard had basically nothing to go on, outside of the bullet removed from Abernathy's head and a partial print discovered on the gate to his front yard.

"Jog your memory?" Mary Stevens asked, blotting the perspiration off her face with a white cotton scarf. The scarf served multiple purposes. If the stench was intolerable, the detective used it to cover her nose and mouth. If she got close to a body, she tied it around her head to make certain no hairs would contaminate the crime scene. Today, however, she was wearing a cap, probably at the insistence of Dr. Ferguson. The Santa Ana winds had blown in Saturday, and the temperature had risen into the mid-eighties. That, coupled with the intensity of the sun, made it seem like summer instead of fall. But, of course, Southern California didn't really have seasons. "Excuse me, but I'm sweating buckets," Mary continued. "According to Hank, this is where Carl Holden buried his first victim. A guy staying at the Pierpont was out walking his dog Sunday when he got loose and jumped through a hole in the fence. He had to chase him to keep him from getting hit by a car on the freeway. He twisted his ankle when the soil caved in on top of the grave." She chuckled. "The man, not the dog. I'm sleep deprived, okay? Excuse me if I don't make sense."

"I know Holden buried Tracy Anderson somewhere out here," Carolyn said, glancing around the area. "I'm not sure it was in this same exact spot, though. Hank should know better than me. I only saw the crime-scene photos." Surprisingly, not much had changed. The trees had grown taller next to the freeway, and the scrub brush was denser. A sign was now posted that read *Alessandro Lagoon*, as if it were something other than a swamp. The naturalists had probably turned it into a refuge for some type of animal life. What it looked like was a breeding ground for the West Nile virus.

The area was far from the perfect place to bury a body, being this close to a heavily traveled highway. If the victim had been tossed out of a car, it might make more sense. But, then again, Holden had picked this location to bury Tracy Anderson. There were no street lights, so at night the area was dark.

Carolyn adjusted her sunglasses on her nose. She assumed the CSI team had already photographed the position of the remains, but Dr. Ferguson was standing inside the grave taking her own shots in case the police screwed up theirs or somehow misplaced them. Determining cause of death was always difficult in cases like this, and knowing the exact position of the remains was mandatory.

"How long do you think she's been dead?" Carolyn asked Mary, swatting a mosquito away.

Hank heard her voice and turned around. His white suit was soaked with perspiration and stained with mud, his hands encased in plastic gloves. "Glad you could come," he said. "Charley and Ferguson believe the body has been here for some time, but we can't be certain. She's going to start packing up the bones soon, so maybe we can clear before dark."

"Bringing in someone like Ferguson was a good call," Carolyn commented.

"That woman's something else, let me tell you," Hank said. "She wouldn't even let *me* get near the body until a few hours ago. She personally took samples of all the vegetation over the grave." His eyes were outlined with dark circles. "You know how long we've been wading around in this shit? Since two o'clock yesterday. Ferguson's been using dental picks and bamboo sticks. She insisted we remove the soil five inches at a time instead of the normal ten, then put it through six or seven different sized sieves. I don't know why Charley insisted on calling in this obsessive broad. We're not exhuming King Tut here."

Mary Stevens's eyes flashed. "It's demeaning to refer Dr. Ferguson as an obsessive broad. You refuse to accept the way things are done today—you know, *right*. What did you want us to do? Dig the body up with a backhoe?"

The detective scowled. "I'm tired, I'm hungry, and I'm sick of being bullied by women. Smart off to me again, and it'll show up on your next performance review."

After Mary dropped her head and ducked behind another officer, Carolyn asked, "What can I do here, Hank?"

Hank ignored her question. "The victim may have been killed, buried somewhere else, and then dug up once the body decomposed. Her teeth are gone. Looks like he's trying to keep us from identifying her. He waited until the gums were soft enough so he could pluck out her teeth with his hands, sort of like picking kernels off an ear of corn. Lazy bastard, huh?"

"Your garden-variety killer wouldn't revisit the body," Carolyn noted. "Someone could have seen him. This crime could have been committed by someone other than Holden, Hank. The location is probably nothing more than a fluke."

"Fluke, my ass," he said. "We checked the coordinates, and the grave is within fifteen feet of where Holden buried Anderson." He removed the plastic glove on his right hand, then pulled a toothpick out of his pants pocket and placed it between his teeth. "Want one?" he asked, producing a small plastic container. "I dip them in cinnamon. When I was a kid, they sold them this way. Now I have to do it myself."

Carolyn accepted, hoping it would help calm her churning stomach. Usually, it was the stench of the body that made people sick. There was a stench floating around this case, but it had nothing to do with rotting flesh. As hard as she'd tried to warn everyone that Holden would kill again, the reality of it actually having happened was so horrifying, she found herself trying to believe it wasn't true.

"I doubt if he came back," Carolyn said. "It seems more logical that he knocked her teeth out when he killed her."

"All her teeth are missing, not one or two. And her jaw isn't cracked. You've had a tooth pulled, haven't you? It's not easy to get those suckers out. He'd have made a mess of her if he'd used a pair of pliers or some other crude tool. He waited until her gums began to decay before he removed them."

"Don't they just fall out when the body decomposes?"

"Yeah," Hank said, "but the teeth aren't here. We thought they might have floated away, but we've searched every inch of this place and we can't find even one tooth. They could be in the first grave, although this guy probably kept her in the cellar or something until she ripened."

Carolyn's cell phone rang and she excused herself, stepping a few feet away. She had thought about Marcus ever since they'd met. When she'd called the garage that morning to check on her car, Emilio had told her the car was ready and the repairs had already been taken care of by Mr. Wright. Such a magnanimous gesture was a good reason to call and express her gratitude. "Is this Carolyn Sullivan?" a low male voice said. "You left a message on my voice mail. Something about your car."

"Hi, Marcus," Carolyn said, excited he had returned her call so soon. "I'm going to pick my car up after work. I drove my son's Honda today. You must let me reimburse you for the repairs. If you refuse, the very least I can do is take you out to dinner. I was supposed to pick up the tab for our lunch yesterday, but I forgot. You know, the run-in with Troy Anderson was upsetting. Now things are going to really blow up. Ventura PD exhumed the remains of a woman yesterday in almost the same spot where Holden buried Tracy Anderson. I'm at the Alessandro Lagoon now."

The line fell silent. Carolyn could hear phones ringing and people talking in the background. *He must be busy,* she thought. He'd asked her so many questions about herself and her job that she'd failed to ask what he did for a living. When he still didn't say anything, she decided they must have a bad connection. "I can't hear you that well," she said. "Did you say something?"

"You said they found a woman's body. What happened to her?"

"She was murdered, Marcus," Carolyn said, thinking it was odd he hadn't made the connection. "The police think Carl Holden killed her." *He must have a lot on his mind,* she told herself. And some people who were talkative in person clammed up when they were on the phone. She glanced at the caller ID, but his number was blocked. "I thought we might be able to get together tonight. That is, if you don't have other plans." Again, the line fell silent. This wasn't going very well. Now she knew how guys felt when they called girls up for a date. "I can tell you're busy. Anyway, I just wanted to thank you. If you're in town again, give me a call. "

"Don't hang up," he said. "Where do you want to meet tonight?"

"Oh," Carolyn said, happy that things were turning around. "You could pick me up at the house. Is six too early?"

"Yes," Marcus said. "I'm in LA right now. Where is this lagoon?"

"In Ventura," she said.

"Depending on traffic," he said, "I think I could get there by eight. Since I might be running late, why don't I meet you in the bar at the Holiday Inn, the one next to the pier? Is this your cell phone?"

"Yes, but eight's a little late for dinner, don't you think?" Carolyn said, not wanting to sit around in a bar waiting for a man who might not show up. "Why don't we get together another time?"

"Make it seven," he said. "I'm sorry, but I have to go to a meeting. I'll see you tonight. What will you be wearing?"

"Clothes," Carolyn said, laughing. "I don't know, something casual." She knew she couldn't wear what she had on, as she was standing in a foot of mud. He was probably trying to find out if he should wear a jacket. "A dress," she told him, "a red dress."

"Fine," he said. "Seven at the bar in the Holiday Inn."

Realizing he'd disconnected, Carolyn remembered the problems she was having with Rebecca, and wished she hadn't arranged to go out tonight. Too late now. She wasn't going to call him back, not when she'd almost begged him to see her. At least John didn't work on Mondays, so he could play policeman and make certain her wayward daughter didn't fire up another joint.

She'd called Veronica on Sunday to ask her how she thought she should handle the situation with Rebecca. Veronica's seventeen-year-old daughter, Jude, drove her crazy, and she'd become a master at innovative parenting. Veronica knew how vain Rebecca was about her appearance, so they'd concocted what might turn out to be a unique form of punishment. When Rebecca left to walk to school that morning, she'd been dressed in the tackiest and most unflattering outfit Carolyn could dig out of the back of her closet, a pair of striped bell-bottoms and a blouse with an empire waistline that made her look like she was pregnant. "I hate you," Rebecca had shouted. "If you make me wear this, I'll ditch school, run away, and you'll never see me again."

"I'll be calling the principal's office in about an hour," Carolyn had told her. "If you're not in class, I have another outfit you can wear tomorrow."

Pulling herself out of her thoughts, Carolyn turned around and saw Hank standing right behind her. "My office needed some information about one of my cases," she lied, watching as Dr. Ferguson bagged, labeled, and sealed each bone, handing them up one by one to a CSI officer, who then carried them to one of the tables to be placed in an evidence box. "Do you think they'll be able to tell how the victim died?"

"Don't know," Hank told her, frowning. "Charley thinks she may have been strangled. The killer dumped trash on top of her to make things more difficult for us, particularly as to DNA." He looked around, then added, "As if it isn't bad enough. We're not catching any breaks here, know what I mean?"

"How would Charley know if she'd been strangled?"

"Just the words I love to hear," he said, his voice tinged with sarcasm. "Diagnoses of exclusion. There's a slight chance of a fractured bone either in the neck or the spinal vertebra. Won't know until we piece her back together. No sign of gunshot wounds. She could have been stabbed, of course. Once the Ferguson woman and Charley examine the bones under a microscope, they might find some nicks to indicate the killer used a knife. A person can be stabbed numerous times, though, without any of the wounds penetrating to the bone." He paused, then added, "You know, now that I think about it, Holden did the same thing."

"He didn't use a knife, Hank," Carolyn said, thinking the detective should have spent more time reviewing the old case file. As dangerous as Holden was, they couldn't use him as a scapegoat for every crime that came along. She wanted to get him behind bars, but this time she wanted him to stay there. "Tracy Anderson was strangled, not stabbed."

"That's not what I meant," said Hank, scratching a mosquito bite on his wrist. "We decided Holden emptied a pile of trash on top of her before he buried her."

"I remember." Of course, back then, Carolyn thought, the spot of land they were standing on hadn't been a lagoon, and homeless people had been known to live there in cardboard boxes.

Just then her eyes focused on something white on one of the tables across from where they were standing. Mary was helping the CSI officers pack everything up so it could be logged into evidence. She acknowledged Carolyn with a nod but refused to look at Hank. "What is that? A golf glove?"

"How the hell do I know?" Hank grumbled, moving the toothpick to the other side of his mouth. "We've got every kind of trash imaginable. It'll take us weeks to sift through all this crap. We don't have the manpower. There's some kind of gang war going on in Oxnard that's spilling over into Ventura. Two kids were shot last weekend on the West Side. I've also got a masked perp robbing convenience stores. At least Abernathy wasn't killed in our city. My guys are working six days already. Guess they'll have to work seven. Such a deal, huh?"

Carolyn remembered the crime-scene photos from the first homicide. She distinctly recalled a white golf glove resting on the Anderson woman's stomach. The police had been unable to lift any prints because no one had ever worn it. They decided it was just another object someone had tossed out. It had stuck in Carolyn's mind because the glove was brand-new, and she couldn't understand why a person would discard it. "The golf glove," she said, animated. "Don't you remember, Hank?"

Hank rubbed his forehead. "Now that you mention it, there was a glove similar to this one. Didn't we decide the person threw it away when they lost the matching glove?"

"Golf gloves don't come in pairs," Carolyn said, raising her voice. "A golfer only wears one glove. God, Hank, everyone knows that."

The detective's jaw thrust forward. "I'm not an idiot just because I don't know golfers only wear one glove. And I don't take personal calls when I'm working a homicide."

Carolyn was hurt. "That was uncalled for, Hank. Why did you call me out here if you didn't want my opinion?" Then she blurted out, "Holden has to be the killer. The glove is his calling card. This is tantamount to a confession. He's boasting, don't you see? He wants us to know he murdered this woman. At the same time, he's either eliminated or contaminated all the evidence."

The detective glared at her, spitting his toothpick out onto the ground before turning to walk back to the grave. Their loud voices had caught the attention of the officers gathered around the evidence table.

"You may never be able to identify the victim," Carolyn yelled after him, heedless of their audience. "Unless you manage to locate an eyewitness who saw Holden bury the body, no prosecutor will ever be able to convict him. If you don't arrest Holden immediately, you're going to have more water, mud, and blood on your hands. This is his dumping ground."

"You don't think we've been busting our butt trying to pick up Holden ever since we discovered the body?" Hank shouted back. "Since you seem to know so much, why don't you track him down? Or let your new boyfriend, Marcus, find him."

Carolyn placed her hands on her hips. "I can't believe you eaves-dropped on my conversation."

"If you don't want people to hear you," Hank said, "make your damn phone calls in private. You think the officers working out here want to listen to you making a dinner date when they haven't slept since yesterday?"

"Whatever," Carolyn said, tossing her hands in the air and stomping off.

CHAPTER II

Mary Stevens caught up to Carolyn before she reached her car. "Want to grab a quick lunch?"

Carolyn needed to get back to the government center, but she wanted to see what else Mary knew about the case. "Sure," she said. "I'll follow you."

"Is the Habit okay?"

"Fine with me." Getting into her car, she waited until she saw Mary pull out in her unmarked police unit.

Ventura had grown up around the historic San Buenaventura Mission, founded in 1782. On one side were miles of sandy beaches, along with multimillion-dollar homes with boat slips. The rest of the city had sprawled upward into the foothills, where the residents had panoramic views of the ocean. But unlike Santa Barbara, a similar city approximately twenty miles north, Ventura hadn't developed into a playground for the rich and famous. New shops and restaurants had slowly appeared throughout the years, but most things had stayed the same. Carolyn thought there was a tired feeling to Ventura, as if a dusty bubble had been placed over it, trapping it twenty or thirty years in the past. The Spanish influence was still present, but it hadn't been cultivated as it had in Santa Barbara, where lovely mission-style homes and buildings had been built to harmonize with meticulously renovated existing ones. And, unlike Santa Barbara, Ventura had a sluggish economy. When a new business opened in Ventura, it was a major event.

As they stood in line at the Habit, a popular burger joint only a few blocks away from the mission, Mary turned to her with a smirk. "If Hank hadn't jumped on me back there, I would have brought him something to eat. He's a great guy, you know, but I can't stand by and listen to him denigrate women, even if he is my boss."

Carolyn wasn't interested in burgers. What she craved when she was upset was chocolate. Knowing there was a Starbucks next door, she told Mary she'd be right back and went to order a Chantico, a deliciously rich chocolate drink that came in a small container the size of a Dixie cup. She was so addicted to it that she sometimes made a cheap substitute at home, as she and John had done when they'd melted down four Hershey bars in the microwave. While she was waiting, she was tempted to buy a low-fat sticky bun, but the mere thought that a sticky bun could be low-fat seemed absurd. To keep the calories down, she decided to forgo whipped cream on the Chantico.

Mary was already seated at a table, about to dig into her double cheeseburger, large fries, and strawberry shake. "Where's your food?"

Carolyn took a sip of the chocolate, instantly feeling better. "This is all I need."

"Suit yourself," Mary said, unwrapping her burger and taking a bite. "It seems like nobody eats anymore but me. Are you on one of those low-carb diets like Hank? Lettuce wraps. Who in God's name wants to eat a hamburger wrapped in lettuce? What is that anyway, an espresso or something?"

"Take a sip," she said, sliding the cup across the table.

"Jesus," Mary said, "this is sinful. I might have to go next door and get one."

Carolyn smiled. "It's like crack, only chocolate. Don't start, or you'll be addicted." Quickly consuming what remained when Mary handed her the drink back, she let her thoughts return to Holden. She'd known he would kill again. The entire system was responsible, not just Abernathy. The DA's office should have listened to her eight years ago when she'd told them she suspected Holden had killed other women. Maybe the skeletonized woman had been murdered before Holden went to prison, and he'd buried her in the lagoon, thinking that would be the last place anyone would look.

"I haven't talked to you in months," Mary said, sucking down her shake. "You got a new boyfriend, right? That's why you changed your hair. You're looking good, girl. You're such a dainty thing. With that new haircut, you look like a teenager."

Carolyn smiled. "Thanks. I did meet someone. That's who I was on the phone with right before Hank jumped on me."

"Ah, now I understand. You're not eating because you want to look good with your clothes off," Mary said, a mischievous glint in her eyes.

"What I just drank probably has more calories than a five-course meal. You *can't* eat anything else when you have a Chantico."

"Tell me about the guy."

"It happened so fast." Carolyn stuck her finger in the empty cup and licked a few remaining drops of chocolate off her fingers. "I was thinking about Holden and ran a stop sign. Another car crashed into me."

"No one hurt?"

"No, but my car is in the shop. Marcus insisted on paying for the repairs." She wiped her hands with her napkin.

"He's setting a good first impression," Mary said, nodding her head. "So what does he want in return?"

"Nothing that I wouldn't give him eventually," Carolyn told her, laughing. "I guess the only way to meet a man these days is by accident."

"That's for sure. What's his last name? Is he black, white, Hispanic, Jewish?" She rubbed her thumb and forefinger together. "Details, babe, give me some juicy details."

"He's white, and his last name is Wright," Carolyn said. "He looks like he could be European. It's probably just his clothes. What about you? Are you seeing anyone?"

"No, not right now, so I'm taking advantage of it. Besides, whenever I get annoyed, I binge out on junk food. Works every time. Anyway, do you know why Hank ripped into you?"

"Not really," Carolyn told her, staring out over the restaurant. "I think he was mad at himself for not remembering the golf glove. He also didn't realize that golfers only wear one glove. We're so close, you know. He's never talked to me like that before."

Mary leaned forward. "Hank thinks the world of you, Carolyn. He hasn't slept in days. We had two robberies go down last night within an hour. And the two boys who were shot last weekend weren't gang members. Their parents are crawling all over us, demanding we find the killers. You know how hard it is to solve a random gang murder, especially when the victims aren't linked back to the shooters. The last thing we needed was an unidentified murder victim floating around in a swamp."

"I'm not involved in this investigation," Carolyn said, still miffed. "I came out there today as a favor to Hank. He had no right to criticize me for taking a phone call, business or otherwise."

"Hank's jealous, that's all. Try to understand."

"Why on earth would he be jealous? Hank and I are friends, Mary. I don't know where you got the idea that there was anything else going on between us."

Mary glanced over her shoulder to make certain someone from the department wasn't sitting within earshot. "Why do you think he whipped himself into shape? Maybe he thought if he spruced up his image, you would see him in a different light. If he overheard you talking to a guy, that's probably what set him off."

Carolyn was stunned. Hank had never given her any reason to think he was interested in her romantically. "I thought he had something going on with that waitress. Don't they go dancing every Saturday night?"

The look in Mary's eyes was wiser than her years. "What a man does isn't the same as what a man wants." When the probation officer just stared at her, she continued, "I shouldn't have said anything. Please don't mention it to Hank. I just thought if you knew how he felt, things might go more smoothly." She wiped her mouth with her napkin. "What you said back at the lagoon was right, by the way. When I heard you mention the golf glove, I remembered reading something about it in the Anderson file. But the first thing we have to do is identify the new victim. I've been checking all the missing persons reports. There're three or four that sound promising."

Carolyn set her emotions aside. "Three or four? There're thousands of people reported missing every day. How could you narrow it down this fast?"

"I used Tracy Anderson," Mary explained. "I pulled her DMV photo off the system and had the computer try to match it to any missing females with similar features within a two-hundred-mile radius of Ventura. Since Holden's victims were blond housewives in their mid-thirties, most of them fairly attractive, it seemed reasonable to think he would pick the same sort of woman."

Carolyn listened while the detective rattled off the particulars of four missing females the computer had selected, then began stringing the case together in her head. "I managed to extract some worthwhile information from Holden during the presentence investigation on the Anderson homicide. Didn't do me any good, did it? He's back on the street. Why didn't anyone realize that Abernathy had lost his mind?"

"Forget Abernathy," Mary said, one side of her mouth curling in contempt. "The guy's dead. You can't stay mad at a dead guy. Besides, everyone gets out. You think it drives *you* crazy? How do you think *we* feel? We risk our lives to catch these assholes. Then a few months or a few years later the same guy surfaces again, committing even worse crimes. Bitching about it doesn't do any good. If you've got rats in your house, you gotta keep killing them."

Carolyn fell silent, thinking. "I'd be willing to pick Holden apart again when you manage to find him. That must have been why Hank wanted me involved? Did he tell you Holden walked out on his interview with me Friday?"

"Yeah," Mary said, nodding at two uniformed officers who walked in the door. "Do you know Daniel Thorn, the county's general counsel?"

"I've heard of him," Carolyn said. "I thought he had a heart attack and was out on sick leave."

"You're thinking of Patrick Green," Mary told her. "So Thorn caught me in the office Saturday, demanding that I send him everything we had on Holden. Guess Tracy Anderson's husband went through the roof when he found out Holden's conviction had been overturned. He hired an attorney to sue the county, and they're pissing in their pants. I don't blame Anderson. I mean, I'd sue, too, if the maniac who killed my wife got away with it."

"I know," Carolyn said, rubbing the side of her neck. "Troy Anderson recognized me while I was having lunch at the Olive Garden on Saturday. He's not a happy camper, that's for sure. I thought he was going to rip my head off right there in front of Marcus."

"When are you going to see this guy again?"

Carolyn wiggled in her seat. "Tonight."

"He must be doing something right," Mary answered. "Even with all this about Holden, you're lit up like a Christmas tree. You've slept with him already, haven't you? Come on, you can tell me."

"No," she said. "I don't make it a practice to have sex with strangers. To be honest, I haven't had sex with anyone in over a year."

"When the pickings are slim," Mary told her, "you gotta get it whenever you can. What does he do for a living?"

"I'm not sure what he does. I'll call you tomorrow and let you know how it goes tonight."

"Holden's DNA should already be in the CODIS system." Mary yawned. "I need coffee, but my stomach's been killing me. I think I may have an ulcer."

"Join the crowd." Carolyn heard her own stomach gurgling. Food might help, but she didn't think she could handle a hamburger. She decided to pick up something from the courthouse cafeteria when she got back.

"The FBI's DNA database has genetic samples from almost two million criminals now, taken as soon as they enter prison," Mary went on. "They also have over eighty thousand samples gathered from unsolved crime scenes. We'll nail him, Carolyn. Dr. Ferguson is highly esteemed in her field. That's why I got bent out of shape when Hank said such stupid things about her. So what if Ferguson pushed us to go the extra mile? It's exhausting work, but the payoff is worth it."

Carolyn was impressed by Mary's confidence. She was a realist, though, and knew the investigators had a difficult road ahead of them. In most instances, the police could focus all their attention on tracking down the killer and building their case. This time they had to figure out who the victim was, and from what Mary had said, the department was already stretched far too thin. "Did you put out a national bulletin on Holden?"

"Of course. All we can do is list him as wanted for questioning, though. As soon as we get a positive ID on the victim, we can ratchet up the heat and get everyone's attention."

Carolyn rested her head on her hand. "Tell me more about the woman in San Diego."

"Okay," Mary said, struggling to keep her eyes open. "Holden's been out of prison for two years. San Diego PD reported a white thirty-six-year-old blond computer technician missing from her home approximately a year ago. The husband later called in and claimed his wife had gone to live with her mother in St. Louis. The police wanted to close the case, so they went over to talk to the husband in person. By then the neighbors told them the couple had packed up and moved away."

"Maybe the husband walked in while Holden was raping her, and he killed him. Did you search for other possible bodies in the lagoon?"

"Thoroughly," she said. "What makes the San Diego case unusual is the couple left all their furniture. Even if the husband killed her, why would he leave everything behind?"

"He didn't, don't you see?" Carolyn told her, speaking rapidly. "The killer probably took the things he knew could be used to identify him. There's only so much you can do to clean up a crime scene. Clothes have hairs on them, toothbrushes have saliva. Nightgowns and underwear sometimes have semen stains. You're dealing with a sophisticated, devious criminal, Mary. He's smart, and he knows as much about forensic science as most police officers. Maybe the husband hired Carl Holden to kill his wife, then dispose of the body out of town where no one would find it."

"Possibly," Mary said, squinting as she thought. "They never found the husband, so I'll put in a request for Holden's phone records from Chino. But, Carolyn, I don't think Holden could be considered a sophisticated criminal. He was a construction worker. Hank said his brain was fried from booze."

"Well . . . he should know." Hank had been trying for years to live down his battle with the bottle. Most of the people at the department knew he was a recovering alcoholic. The detective had gone into a nosedive when his younger brother had been killed in a car accident. "Carl Holden might have been a construction worker, but he was an extremely bright man. When I interviewed him the first time, he quoted Greek philosophers. Also, remind Hank that he had eight years to sober up. You know how a lot of guys pass their time in the joint?"

Without answering, Mary folded the paper the hamburger had been wrapped in, grabbed their empty plastic cups, and walked over to place them in the trash bin. "Ready to get out of this dump?" she said, placing her hand on her stomach. "That was gross. If you ever see me order this kind of junk again, you have my permission to shoot me."

"I thought it made you feel better."

"I lied," Mary said, walking beside her toward the front of the restaurant. When the two women stepped outside, they felt a blast of hot air. "Both of us gave Hank a hard time, now that I think about it. Women tear into guys, then act like they're the injured party when the guys strike back. I don't know about you, but I'm feeling like I owe him an apology." She moved to let another person pass, looking as if she was waiting for Carolyn to come to the same realization. When Carolyn didn't respond, Mary picked up where they had left off, "You asked me what I thought prison inmates did to pass time. Jerk off. Pump iron. Who the hell cares?"

"They do that, too," Carolyn said. "A person has to be strong to carry a dead body. That's not the point I'm trying to make, though. Inmates study law books and read crime fiction. And what about all the cop and forensic science shows on TV? Some prisons even give them access to the Internet. That's like having every resource in the world at your fingertips."

"I never thought of it that way," Mary said, opening the door to her unmarked police unit. "I'll tell Hank that you said you were sorry. And don't worry about the other stuff I told you. You know, about him having the hots for you. He'll get over it. It's funny you didn't know. Everyone else does."

Carolyn started to say something, then stopped, trying to figure out how she felt about Hank. "I'll see what kind of information I can dig up on Holden," she said, deciding it was better not to dwell on Hank's feelings. They both had more important things to focus their attention on.

"Find out if you still have the original glove in evidence," Carolyn said. "Tell Hank that since we've now got two gloves, we don't have a pair, but we may have a match."

"Yeah, right," Mary said, scowling as she slid behind the wheel. "Tell him yourself. I don't want to end up back in patrol. The way I've been eating, I won't be able to squeeze into my uniform."

CHAPTER 12

Monday, September 18—5:42 P.M.

When Carolyn got home that evening, Rebecca was sitting on her bed, her room clean and her laundry folded and stacked neatly on top of her bureau. Their eyes met and lingered. "You'll never find pot in my room again, Mom, I promise."

"Good," Carolyn said, feeling she'd made a breakthrough. Rebecca contrite—she hadn't seen her like this since she was ten. She was just the product of a broken home, after all. She'd learned to bury her feelings by rebelling and acting tough.

"Seriously," Rebecca continued, "I had a long talk with John when he gave me a ride to school this morning. I told him if he wants to smoke pot, he'll have to do it outside or in his own room."

Carolyn's jaw fell open. "I can't believe you'd make up a story like this about your brother. John would never defy me. He knows how I feel about drugs."

"And John does everything you tell him, right?"

"I guess I'll have to find something worse for you to wear tomorrow. I have a green taffeta bridesmaid's dress in the garage. How does that grab you?"

"Super," Rebecca said, challenging her mother with a cold stare. "My friends went wild over the clothes I wore today. Empire waistlines are back in style, and so are striped pants. You're a real trendsetter, Mom."

"You're grounded for the next month, young lady," Carolyn exploded, suppressing the urge to walk over and slap her. Instead, she snatched her iPod off the end table as well as her portable phone. "I'm also going to turn off your cell phone tomorrow. I can't believe a child of mine would tell such terrible lies."

"Hey," Rebecca said, tossing her hands in the air. "Knock yourself out. I may not tell the truth all the time, but I wasn't lying about John. He's been smoking pot for years. I know he's your favorite. You think he's gonna win a Nobel Prize while I'm waiting tables or something. I make good grades, too, you know." She stood and faced her mother, only a foot away. "Physics Boy isn't as perfect as you think," she told her, her breath warm on Carolyn's face. "Maybe you should pay more attention to John, and quit ragging on me all the time."

"I'll get to the bottom of this right now," Carolyn said, experiencing a sinking sensation. If what Rebecca said was true, not only was John smoking marijuana, he had lied to her and laid the blame on his sister. And this was the kid she was giving up her home for. Talk about being disillusioned. A muscle in her eyelid twitched. "Where is he? Is he in his room?"

"Heck, no," the girl said, tucking her thumbs inside the waistband of her mother's striped bellbottom pants, then rocking back on her heels like a cowboy. "It's kind of like that saying about cops, Mom. A guilty person is never around when you need them."

Carolyn handed the iPod to her. "If I made a mistake, I'm sorry. I'll find a way to make it up to you." She started to leave, then spun back around, certain she'd been had again. "But I have John's car. How could he have driven you to school if he didn't have a car?"

"Semantics," Rebecca said, arching an eyebrow. "See? You never listen to me. I didn't say John *drove* me. I said he *gave* me a ride. Turner picked us up."

"Is that who John's with tonight?"

"Yep," Rebecca said, opening her underwear drawer and shoving in a stack of bras and panties. "They're probably out cruising for drugs." She glanced over her shoulder at her mother with a sly smile. "It's only pot, Mom. You used to smoke it."

"Twice," Carolyn said, realizing that not being forthright with your children might have its merits. "Your father was a writer. He said it helped his creativity. He wanted me to smoke it with him, so I did a couple of times. Back then I would have done anything for him. I decided it wasn't good for a person's lungs, nor for their motivation. Maybe if your Dad hadn't smoked so much marijuana, he would have written a book someone wanted to publish. Anyway, I didn't want to go to jail."

"If they catch you today," Rebecca told her, "they just give you a ticket, as long as you're not carrying around a brick or something. Half the kids at my school smoke weed." She slammed one of her drawers closed. "Except me, of course. Why would I want to pig out and gain twenty pounds? All stupid pot does is give you the munchies."

Carolyn looked at the clock and realized she had only thirty minutes to shower and get dressed. "I have to go out," she said. "Will you be okay here by yourself? Surely, John will be home in a few hours?"

"Mom!" Rebecca yelled, "I'm almost sixteen. I swear I won't do anything wrong. I have tons of homework. Hillary is coming over in a few minutes so we can study together."

Carolyn moved her feet around on the floor, trying to decide if she should call Marcus and cancel. Then she remembered that the only number she had was for his office. If he expected to reach Ventura by seven, he would have had to leave LA around five-thirty. "You can always reach me on my cell.'"

"Duh!" the girl said, holding out her palm and wiggling her fingers. "You might want to give me my phone back. Your room is off-limits, remember, and I can't hear the one in the kitchen when I'm concentrating."

"I love you, honey."

"I know," her daughter said. "I love you, too. You shouldn't have cut your hair, though. It makes you look like a butch."

"You're getting back at me, aren't you?"

"Yep," the girl said. "I was telling the truth about John. If you hadn't made me wear that hideous outfit to school, I wouldn't have ratted him out. Now he's gonna find a way to get back at me."

Carolyn slouched against the wall by the door. "Not if I can help it," she said. "I'm sorry I doubted you, honey. Do I really look like a lesbian? Not that there's anything wrong with being a lesbian, but . . ."

Rebecca said, "You try too hard, Mom. I love your hair. Everyone's getting their hair cut short. The guys at my school think you're hot. I don't know why you're so freaked out about turning forty."

Carolyn walked over and hugged her. "Thanks," she said, "I needed that, even though I'm sure you made it up."

"Anytime," Rebecca said, putting her headset on and turning on her iPod.

Mary Stevens had slept for a few hours, made herself a peanut butter and jelly sandwich, then soaked in a hot bath. She was bone-tired, but she couldn't stop thinking about poor women they'd found in the lagoon.

When she'd moved out of her apartment in Los Angeles after re-signing her position with AMS Biotech to concentrate on finding her father's killer, Mary had been fortunate to be able to purchase a home of her own. Ventura PD had offered her a job, and she'd been attracted to the area because it was close to the beach.

She lived a few streets over from Carolyn Sullivan and passed the probation officer's house on her daily jog. Since she'd purchased her home outright with the proceeds from her father's life insurance, along with the money she'd saved from her job in the private sector, she didn't have to worry about payments. This was good, as she was used to living on a comfortable salary, and police officers were paid barely enough to survive. She wasn't certain how Carolyn pulled it off, particularly with two kids. The probation officer told her once that she and her former husband had purchased her house years ago, when California real estate was still affordable.

Mary had converted her guest room into a small office. Wearing her turquoise-colored bathrobe, with a towel wrapped around her head, she plunked down at her desk to begin the arduous task of searching through as many missing persons' reports as possible. An unidentified body was the stuff of nightmares. Already, the dead woman seemed to be haunting her. She heard a faint but desperate voice inside her head, pleading to be reunited with loved ones. Somewhere a mother, a father, children, a brother or sister were vig-ilantly waiting and praying. Not knowing placed all their lives in an extended state of misery. It was her job to answer that call and re-solve it as quickly as possible.

The detective booted up her computer, then rubbed her hands together to warm them. As hot as it had been during the day, the past two nights at the crime scene had been cold and damp. Of course, digging up a body created its own kind of chill.

Now that the evidence had been collected, Mary could begin to work her magic, as Hank called it. She was by far the most techno-logically advanced detective assigned to homicide. While other, more seasoned officers had been passed by, she was certain Hank had re-cruited her because of these specific skills.

The computer in front of her was a Silicon Graphics Platform, which ran on the UNIX operating system and had the power to do accelerated 3D animations. Computer imaging was becoming an ac-cepted alternative to more traditional modes in the practice of foren-sic anthropology. Mary also used Encase Forensic, a program specifically designed for law enforcement agencies, enabling the various agen-cies to securely share sensitive information and communicate their findings immediately.

Mary felt as if she'd already made her mark in life. She had man-aged to put the man who had shot and killed her father behind bars, something every cop in LAPD had failed to do. And she had done it without leaving her apartment.

With the use of DMV photos and mug shots, Mary had first tried to match them to a composite drawing of the suspect made from the input of her father's fellow officers, those who were present when he was killed. The technology to run such a search on a national level had not been implemented at the time; therefore, she'd gone through hundreds of thousands of records in each state, superimposing them over the composite sketch. Because the killer had never been ar-rested, his mug shot and fingerprints were not on file. DMV now made it mandatory that every person holding a California driver's li-cense be fingerprinted and the information shared with all law en-forcement agencies. Many states had followed suit, which would have made Mary's quest to track down her father's killer far less time-con-suming if it had been the practice back then.

After a year of fifteen-hour days and many dead ends, she had finally tracked down Leroy Collins in Florida. Once he'd been convicted, Mary decided to become a police officer in tribute to her father.

For this case, she had asked Dr. Ferguson's office to send her the electronic file containing the information necessary to reconstruct the face of the victim on her computer. The forensic pathologist had informed her that once she got the bones back to the lab, she found evidence of a broken femur. Since they didn't have access to the victim's medical records, this information didn't do them much good.

Using an X-ray and the weight of the skull, the detective could get a numerical value. Then, with the help of her sophisticated software, she could set specific tissue-depth markers. There were thousands of variables in the predefined database, based on NURBS curves—Nonuniform Rational B-Splines—which used mathematical equations to create shapes to be applied to the skull. The result would be a close approximation of the facial features of the victim, the same as Dr. Ferguson could do with clay in her lab.

Using computer imaging was more flexible, as features could be changed with a stroke of the keyboard. The majority of forensic scientists were now using the same technology, but Ferguson liked to do things the old-fashioned way. The problem for Mary's work was that she didn't have the credentials, and if a match was made and a suspect brought to trial, a forensic expert would have to testify in court as to anatomical landmarks of the cranial and facial bones. Yet, experts like Ferguson, whose reputations were at stake, had been known to bog a case down for months, even years. In a homicide investigation, the first few days following the crime were the most crucial. This was Mary's way of getting critical information fast, hoping the experts would later validate her findings.

Although Carl Holden was a viable suspect, even with the similarities in the two homicides Mary knew he might not be their killer. The clock had begun ticking the moment the body was discovered. That was when the killer knew he was being hunted. If he was going to make a mistake, he would make it then.

After four hours, she had eliminated Janice Foster, Marilyn Wells, and Betsy Styles as victims of Holden. The face of Lisa Sheppard, however, the missing woman from San Diego, fit almost perfectly when superimposed over her computer model.

Nothing that easy could be right, Mary thought, but every now and then a person got lucky. She would still have to eliminate thousands of other possibilities. She stood and stretched, knowing she couldn't ask her aching body and burning eyes for anything more tonight. Now that she had a possible match, she was ready for a trip, but it wouldn't include tropical drinks, a bikini, or action from a warm-skinned island guy. This would be a serious fact-finding mission to San Diego.

When Marcus Wright walked into the dimly lit bar at the Holiday Inn, Carolyn knew this was the man she wanted.

He was dressed in a beautifully tailored business suit, a white shirt, and a blue and red striped tie. Even the way he walked intrigued her. His long legs and torso moved purposefully forward, while his head seemed to remain motionless. It was a trick of the eye, Carolyn told herself, created by his graceful but deceptively fast pace. This was the walk of a man who didn't like to waste time.

Since she'd raced out of the house without makeup on the day of the collision, she'd made an attempt to look as good as possible tonight. Her red dress had been purchased from the markdown rack at Macy's for twenty-nine dollars. Her figure made the lightweight knit an eye-catching garment, regardless of the modest price. The V-neck showed a tasteful amount of cleavage, and the fabric hugged her hips. As much as she complained about her weight, she still fit comfortably into a size six. She wouldn't much longer, however, if she didn't find a way to curb her newfound addiction to chocolate.

Certain she'd been stood up, Carolyn had been sipping on a glass of red wine when Marcus arrived almost thirty minutes late. Thirty minutes wasn't a long time unless you were waiting.

As soon as he took a seat on the bar stool next to her, Marcus ordered her another glass of wine and a cup of hot tea for himself. "I can't thank you enough for paying for the repairs on my car," she told him, a slight tremor in her voice. She'd hadn't been nervous on Saturday when they'd had lunch, but this was more along the lines of a date.

"It was nothing," Marcus said. "Did you pick it up already?"

"No," Carolyn said. "Today was a hectic day. I'm borrowing my son's Honda. I left it in the parking structure so I wouldn't have to pay the valet."

The parking structure next to the hotel was a popular place in Ventura. People left their cars in the high-rise structure when they went to the beach, kids congregated and partied there, and car thieves ditched stolen cars. The police officers assigned to that beat made it a habit to drive through the structure several times during their shift. If nothing else, they would run all the license plates for warrants, then wait for the guilty parties to return so they could arrest them.

She told Marcus about finding the marijuana cigarette in Rebecca's room and then learning that it was her son who was allegedly the culprit. She went on to tell him about John's desire to become a physicist and attend MIT. "If what my daughter said is true," she added, asking the waiter for a glass of water, "I don't think my son's going to be driving for a while."

Marcus laughed, tossing a handful of peanuts from the small bowl in front of him into his mouth. "I had a similar problem with my son a few years ago. He didn't aspire to become a physicist, though. Your boy must be highly intelligent. It takes a fine mind to get into MIT."

Carolyn was taken aback. "But you told me you'd never been married. You're not married now, I hope."

"No," he said, self-conscious. "I've been divorced for seven years. I don't like to talk about my divorce. Do you generally discuss your failed marriage with someone you've just met?"

"No," Carolyn said, disenchanted, "but I did with you." No matter what the situation, she wouldn't have lied about something that important. Then again, she'd told Marcus she had just broken up with a race-car driver, not a supervisor from work who drove cars as a hobby.

Carolyn stared at the fancy alcohol bottles behind the bar. She decided to speak her mind. "I'm more or less an open book," she said, turning her bar stool around to face him. "I practically told you my life history an hour after we met. And I also gave you a fairly extensive overview of the judicial system, as well as the Holden case." Her lower lip protruded. "In case you've forgotten, you found it fascinating."

"Tell me about this woman who was murdered," Marcus said, asking the bartender to bring him more hot water for his tea. Seeing that her wineglass was still full, he asked, "Would you like something other than wine?"

"No," Carolyn said, reaching over to snatch another bowl of peanuts, since it appeared that they weren't going to be having dinner. Her stomach was kicking up such a ruckus, she cursed herself for having guzzled liquid chocolate for lunch and, instead of picking up a salad at the cafeteria, snacking all afternoon on nuts and raisins. She filled Marcus in on what had transpired that morning at the lagoon, explaining why she felt certain the killer was Carl Holden.

"Aren't you concerned this man might hurt you?" he said, spooning sugar into his tea. "You said he has some kind of vendetta against you because of the things you put in your report."

"Sure," she said, shrugging, "but I'm good at what I do. There's nothing in my job description that says I have to pry information from offenders. I just want the court to be fully informed before they impose a sentence. Although the margin isn't as great, I also try to help people who I believe have been wrongly accused. A lot of probation officers simply don't care. They write their reports, make whatever recommendation they feel like, and promptly forget it. It's easy to burn out in this type of work."

"Why don't we get out of this place?" Marcus said, removing his wallet and handing a twenty-dollar bill to the bartender. "Are you hungry?"

"Not anymore," Carolyn said, excusing herself to go to the restroom. She felt his eyes on her as she walked away. She'd gone to a lot of trouble to look sexy, and this was the first time he'd looked at anything other than her face. Of course, it was hard to notice a woman's body when she was perched on top of a bar stool.

Once she'd used the bathroom, she washed her hands and freshened up her lipstick. The man she'd been so dazzled by Saturday now seemed ordinary and boring. Marcus Wright was an illusion, just someone she'd fabricated in her mind. That's what happened when a woman became desperate. Any man that came along was filtered through her fantasies.

When Carolyn returned, Marcus was leaning against the wall waiting for her. He glanced down at her high heels. "I was going to suggest a walk on the beach, but not in those. What about the pier?"

Carolyn kicked her shoes off, swinging them back and forth in her hand. "The beach sounds better," she said. "That's where I was headed the day I met you."

Marcus looked uncomfortable. "I want to apologize. It just dawned on me that you may not have had dinner yet. Didn't you say something on the phone about it being too late to eat?"

"I'm fine," Carolyn said, peering up with a wide-eyed look. She'd forgotten how tall he was, and in the light, he was even more attractive than she remembered. His eyes were hazel, with flecks of green in them. His hooded lids gave him a seductive look. Bedroom eyes, her mother used to call them.

Marcus steered her by the elbow as they made their way out of the hotel lobby. "We could go somewhere and eat now, if you'd like. The Pierpont Inn is only a few miles away."

"The past couple of days have been terribly stressful," she said, enjoying the brisk night air. "I'd rather walk on the beach than spend what's left of the evening in a restaurant."

Fifteen minutes later, they were standing beside each other in deep sand. Carolyn began shivering in her thin dress. The Santa Ana conditions they'd experienced for the past several days had passed, and the damp ocean air was chilling. Marcus opened his jacket and pulled her to his body, wrapping it around her to keep her warm.

They stood without speaking, watching the waves roll onto the shore. She could feel the warmth of his body through his shirt. His erect posture made him seem even taller, and his abdomen and back were lean but muscular. She felt safe with this man. Together, they seemed somehow whole. "Thanks for suggesting we come here," she said. "I live close by, and I seldom take time to enjoy the beach. My work and my children consume me. I take all this beauty for granted."

Marcus sighed. "You're not the only one. I don't know where the last ten years went. I was so busy building my business, I forgot the things that are really important. That's why my wife divorced me. The worst thing was I didn't even miss her. I was relieved because I had more time to devote to my work. Now my life seems meaningless."

"What about your son?"

"He and my daughter live back east with my ex-wife," he told her, a tinge of sadness in his voice. "We're not on the best of terms. Children in the midst of divorce usually take sides with one parent or the other. I suspect it's a survival skill. Ethan did the right thing by siding with his mother. I'm the one who broke up the family. For all practical purposes, I abandoned them."

His words made Carolyn feel as if she were conspiring with the enemy. Frank had abandoned her and the kids for drugs. Marcus's excuse should make him even less sympathetic, yet for some reason, she didn't blame him. She sensed he was a decent man who had somehow lost his way while trying to provide his family with the finer things in life. When a person became involved with hard drugs, as Frank had, they intentionally plunged themselves and everyone who loved them into the gutter. Her children's father was an educated man who knew all too well where drugs would take him. All Carolyn hoped was that John wouldn't follow in his father's footsteps. He was an intelligent young man who appeared to be extraordinarily gifted in math and science. Nonetheless, becoming a physicist could still be beyond his reach, and since junior high nothing else had ever interested him. "Your ex-wife," she said, turning her attention back to Marcus, "do you still love her?"

"No," Marcus said wistfully. "I don't think I ever loved her. I didn't know how."

"Sad." Carolyn's face was pressed against his chest. She felt as if she were surrounded by him—his smell, his skin, his maleness. He wasn't boring at all, she decided. His quiet, introspective manner was even more endearing than the fast-talking, flashy persona he'd exhibited when they had first met.

Marcus turned and gazed at her. "You're beautiful," he said, running a finger down her jawline. "And you're natural, not plastic, like so many women today. I bet you're beautiful even without makeup."

"I beg to differ," she said. "That doesn't mean I won't accept the compliment. Men always think women look better without makeup, for some reason. All these years, and I've never figured out why. It isn't the women without makeup who attract their attention."

"I'm glad I came tonight, Carolyn," he told her. "What started to be a disaster seems to be headed in the opposite direction."

"I didn't smash your car up that bad," she said, assuming he was referring to the accident. "We weren't even going that fast, remember?"

"That's not what I was talking about," Marcus said. "I've never met anyone quite like you before. You're complex, and at the same time, simple. Your passion for your work is admirable, as well as your concern for your children. I'm sure you can be fierce when necessary, yet you exude femininity."

He turned his body so they were facing each other. Carolyn released him, thinking he was ready to head back to the hotel. To her surprise, he embraced her, engulfing her in his arms and kissing her. She shut her eyes, relishing the fresh taste of his mouth and the intimate touch of his tongue. His lips were soft and moist, and she returned his kiss with fervor, placing her hand at the base of his neck and standing on her tiptoes to reach him. His hand cupped the back of her head, his other hand pressed into the small of her back.

Carolyn felt his hands slide over her hips as he effortlessly lifted her off her feet. The next thing she knew, he had swept her up in his arms. He carried her a few feet before he carefully laid her down in the sand. First, he dropped to his knees, then he stretched out on his side beside her. He looked strange in his business suit lying in the sand, with not so much as a towel beneath him.

They were both breathing heavy, but they didn't speak. The moon reflected off the water a short distance away. Coupled with the soothing sound of the surf, the moment took on a magical quality. With the tips of his tapered fingers, Marcus stroked her face, her hair, the nape of her neck. His touch and the expression on his face was so tender, tears spilled onto Carolyn's cheeks. "Tell me this is real?" she whispered, emotion welling up inside her.

"It's real," Marcus told her. "I'm not certain what it is, but it's monumental. I want you, but I don't want you here. What I feel for you is more than sexual desire."

Carolyn reached out and took his hand, guiding it to her eyes so he could feel the wetness of her tears. "I'm not crying because I'm unhappy," she said. "It's like I've been waiting for you for a long time. Does that make sense?"

"Yes." Marcus cradled her in his arms. She slipped her leg through his, tossed her arm over his shoulder, and curled herself around him. When she fell asleep, he remained still in order not to wake her.

After an hour Carolyn's eyelids flickered open. Confusion gave way to contentment as she realized where she was and saw his tender gaze. "I've been watching you sleep," he said. "I think I could watch you forever."

Her hair had formed into tight curls from the moist air. She never napped or even dozed off while watching television, and certainly not on the beach with a man beside her. "Will you?" she asked, stroking the lapels on his jacket. "Will you watch me forever?"

"I might," Marcus said, smiling. He stood and helped her to her feet as he continued, "Right now, though, I think we need to head out. It's past one, and I have to drive back to LA. I own a house in Santa Rosa, but I don't want to fight the traffic in the morning. I have a conference scheduled for eight."

Carolyn felt strange but wonderful, as if they'd made love dozens of times and knew everything there was to know about each other. She could already picture him in her house, laughing and talking with Rebecca and John, wrapping presents for Christmas, planning family vacations. How could something so new feel so comfortable? "Where do we go from here?"

Marcus removed his jacket, draping it around her shoulders as they walked through the sand toward the lights of the hotel. "We'll figure it out. The next time I see you, the first thing I'm going to do is buy you a decent meal. Somehow we got our signals crossed tonight, but I'll do my best to make it up to you."

"I don't know if I can see you tomorrow," Carolyn told him. "I have problems at home I need to take care of . . . my son . . . and I leave the kids alone a lot because of my work. Maybe that's why . . ." She was tongue-tied, infatuated. He had wrapped her up in a box, put a bow on her head, and she didn't care.

Marcus gave his ticket to the valet, then pulled Carolyn close. "I'm going away on business tomorrow," he said. "When I call you, though, you have no choice but to see me."

Each time Carolyn saw him in the light, he seemed more handsome. It was hard to pay attention to what he was saying when what she wanted was to drink in every inch of him and commit it all to memory. "What does that mean? Why don't I have a choice?"

Marcus smiled. "Because your future depends on it."

She swallowed hard. He might be smiling, but she could tell he was serious. "Really? Elaborate, please."

"I'm a decisive man," he said, a confident look on his face. "What's happening to us doesn't happen every day. You're not going to let it slip through your fingers, are you?"

Carolyn shook her head. When they brought his car around, she wasn't even certain what make it was, just that it was metallic blue and looked outrageously expensive. She'd been expecting the Jaguar. "What is this, a Rolls Royce? How many cars do you have?"

"It's a Bentley," he said once they were both inside. "Don't get used to it. It's going on the auction block next week. Business isn't so great right now, and I may need the money to live on."

"Do you sell cars?"

Marcus laughed. "Not exactly."

Since he didn't remember how to get to her house, Carolyn gave him directions while she marveled at the interior of the car, which was considerably more lavish than his Jaguar. The seats were large and plush. She could tell the engine was powerful when he accelerated, but instead of roaring, it made hardly any sound at all. And she couldn't feel the road. The sensation was similar to floating on a cloud of air.

"Later on," he told her, stopping at a light, "I'll give you a code and a secure cell phone number. You probably have a GPS system on the phone you're using now. Almost all the new phones have them. When we talk, our conversations will be encrypted."

Carolyn thought he was joking. "Are you with the CIA or something? I don't even know what you do for a living."

"I work for a company that designs custom software for the military," he told her, turning the Bentley onto her street. "My work is classified, so I can't really discuss it. Rival companies, as well as people working for foreign entities, attempt to hack into our system on a regular basis. Sometimes they plant viruses that send out e-mails or make phone calls from our contact lists."

"I see," Carolyn said, pointing out her house before he drove past it.

"I'm not going to walk you to the door." Marcus's voice was deep and resonant. "I don't think your kids should see us together until we're both certain where this is going." He kissed her as he reached across her to open the passenger door.

When she turned to get out of the car, her fingers slid out of his hand and across the seat. She heard a pop and saw Marcus's hair lift a bit.

"Is this what they mean by chemistry?" he asked with a grin.

"Afraid not." Carolyn smiled back at him as she closed the car door, then stuck her head inside the window. "Just the imbalance of positive and negative charges. You know, static electricity. My son's an aspiring physicist, remember?"

"I'll call you tomorrow," Marcus said, laughing.

As soon as he drove off, Carolyn felt the dew-covered grass tickling her toes. She had sand in her hair, inside her dress, and her back itched as if she'd been attacked by fire ants. Not only had the sand not bothered her as long as she was with Marcus, but neither of them had realized that she'd walked to the hotel barefoot. She unlocked the door and stepped inside, leaning against it to relish the moment. Not having money had its benefits. The shoes had been purchased at Payless for fifteen dollars. Not a big loss for such an eventful and promising evening. She headed to the kitchen and grabbed the box of Kellogg's Special K cereal from the pantry, pouring it into a large coffee mug and filling it with milk so she could munch and drink it while she got ready for bed.

It wasn't until Carolyn stripped off her clothes, set her alarm, and slid underneath the covers that she remembered something else she'd forgotten. John's Honda was still in a stall at the parking structure. She would have to call Veronica in the morning and ask for a ride to work.

CHAPTER 13

Tuesday, September 19—8:15 A.M.

"Devil keep you up all night?" Hank Sawyer asked Charley Young in the reception area of the Ventura County Coroner's Office. He had stopped by to see if the pathologist had any information for him on what they were referring to as the Alessandro Lagoon homicide.

"Always," Charley said in a slight Korean accent. "How could you possibly think we've had time to work up your case, Hank? I don't have the remains, anyway. Ferguson has them. I was just about to leave to go to her lab in LA."

Charley was only in his mid-thirties, but this morning, he looked several years older. Even his crisp white lab coat and neatly combed hair couldn't hide the fact that he was exhausted. "Now isn't this grand," Hank teased, knowing Charley didn't want him to tag along and get in his way. "We can visit on the drive down. Get caught up on all the gossip."

"No way," Charley said, making a sharp horizontal gesture with his hand. "Martha and I need to concentrate. This is tedious work, Hank."

"Martha, huh? Isn't that the lady with all the bucks who went to prison?"

"Martha Ferguson. You mean you don't even know who you were working with the past two days?"

"Two very long days," the detective said, grimacing. "I'll drive. Get your things. I can't wait to see old Martha. We got real close at the scene. You know, standing around up to my knees in mud, inhaling fumes from the freeway, listening to her bark orders and humiliate me in front of my men. She'll probably want me to scrub the toilet out when we get there."

A corner of Charley's mouth lifted, causing his left eye to narrow. "Go there with that attitude and she'll pitch you out on your head. Martha doesn't like outsiders in her lab, Hank. Ferguson Labs has one of the highest ratings in the country. Nothing gets contaminated. I'm serious, you shouldn't go with me. Concentrate on catching the killer, and let us handle the rest."

Hank draped an arm around the smaller man's neck, hugging him tight against his body. "I'm your daughter's godfather, remember? When you get called out late at night and Kim gets scared, who does she call? I'm your man, Charley. You gotta take me." He released him when he saw a look of acceptance appear on the pathologist's face. "Don't take this the wrong way, guy, but after the Abernathy fiasco, I'd like to keep tabs on the evidence. You know where this place is?"

"I've been there several times. The building is on a side street off Wilshire. To be sure, I mapped it on the computer."

An old-school detective, Hank had a high school diploma and a lifetime of experience. Today's cops were college grads; some even had master's degrees. Too much education gave a guy a swelled head, in Hank's opinion. When an officer thought too highly of himself, he was sometimes blind to the obvious. To catch a killer, you had to sink down to their level, muck around in their filth, learn to think with their brain. After handling a particularly gruesome case, some of the younger officers had to visit the department shrink. Hank, on the other hand, lived for those cases.

Charley swiped a card to open the security door, and the detective followed him down a long corridor. Most of the autopsy rooms had glass windows, and there always seemed to be a body or what was left of one on the table. Charley unlocked his own room with a key, and the two men stepped inside.

On one wall was a workbench, fitted with a drill press, anvils, saws, screwdrivers, wrenches, mallets, and all kinds of assorted tools

Hank wouldn't have associated with forensic pathology. Charley said the abstract shapes came in handy. He occasionally became stumped as to what kind of instrument had been used to kill a victim, then discovered that one of these tools matched up perfectly. He also had catalogs from various hardware stores that he would flip through when he had a free moment, always looking for everyday objects that could be used as instruments of death.

Then there were the machines used to grind down bones for samples: diamond-backed saws used to cut thin sections from bones and teeth in order to view them under a microscope, and the vibrating Stryker saw that Hank had nightmares about. The Stryker was used to slice off the top of the skull so the brain could be removed. Garden tools such as branch cutters were used to cut through ribs.

In one of the larger rooms there were various types of cameras and photographic equipment, a miniature X-ray machine, as well as an X-ray duplicator that could copy X-rays like a Xerox machine.

The place gave Hank the willies, but he'd learned to keep his repulsion off his face. How could a man supervise the homicide division if he got queasy around dead bodies? They didn't bother him at crime scenes, no matter how gory. That is, unless the victim was a child. Children were the worst, even if the scene was only a traffic accident, not a murder. A child was like a spotless canvas. None of them deserved to die.

It was something about the tiled floors at the morgue, the chemicals, the grinders and slicers. Hank decided that after a person got killed, he or she went through a second butchering on a frigid autopsy table. He wouldn't want his organs to end up as hamburger in one of Charley's grinders.

"Okay," the pathologist said, covering up a partially dissected young male on the table, pocketing his cell phone and keys, and stuffing some papers into a black leather satchel.

Hank stared at what looked like a small roast sitting on top of the scales. "What's that?"

"A heart," the pathologist said, rushing over to take care of it. "Thanks for reminding me. I started working on one of your shooting victims from the gang case. Everything needs to go back in the refrigerator until I get back." He started to package up the heart himself but then hit the intercom and gave instructions to an assistant to finish the job.

Leading the detective out of the room and heading back the way they had come, he said, "I told you we had a problem with your case yesterday." Their heels tapped on the floor as they walked. "It's even worse than I thought. I spent an hour teleconferencing the case with Martha last night. She called me at midnight, and she was still at her lab. I was so tired, I passed out as soon as I got home. Martha's a machine. She can work for days without sleeping."

"You're just bursting with good news," Hank said, pulling out a toothpick and placing it between his teeth. "Lay it on me."

"I don't know how the hell we're going to identify this woman. We can't profile her by nuclear DNA typing like we normally do. The remains were in the Alessandro Lagoon for an unspecified period of time. Depending on rainfall and other factors, they were more than likely submerged, then exposed to high temperatures and humidity from the miserable summer we had."

They stepped into the sunshine, and Hank slipped on his dark glasses. When they reached his unmarked black Crown Victoria in the parking lot, he hit the alarm button and unlocked the doors. "Didn't you find some maggots in the grave? I thought you could tell something from what those nasty little suckers had eaten."

"Unfortunately not," Charley told him, climbing into the passenger seat and strapping on his seat belt. "The tissue the insects were consuming turned out to be cat gut. There was a partially decomposed cat a few feet away."

"Partially decomposed? Why wasn't the cat reduced to bones like the victim?"

"A rodent probably burrowed in with it. Then it later floated to the surface. Obviously, I haven't had time to go over every detail. We have nothing more than the woman's height and a speculation as to her general weight. There's no sign of degeneration in her knees, so let's say five four, weight between one twenty to one forty. Martha agrees that she's probably in her thirties or early forties. Let's hope she can come up with something more definitive."

Hank turned the key, and the big engine engaged. "The last time we brought in an anthropologist, we didn't hear back from the guy for over a year. He charged us a fortune to reconstruct the dead guy's face with clay. In my opinion, it didn't even look like a person, more like a doll or something, and an ugly one at that. That was five years ago, and we still haven't identified the victim." He pulled out of the parking lot and headed toward the 101 freeway. "Did Ferguson see anything that would give us the cause of death?"

"I already told you there was no blunt force trauma," Charley told him. "Martha didn't find any knife scrapings on the bones, which lowers the chances that the victim was stabbed. Her jaw was gaping, but there's no way to know if her mouth was open at the time of death or if it just collapsed that way during decomposition. It could have also happened when the killer moved her. I'd say strangulation or suffocation, but the killer could have held her head underwater out there until she drowned, along with dozens of other scenarios. Without tissue, for all we know, she could have starved to death, or the killer may have buried her alive."

"Now that's a pleasant thought," Hank said, directing a harsh glance toward the pathologist. All this fancy equipment and brain power, and they knew nothing more than the day before.

They made it to the 405, one of the most heavily traveled freeways in the country, and headed south toward Los Angeles. Early afternoon, and already the traffic was bumper to bumper.

Charley said, "Now that we're on the subject, are you still dieting?"

"I watch what I eat." Hank proudly sucked in his stomach, then pounded it with his fist. "That's solid muscle, my friend. I run two miles every other day, do a hundred sit-ups every morning, and lift weights for an hour. I feel like I'm twenty again. The only problem is my belly feels like a tin drum with a dime rolling around inside. Right now, it wouldn't be satisfied if I fed it an entire cow."

"Ah," Charley said, "that's why you're so anxious lately. Don't lose too much weight. It isn't healthy. You might be trying to push your body below its set weight. If that's the case, you'll be battling this forever."

"It's more like a war than a battle," Hank said. "If I let myself, I could pack on ten pounds in a week. Forget about me. You had to find something worthwhile about our Jane Doe."

"CSI recovered a few hairs, but they're missing follicles and roots. One of the reasons we think she was buried somewhere else, then moved, was there wasn't any sign of clothing."

The detective was tempted to turn on his lights and siren to navigate around the traffic. Insisting on accompanying Charley may have been a poor decision. But now that he was a lieutenant, he had other officers to do the grunt work. And he had a vested interest in this homicide. Most murderers he didn't know. Carl Holden was the scum of the earth. The man didn't suffer from a mental illness, nor was he retarded. Although Carolyn said his mother may have abused him, causing him to develop a hatred for women, who gave a damn? Every killer out there claimed a history of abuse. Hank's mother used to lash him with a belt, and he hadn't turned into a murderer. That psychological stuff was nothing but bullshit. Tracy Anderson had been a beautiful young woman with an adorable four-year-old boy. If the child hadn't been at Tracy's mother's house on the day Holden murdered her, he would more than likely have been killed as well.

Sammy Anderson would be twelve by now. He recalled Carolyn telling him about having seen the boy with his father at the Olive Garden. How would the poor kid feel when he learned that the man who had murdered his mother had been released from prison because of an incompetent scientist?

"Any news on the Abernathy homicide?" he asked Charley. Even though Oxnard had its own police department, it was still part of Ventura County, and their crimes were processed at the same labs.

"I'm not handling it," Charley told him. "From what I understand, dozens of people wanted him dead."

"Dozens is an understatement. It looked like an execution to me. They tried to get a match on the partial print and came up with nothing. The shooter had grease or something on his hands, so the print was distorted. The kill shot was perfectly placed. And unlike most people, he didn't pump the guy full of bullets to make certain he was dead. He only fired one time. My guess is that the murderer served time in the military. If not, someone might have hired a professional assassin."

"Where are you going, Hank?" Charley asked, looking out the window. "We were supposed to exit on Wilshire. You drove right past it."

Hank took the next exit and used the side streets to make his way back over to the right street. "Were the hairs the CSI guys found human?"

"Yes. They had to sift through a ton of cat hair to find them. The hairs are only a few centimeters long, and we don't know if they're from the killer or the victim. That's the only break we've caught so far."

Big break, Hank thought facetiously. "What's next?"

"Mitochondrial DNA typing is all that's left. Belinda Connors will have to get approval from the top." Connors had replaced Robert Abernathy as the new chief of forensics. "We use an outside lab, and it's extremely costly. Mary Stevens called me this morning. She said our victim might be a woman who disappeared from San Diego about a year ago. The height and weight match, and the woman was thirty-six years old. I can't be certain about time of death. That's another thing we might learn if we run mtDNA on the remains. We can compare the findings to a body whose time of death is known. A year could be on the money, and then again, we might be looking at five or ten years. If she'd been buried in a cooler, dryer place, the bones would have been able to tell us more."

Hank wasn't impressed with Mary's assumption that the missing woman in San Diego was their murder victim. Mary was smart all right, and a damn hard worker, but she had a tendency to jump to conclusions. "Most of the females aren't even missing. They know where they are. They just don't want anyone else to know. Half the time they're running from an abusive spouse or boyfriend. We can't find anyone these days. You know what I think?"

"No," the pathologist said, pressing his glasses farther up on his nose, "but I'm sure you're going to tell me."

Hank thought about how many people were killed every day, and his mind summoned up images of his own body on one of Charley's autopsy tables. "Promise me something, okay? If some asshole shoots me, don't grind me up or put me through one of your slicers."

Charley laughed. "I'll use the Stryker saw instead."

"You're a prick, you know," Hank told him, his body twitching with tension. "I don't know how you can do what you do. I don't have the stomach for it. Anyway, what was I saying?"

"Something about why you can't find anyone." Charley saw a street sign just then that prompted him to call out, "Turn here."

Hank careened around the corner, picking up where he'd left off. "It's the Internet. It's taught everyone to lie. Even old ladies have dozens of AKAs. They're in chat rooms, trying to pick up men, or using their kid's credit cards to buy stuff they don't need. Sex Starved Wanda or Lizzy Big Boobs can turn out to be ninety years old. Can you believe this crap?"

"So, you've finally learned to use the Internet?"

"Just because I know how to use it doesn't mean I like it. Jesus, Charley, a monkey could use the Internet." The detective spat his toothpick out the window. "We busted one guy who'd gone to court and legally changed his name to the one he used on his e-mail. Cyberspace, my ass. It's a hotbed of criminal activity."

"Thanks for reminding me," Charley said, opening his briefcase and pulling out his Blackberry. "I need to check my e-mail."

"Put that away," Hank barked. "Check your e-mail later, damn it. How long is this other test going to take?"

"Don't you ever use your onboard computer?"

"I use it now and then. Just answer my question."

"Okay, mtDNA typing can take two analysts almost a month per case. That's why it's expensive. And there's also a risk of consuming the sample. Then if they come up with a different result, they don't have anything left to test. This was probably what caused Abernathy to do the things he did. He consumed samples, making it impossible to verify his conclusions. And in his case, it wasn't that he didn't have an adequate sample. He failed to collect the necessary material, and he handled it incorrectly in the lab." The pathologist rubbed his palms on his thighs. "Back to your Jane Doe. The thing is, even after we get the results, we still might not know who she is, unless she happens to come up in the FBI's DNA database, which is probably a long shot since she's female. Check and see what the San Diego PD collected as evidence from the missing woman's residence. Get me some decent samples, and maybe we'll eventually arrive at some answers. If nothing else, it'll give me a stronger reason to push the county into footing the bill for mtDNA analysis."

"I'll get Mary on it right away," Hank said, parking in front of a three-story brown brick building and getting out. The street was lined with mature trees, and it was far enough away from Wilshire that the traffic noise was minimal. "Does Ferguson own the building? How much does this broad make?"

"Her company owns it," Charley said, somewhat enviously. "She makes more than we do, that's for certain. They called her in to identify victims from nine-eleven. She started out at the CILHI, the US Army Central Identification Laboratory in Hawaii, working on the remains of Vietnam vets. Her father went MIA in 'Nam. His body has never been located."

Hank fell silent as they walked down a sidewalk leading to the front of the building, his original assessment of the redheaded anthropologist changing. Like Mary Stevens, Dr. Martha Ferguson must have decided to enter her profession due to the tragedy surrounding her father's death, something a man had to respect.

After they spoke to a receptionist, they took a seat in the waiting room. The sofas were worn, and the surfaces of the tables bore circles where people had placed leaking cups of sodas or coffee. The anthropologist might own the building, Hank thought, but she didn't appear to have a desire to impress anyone. He slouched in his seat, his stomach growling from hunger. He'd learned to accept the hunger pains, knowing they meant he wasn't overeating as he'd done in the past.

"Any luck tracking down Holden?" Charley asked.

"Not yet," Hank said, cracking his knuckles.

"Did you see the paper this morning? Your murderer already has a name. Since Holden was cleared in the Tracy Anderson case, they're leading up to classifying him as a serial killer." He opened his briefcase and removed the *Ventura Star*, handing it to the detective.

Hank sat up in his seat, glancing at the headline on the front page: SWEEPER STRIKES AGAIN. "Goddamn reporters," he said, scanning the article. "All I said was the killer hadn't left us much in the way of evidence. Sadistic bastard is probably eating this up. I never said he meticulously cleans up after himself, or any of this other shit they printed."

"He does, though." Charley told him, closing his briefcase. "Why do you think Abernathy perjured himself in Holden's trial? What he found under Anderson's fingernails might not have been enough to test properly. Holden must have spent hours going over that body. And dumping the garbage in the grave was brilliant. Consider yourself lucky that this man spent eight years behind bars. He could have killed a dozen women in that length of time."

Martha Ferguson burst through the doors, and both men stood. She was wearing a white lab coat, its top buttons undone, and her ample breasts looked as if they were about to pop out. Her red hair was tousled, her green eyes blazing, and her freckled Irish skin was beet red from the days they'd spent at the lagoon in the sun. "Hello, Charley," she said, pumping his hand. Then she stared at Hank. "What do you think *you're* doing here?"

"Nice to see you, too," Hank answered. "I'm trying to solve a homicide. That's my job, in case you've forgotten."

"I sent my progress reports to Detective Stevens last night," she advised. "Maybe by the end of the day we'll have more. Right now, Dr. Young and I need to get to work."

"I'm sorry, Martha," Charley said, his face flushed. "Hank and I came in the same car. I don't have a way to get home. I can only stay a few hours, anyway. He's a good man. He'll stay out of your way."

"Humph," she said, her eyes drifting up and down Hank's body. "Well, it looks like I don't have a choice. This way, gentlemen."

She gestured toward the door she'd come out of, and waited for the two men to enter. When Hank stepped into the hallway, he felt something and whipped his head around. The anthropologist winked at him and smiled. Hank didn't know if he should be mad or flattered. The esteemed Dr. Martha Ferguson had just pinched his ass.

CHAPTER 14

Tuesday, September 19—9:45 A.M.

Kathleen Dupont Masters sat in her blue Mercedes SL500, waiting for her husband's private jet to land at the Monterey Peninsula Airport. Standing five ten, she had shoulder-length curly blond hair and blue eyes. She'd always been self-conscious about her height and therefore had a tendency to roll her shoulders forward in order to appear smaller. Her most distinguishing feature was her manner of speaking. She was incredibly articulate, each word perfectly formed, delivered with a slow and measured tempo. People sometimes thought she was a newscaster or radio commentator.

Kathleen's husband, Dean, had made a million-dollar commitment to Jet USA. She would have never spent that kind of money when airline fares were so cheap. But to his credit, with only a phone call he had access to a fleet of jets to take him anywhere he needed to go. He used the plane primarily to fly from one golf tournament to another, chasing his childhood dream to become a PGA pro. He'd failed to make it through qualifying school the previous year. Right now, he played on the smaller, less lucrative tours. She knew he wouldn't be satisfied until he made it to the big time.

Even though her husband was independently wealthy, their spacious home had been a part of her divorce settlement, and she took care of most of the ancillary expenses. When two people knew they had more money than they could spend in a lifetime, it didn't matter who wrote the checks.

Today was Kathleen's forty-third birthday. Because her job selling real estate necessitated that she entertain clients, she'd recently picked up a few pounds, most of it around her waist. Her weight was still below average for her height and age, but her husband thought she looked best when her ribs showed and her stomach was concave. She attempted to camouflage the extra inches by wearing loose-fitting jackets over short skirts that showed off her long legs.

Kathleen was still recovering from her divorce from her first husband, George Dupont, who had traded her in for a younger woman after seventeen years of marriage. The situation was especially painful because she and George had no children. The little twit George had remarried had just delivered the couple's second baby.

Dean had come along at the lowest point in Kathleen's life. He was an intelligent and charming man, as well as a wonderful lover. Emotionally insecure, Kathleen always worried that he would tire of her and the events of the past would repeat themselves. Consequently, she was constantly fighting for Dean's attention. He was usually home only one week per month. Even with her busy professional life, she got lonely. The convertible top on the Mercedes was down because the midday sun was out—unusual in September, when most days were gray and foggy. Looking toward the runway, Kathleen saw the private jet arriving. Her husband walked down the exit stairs, looking great in his tan pleated pants and matching red golf shirt and cap. Six one, lean and fit, his skin burnished by the sun, Dean cut an impressive figure. He had dark hair, beautiful eyes, and looked much younger than his forty-five years. "Hi, handsome," his wife said, smiling.

They threw their arms around each other and kissed. "I missed you," he said. "It's good to be home."

"Liar," she chided.

They walked toward the Mercedes, Dean opening the driver's-side door and sliding behind the wheel. His own car, a Porsche 911, was stored in the long-term parking lot. "I'll pick the Porsche up later. Right now, I'm starving. Why don't we go over to Pebble for brunch?"

"It's my birthday," Kathleen complained. "Can't we eat somewhere that doesn't overlook a golf course?"

"Happy birthday, sweetheart," he told her, patting her thigh as he steered the car out of the parking lot. "Then I guess I'll have to cancel the eleven o'clock facial and massage I booked for you at the spa. I thought you might want to relax a little. You're not that young anymore."

She hit him in the arm. "Younger than you, old man."

"Careful, I need that arm to win the U.S. Open next year. Are you going to keep your appointments at the spa or not?"

Kathleen knew he wanted to hit some balls. Besides, her birthday wasn't important. She had one every year. "An afternoon at the spa sounds great, darling. You picked a thoughtful and practical gift. I've been under a lot of stress lately."

A short time later they entered the famous Lodge at Pebble Beach. "Beach Club okay?" he asked without looking at her.

"Fine," she said, linking arms with him. Dean had a way of asking for her opinion, but not really asking. He knew she would go along with anything he suggested.

The restaurant was wise to put mirrors on the inside walls to reflect views of the ocean from every table. Looking toward the water, she could see the vistas of Carmel Bay. The green fairways at Pebble Beach extended to the edge of the ocean cliffs. The natural beauty was breathtaking, no matter how often you saw it.

As soon as they were seated and had ordered their food, Kathleen told him, "I've decided to travel with you and put my real estate career on hold."

Dean turned sideways in his seat and spat out, "When did you come up with this bright idea?"

Kathleen twisted her napkin in her lap. "Between the two of us, we have more than enough money. I want to be with you, honey. I can go to your tournaments and root for you. It's not right for a husband and wife to be apart all the time. I've already spoken to Elaine Caldwell. She can run the office for me, and I can do a lot by phone."

His jaw locked, and he spun around, almost knocking over his coffee cup. She was relieved when her cell phone rang. "What do you mean they're canceling the escrow?" Kathleen said, her voice carrying out over the restaurant. "Call Larry in Legal and have him fire off a letter reminding the buyer of the liquidated-damages provision in the purchase and sale contract. If they think they're going to lose their hundred grand, they may think twice before backing out. Tell Larry not to sit on this. I'm expecting it to be done before I finish my lunch." She terminated the call, slipping the phone back into her purse. "Larkin deal. Major problem, but that means the deal's almost done."

"How much is the commission?" Dean asked, tapping his fingers on the table.

"Just over a hundred and fifty thousand."

"And you're going to walk away from that kind of money? Come on, Kathleen. You've worked for years building up that business. Elaine can't handle it without you. You're the one with the contacts."

"I don't care about the business," she insisted. "I want to be with you. Is that so wrong?"

Dean's face softened and he smiled, reaching over and clasping her hand under the table. "We'll discuss this later. Today we're celebrating your birthday."

"How was the tournament?" Kathleen asked, deciding to change the conversation to his favorite topic.

"Disappointing," he said. "Monday and Tuesday I played well enough to make the cut. Then I lost my swing and shot seventy-eight. All the guys out there hit the ball well. The difference is their mental game. If I improve in that area, no one will be able to touch me." He paused, looking around for the waiter. "I should have ordered a Bloody Mary." Turning his attention back to her, he added, "I can't afford any distractions right now. Even when I'm not playing, I'm working on my game. If you travel with me, I won't have any more time for you than I do now."

Kathleen lowered her eyes. "I thought we weren't going to discuss it right now."

The waiter came over with their food. Dean asked her if she wanted a cocktail, but she declined, so he ordered one for himself. "Don't give up on me, Kathleen," he said. "Golf is the hardest sport in the world to master. It takes work and sacrifice to make it."

"It seems like you're punishing yourself as well as me," she told him, her voice trailing off. "Maybe you're just not cut out to be a professional golfer. There are more productive things you could do with your time. You'd be a great addition to my business. Getting your real estate license would be a piece of cake. You could still play golf in your spare time."

Dean gave her a dark look, but he didn't reply. At some point, she had to decide if they had a genuine marriage, or if she was nothing more than Dean Masters's adoring fan. How could she leave him, though? She was in love with him. He called her every day, but phone calls didn't satisfy her need for a physical connection.

"You're just feeling neglected," he told her, taking a sip as soon as the waiter brought his Bloody Mary. "I flew all the way back from Atlanta to be with you on your birthday. Why can't you ever appreciate the things I do for you?"

"I do, Dean," Kathleen said, reaching for a roll from the bread basket.

He reached over and snatched the roll out of her hand. "Stop eating, for God's sake. You're getting fat. What size is that suit, anyway, a fourteen? You might think you're hiding the weight, but you're not. If you went on the road with me, you'd probably stay in the hotel room all day and eat. Then I'd have to haul around a cow. "

Kathleen was crushed. She felt her eyes moisten with tears, but she refused to cry. There was something far more serious than his hurtful remarks on her mind. How could Dean have been in Atlanta when one of her friends saw him at a restaurant in Ventura? The worst of it was that he'd been having lunch with an attractive woman. She stood and threw her napkin down on the table. "I'll see you back at the house. I don't want to be late for my massage."

"Stop it," Dean whispered, seeing the couple at the adjacent table staring at them, "You're acting like a child. Sit back down and eat your lunch. You have thirty minutes before you have to be at the spa."

"Eat it yourself," Kathleen said, walking out of the restaurant.

The garage door opened. Dean would be coming through the kitchen directly into the living room. Kathleen was seated on their white leather sofa, her hands clasped tightly in her lap. As soon as she heard his keys turn in the lock, she flinched, resisting the urge to make up with him so they could enjoy the evening. Instead, she took a deep breath and steeled herself for the argument that was sure to come.

"How was the spa?" Dean said, walking over and planting a kiss on her lips. "I'm sorry if I was abrupt at lunch, honey. I was annoyed because you were nagging me again about the time I spend on the road. Just so you'll know, I don't usually shoot seventy-eights. This was a tougher course than I expected."

Kathleen straightened her back. "Just so *you'll* know, I've never worn a size fourteen in my life." She gulped oxygen, then blurted out, "What were you doing in Ventura Saturday? You were supposed to be in Atlanta."

Dean moved away from her, his face shifting into hard lines. "What are you talking about? Why would I be in Ventura?"

"Andrea Worthington saw you," she said. "She said you were having lunch at the Olive Garden with a woman. Are you having an affair, Dean?"

"Andrea's an idiot!" he said, pacing in front of her. "Of course I'm not having an affair. I've only been to Ventura once, and that was ten years ago."

"She knows you, Dean," Kathleen said, certain now that he was lying. If he'd admitted being there, he might have provided a justifiable reason for having lunch with a woman. She could have been a female golf pro, or someone involved in organizing the tour. Maybe there'd been some problem with the jet that had necessitated his stopping in that area. For all she knew, the pilot could have been a woman. He felt so confident that he could get her to believe anything he told her that he hadn't even taken the trouble to make up a believable story. "She said you were only two tables away from her, but you were too engrossed in your lunch date to notice. She even described the clothes you were wearing—that black Gucci turtleneck I bought you last Christmas."

"I don't have to listen to this," Dean barked. "You and your peabrained women friends. Black turtlenecks are a dime a dozen, for Christ's sake. Even if Andrea did see me out somewhere, do you really think she could tell if my turtleneck was a Gucci? Frankly, it looks like it came from Target. I hate that stupid shirt. I only wear it because you gave it to me."

"Who is she?" Kathleen said, lowering her chin and peering up at him. "I was already married to a man who cheated on me, remember? I blame myself for not figuring it out before now. Because I don't pay attention to golf, I can't be certain what you do when you take off in your jet." The more she thought about it, the madder she became. "I bet the girls are really impressed, Dean. With your looks, and the way you like to spend money, you should be able to get anyone you want." She stood and turned to leave the room.

"Get back here!" he shouted, his hand clutched in a fist. "I'm talking to you. . . . I've never been unfaithful. Do you know how it makes me feel to be accused of something I didn't do? And what's this shit about me working for you? I play golf, you sell real estate. What are you trying to turn me into, some kind of office boy?"

"This will probably come as a shock to you," Kathleen said, refusing to move, "but everything doesn't revolve around you. There are more important things than you and your stupid golf. Traveling around the country to shoot seventy-eights. Face it, Dean. You're a mediocre golfer and a lousy husband."

"That's bullshit," Dean said, throwing his arms into the air. "I have an important tournament this week. You're trying to ruin my career by making me a nervous wreck. I *am* good enough. You'll see. What I do is what I do. You're just going to have to deal with it."

"Not on my nickel, I don't."

"I've got my own money, remember?" he said, lowering his voice. "When we decided to get married, we had an agreement. I wouldn't interfere in your real estate business, and you wouldn't bother me about my golf. What happened, huh? You knew what kind of relationship this was going to be going in."

"Leave!" Kathleen said, her voice laced with venom. "I refuse to live with a man I can't trust. Go ahead and scream, Dean. Yell. Stomp your feet. It won't do you any good. This is my house, and I want you out. I'm going to my attorney tomorrow morning and file for a divorce. Then you can play golf to your heart's content."

A look of shock registered on his face. She'd won the fight, and lost her husband. It didn't matter. From the way things looked, she'd lost him long ago. She went to the door and flung it open. "Get out of my damn house before I call the police."

"You can't call the police," Dean said. "You have no grounds. And, besides, we're married."

"I'll tell them you hit me."

"But I've never laid a hand on you."

"I'll lie," Kathleen said, "just like you did when you said you were in Atlanta instead of fucking some girl in Ventura."

Dean was blinking repeatedly in his attempt to control his rage. He didn't even look like the man she had married. She'd finally caught a glimpse of who he really was—a person she could learn to hate.

CHAPTER 15

Brad Preston walked up to Carolyn as she banged open the door of Department 46 of the superior court after having appeared at a sentencing hearing on a robbery and shooting. The department's court officer represented the probation officers' recommendations on minor cases, but the more serious offenses required the officers to appear in person and verbally present their recommendations to the court.

"Do you think Carl Holden murdered the woman they found buried in the lagoon?" Brad said.

"It certainly looks like Holden's handiwork to me," Carolyn responded, continuing down the carpeted corridor at a fast clip. "I'm not sure the police are convinced, but there are far too many similarities. Every cop in town is looking for him. He's still a registered sex offender, and no one knows where he's presently living. When I interviewed him, he said he'd stayed at the shelter after he was kicked out of his apartment in LA. I called every shelter around, and no one has ever heard of him. They should have kept him in jail until he established a permanent residence. How many times can the system screw up?"

Seeing an attorney she didn't care for conferring with his client, Carolyn turned around and began walking back down the same corridor they had come from.

"You want to tell me where you're going?" Brad asked, stopping.

"The long way," Carolyn told him, glancing over her shoulder. "That was Don Pinehurst, the asshole who's representing Benjamin Abbott, the twelve counts of child molest you assigned me. I'm not in the mood to listen to his opinions on the sexuality of prepubescent boys. "

"Listen to me," Brad said, catching up to her. "Judge Reiss couldn't hold Holden without cause. The other guy started the fight in the bar and pushed Holden into the window. I'm surprised Reiss even convicted Holden. As far as being a registered sex offender, that's leftover red tape from the old charges. He's been cleared on those crimes."

"Reiss knew who Holden was," she argued. "He's a damn judge. He could have figured something out."

They took the elevator to the first floor, crossed the lobby, and stepped outside into the morning sunlight. People were streaming in and out of the courthouse or sitting around the ledge of the fountain. It was a gorgeous day, but Carolyn didn't notice.

The defendant in the case she'd appeared on would turn twenty in two weeks. A former surfer, Cory Slaver wasn't old enough to buy booze, but he would spend his birthday, along with the best years of his life, inside a prison cell. He had an extensive record, most of the prior offenses related to drugs. This time he'd moved into the big time, robbing a pawnshop and killing the owner, a Russian immigrant with a wife and five children. The law afforded victims the right to make a statement during the sentencing hearing. The dead man's wife had appeared, surrounded by their young children, tearfully telling the court in broken English of the desperate life they'd led in Russia and the many dreams her husband had held when he'd moved his family to this great land of opportunity. The only opportunity her husband had now was to spend eternity in a cemetery on U.S. soil.

Carolyn and Brad continued walking toward the adjacent building where the probation department was located. "I want Holden in prison until he dies, Brad. Like it or not, once he's in custody, you're going to help me."

Brad opened the door for her. "And how am I going to do that?"

"Whatever it takes," she said. "We have to get this animal off the street any way we can."

They passed the headquarters for the sheriff's department, and then hiked up the stairs to the second floor. Once they'd entered the secure area behind the reception console, Preston placed his hand on her elbow and steered her toward his office. He kicked the door shut behind them with his heel.

"Calm down," he told her. "Holden will eventually get what's coming to him."

"I'm just so tired, Brad," Carolyn said, an anguished look on her face. "I feel like I'm surrounded by evil, fighting this enormous battle that I have no chance of ever winning. I mean, you should see my bed in the morning. I thrash around all night like someone is chasing me."

"Your children aren't evil," Brad told her, moving closer and clasping her hand. "Children are the essence of good. Your family loves and needs you. I care about you. There's your mother and Neil. You take too much on your shoulders, Carolyn. You always have."

She pushed him away and started pacing. "This thing with Abernathy . . . I was consumed with hatred and indignation. But I didn't want someone to blow his head off, for God's sake. . . . Then the poor woman reduced to bones at the lagoon . . . " She stopped walking and grabbed the back of a chair. "At the sentencing hearing this morning, I was so conflicted. I knew Cory Slaver got what he deserved, but he was just a kid, only a few years older than John. He threw his life away. And for what? A few watches, some gold chains, a handful of cash. I felt such compassion for the victim's wife and family. All these lives destroyed. It never ends, even when I'm not at work. The other night I stopped off at El Pollo Loco to pick up some food. These two thugs came in. I was certain the restaurant was about to be robbed. Earlier I saw a father abusing his five-year-old right across from the church. The whole world has gone mad."

"Look at me," Preston said, seizing her by the shoulders. "You are *not* having a meltdown, understand? You've been in this business long enough to know that this kind of stuff sometimes comes in waves. You're one of the best investigators we have. We need you,

Carolyn. You *are* making a difference. Sure, the system isn't perfect, but it's all we have."

They stared at each other. She thought of the night before with Marcus, and her sense of panic began to ebb. "I'm fine," she said, taking a seat in a chair. "Thanks for letting me rant, Brad."

"Are you sure?" He walked over and sat down behind his desk. "Your eyes looked a little psycho a few minutes ago. I don't want you stripping your clothes off and running naked out of my office. I have a bad enough reputation as it is."

Carolyn laughed. "Really, I'm fine. Why did you come looking for me?"

"I didn't," Brad said. "I was in a conference at the DA's office. A woman named Helen Carter was arrested last month for shooting her former lover. Victor Paglia at the DA's office thinks Carter's attorney may be planning an insanity defense. The lover, you guessed it, had a restraining order. Carter was convicted on that count this morning. When you talk to her for the presentence report, try to find out if she's faking. If you do, Paglia will give you a medal."

"Yeah, sure," Carolyn said, scowling again. "And then when she's convicted on the homicide charges, you'll assign me the case. I'm up to my eyeballs in work right now, Brad, and I'm trying to help the PD track down Holden."

"Paglia wants to know where they stand before they get in too deep on this thing. He asked specifically for you, Carolyn. I know I've been hitting you hard lately. I'm trying to cut you some slack by assigning you lightweight cases. Why worry about the homicide count now? The preliminary hearing isn't scheduled for another two weeks. The way the courts are bogged down, it might be a year before Carter's convicted."

"Helen Carter isn't insane," she tossed back. "I handled her seven years ago for nineteen counts of welfare fraud. She was only twenty-three, and she knew how to work the system better than most people twice her age."

"Your memory is phenomenal," Brad remarked, pleased to see her feisty spirit returning. "Since the computers are always crashing, we should just tap into your brain. You remember every case you've ever handled." He put his feet up on his desk. "Guess I picked the right person for the job. I wonder if Carter will respond to you the same way men do. Be sure to dress up in a short skirt and show your tits. She likes girls. Of course, maybe you're not her type."

"I know you're trying to be cute, Brad," Carolyn said, snatching the file off the corner of his desk. "But if you make any more obscene remarks, I'll do more than strip naked and go running out of your office."

Dean Masters left the Porsche in the garage, jumped into Kathleen's Mercedes and squealed the tires, propelling the car backward out of the garage. He was so consumed with rage, he slammed into the trash cans at the curb, causing one to roll down the hill.

How dare she order him out of their house and threaten to call the police?

Kathleen had summoned the past. He'd sworn to himself he would never be vulnerable to a woman again. He was in the same position he'd been in fourteen years ago, only worse. He couldn't afford the scrutiny of a divorce, particularly not now.

As he drove, the rage grew stronger until he could think of nothing else. He turned the radio on at a deafening level, hoping to drown his thoughts out with sound. He had no choice. He had to . . . had to . . . His fingers tightened on the steering wheel; the road blurred in front of him. He had to . . . must . . . he couldn't tolerate . . . he had to . . . kill her. Okay . . . okay, he thought, the decision was made. Now he could take action.

Dean's mind changed gears, the coolness of logic replacing the irrationality of anger. He was smarter this time. All he needed was to formulate a solid strategy. Someone had to take the fall. Then he would stick around, play the grieving husband, put on a good funeral.

The sun had disappeared, and dark clouds loomed overhead, spitting forth moisture. With a cold wind blowing off the ocean, the temperature had dropped into the fifties. Already the smell of firewood filled the air. In Carmel, people used their fireplaces even during the summer.

Dean needed a drink, so he took a sharp right into the parking lot of Twin Pines Liquor. When he stepped out of the Mercedes, a voice broke the silence. "Can you spare a few dollars?" a man asked, his words slurred. The plea came from a drunk with a long beard and matted hair. He was wearing a ripped Charlie Manson T-shirt.

There are times when solutions come out of nowhere, Dean thought. This appeared to be one of them. The drunk, sitting on a cardboard box behind the building, could be part of the framework of a perfect plan. "What's your name, guy?" he asked, squatting down to the man's level. His stench was almost unbearable. Alcohol seemed to be oozing through his skin, and he smelled as if he'd been lying in his own excrement.

"Arnie," he said. "You've got to help me, man, I'm really hungry."

"Are you hungry or thirsty?" Dean asked, his eyes scanning the parking lot to make certain no one was around. "Be honest with me, Arnie, and I might help you get what you need. Isn't that what you want, money for booze?"

"Yeah, man," Arnie said, becoming more alert. "I'd give my right arm for some whiskey. Warms me up, you know. I ain't got no place to live."

"Sure you don't," Dean said, repulsed that he'd been reduced to conversing with the lowest level of humanity. "I can drive you to the homeless shelter. You don't want that, do you? Come on, be honest, pal. All you want is to get drunk."

One thing he had in common with Arnie was an addictive personality. Women were an addiction, something he needed as badly as this disgusting man needed alcohol. If his mother and father had not rejected him, if people would only appreciate him and do the simple things he asked of them, he might not be in the position he was right now. There was no halfway house, no pills he could take to cure himself. He craved the attention of women, and at the same time, he often wanted them to shut up and leave him alone. He wanted *his* kind of attention—praise, affection, a desire to do anything he asked of them. In the case of Kathleen, she'd seemed like the perfect candidate. Then she'd become overly clingy and inquisitive. "Wait here," he told the man. "What kind of whiskey do you drink?"

"Whatever you're buying, I'm drinking," Arnie said, salivating. He brushed a filthy hand across his mouth and slowly pushed himself to his feet.

"No," Dean said, reaching into his pocket and pulling out two twenties, "you're buying and I'm paying. Get a gallon or something. That way, you won't run out."

Arnie glanced over at the Mercedes. "That's a beautiful car you got. Is it warm in there?"

"Of course," Dean said, smiling. If nothing else, he'd lost his desire to drink. "We'll party in the car. I'll be waiting for you, buddy."

"God bless you," Arnie said, staggering around the corner.

God wasn't going to save this man, Dean thought, even if there was a God, which he seriously doubted. Only a matter of time, and old Arnie would be scraped off the street like a dead cat. Winter was coming, and this area of California was far colder than Los Angeles. If Arnie didn't die of hypothermia or dehydration, cirrhosis of the liver would surely kill him. The man's skin had a yellowish cast. What Dean had in mind would give Arnie's worthless life some degree of meaning.

When Arnie emerged from the store, Dean realized he had a problem. How the hell was he going to get this guy into the trunk? The man struggled to open the bottle.

"Where's my change?"

"Here," Arnie said, handing Dean both the change and the bottle. "Open it for me, will you?" Losing his balance, he toppled over to find his old familiar friend, the pavement. "Shit."

As Arnie's eyes zeroed in on the bottle, Dean pressed the button on his key to open the trunk. "Can you get up?"

"I don't think so," the drunk said. "A sip of that whiskey sure would help."

"You'll have plenty of that in a few minutes. You're going straight to whiskey heaven." Dean placed the bottle next to the open trunk. The rain was coming down harder now, and his clothes were getting soaked. "Let me give you a hand." He grabbed Arnie's arm, using his own weight to pull the man upright. Arnie's momentum and his weak legs brought him into Dean's arms. All he needed was some stinky bum's arms wrapped around him! He pivoted and dropped him into the trunk. The bottom half of Arnie's body sank, but his feet still dangled outside the car. "Pull your feet in."

"I ain't going to ride in this here trunk, am I?"

Dean shoved the bottle at him. "Here's your booze."

Arnie's eyes got big, his feet retracted, and Dean slammed the trunk closed. "You all right in there?" he asked, not wanting the guy to start screaming before he managed to get on the road. The man was too busy taking large gulps of the alcohol to care where he was. It would only be a matter of time before he went into an alcoholic stupor.

When Hank called and told Carolyn he was sending Mary Stevens to San Diego to talk to the local authorities and examine their evidence on the disappearance of Lisa Sheppard, she called the detective and asked if she minded if she tagged along. "A little company would be great," Mary said, in high spirits. "I'll swing by the courthouse and pick you up. Be downstairs in fifteen minutes."

Carolyn packed up her briefcase and walked down to Brad's office again. "I'm going to interview two defendants at the jail today," she said, not wanting him to tell her she couldn't take the afternoon off to go with Mary. "Then I'm going to lock myself up somewhere and see if I can knock off a few reports. If you need me, I'll be on my cell."

Brad gave her a curious look before slapping his hands on the desk. "You're the worst liar I've ever seen," he said. "Never play poker, baby, or you're going to lose your shirt. What's going on?" He continued with a devilish smirk on his face, "You got some new man you're taking to the house while your kids are at school?"

Carolyn was accustomed to Brad's jokes and innuendos. Although she protested, she actually enjoyed their banter. With the kind of control she needed in her job, it was good to occasionally have someone to butt heads with and release her frustrations. She stepped closer to his desk, apologizing and telling him the truth about the trip to San Diego. "I want to nail Holden so bad, I feel as if I'm going to jump out of my skin. I can still hear his voice inside my head. No one else knows him like I do, Brad. That's why the police aren't going to catch him without my help. I promise, I'll keep up with my caseload. You know me. I can juggle a million things."

"Humph," Brad said, checking his fingernails. "As your supervisor, I have to advise you that you could be jeopardizing your job. The agency doesn't pay you to investigate murders until the person is convicted. Now as . . ."

She waited for him to finish, but he nonchalantly glanced around the room. He was baiting her.

"What, for God's sake? If you've got something to say, say it."

"Well," he said, undoing his tie and tossing it on top of a stack of files on the floor, "as the magnanimous individual that I am, I'd say forget the rules. We can't do much to stop crime after the fact. If you think you can help bring Holden in, go for it, but you'll owe me."

"Put it on my tab," she said, rushing toward the door, knowing Mary was probably waiting.

"All this and I don't even get a thank-you."

"Thanks, Brad. I'll buy you lunch or something."

"Can't you do better than that?"

"I'll frame your picture and hang it up next to the pope," Carolyn tossed over her shoulder as she disappeared through the doorway.

CHAPTER 16

Tuesday, September 19—12:45 P.M.

Mary Stevens should have been a race-car driver instead of a cop, Carolyn decided, having white-knuckled it all the way to San Diego as the speedometer barely dropped below ninety and several times inched its way past one hundred.

When the two women arrived at the San Diego Police Department, Detective Pete Fisher met them in the lobby and led them down a corridor to the detective bay.

Mary looked stunning, so much so that several of the officers stopped and stared. Wearing a clingy pink dress and sling-back pumps, she had straightened her usually curly shoulder-length hair for the day and carefully applied her makeup. Her sensuous lips were a bright, shiny coral. She leaned over and whispered in Carolyn's ear, "A little glam can open a lot of doors, know what I mean? Particularly when we're poking around on another department's turf."

"I agree," Carolyn said, asking herself if Mary knew that she herself occasionally dressed provocatively when she went to conduct an interview with a violent offender. Anything to get them to spill their guts. No wonder she and Mary got along.

Detective Fisher gestured toward two chairs, then sat down behind his paper-strewn desk. He was a tall, thin man, with dark, unruly hair, his face pockmarked from acne. Inside the open room, phones jangled, men and women chattered, and plainclothes officers rushed in and out. "I'm sorry if I gave you the wrong impression over the phone," he said. "I handled the missing person's report on the Sheppard case, but that case is closed. We didn't find any evidence of foul play."

Mary's jaw dropped. "The woman disappeared, didn't she? Didn't you send your CSI team to her house? There's a possibility she's our murder victim."

"I doubt it," Fisher told them, standing. "Hey, can I get you two some coffee?"

"No," Mary said, pissed. "What I drove all the way down here for is answers. We have an unidentified body. Our computer models show that it's Lisa Sheppard. We need to confirm this, understand? How could you handle this as a simple missing person's report? Lisa Sheppard is still missing, am I right? That's because she's dead. In Ventura, we call that a murder investigation."

"Don't get huffy with me," Fisher said, flopping back down in his chair. "You know how many people go missing every year? This isn't your victim. The couple had a falling out, that's all. The husband reported her missing, then called a week or so later and said she'd phoned him from her mother's house in Missouri, and they were more than likely going to get a divorce. No more missing person. Now if it had been a kid or a retard or something . . ."

The two women exchanged tense glances. "Did you speak to Lisa Sheppard and make certain she was okay?" Carolyn asked, deciding to step in before the detective threw them out.

"Nah," Fisher said, wadding up a piece of paper and tossing it into the trash can. "Mr. Sheppard was the party who reported his wife missing. If he says she's accounted for, case closed. When a guy calls and tells you his car is stolen, then calls back and tells you he's found it, it's no longer police business."

"A wife is not the same as a car," Mary said, even more annoyed. "Give us the contact information for the husband and the woman's mother in Missouri. Please don't tell me you don't have it."

"Listen," he said, leaning forward, "I drove by there a week or so after the husband contacted us to say his wife was no longer missing. The house was up for sale. One of the doors was unlocked, so I went inside and looked around. At first I thought there might be something going on. All their furniture was still there, like I told you. Since their clothes and miscellaneous personal items were gone, I decided the husband packed up and left after the wife dumped him. The furniture was shit, anyway. They probably split up because they couldn't make the payments on the house. Do you know money is one of the most common reasons why people divorce?"

"Let me get this straight," Mary said, counting on her fingers. "You didn't collect any evidence. You didn't talk to Lisa Sheppard to verify her husband's story, and you didn't call her mother in Missouri. What exactly *did* you do, Fisher, other than walk through the victim's house without the benefit of a search warrant?"

"Tell you what," he said, "I'll make copies of the file and you folks can go at it anyway you want. Will that get you off my back? I don't know about Ventura, but San Diego is a big city. We probably had twenty crimes go down since you got here. You know, real crimes, things that are happening right now."

Once Fisher left to make the copies, Mary turned to Carolyn. "Hope he doesn't handle his other cases the way he handled Lisa Sheppard's disappearance." She glanced at her watch. "Want to stop by the place where they lived and question some of the neighbors?"

"I'm game," Carolyn told her. "If Lisa answers the door, though, we might owe Detective Fisher an apology."

"Shit, that lazy fool," Mary said, scrunching up her face. "I'm not apologizing for nothin'. He's the poorest excuse for a cop I've ever seen. Besides, I don't like him."

"You don't even know the man."

"Oh, yeah," Mary said, lowering her voice so the other detectives couldn't overhear. "I know enough to know I don't like him. My guess is he didn't even write a missing person's report. He might have only filed an incident report that can be written in five minutes. Right now, he's probably back there scribbling down whatever he can remember."

The minutes ticked off. Mary started swinging her leg. Her sling-back shoe made an annoying sound as it slapped against her heel. After twenty minutes, she said, "Told you, didn't I? How long does it take to copy a file? Bet he steals, too. I can smell a thief a mile away."

Pete Fisher returned with a harried look on his face. He handed Mary a thin manila folder without speaking. She knew the contents of the file were going to be worthless to them. Carolyn had to admit that the detective looked guilty. For what, she wasn't entirely certain. Maybe because he was standing in front of a dedicated police officer who would work a case until there was nothing left to work, who had even tracked down her father's killer. Perhaps he merely sensed that Mary was a woman of integrity, a quality Detective Fisher didn't appear to possess.

Mary and Carolyn went back and forth about where to have lunch. Mary wanted to go to the drive-through at Carl's Jr., and Carolyn wanted to stop off at a health-food store that served soup and sandwiches. "You're going to lecture me about junk food?" the detective said, pointing a finger at her. "You're the one who guzzles liquid chocolate for lunch. That's not exactly health food."

"I don't do that all the time," Carolyn protested, tugging on the strap of her seat belt. "I was on a chocolate binge, okay? I'm going through withdrawal now, and I have to eat something other than hamburgers."

"You'd have a hard time being a cop," the detective told her, turning into the shopping center where the health-food store was located. "We have to eat whenever and whatever we can get our hands on. By the time we finish eating, it's going to be close to three o'clock. We're going to get stuck in traffic on the way back."

"Then maybe you'll have to drive the speed limit," Carolyn said, as Mary parked. She looked up and saw a familiar blue sign. "Do you realize this is a handicapped slot?"

"Oops." Mary backed up and parked a few rows over. "I did that once in a black-and-white. Doesn't go over well with the public. I got written up."

Carolyn told Mary about her evening with Marcus over lunch.

"Now I know why you're watching what you eat," the policewoman said, finishing off her egg salad sandwich and splitting their bill. "I still can't believe this whole scenario you described. Man's got a good-looking woman on the beach. Moon's out, waves splashing, and all he does is watch her sleep. Pretty weird, if you ask me. Guy should have been all over you."

"It was wonderful," Carolyn told her, a dreamy look in her eyes. "I can't explain it, Mary. There was something so honest about him, so deep, so unique. Most men are either rushing at you ninety miles per hour or they're running the other way. He let me remain in my own space, but somehow we connected at this profound level."

"Quiet, mysterious type, right?"

"I guess," Carolyn agreed, putting on her sunglasses as they exited the restaurant.

"Here's what I've learned about men like that," Mary said as they walked to her car. "The silent types are silent for a reason. They're stupid. They haven't got anything to say. Women fill in all the blanks and end up married to a knucklehead who looks good and knows how to keep his mouth shut."

A half hour later, they pulled up in front of a modest house on Grove Street, not far from Balboa Park. As they made their way to the front door, Carolyn said, "The Sheppards could have made up, then taken the house off the market."

"We'll know shortly." The detective indicated a person moving past a window toward the door.

A portly middle-aged man wearing a tank top opened the door. Mary flashed her badge and quickly slipped it back into her purse before the man figured out she was working outside her jurisdiction. "I'm Detective Stevens and this is Officer Sullivan," she said, peering through the screen. "We'd like to ask you some questions. Do you mind if we come in?"

"Sure," he said, opening the door wider. "I'm Owen Richards. What's this about?" After the women stepped inside, he continued, "Have a seat. Do you want something to drink? Some water or a soda? I'd offer you a beer, but I guess you can't drink while you're on duty."

Shaking her head "no" to the offer of a beverage, Mary said, "When did you buy this home?" and took a seat beside Carolyn on a dirty beige sofa. The only other chair in the room was a recliner, and the owner was already sitting in it. The house was fairly neat, but it reeked of perspiration, beer, and, from the kitchen, grease.

"I reckon it's been about five months now," Richards told them, taking a swig of his Budweiser. "Got a good deal on it, too. I'm a bachelor, see. I never owned my own home before. Drive a truck for a living. Guess that's why I never got hitched. Women don't like it when you're gone all the time. They always think you're cheating on them."

Carolyn asked, "Did you buy the furniture as well?"

"What furniture?" he said, looking puzzled. "I just moved my stuff out of my old apartment. I'm not here that often, so why bust my budget to buy new furniture? Don't you think it's time you tell me what this is all about?"

"One of the former owners of this house was reported missing about a year ago," Mary informed him. "The couple's name was Sheppard. Did you meet them, maybe speak to one of them on the phone?"

"You gotta be mistaken," Richards said, belching. "I've never heard of anyone named Sheppard. I bought this from a real estate investor named Mark Thomas. Nice guy. Gave me a real good deal, knocked twenty grand off the asking price. He'd sold it to some other people before me. They turned out to be deadbeats, so he kicked them out. I think their name was Wagner. I occasionally get mail addressed to them. Never got mail for anyone named Sheppard, though."

"Have any of your neighbors lived here a long time?" Carolyn asked, knowing Mary was disappointed. If he'd bought the furniture from the Sheppards, they might still be able to locate some kind of evidence. "You know, a busybody, someone in a neighborhood watch."

"You got it right the first time," Richards said, chuckling. "That's got to be Mrs. Kirkland. Lived here about twenty years, they tell me . . . always looking out her window. First time I saw her, I thought it was a cat." He cupped his hand in a circle and held it to his ear. "Do you hear that racket? She plays her TV so loud, I almost reported her for disturbing the peace. Poor old thing is deaf, though." He shrugged, picking up his beer can and placing it back down when he discovered it was empty. "Nothing I can do but tolerate it. Don't have the heart to sic the cops on her."

"Thanks for your time," Mary said, standing to leave. "Here's my card. If you think of anything else, please call me."

"You're a Ventura cop," he said. "Shoot, I thought you were local.

You said one of those people was missing. Was it the husband or the wife?"

"The wife," Mary said. "We found a body we believe may be Lisa Sheppard."

At the door, Richards became animated. "You know what? Now that I think of it, I read that name on some papers. Guess I had a few too many beers this afternoon. I gotta pick up my rig and hit the road in the morning, so I usually indulge the day before. Can't drink when I'm driving."

"What kind of paper?" Mary asked, spinning around.

"Well," he said, scratching his stomach, "I was storing some of my stuff in the attic when I found a cardboard box over in a corner, the kind you store files and things in. Under it was another box that had old clothes in it. I was going to throw them out, but I didn't want to take the trouble of hauling them down. Most of the papers had the name Elizabeth Beckworth on them, but one of them was a certificate for some kind of computer school. The name on that was Lisa Sheppard. Maybe Lisa was a nickname for Elizabeth, and the boxes belonged to the woman you've been asking about. I sure as heck don't have any use for them. You want, you can have them."

"You bet," Mary said, shifting her eyes to Carolyn.

Once Richards pulled the boxes down from the attic, the two women carried them to Mary's unmarked police unit. They were so eager to see what was inside, they immediately started digging through the boxes inside the trunk. "Thank you, Jesus," Mary exclaimed, a paper fluttering in her hand. "This is an emergency room report from a hospital in St. Louis. The name on it is Elizabeth Beckworth. The next of kin was the girl's grandmother, Eleanor Beckworth. We even have an address and phone number for her. Beckworth must have been her maiden name. She probably started calling herself Lisa when she got older. She broke her leg ice skating when she was seventeen. It was such a bad fracture, they had to pin it. Dr. Ferguson found a similar injury on our Jane Doe. The pins had fallen out, but there were holes in the bone where they'd been inserted."

"We're getting closer, then."

"No shit," Mary said, smiling. "You must have brought me luck."

Wearing rubber gloves, Carolyn had been sorting through the various clothing in the box labeled *Goodwill* in magic marker. "This is a forensic goldmine," she said, as excited as the detective. "There's men's clothes, women's clothes, even old underwear. Goodwill doesn't take underwear, do they?"

"This was probably the stuff she was going to toss." Mary asked Carolyn to stand back so she could close the trunk. As soon as both women were inside the car, the detective dialed Eleanor Beckworth's phone number. "Damn," she said, ending the call, "the number has been disconnected. We'll call the St. Louis PD and have them send a unit to her house. Because of all the junk calls, people change their number all the time."

"Are you going to have the police tell the grandmother her daughter is dead?" Carolyn asked, removing the rubber gloves and placing them in her pocket. "Let's think this through before we jump to any conclusions. Shouldn't we wait until Charley Young or Dr. Ferguson confirms it's the same injury? There weren't any X-rays in those files, were there?"

"No," Mary said, dropping her hand holding the phone, "but we should be able to get them from the hospital. Anyway, you're right. I'll take you home and start fresh tomorrow morning. I'm fairly certain we've identified our victim. Pretty good for a day's work. Now all we have to do is find out who killed her."

"We have Holden's DNA on file," Carolyn reminded her. "Those clothes looked pretty old, though, and there's no telling how many people have handled them." She watched Mary insert her key in the ignition. "Aren't you going to talk to Mrs. Kirkland? She might have seen the killer."

"You're pretty good," the detective said, smiling. "Hank thinks I move too fast. Guess he's right."

A few minutes later Mary rang Mrs. Kirkland's doorbell. "Good Lord, do you hear that? She must have some kind of amplifier hooked up to her doorbell. No wonder the guy next door is complaining."

A petite gray-haired woman opened the door. She couldn't have been over five feet tall, and her feet were the size of a ten-year-old's. She fiddled with her ear, adjusting her hearing aid. When Mary held her badge up, the woman invited them in. Her home was tastefully furnished, but crammed with knick-knacks, making Carolyn feel claustrophobic. "What can you tell me about the Sheppards, the couple that used to live next door?"

"Oh, yes," Mrs. Kirkland said, perching herself in a faded blue chair. "I didn't know them personally, of course. They were young people. Young people don't have any use for a person my age."

"Can you describe them?" Carolyn asked, while Mary held her pen over her notepad.

"I'm sorry—you'll have to speak louder."

Mary shouted, "What did the husband look like?"

The woman rubbed her hands on the arms of the chair as she searched her memory. "The man was nice-looking. He was tall, and he always wore a black cowboy hat and sunglasses. I believe he had a mustache. The girl was pretty. She had blond hair. I don't think she had a job because she didn't go out that often."

"It would really help if you could provide us with more specifics," Mary told her. "Was he six feet tall? Was he over six feet? What about his build? Was he heavy, thin, or medium? Did he have any noticeable scars or tattoos?"

"So many questions," the woman said, her brow furrowing. "I can't tell you exactly how tall he was. Everyone looks tall to me. He wore long-sleeved shirts most of the time. I didn't see any scars or tattoos." She took a breath. "Is that all, officers?"

"No," Mary said, her voice booming out over the room. "Can you tell us what kind of car he drove?"

"The husband drove a black pickup truck. I'm not sure they had another car, unless they kept it in the garage." The elderly woman smiled demurely, pulling her skirt down over her knees. "I don't pry into other people's business, officers. That wouldn't be polite, now would it?"

"Did they get along?" Mary drilled her. "Did they fight? Do you know why they moved away? Lisa Sheppard was reported missing by her husband thirteen months ago. No one has seen her since."

"Good heavens," Mrs. Kirkland exclaimed. "This is really serious, isn't it?"

"Absolutely," Mary shouted, her voice already getting hoarse.

"I have some minor hearing problems," Mrs. Kirkland answered.

"I might not have been able to hear them if they were fighting." She looked down, then slowly raised her head. "The last time I saw them the husband was putting some things in the back of his truck. I don't remember seeing the wife that day."

"Do you know what day that was?"

"Gosh, no," she said, sliding off the chair to her feet. "I'm sorry I can't help you more. My shows are on now."

Mary remained seated, refusing to be brushed off for a soap opera. "You wouldn't know the license number of the pickup, would you?"

Mrs. Kirkland shook her head, then walked over and turned on the TV as if they weren't there.

Letting themselves out, they headed back to Ventura. Carolyn asked Mary, "Can't you get DMV records on the husband?"

"I've already tried. There are hundreds of vehicles registered under the name of Matthew Sheppard in California. We'll try to narrow it down now that we know he drives a pickup. I couldn't locate a driver's license with the date of birth that Sheppard listed in the missing persons report. I even checked Missouri. I'm going to try to track him through social security. If we don't come up with something there, we've got ourselves a phantom. That means Sheppard is probably our murderer."

"But how did he get married?" Carolyn asked. The case had taken another perplexing turn. "Most states require that you have two pieces of identification, your birth certificate, passport, or driver's license."

"Maybe they weren't married," Mary said, entering the onramp to the freeway. "Some people don't care about the legalities. At least, we've got Lisa's grandmother. She should be able to give us some answers."

CHAPTER 17

Tuesday, September 19—5:15 P.M.

Dean picked up his cell phone and dialed his home number. "Sweetheart," he said when Kathleen answered, "I'm sorry about what happened earlier. I ruined your birthday. Now that I've had time to think, I'd love to have you with me when I travel." He could hear a long sigh on the other end of the line. He hoped she couldn't tell by the tone of his voice that he was lying.

"Oh, Dean," she gushed. "I'm so happy. I'm sorry for the things I said, too. Andrea must have mistaken you for someone else. She's jealous because she doesn't make anywhere near the money I do. Elaine told me the reason she was in Ventura is that she and her husband were shopping for a less expensive place to live, some area with large homes. How could anything in that area be decent?"

Dean gritted his teeth, barely able to unclench his jaw long enough to speak. "I'll be there in about twenty minutes." At least she was receptive to his apology. She believed what he had told her because she wanted to believe. Simple human nature. "We have that bottle of cognac, don't we? Will you join me in a drink to celebrate?"

"Yeah, we have it, Dean," she said, then hesitated. "But I'm going to stay off the sauce. I want to start my diet tomorrow and go back to the gym. Alcohol has lots of calories."

Kathleen had just ruled out his chance of drugging her with a glass of booze. Now he would have to resort to more violent means to render her unconscious. With a man in his trunk in a drunken stupor, he couldn't waste any time when he got home. Arnie could wake up at any moment and blow the whole thing. If something happened, though, Dean knew he could fabricate some kind of story. He was a master at working his way out of tight spots.

"Hello, are you still there?" Kathleen said.

"Yes, I'm here," Dean told her, gripping the steering wheel with both hands. "The cell connection is crap around here."

His mind was drifting. She sounded so happy. He looked in his rearview mirror and expected to see Arnie hanging halfway out of the trunk. "I'll see you soon, honey. We're breaking up."

"I love . . ." Kathleen said, no longer audible.

He clicked off the phone. The grim reality of what he was planning began to creep into his consciousness. It would be much harder if Kathleen hadn't turned into such a bitch and demanded to travel with him. Now she had learned things she wasn't supposed to know.

Kathleen had begun to drain him rather than sustain him. He was sick of calling her every day and micromanaging her foolish life. How could she criticize anything he did? The stupid woman had no idea what he was capable of doing. Besides, she actually believed selling real estate was important. How dare she suggest that he work for her?

Kathleen was the type of woman that he used to treat when he worked as a psychiatrist. They came to him to complain about the failure of their personal relationships, but their real problem was that they were power-hungry, carnivorous men haters. They played along until they had a man by the balls, and then they started nagging and ordering him around.

It wasn't as if Kathleen contributed anything to society. The only contributions she made to charity were to attend fancy benefits where she could attract more wealthy clients. One less Kathleen in the world sounded fine to him. Who would really miss her? Her friends were superficial, her clients would forget her, and her only relative, a sister who resided in Los Angeles, hadn't spoken to her for years.

Parking in the garage, Dean quickly opened the back door of the Mercedes, peering into the trunk through the opening between the seats. The drunk's rancid smell permeated the car. Placing his knee on the seat, he reached through the hole and poked him. He was startled when Arnie latched onto his hand. The door to the house sprang open.

"What are you doing, Dean?" Kathleen asked, standing in the doorway.

The fingers that were curled around his hand went limp and released him. "Nothing," he said, perspiration soaking his shirt. "Just picking up something I dropped." He got out and slammed the car door. His ears perked, dreading a sound from the trunk. "I've been out in the rain. Let's go inside."

Kathleen had already changed into a blue silk nightgown. Once he stepped inside the hallway leading to the kitchen, she took him by the arm, then rested her head on his shoulder as they continued walking. "I have so many deals in the fire, Dean. If I go on the road with you, I'll have to hire more people. Elaine can't possibly handle everything by herself. There's the banking, making arrangements for someone to look after this house. You'll have to help me with the . . ."

Fucking bitch, Dean thought, tuning her out. "Everything's going to be fine, darling," he said, stopping and peering at her eyes. Her pupils were constricted. He should have known she couldn't give up her addiction to Valium. To cover up the fact that she'd sedated herself, she'd turned into a motor mouth. He struggled to keep a pleasant expression on his face when inside his stomach was doing cartwheels. His eyes came to rest on the long curve of her neck. He imagined choking the life out of her.

Kathleen went behind the marble bar in the family room. "I'll make you a drink. Tall or short?"

"Neither," Dean said, sniffing his hands. He could still smell the stench of the homeless drunk. He couldn't take a chance Kathleen might notice. "I need to go to the bathroom."

"Damn it, Dean," she said, "you tracked in mud. Why didn't you take your shoes off before you came in the house?"

"I forgot," he said, slipping them off his feet.

"Don't leave them in the middle of the room," Kathleen said in a shrill voice. "Take them to the laundry room, where they belong. And bring me the carpet cleaner and a clean rag."

"Don't scream at me like that, Kathleen," Dean said, placing his hands over his ears. "You know how it annoys me."

She lowered her voice, smiling sweetly. "Will you *please* bring me the things I asked for?"

"Can I take a leak first?" he said, continuing on to the bathroom. As he scrubbed his hands in the ornately decorated guest bathroom, he caught sight of his reflection in the mirror. His lips were compressed, the muscles in his face rigid, his eyes cesspools of hate. Kathleen was so caught up in herself, she hadn't noticed that she'd opened the door to a murderer.

The cleaning crew had come yesterday, Dean remembered, mentally running through his checklist. Kathleen was obsessed with keeping the house clean. She claimed she had allergies, but he thought it came from being in real estate, where everything had to look perfect. Her friends joked that her house was hermetically sealed.

Before he'd left earlier, Dean had gone upstairs and collected all the photographs of them together, pulling them out of the frames and shredding them. Leaving the store pictures inside, he'd shoved the pieces of their photographs into his jacket pockets. The police would assume the store photos were of relatives or friends. He always tried to keep anyone from taking pictures of him. Sure, people in Carmel had seen him, but he was certain no one had snapshots outside of Kathleen. Composite drawings weren't nearly as threatening as photos, which could be placed on the Internet and viewed by every law enforcement agency in the country. He was constantly changing his appearance, but there was no reason to take a chance.

Dean realized he would have to take the trash and dump it somewhere away from the house. Kathleen insisted the vacuum cleaner bags be replaced every week. Of course, he would have to go over the house again. It shouldn't be that difficult to remove any remaining sources of his DNA. Other than a few of his suits, the walk-in closet in the master bedroom was crammed full of Kathleen's clothes. The rest of his clothing had been washed the previous day. He hadn't showered or used the upstairs bathroom since he'd returned, which made his job fairly easy. All he needed to do was run the handheld vacuum over the suits.

If Dean hadn't stumbled across the drunk, he would have been forced to go to far greater lengths to cover his tracks. Since he would make certain the police had overwhelming evidence to convict his unwilling accomplice, whatever they found that didn't link back to old Arnie would soon be discarded. There was no statue of limitations on murder, and recent circumstances had forced him to take every possible precaution. His past deeds might never surface, or, then again, the police might catch up to him any day.

Before leaving the guest bathroom, he dropped to his hands and knees, checking for hairs and finding nothing. Fingerprints weren't a problem, as he'd never been printed. The driver's license he used was phony, and he always made it a point not to speed. Thus far, he'd been lucky and had never been stopped by the police. The only place he'd held a valid license was in the state of New York, and it had long ago expired. Fourteen years ago the DMV didn't collect fingerprints.

When he returned to the room, Kathleen was stretched out on the sofa. "I confess," she said, stretching her arms over her head. "I've been a bad girl, darling. After you left, I was so upset that I took half of a Valium. I just wanted to forget everything and sleep. I promise I'm not going to take them anymore."

Half, Dean thought. She had probably taken ten. Her lids were dropping, her words uncharacteristically slurred. Nothing she did mattered, though, and without knowing it, she had made it easier for him to kill her. Valium was also a muscle relaxant. "You should probably go upstairs and try to rest. We'll celebrate your birthday tomorrow night. I have some things to do. Here . . ." He placed his arm around her shoulder and escorted her up the stairs.

The master bedroom was over five hundred square feet. A floor-to-ceiling window provided magnificent views of the ocean. When the fog rolled in, as it did almost every evening, they were lucky to be able to see an occasional star.

"Why don't you join me?" Kathleen said seductively. "I'm the one who threw a wrench in our party plans. You deserve a little loving."

He looked at her as if she was crazy. Seeing her cheerful demeanor was like having someone hammer nails into his forehead. "We'll have plenty of sex later."

Kathleen stood at the edge of the bed, letting her silk gown fall to the floor. "Come on . . . I want you. I was so mean to you earlier."

"The Valium should be taking effect soon," Dean told her. "If we make love, I want us both to enjoy it."

"Are you sure, honey?" she asked. "I could take care of you if you want."

"No," he protested. "I have to make a trip to the store to pick up some things for breakfast."

Dean left and stood outside the doorway. Did he hate her enough to kill her? Even if he didn't hate her, she knew too much. But for his plan to work, it had to look like a random act of violence.

In sleep, Kathleen looked demure and sweet. Her confident facade was his creation. When they'd met, she had been miserable. After being tossed aside for a younger woman, she'd taken to spending her nights in the bar at the club, guzzling booze and chasing it with tranquilizers. Her hair had been dry, her nails ragged, and she'd been twenty pounds overweight. Turning a woman on the skids around wasn't easy. Dean had put a lot of time and effort into Kathleen Dupont, and for what? To end up with a woman who'd been ready to call her lawyer and eradicate him from her life because she couldn't get what she wanted. She should have bought herself a damn poodle.

Creeping into the bathroom, he found a plastic cap Kathleen used when she conditioned her hair, placing it on his head to catch any hairs that might fall from his head. The truth was he didn't need Kathleen anymore. During what he called the rehab phase of their relationship, she had idolized him. Until today he hadn't considered killing her, just taking off whenever he tired of her. But like his other wife, she'd turned everything he'd done for her against him, thinking she could get along fine without him. She was beautiful because he had made her beautiful, and not simply by picking out her clothes or putting her on a diet and exercise program, or insisting she cut back on her consumption of alcohol and tranquilizers. Women felt beautiful and projected beauty when they were loved and constantly reassured by an intelligent, successful man.

His days as a psychiatrist seemed far away, but Dean didn't need another shrink to tell him that he was a narcissist. They even had a name for what he craved—narcissistic supply. He would secure another source, one that could provide him with far more than Kathleen.

Dean went downstairs. Before heading to the garage, he pulled on a pair of black leather gloves. In the garage he grabbed a towel and at the utility sink, ran water over it.

Releasing the latch to the trunk of the Mercedes, Dean stared down at the unconscious man. Arnie was curled up like a baby holding a bottle. It was good he was still out, but he needed to let go of the evidence. "Arnie, Arnie," Dean said in hushed tones. When there was no response, he checked the man's pulse, detecting the faint beating of his heart. He grabbed the empty bottle and gave it a yank. It didn't budge. Arnie wasn't going to give it up easily.

He ran into the kitchen and found the bottle of cognac, then rushed back to the car and jabbed Arnie in the ribs. The man's eyes opened. "You're almost empty," Dean told him, waving the other bottle in the air. "Wanna trade?"

"Sure," Arnie said, taking the alcohol and drinking it as if it were apple juice.

As Dean yanked the cognac bottle away from Arnie's lips with one hand, he pulled back his other in a fist and punched the man, sending him back into dreamland. Blood dripped out of Arnie's nose. When the police investigated the crime, the drunk's injury would make it look as if Kathleen had suffered a spasm and her fist had inadvertently connected with her assailant's nose when he forced the knife through her abdominal wall.

Dean took the Old Crow whiskey bottle, wiped it clean of his fingerprints, and pressed Arnie's fingers against it before he carried it back inside the house. He even removed several doorknobs and brought them to the car.

In the next hour, he carted various items from the house to the car in order to place Arnie's prints on them. He even plucked several matted hairs from the man's mangy head.

Next was a sweep of the house. The bed linens had been changed the day before. Finding the portable Dust Devil in the cleaning cabinet, he vacuumed the sofas and carpet in the family room, then went upstairs and ran it over his suits and the carpet on the closet floor. He cleaned out the drains in the bathroom shower and sink. Afterward, he emptied the Dust Devil and scattered its minute contents in the backyard, where he knew the wind would blow them away.

Dean knew the clock was now ticking. He had to move fast, but he couldn't be careless. He reached in and lifted Arnie's right arm out of the filthy wool jacket, then pulled until the man rolled over and the clothing came free. Next he removed Arnie's boots and reluctantly stepped into them.

Selecting a twelve-inch stainless-steel carving knife in the kitchen, he removed it from its wooden holder and climbed the stairs to the master bedroom, leaving a trail of muddy footprints.

The room was dark and silent, except for the faint sounds of Kathleen's breathing. If she awoke and he couldn't continue, all she would remember was the putrid smell of Arnie's wool jacket. That way, he could cover himself by telling the police that he'd come home and chased off the attacker. Taking the strands of hair, he separated them and placed some on the bed and a few others on the floor.

DNA testing was both his friend and his enemy.

The toughest part of any journey was the beginning. Kathleen had always looked good with her mouth closed. Her expression was pleasant, and her features bore a softness he never saw when she was awake. She was stretched out on her back, her curly blond hair fanned out on the pillow.

With only a slight hesitation, Dean raised the bottle high and crashed it into her skull. After she whimpered a few times, her head fell to one side, and he felt certain she was unconscious.

The shattered shards of glass sliced into the skin on the left side of her face. Blood streamed from the multiple abrasions. "It's your fault it has to end this way," Dean said, twirling the knife in his gloved right hand.

He began to shake uncontrollably. The room was spinning. He found himself on his knees on the floor next to the bed, perspiration oozing from his pores. He pushed himself to his feet, taking off the tan wool jacket and covering her head. Looking at the face of someone whose life he was about to end wasn't something he relished. It wasn't the blood, but the squinting eyes, curling lips, the excruciating pain he'd inflicted. And this wasn't the face of a stranger. Of course, he'd never killed someone he didn't know. That's what separated him from the others. When he took a life, he always had a reason.

There was no turning back now.

Dean stared down at her, tears pooling in his eyes. Instead of Kathleen's face, he saw the soft face of his beautiful baby sister. When he felt the dampness on his cheeks, he panicked and wiped them on his shirt. Whipping the satin comforter off, he placed his hand on her stomach. When he moved the knife a few inches from her skin, his hand trembled as if he had Parkinson's. He tried to emotionally detach himself. There were dozens of other ways to kill. A carefully placed bullet was one of the easiest. You didn't have to get that close to the victim, which made it less gruesome and messy. The only problem was it left evidence, and digging out a bullet could be tricky. Strangulation was good under the right circumstances. It did require a lot of strength, however, and while people were resisting, they could scratch you and draw blood. This time the murder had to fit the murderer, a lowlife bastard like the man in his trunk.

The tip broke the skin. Taking his free hand and clasping it tight over his other on the knife handle, Dean raised his chin and squeezed his eyes shut, trying to mimic the actions of a psychotic maniac, merely lashing out in a murderous fury.

Taking several deep breaths, he plunged the blade downward. Kathleen let forth a bloodcurdling cry as she buckled forward. Dean grimaced as he pulled the knife out and watched as her body collapsed back on the bed, still and limp.

CHAPTER 18

Tuesday, September 19—7:00 P.M.

Mary dropped Carolyn off at home after their trip to San Diego. Veronica had come over at seven that morning, dropping her off to pick up John's car from the parking structure. Then she followed her to the house and drove her to the body shop to get her Infiniti.

John was at work, so Carolyn and Rebecca prepared dinner together. The girl poured frozen corn into a pot to boil while her mother defrosted two chicken breasts in the microwave. Carolyn cut up vegetables for a salad, plunked the wooden bowl down on the table, and carried the chicken to the barbecue grill in the backyard.

Her thoughts still on Carl Holden, Carolyn reflected again on the alarming scenario they had to consider, as she'd discussed with Mary on the drive home. What if Holden and Matthew Sheppard turned out to be the same man? As yet, no one knew how long the Sheppards had been married, or even if they were in fact husband and wife. Since Holden had been out of prison for two years, it was possible that he and Sheppard were the same person. Holden wasn't a bad-looking man, and he could come across as an educated individual.

When Carolyn had entered the house, Rebecca met her at the door with a curious stare. "I can't believe you planted artificial flowers in the front yard. You might need to see a shrink, Mom. I'm serious. That's totally weird."

Carolyn sat down at the table, burying her head in her hands. She was certain Marcus would have called by now. "You didn't erase any messages from the answering machine, did you?"

"One," Rebecca said. "It didn't sound important."

"You have to stop erasing my messages," her mother said, standing and angrily placing her hands on her hips. "I've told you a dozen times, Rebecca. How would you like it if I erased your messages?"

The girl removed the pot of peas from the stove, and carried it to the sink to drain the excess water. "I was going to write it down, but I figured it wasn't a big deal. He didn't leave a phone number or ask you to call him back. It was probably one of those people trying to get you to refinance the house. His name was Mark or Marcus. He said he'd get in touch with you tomorrow."

He called, he called! Carolyn thought. It was amazing how a simple phone call could change her world from bleak to wonderful. She felt like twirling around in circles. Instead, she rushed over to her daughter and kissed her on the forehead, then wrapped her arms around her waist and squeezed her.

"Mom," Rebecca yelled, "you're hurting me. What's wrong with you?"

"I just want you to know how much I love you," Carolyn told her, kissing her again before she darted outside to get their food before it burned.

When they sat down to eat, the girl leaned forward over the table. "Rapid mood changes can be a sign of mental illness, you know." She held the bottle of blue cheese dressing over her salad, waiting for it to dribble out, then slapped it hard with the palm of her hand. A fourth of the bottle came gushing out. "Well, that didn't work out, did it?" She went to the cabinet to get a clean plate for another serving of salad. When she returned, she smiled at her mother. "Are you going to tell me who this guy is? I mean, he's obviously someone special. You almost peed in your pants when I told you he called."

"He's just a guy, honey," Carolyn said. "He's nice, though, and I like him."

Rebecca slouched in her seat. "Oh boy, here we go again. He doesn't have a daughter, I hope. If he does, I don't want to meet her."

Slightly over a year ago, Carolyn had become involved with a physics professor who'd moved in down the street. Rebecca and the professor's daughter, Lucy, had become best friends, only to be separated when Carolyn and Paul stopped seeing each other and he moved back to Pasadena. "He does have a daughter, but she lives back east with her mother. I barely know the man, honey. Nothing will probably come of it."

They cleaned up the dishes, and Rebecca asked her mother to come to her bedroom. "The reason you don't like your hair is you don't know how to fix it," she informed Carolyn, sticking her fingers in a jar and removing a small portion of the contents, which she rubbed into the palms of her hands.

"What is that stuff?"

"Styling putty." Rebecca pushed her mother down into a chair in front of the mirror. She used her fingers to rub the cream into various strands of Carolyn's hair, carefully shaping it so they flipped out, while the rest of her hair remained straight. "Look in the mirror," she said. "This is the way it's supposed to look."

Carolyn was amazed at the transformation. She touched the ends of the protruding strands of hair. "Was that glue? It's as stiff as a board."

"It softens up when you brush it," Rebecca told her, leaning over her mother's shoulder and smiling. "Don't you love it? You can keep it. I hardly ever use it. I think Hillary swiped it from her brother. See how pretty you are, Mom?"

Carolyn reached up and clasped Rebecca's hand, meeting her gaze in the mirror. "Do you have a boyfriend?"

"Three. None of them can drive, so don't worry."

"But aren't they jealous of each other?"

"Who cares?" the girl said, flopping down on her bed. "I'm not going to *go out* with one guy. Think of how dumb that sounds. You tell people you're 'going out' with a guy. Okay, they say, where are you going? What're you gonna say now? The guy can't drive. So we meet now and then at the mall. Every once in a while, I let one of them kiss me. They can't get carried away because we're in a public place."

Carolyn realized how wrong she'd been about her daughter. "Sounds like you've got everything under control."

"You bet!" Rebecca exclaimed, raising her knees to her chest and then extending them over her head. "No way am I gonna end up with a baby or an abortion. Babies stretch your stomach muscles, and birth control pills make you break out. What do I need a dickhead guy for, anyway? My friends who've had sex say guys don't even know what to do. Masturbation is better. At least you know you're going to enjoy it."

"Good for you," her mother said, thinking things had most definitely changed since she was fifteen. She would have never spoken so openly to her mother.

After Rebecca went to bed, Carolyn sat in the kitchen working on some of her cases. She still needed to talk to John about his use of marijuana. He must have gone somewhere after work with one of his friends. When she tried his cell phone, he didn't answer, and she hung up without leaving a message. He was eighteen now and paid his own expenses, so it was hard to keep him from coming and going as he pleased. She reminded herself that he would be in Massachusetts soon and then she would have no idea what he was doing. She had to start the process of letting go. Rebecca had probably warned him about the marijuana conversation, and John was intentionally avoiding her. Not knowing when he would show up, Carolyn gave up on waiting and headed off to her room.

The first thing he had to take care of was the knife.

Dean rushed to the garage, opened the trunk, and pressed the handle of the knife into Arnie's right palm and fingers. Then he did the same with the man's left hand. He hadn't noticed if Arnie was right or left-handed, but it didn't matter. A madman would have probably clasped the knife with both hands the way he had. What Arnie wouldn't have been able to do was stab someone with his less dominant hand. The police could easily determine which hand he used. Nothing could be left to chance.

Taking the stairs two at a time, Dean threw the knife on the carpet near the doorway, wanting it to look as if the killer dropped it when fleeing. He stepped toward Kathleen and into a puddle of blood. The dimmed lights reflected off the comforter on the bed, causing the predominant color in the room to appear red.

With his index finger and thumb, he reached down to remove Arnie's jacket. When he saw Kathleen's face, he jumped back. The whites of her eyes were staring up at the ceiling.

She blinked!

Letting the jacket fall to the floor, Dean rushed downstairs, leaving a trail of Arnie's boots imprinting their pattern in blood. Kathleen was dead, or would be within minutes. No one could survive such a violent attack. The movement of her eyelids was a reflex. Dead bodies did all kinds of strange things.

He grabbed a log from the holder next to the fireplace, went out the French doors leading to the backyard, but then momentarily forgot what he was doing. The swimming pool lights were on, and the serene beauty of the water made the events that had occurred inside the house seem even more macabre.

The police should find Arnie's prints on the point of entry, Dean remembered, and transferring them wasn't impossible, just time-consuming. A quicker way was to wrap his jacket around the log, which he did, and smash the glass pane near the locking mechanism. Wanting to make certain some kind of evidence was left that would link the crime back to Arnie, he purposely snagged the man's jacket on the jagged edges of glass before reaching inside with his gloved hands and unlocking the door.

When he returned to the living room, he felt light-headed, so he put his head between his legs. He had to make sure he didn't pass out. He felt dark and tortured, as if he'd become evil incarnate. The other times he'd killed, he'd been exhilarated, drunk on power. This time was different. His actions had been more calculated, and he'd spent too much time preparing.

Now he had to take care of Arnie. *Shit*, he thought. Till now he hadn't considered that physical evidence would be left in the trunk. He ripped the plastic cap off his head, going outside to wash it with the garden hose. After he was certain all the evidence had been removed, he walked to the edge of the yard. The plastic was similar to Saran Wrap and he easily shredded it with his teeth. Then he dug a hole and buried it.

He had to think fast. He couldn't make both the Mercedes and the man he was pinning the crime on disappear into thin air. Maybe if he washed out the trunk with water, he could eliminate or contaminate all the evidence. The issue was time. He had to finish the job before something unexpected happened. As his panic increased, the solution suddenly appeared.

Opening the trunk, he found Arnie still out cold. Dean moved his legs so that he could put his boots back on his feet. "Wake up, Arnie," he said. "The police are coming to arrest you. Don't worry, I'm gonna help you."

"I ain't done nothin' wrong," the dazed man said. "I'm bleeding. My nose, man. Who hit me? Jesus, how long I been out?"

"You'll survive," Dean told him, "but only if you get out of here. You've done something terrible. You killed my wife."

Arnie's runny eyes flashed in fear. "I didn't, I swear."

"Get out of the trunk," Dean commanded, reaching in to give him a hand. "You need to get away from here fast. If you don't do exactly what I tell you, you'll spend the rest of your life in prison without alcohol. Can you drive?"

"Maybe," Arnie said, standing, then staggering over to the driver's side of the car.

"Get in," Dean told him. As he attempted to obey, Arnie lost his balance and barely caught the edge of the seat. "Grab ahold of the steering wheel and brace yourself."

Arnie did as he was instructed but then muttered, "I can't do this," and tried to climb back out of the car.

Dean blocked him with his body. "Relax, buddy, all you have to do is listen to me. Place the shifter to the D. Then put your foot on the gas." He knew if the momentum was great enough, the car would plow through the garage wall into the backyard. Ten paces, and Kathleen's Mercedes would be in the pool with Arnie trapped inside it. No way could this inebriated fool manage to free himself and swim to the surface. "Here we go. Press on the gas."

Back in the driver's seat, Arnie looked over at him as he tapped the accelerator. "Like this?"

"No, harder," Dean instructed. "I want to hear that engine running. Okay, now slide that handle away from you." He stood impatiently as the man fumbled to find the gearshift. "Press the button on the top and move the handle to D."

In a sudden torque of the engine, the back tires screeched as the car was propelled forward. Dean was engulfed in an explosion of sound. He fell to the pavement, sheltering himself from flying drywall and wood. When he looked up, there was a large hole that went all the way through to the backyard.

The Mercedes splashed into the blue water.

Dean sped to the edge of the pool, watching as both the car and the man inside sank to the bottom. He dusted his hands, satisfied that he'd removed or destroyed all the evidence.

The horror of what he'd done to Kathleen was drifting deep into his subconscious. Arnie was the murderer, not him. By the time the police arrived, he would believe it. If they gave him a lie detector test, he would pass. With sufficient willpower, this feat was possible, but only with a mind as powerful as his. As he basked in the knowledge of his own brilliance, he considered what a shame it was that no one else could know. He had committed the perfect crime, and now he had to forget it.

As he returned to the house, Dean was overcome with emotion. Playing the grieving husband would be easy—the blood, the horror, hearing Kathleen's bloodcurdling screams. He picked up the portable phone, his hands shaking as he speed-dialed the number of his closest neighbor in the house over an acre away. With the dense trees, and the surf crashing into the large rocks below them, there was no chance the Kaufmans could have overhead the commotion. "Dr. Kaufman," he said, his voice cracking. "This is Dean. . . . Thank God you're home. Someone broke into our home and . . . s-stabbed . . . Kathleen. Come, please! Have Esther call the police and an ambulance. I-I don't know what to do."

"I'm on my way," the doctor said. "Is it safe? Did the attacker leave?"

"Hurry, there's blood everywhere."

Ending the call, Dean sat on the stairs and placed his head in his hands. It would have been cleaner if he could have merely fled, but he couldn't afford to create suspicion by being absent. He forced himself to return to that terrible day in late September.

At five, he'd been an impulsive, inquisitive child, always getting into trouble. When he didn't get what he wanted, he threw temper tantrums, and his mother scolded him and made him sit in the corner. That afternoon she'd taken his six-month-old baby sister for a walk in her stroller. He'd asked to go, but she'd told him to stay behind and play with his toys. Their large house in Tarrytown was situated on top of a steep cliff overlooking the Hudson River.

The backyard was fenced, but his father had decided against erecting a fence in the front as he didn't want anything to obstruct the dramatic view. To keep the children from getting out, the doors all had interior padlocks. This day, however, while the maid was upstairs, Dean had turned the handle on the front door and been surprised when it opened. His mother must have forgotten to lock it.

Every fall his mother made a wreath for their door, using twigs and multicolored leaves she picked up off the ground and placed in a big wicker basket. She was engaged in that pleasant task, wandering farther from the baby's stroller, parked under a sycamore tree, than she had planned, when Dean found his sister there. Iris was such a cute baby, with her round face and rosy cheeks. He loved the way her soft hair tickled his chin when his mother let him hold her in his father's big chair. But most of all, he liked to make Iris laugh.

He shook the stroller, and Iris started giggling. After a while, he got bored and jumped on the back, dangling from the push bar like he did on the jungle gym in the backyard. The stroller suddenly toppled backward, pinning him beneath it. His stomach and head hurt, and Iris was shrieking. She was dangling upside down, her body held in place by the strap. He called out for his mother, but she didn't come, his cries muffled by the sound of the wind rushing through the trees.

That's when he got mad.

He strained with all his might, managing to push the stroller off. It landed in an upright position, the wheels locked in place. He knew how to unlock them, as his mother sometimes let him push Iris around inside the house. He couldn't stand it when she cried, especially the high-pitched sound she was making now. He suffered from repeated ear infections, and certain sounds made his ears hurt.

He only remembered bits and pieces of what followed—the stroller disappearing over the side of the cliff, the sound of it slamming into rocks on the way down, Iris's shrill voice becoming fainter, then a muted splash as it landed in the river.

A few days later, they buried baby Iris, and a month later, his mother moved out of the house without even saying good-bye to him. She blamed herself for not locking the door and leaving Iris alone. But his father never blamed his mother, nor did he take responsibility himself for not erecting a fence in the front of the house. He blamed his son, and every day his loathing for that son grew stronger.

Warm tears rolled down Dean's face. The real blow came after his father's death. Although his estate was valued at over three million, he left Dean only a paltry twenty thousand, his final payback for killing baby Iris and destroying his mother.

Prior to his father's death, Dean had done everything possible to win his love and respect. He'd graduated from medical school, then gone on to specialize in psychiatry, wanting to understand how a man could exhibit such irrational hatred as he felt his father did toward him. The relationship was never restored.

He wiped his tears with the edge of his shirt. The silence was broken by his neighbor slamming through the front door, carrying a black medical bag.

"Where is she?"

"Upstairs." Dean heard the sirens in the distance. "I-I think she's dead. I came home and found her this way. The killer must have tried to escape in Kathleen's Mercedes. He crashed through the garage wall. The car is in the pool. I'm not sure if he drowned or got away. Should I go out and check?"

"No," Kaufman barked. "The police will be here any minute. Don't take any chances. I'd rather him get away than you get hurt. Take me to Kathleen."

The two men moved quickly into the bedroom, approaching the motionless figure lying in a bed of blood. "My God, the bastard butchered her," the doctor said, examining the jagged wound in Kathleen's abdomen. He put his fingers on her neck, seeing the gashes on her face.

"She's got a pulse!" The doctor grabbed one of the pillows and positioned it underneath Kathleen's knees. "This will help relax the abdominal muscles. I need a wet towel so we can cover her organs." He pried open her mouth to check for vomit.

Forcing himself not to think beyond the moment, Dean went to get the towel, carried it to the sink to wet it, and walked back to hand it to the doctor. "Please, don't let her die. She's all I've got."

"She might make it," Kaufman said, laying the towel over the wound. "Depending on how much internal bleeding the injuries caused. I wouldn't get your hopes up, though. This is a massive wound."

"I'm sorry," Dean said, looking anguished, "I can't stay here and watch her die." He left the room just as two paramedics were ascending the stairs with a stretcher. "She's in the bedroom . . . straight ahead." He suddenly clutched his chest, his face twisted in pain.

"You all right, sir?" a tall redheaded paramedic asked.

"The pressure . . . it feels like a heavy rock on my chest." Dean fell to the floor, writhing in agony. "I can't . . . breathe." He grabbed his left arm. "My arm . . . please help me!"

"Shit, Jason," the redhead said, "this guy's having a heart attack. Get another unit out here fast. We're gonna need the 'copter. I'll try to stabilize him while you take care of the woman. The dispatcher said there's a doctor on the scene. Let's hope he was right."

CHAPTER 19

Carolyn finished the report she'd been working on and stored it in her computer to proofread later. Studying her notes again from her original interview with Carl Holden, she remembered that the address she'd scribbled down, 4005 Park Avenue, had been his mother's. She picked up the phone and called Hank. "Have you talked to Mary?"

"Yeah," he said. "Ferguson said as soon as we get the X-rays from St. Louis we should have a positive ID. Good work, Carolyn."

"I may have a lead as to where Holden is hiding."

"That's one of the reasons I wanted you involved," he said. "What have you got?"

"He may be staying at his mother's house," she said, her excitement flowing through the phone. "Did your men check it out already?

"Nope. I didn't know he had a mother. For God's sake, woman, don't go there by yourself. If this guy's our murderer, I don't want you to be his next victim."

Carolyn had never been one to put something off that needed to be done. In fact, she filed all her reports early, fearful she could get sick or something might develop with John or Rebecca that required her attention. Being so efficient worked against her in one way, as she ended up handling twice as many cases as most of her coworkers. The situation with Holden wasn't just a report, though. They were trying to track down a rapist and murderer before he struck again. "When can you meet me there?"

"I'm waiting to testifying in the Sanchez homicide," Hank said. "I was scheduled to testify at three, but they're running behind. Judge Shoeffel has ordered the state to conclude their case today even if we have to stay over. She won't allow me to leave the courthouse. If you want to talk, walk over and keep me company. I'm outside department thirty-three." He paused, then added, "Don't worry. I'm in a better mood than I was last week. I guess everyone knows golfers only wear one glove but me."

"The only reason I knew is that Neil had a friend once who played," Carolyn told him. "Mary told you about the box of clothes, didn't she? Maybe you'll find Holden's DNA on some of that stuff. If Holden wasn't posing as Sheppard, Sheppard's DNA may be on file."

"Sounds promising." After a pause, he added, "When I sit around like this, all I think about is food. The skinless, boneless, tasteless chicken breast I had for lunch didn't quite cut it. I may have to strangle someone just to release my frustrations."

"You're looking great. Your new wardrobe is really stylish. I intended to mention it the other—"

The detective jumped in with, "You really think so?"

"Yeah," Carolyn said. Hearing his need for her reassurance confirmed what Mary had told her. She looked down at her watch. "Call me when you get out of court. After we check out Holden's mother's place, we can pick up some Chinese food and eat it at my house. I'm sure Rebecca and John would like to see you."

"Look, Carolyn, instead of us going over there, I'll have a couple of patrol units drive by and see if they spot Holden in the area. We can't go inside the house without a warrant. Why tip him off? Give me the address, and I'll get Mary to write up a request for a search warrant. We should have it signed by tomorrow morning."

Carolyn rubbed her forehead. Most criminals worked at night. Sundown to sunset was a long time. "Are you telling me not to go?"

"Yes," he answered. "You can tag along when we search the house tomorrow. Why don't you see what else you can dig up on Holden? I'll touch bases with you in the morning, let you know how things are coming along with the warrant. Oh, and thanks for the invite. If I get out early, I'll give you a jingle. "

"Sure," Carolyn said, sighing as she disconnected.

Sipping on a bottle of mineral water, she turned to her computer and went to a real estate foreclosure Web site. One of her friends had taught her how to search for the status on a property by typing in an address. She discovered the residence at 4005 Park Avenue was slated for a bank auction in twenty-two days.

Perhaps she shouldn't be present when they searched Holden's residence. Maybe he wasn't their killer after all and prison had done him some good. *No way,* she thought, recalling the hostility he'd shown the day he'd walked out on the interview. When an offender committed as many acts of violence as Holden had, thinking he might have been rehabilitated was inane. Prisons had gone out of the rehabilitation business long ago. Today they were merely human warehouses, not much different from the local zoo. She'd visited a number of prisons and had been appalled at what she'd seen. At the maximum security level inmates acted and were treated like animals. They jumped up and down in their cells, spouting the foulest of profanities. They threw their food at passing guards and urinated through the bars. Then they were released, under the assumption that they could be integrated back into society. How was this magical transformation from caged animal to upright citizen supposed to take place?

Her phone rang. Marcus said, "I called you yesterday. Did you get my message?"

"Yes," Carolyn told him. "How was your trip?"

"They ran me ragged," he said, a voice on a loudspeaker saying something in the background. "I've been thinking about you, though. When are we going to see each other again? I'm at the airport now, trying to get a flight out."

"Gosh, you do sound tired." She wanted to see him, but her work was far more important than her social life. "The other night was wonderful, Marcus. I can't see you tonight, though. I went to San Diego yesterday, so I've got to play catch-up. We're almost certain we've identified the woman at the lagoon. I found another new lead as well."

"The way you're going at it, you'll get your man in no time."

"We found a hair fragment, which might be our biggest piece of evidence," Carolyn said, her voice tinged with excitement. "If the DNA matches Holden's, he'll be headed back to prison where he belongs. That is, as soon as we arrest him."

"Is that your new lead?"

"No—I'll fill you in later. Why don't you call me tonight at the house when I have more time to talk?"

After they said good-bye, she opened the Helen Carter file. A former heroin addict and high-priced call girl, Carter knew the law better than most attorneys. Could she have legitimately gone mad? Sure, but Carolyn doubted it. The conviction she was writing the report on for Carter was inconsequential: violation of a restraining order. Later, if the woman was tried and found guilty of murder, the restraining-order offense would be dismissed, as it would be deemed a "lesser" or "included" crime—meaning she couldn't have killed her lover without getting close enough to violate the restraining order.

Another factor the court had to consider was whether the crime was part of a single period of aberrant behavior. Judiciously interpreting the laws as they applied to some criminals was a joke. Helen Carter's entire life had been one continuous act of aberrant behavior. But the minor conviction opened a door by which Carolyn could slip through and do what she did best—get inside a criminal's head. If Helen Carter thought she was going to outsmart the court and plead not guilty by reason of insanity, she better damn well be crazy. If she wasn't, Carolyn would find a way to expose her.

Carolyn was amazed at how well Helen Carter had held up in the seven years since she'd seen her. She was only thirty, but women with her past generally aged poorly. Even though her dark hair was disheveled and her demeanor flat, traces of the beautiful young woman she'd once been were still visible. "Do you remember me, Helen?" Carolyn asked, sitting across from her in an interview room at the women's jail. "I was the probation officer assigned to your welfare-fraud case."

"Yeah, I remember you. Why are you here? They're certainly not going to put me on probation for murder."

Technically, Carolyn couldn't interrogate the woman on the homicide charges as she had not yet been tried and convicted. The restraining-order violation did give Carolyn a legal reason to ask questions regarding the night of the murder, though. If Carter was malingering in an attempt to plead insanity, she didn't appear to have given it much thought. When most inmates tried to fake mental illness, they went overboard, acting silly instead of insane. Helen Carter hadn't refused to communicate and now had openly acknowledged that she and Carolyn had met on a previous occasion, demonstrating that she was alert to her environment and her memory was intact. Her statement about not getting probation for murder meant she knew the seriousness of her actions. The primary test to determine if a person was legally sane was whether they were aware that their actions constituted a crime. As far as Carolyn was concerned, Carter had already passed the test.

"What happened, Helen? The DA has filed murder charges against you. That's a long way from welfare fraud."

Carter stared at a spot on the wall. "I don't want to talk about it."

The door had just closed. If Carolyn continued to press her into discussing the crime, she would be stepping over the line, and nothing Carter told her could be introduced at her trial. "Okay," she said, quickly asking the customary questions so she could complete the report and go home. When she finished, she stood, then walked over to press the buzzer for the guard.

"I loved Grace," Carter blurted out, tears spilling from her eyes. "She was the only person in the world who ever really cared about me. I would have cut my arm off before I would've hurt her."

Carolyn sat back down, pulling out some tissues from her purse and handing them to her.

"He killed her."

"Can you be more specific, Helen?"

"That asshole guy she'd been seeing."

"Does this person have a name?"

"Martin," Carter said, her hair obscuring one of her eyes. "I'm not sure if that's his first or last name. I was jealous, so Grace wouldn't tell me much about him. It all started because of her family. She was only twenty, and her father went nuts when he found out she was involved with a woman. She decided she wanted to get married to make her parents happy."

"This must have been hard on you, Helen," Carolyn said, working her now that she was volunteering valuable information. "I can see why you're depressed."

"I'm more than depressed," Carter tossed back. "They're going to try me for murder. If they file first-degree, they could give me the death sentence. Jurors don't have much sympathy for lesbian killers, in case you haven't noticed. Look what happened to Aileen Wuornos."

"Aileen Wuornos was a serial killer, Helen," Carolyn said. "Tell me about this man Grace was seeing."

"The dick had some bucks," Carter said, taking on a tougher demeanor. "I know, because he paid the rent on her apartment and bought her expensive things. I tried to talk some sense into her, that's all. He convinced her I was stalking her. Then Grace went to court and got a restraining order."

"Which you violated on the day she was killed?"

"All I wanted was to talk to her." Carter used the tissue to blow her nose. "You know, make certain she was all right. Grace broke down and told me things weren't working out that well, that she was certain this Martin guy was seeing another woman behind her back. They'd only known each other two months, and he'd already asked her to marry him. You know, things like that don't happen, especially with a girl like Grace who doesn't have anything to offer. I told her to get her stuff together and I'd come and get her in an hour. That was the last time I saw her alive."

Carolyn studied the other woman intently. She spoke without hesitation, looked Carolyn straight the eye, and there was nothing in her body language to indicate she was lying. "Have you told the police what you just told me?"

"Yeah," she said, squaring her shoulders. "Someone saw me leaving Grace's place that day. They didn't see anyone else, so they decided I killed her. They found some fingerprints inside that weren't mine, but they said it didn't matter since there was no telling how many people had been inside her apartment." She leveled her gaze at Carolyn. "Just because someone didn't see Martin didn't mean he wasn't there. All it means is they weren't looking out the window at that precise time."

"Did they question this man?"

"They couldn't find him. The bastard must have split after he killed Grace. Her parents met him, but they were certain I killed her. He was some kind of traveling salesman. They believe he took off because he was scared of losing his job. You know, because his girlfriend turned out to be gay." She sneered. "What a crock of shit."

Carolyn collected her paperwork to leave.

"Are you going to help me?" Carter asked, a desperate look in her eyes. "I haven't been a model citizen in the past, but I'm not a murderer. Don't let them railroad me for something I didn't do. After all these years, you must have a lot of pull around here."

"Afraid not, Helen," Carolyn said, standing. The way it looked, the former call girl had courted an insanity defense, then was smart enough to realize it wouldn't hold water. Her new tactic was to create reasonable doubt in the eyes of the jurors by creating a suspect who couldn't be located. "Did anyone see this Martin person other than Grace's parents?"

"Probably," Carter said, fidgeting in her seat. "The police had me, so it was a done deal. Why knock themselves out, you know? I served time in the can. They don't care that I never did anything violent. A record is a record." She leaned forward as if she were going to reveal a secret. "I know one thing, though."

"Oh, yeah?" Carolyn said. "What's that?"

"Grace never told him she was gay. That's why she didn't want me coming around."

"It doesn't look like she was," Carolyn answered. "Not if she was making plans to marry a man. You were a fling, Helen. Young girls sometimes experiment. When you realized that, maybe you got mad enough to kill her. In court, they call that a motive."

"You're wrong about that," Carter said, her jaw protruding. "Grace was raped and beaten when she was fourteen. Being with a man terrified her. She lived with another woman for two years before I met her. If she spread her legs for this Martin character, I can guarantee you she didn't do it because she enjoyed it."

Carolyn left the jail, making her way to her Infiniti in the parking lot. She decided to drive by Park Avenue on her way home in spite of what Hank had told her. Rarely did an opportunity present itself to prevent a crime before it happened. When it did, she went for it.

CHAPTER 20

"Mr. Masters," Detective Brian Irving said, "are you feeling up to answering a few questions?"

The events of the previous evening had worn Dean out. Once he'd distracted the paramedics to the point where he felt certain Kathleen would die before she reached the hospital, he'd refused treatment and told them he was suffering a panic attack. He certainly didn't want the hospital to draw blood.

Hearing his name, he peered up at the gray-haired man standing over him. From his perspective, the man looked like a giant. He must be prematurely gray, Dean thought, as the detective's face was free of wrinkles and his muscles strained inside his patterned flannel shirt.

"God no!" Dean exclaimed, bolting upright. "My wife . . . you're here to tell me my wife is dead, aren't you?"

"Your wife is alive," he said in a deep authoritative voice. "I'm Detective Brian Irving. Mrs. Masters is still in surgery." He rubbed his chin and regarded Dean with curiosity. "Didn't the doctors speak to you? I glanced at the chart and saw your signature on the surgery consent form."

"I-I vaguely remember signing something," Dean stammered. "I thought I was dying. It's embarrassing, officer. The doctors think I may have just fainted. I was certain I was having a heart attack."

"You went through a terrible ordeal," Irving told him, taking a seat beside him. "That was sharp thinking on your part to call Dr. Kaufman. Technically, I guess he's your neighbor. Your houses are a long way apart, though. I'm not used to the kind of spreads you people have here in Carmel. I transferred from Modesto, bought myself a little place about forty miles inland."

"I didn't know what else to do," Dean said. "We live in a remote area. I was afraid the paramedics wouldn't get there in time."

"If you hadn't called the doctor, your wife wouldn't have made it to the hospital."

Dean's eyes drifted downward, dozens of thoughts racing through his mind. Kathleen was alive! And he had to hear it from this lumberjack cop. He would never have called Kaufman if he hadn't thought she was beyond saving. The only hope he had now was that she would die in surgery. His shoulder twitched. He had to figure out an alternative plan. "I'm sorry," he said. He was genuinely distraught. Right now, acting wasn't necessary. "I'm not handling this very well. Did you catch the maniac who did this to my wife?"

"Well," Irving said, rubbing his palms on his brown corduroy slacks, "we didn't have to do much in that department. The assailant caught himself, it seems. He was an ex-con named Arnold Layman. Looks as if he drowned when he drove your wife's Mercedes into the swimming pool. Can't be sure until the coroner gets through with him, but Layman's ID was found in his pocket, and his fingerprints were all over your residence, including the knife he used on your wife."

An ex-con! Dean thought. This was better than he'd expected. "What was he sent to prison for?"

"Breaking and entering. He was paroled four years ago. We had an active warrant for his arrest in connection with two burglaries that occurred in Monterrey a few months back."

"Christ, did he kill someone else?"

"Nope. All he did was eat some of their food and steal a few bottles of booze. He must have thought no one was home at your place. We found a shattered whiskey bottle near the bed, along with some glass shards. When you left, was the alarm set?"

"I don't remember. We don't turn it on until we go to bed at night."

"Your wife *was* in bed," Irving told him. "Do you generally go out at night and leave her alone in the house with the alarm off?"

The cops who came across as the dumbest, Dean reminded himself, were many times the cleverest. He would have to watch what he said around Brian Irving. "No," Dean replied, trying to maintain his dazed expression. "She was in the family room when I left. She might have decided to go to bed early and forgot to set the alarm."

"The coroner believes Layman smashed your wife over the head, then for some reason decided to stab her. Maybe she fought him. He had some bruises on his face, more than likely defense wounds. Guess he didn't want to go back to the joint, so he decided to kill her."

"You believe he's the one, then?" Dean said with a look of righteous anger.

Irving crossed his long legs. "All you have to worry about is your wife, Mr. Masters. We do need to ask you a few questions, though. We can get that out of the way now, if that's all right."

Irving pulled out a small notepad and removed a pen from his shirt pocket. "What time did you arrive at your house?"

Dean cupped his hands over his face. "It's hard to remember anything before this happened. My plane got in yesterday morning. Kathleen met me at the airport, and we had lunch at the Lodge at Pebble Beach. It was her birthday, so I'd arranged for her to have a massage and facial. I met her at the house around six, I believe." He took a deep breath, then said, "We got into an argument and I left."

The detective remained stoic, but it was obvious that Dean had captured his full attention. "What did you argue over?"

"Let me be honest," Dean told him. "Kathleen and I weren't getting along. I thought everything was okay, but then I found out she'd started popping Valium again. She accused me of having an affair. Kathleen was completely out of control last night, screaming and yelling at me like a banshee. I can't deal with her when she gets like that, so I went out for a drive to cool down."

"Did you come to blows? Did you hit her?"

"Absolutely not." Dean acted incensed that Irving would even imply such a thing. "I would never, and I mean never, strike a woman. Kathleen has hit me dozens of times, but I never once retaliated. Her first husband was extremely wealthy, Detective . . ."

"Call me Brian," he said. "People say you're pretty well-heeled yourself, Dean, that you even have your own private jet. Is that true?"

"Not really," Dean answered, uncomfortable with inquiries regarding his financial holdings. "The jet is a co-op deal. If you're wondering if I had anything to gain if Kathleen died, I didn't. When we married, we signed a premarital agreement. Basically, if we divorced, my wife would retain whatever assets she had prior to the marriage, as well as anything she earned during. The same applied to me. Money was never an issue." He stopped and cleared his throat. "What I was trying to say about her first marriage is that her husband treated her like a child. He spoiled her, but he also dominated her. I came along and picked up the pieces. For the first year or so, everything was fine. Then Kathleen's emotional state began to disintegrate."

"I see," Irving said, jotting down a few notes on his pad. "Let's try to focus on the night of the break-in. When you left to cool down, did you go to a bar or stop off at a friend's house?"

"No," Dean answered. "Are you wondering if someone saw me? Is that what this is about? You said you knew who the murderer was . . . this . . . this . . . Arnold Layman person."

"I know it's a technicality, Dean," Irving told him, "but your wife isn't dead yet. Right now, the crime is an assault with a deadly weapon, not a murder. Now, about the time you arrived home and discovered the crime . . ."

Bastard, Dean thought. The detective was trying to make him nervous by challenging him on every detail. Another troubling thought came to mind. What time had he called Kaufman? If they decided to consider him a suspect, which he still felt was unlikely, they would be able to find out he'd called Kathleen from his cell phone around five. But they wouldn't know what had transpired during the conversation. "I didn't look at my watch, Brian," he said, using the man's name in a not altogether pleasant manner. He had every right to be defensive. Anyone would be, under the circumstances. "I guess it was around ten or ten-thirty. I called Kaufman pretty fast, or at least it seemed that way. I was in shock, so there's no telling what I did." He stood. "I've been in this place since last night. I need to get some air. Maybe we should talk about this tomorrow."

Irving slowly pushed his six-five frame to a standing position. "I'll step outside with you."

Great! When was this asshole going to leave? He'd laid the groundwork, though, and when the police finished going over the forensic evidence and the autopsy report on his pal Arnie, the case would be closed. If he didn't stick around and Kathleen pulled through the surgery, they might not think too highly of him, but he knew they couldn't lock him up for leaving his wife, even under the present circumstances. As long as they didn't consider him a suspect, he could do whatever he wanted.

Irving leaned against a wall outside the entrance to the emergency room. When he just stood there, Dean wondered if something was going on he didn't know about. "I thought they operated on Kathleen last night. How could she still be in surgery?"

"There was a problem last night, and they had to postpone the surgery," the detective told him. "She might be in the recovery room by now. I doubt if they'll let you see her right away."

"If you don't mind, Brian, I'd like to check on Kathleen, then go home, shower, and change my clothes. I'm beginning to stink."

"I'm afraid that's not possible. We haven't finished processing the crime scene. It'll be several days before we're done, and the place has to be cleaned. Do you have some friends you could stay with?"

"I'll go to a hotel," Dean said, running his hands through his hair. "I don't want to go back there now, anyway."

"Would you like me to make arrangements for a crime-scene cleaning crew?"

"Sure."

"You'll be billed. Cleaning crime scenes is their specialty, though, so it's worth the money. They have the experience and chemicals to get out blood and other stains. They'll even replace your carpet if necessary."

"Whatever," Dean answered, not sure if he ever wanted to set foot in that house again.

Irving handed him his card. "Call and let me know which hotel you're at."

Dean gave him his cell phone number. He started to walk away when the detective called out to him.

"Oh," he said. "Just one more question. Do either you or your wife drink Old Crow whiskey?"

"I'm not sure," Dean responded, suddenly realizing that this could be the one flaw in his perfect scenario. He hadn't known that Arnie was a burglar who broke into homes to steal booze and food. If he'd known, he would have cracked Kathleen's skull open with a bottle of Jack Daniels. Yet, even that wouldn't have solved the problem. Drunks don't bring their own booze when they burgle a house. "I don't drink whiskey at all, Brian. Besides, it's my wife's home. It was part of her divorce settlement. I was only there one week per month." He started to suggest one of the housekeepers had stashed away a bottle of Old Crow, but he didn't want the police to know the house was cleaned the day before the crime. "If you want to know what Kathleen drinks," he said, shrugging his shoulders, "I guess you'll have to ask her."

"We'll be in touch," Irving said, walking off in the direction of the parking lot.

Not for long, Dean thought, relieved to finally ditch the detective. He'd go upstairs now and see if Kathleen was out of surgery so he could establish himself as the dutiful husband. A few phone conversations with the nurses if she pulled through, a call or two to Irving to see how the case against Layman was stacking up, then he would disconnect his cell phone. After that, Dean Masters would cease to exist.

CHAPTER 21

Wednesday, September 20—4:30 P.M.

By the time Carolyn turned onto the street, the late September sun had disappeared behind a thick wall of fog. She slowed down and checked the numbers on the curb until she located 4005 Park Avenue. The street name alone was a joke. Park Avenue was only a few streets over from the old projects, an area they now called Westview Village. The high cost of California real estate anywhere near the coast meant that even a low-income house could run into the hundreds of thousands.

She wondered if the place might be a crack den. Black wrought-iron bars covered the front door. Rather than put on fresh paint, someone had removed the shingles from the roof and nailed them over the exterior. After last year's rains, a person would have to be on drugs in order to stand walking into the place. It must be like a swimming pool in there.

The window on the right had black lace curtains in front of what appeared to be a yellowed white shade. The window to the left of the main entrance was covered with pink satin curtains, but they had been pulled back to let in the light. Maybe that's where Holden's mother's bedroom was located. No wonder he had been traumatized by the woman. The house looked like something out of a horror movie.

Carolyn assumed Holden's mother had either passed away or was in a nursing home and the state had taken the house for back taxes.

It looked as if it hadn't been occupied for years. The grass had died from lack of water, and weeds had taken over. The sales sign was even leaning sideways. Several other houses on the block were in a similar state of disrepair.

She hadn't been in this area in a long time. Years ago the inexpensive tract had been occupied by young families, thrilled to own their first home. Now, she assumed, most of the residents were renters, people who couldn't care less if the yard was mowed or the house painted. On the opposite side of the street was a storage yard belonging to what appeared to be a trucking company, the property protected by a high curled-wire fence like the ones you saw around prisons.

The place was obviously vacant. There were no furnishings, and Carolyn could see through the window all the way to the backyard.

She hit the autodial on her cell, ending up with Hank's voice mail. *He must be testifying,* she decided. Glancing at her watch, she saw it was after five. Rebecca had a ride home from art class, so she didn't have to worry about that, but she needed to talk to John. Today was his day off.

"Hank," she said, speaking when she heard the beep. "I'm at Holden's mother's house, and it's vacant. Looks like nobody has lived here for ages. Forget about getting a warrant. I doubt if there's anything inside this dump except rats."

After concluding the call, Carolyn drove to the end of the block and turned around. A group of thugs were congregated on the street corner. They stared at her for a second or two but quickly lost interest. Just before she passed Holden's house again, she eased her foot off the accelerator. It couldn't hurt to take a walk around the property, especially since she'd told Hank to forgo securing a search warrant. Removing her gun from her purse, she got out and opened the trunk to get the flashlight she kept there.

Circling to the back, she climbed the stairs to a rotting wooden porch. A noise made her freeze. Taking a step forward, she realized it was probably her own weight that had caused the boards to creek. She peered into what seemed to be another bedroom. Nothing but dirty walls and worn carpet there.

To the side of her, the door was flung open. Spinning around, she found her flashlight pointed at the face of a man. *My God,* she thought, gasping. *It's Carl Holden!*

He was neatly dressed in a blue sweater and black slacks. He shielded his eyes from the light of the flashlight. She clasped her gun tightly, concealing it behind her back. She'd sworn she would never take another life, even if it meant sacrificing her own. Although she wouldn't be unhappy if Holden ended up dead, she didn't want to be the one to do it. She carried the gun only to frighten people or, if someone attacked her, to use as a bludgeon.

Her hand shook as she tried to steady the flashlight beam on Holden's face, hoping it would prevent him from recognizing her. "I'm sorry," she said, speaking in a higher pitched voice to disguise it. "I'm a real estate agent. One of my clients is interested in purchasing this house. I'll come back tomorrow."

The area was suddenly illuminated. It took Carolyn a moment before she figured out the neighbor had turned on his backyard lights.

"How did you find me?" Holden exclaimed, his face etched with fury. "You have no business poking around in my business."

"I'm sorry to disturb you, Carl," Carolyn told him, trying to distract him while she readied herself to flee. "I was just passing by and remembered this was the address you'd given me for your mother. Since you got evicted from your apartment, I thought you might be staying here." Her palms were sweating and her heart racing. Holden's chest was rising and falling, his rage simmering. "I may not be charged with supervising you," she continued, "but I do need to advise the court where you're living."

Carolyn spun around to run. Holden surged forward and grabbed her blouse, leaping on her back and causing her to fall face first onto the edge of the porch. The flashlight flew out of her hand. She tried to crawl away, but his weight crushed her. The pressure released as he bent over and encased her ankles with an iron grip. "You don't want to do this, Carl," she managed to gasp. Her hand holding the gun was dangling over the side of the porch where he couldn't see it. "Assaulting a police officer carries a stiff penalty."

"You're a stupid little probation officer," he said, letting forth a sinister laugh. "No one cares what happens to you. I don't see any police cars anywhere. I bet nobody even knows you're here. That's right, isn't it? Answer me, damn it!" He slammed her head down with tremendous force.

When Carolyn lost consciousness, her fingers opened and the gun fell onto the dried grass below the porch. She awakened as he was dragging her over the threshold into the house. Thrusting her arms forward, she clawed the wood surface with her fingernails. Her head was throbbing, and her muscles already ached from exhaustion. He was too strong. She screamed, thinking she could attract the attention of the people next door. "Help! Someone help me! Call the police!"

"Nice try," Holden snarled, wiping his runny nose with the back of his hand. "The lights next door are on a timer."

His movements were quick and powerful. "What are you going to do to me?" she said, panting as she reached into her pocket of her skirt and pressed the redial button on her cell phone.

"I'm going to give you what you deserve," Holden told her, dropping her on the floor in a small room that smelled of mildew. He placed his foot in the center of her chest as he pulled out a long strip of gray duct tape, ripping it apart with his teeth. "No one will catch me. I learned a lot in prison."

"You're making a mistake, *Holden*," she said, emphasizing his name. "I called for backup before I reached your house. The police will be here any second. They'll shoot you, understand? They know you murdered that other woman and buried her in the lagoon." She prayed Hank had picked up his cell phone this time. If not, she might end up in a drawer at the morgue next to Lisa Sheppard.

"You wanted me dead all along, didn't you?" he hissed, wrapping the tape around her wrists and extending it behind her head. He then secured her hands onto her forehead. "Look at me now. Eight years, and I'm standing in front of a perfectly ripened female, right in my target demographics."

"Stop, Holden," Carolyn pleaded. "I'm not your mother. Nothing you do is going to change the abuse you suffered as a child."

He exploded, raising his arm and hitting her in the face with a closed fist. "My mother's dead. She died alone in this shitty house while I was in prison. They didn't find her body for almost a week.

She didn't abuse me. My mother loved me. I just made that stuff up so the court would give me a lighter sentence."

Carolyn was struggling to remain conscious. The impact of his punch had blurred the vision in her right eye, and she could feel blood from her nose running down her face. He strapped another piece of tape over her mouth. The thought of him raping her was so repugnant, she could feel her stomach coming up in her throat. If she vomited, she could drown in her own fluids.

Holden removed his slacks and let them fall to the floor. Carolyn fought furiously against the restraints as he knelt down in front of her. He lifted her skirt and tore off her panty hose. She kicked out with her legs, but it was no use. "I'm going to show you who's in charge here, you conniving slut."

He pinned her down with his upper body. Then he stuck several fingers in his mouth, wetting them before reaching down to grope her vagina.

Carolyn tried to pray but couldn't. All she wanted to do was kill him. She stared at the ceiling, trying to separate her body into compartments. Whatever was happening between her legs was happening to someone else. She tried to imagine she was listening to her car stereo, about to turn into her driveway. The guttural animal sounds Holden was making made that impossible. His unshaven face scraped against the tender skin on her cheek. She didn't think he'd penetrated her except with his fingers. He was moving his hand up and down on his penis, trying to get an erection. He'd probably subdued her too soon. Many rapists only became stimulated when their victims fought and pleaded for mercy. This was what empowered them.

Carolyn had to keep her mind working on a rational level. If she let her emotions take over, she would not be able to think straight if an opportunity presented itself to escape. He'd taken away one of her strongest weapons when he'd taped her mouth. Now all she could do was remain mentally detached.

Why worry about his raping her? Regardless of what he did, he was going to kill her. If Hank was coming, he would have been here by now. His trial must have carried on into the evening. Because of a judge's decision to move the calendar, Carolyn would die.

Holden's attention was suddenly drawn to something behind her. Climbing off, he picked up her lighted cell phone off the floor where it had fallen. "Fuck," he said. "You called someone."

Carolyn watched as he yanked his pants back on. He rushed around inside the dark room as if he was looking for something. In the distance, she heard the shrill of sirens. Tears of relief gushed from her eyes.

Holden ran out the back door, the screen slamming shut behind him. Minutes later, Hank and several uniformed officers burst through the front.

"Get Romero," the detective barked. "He and Hooper are covering the back." He looked down at Carolyn as the other officers ran out, one of them speaking on his portable radio. "Is Holden armed?"

Carolyn started to shake her head, but then nodded, afraid Holden might have found her gun. It was humiliating to have the officers see her spread out on the floor, but her personal feelings would have to take a backseat to catching a killer.

Hank used his cell phone and called the station, asking the dispatcher to send more officers and the K-9 unit. He squatted down beside her, using his pocket knife to cut off a piece of her skirt. "I'm sorry," he said, covering the lower half of her body with his jacket. "We need this for the dog."

"The tape," Carolyn mumbled.

"This is going to hurt," he said before pulling the tape off her mouth as gently as possible. Seeing the blood near her lip and nose, he took a tissue from his pocket to wipe it away.

"No, Hank." She stopped him by turning her face away. "Don't contaminate me."

"That monster raped you?" he said, overwrought. "Why in hell did you come out here by yourself? Jesus, Carolyn, he could have killed you."

"Calm down," she said weakly, "you scared him off just in time. Put on a pair of gloves, then get the rest of this blasted tape off me. I'm okay, but I was certainly glad to see you." She extended her hand so Hank could help her to her feet. Pulling a pair of plastic gloves out of his pants pocket, he slipped them on, then picked up his jacket and tied it around her waist before he began removing the rest of the tape from her head and hands.

Carolyn stood, unsteady on her feet. The room began swimming, and she slumped against the detective. "I might have a mild concussion," she told him, touching a sore spot on her forehead. "He banged my head against the porch." She felt something pricking her back and yanked it out with her fingers. "A splinter," she said, tossing it on the floor. "The only evidence you'll get out of that one is from me."

"Even if he didn't actually rape you," Hank said, his concern for her showing on his face and in his voice, "you still need to go to the hospital for a medical legal exam. The doctors can also look at that bruise on your head."

"I know." Carolyn grabbed his shirt to keep from falling. "Contact your men and see if they caught him. Holden's our killer, Hank. We can't let him get away." She thought of her kids and searched the floor for her cell phone. "He must have taken my phone. I don't want John and Rebecca to know what happened here." She reached over and took Hank's phone from the clip on his belt, calling her house and reaching her daughter. "I got tied up at the office, sweetheart. Is your brother there?"

"John's barricaded in his room," Rebecca told her. "He made himself a steak. I had to eat leftover pasta. I'm trying to lose weight. Now I'll blow up like a water buffalo."

Carolyn welcomed the normality, her daughter's voice erasing the terror she had just escaped from. "But I defrosted three steaks this morning."

The girl's tone changed. "You're with that new guy, aren't you? I can tell by your voice that something's going on. Are you at his house? Are you going to sleep with him?"

"No," Carolyn said, "I'm not with Marcus." She told Rebecca she'd be home in a few hours and handed the phone back to Hank.

"Marcus, huh?" Hank said, a downcast look in his face. "That's the guy you were talking to that day at the lagoon."

"I need a minute to get myself together, Hank. This isn't the time to ask me questions about my personal life."

"Sorry. I wasn't thinking. As soon as the other units get here," he continued, donning a professional demeanor, "I'll have one of them take you to the hospital. They'll wait and drive you home. I want to stay here and oversee things. There's a field with an old shed on it about a mile from here. Holden might be hiding out there until the heat dies down."

"I'm not going home in a police car," Carolyn argued. "I told you I don't want the children to know what happened."

"I guess you could call your new boyfriend to come and get you?" he said, hands on hips.

Carolyn knew what he was implying, that he'd always been there for her, even if it meant risking his life. The previous year, he had pulled her out of the ocean when she'd driven an arms dealer's car off a cliff. If it wasn't for Hank, she wouldn't be alive. "I'm not going to answer that," she told him. "The kids have been through enough scares in the past. There's no reason for them to know what went on here tonight."

He pulled out a toothpick, shoving it in between his teeth. "Wait here." He stepped outside to speak with the other officers. "No sign of Holden," he told her when he returned. "We're going to canvass the neighborhood, but I doubt if we're going to find him tonight. Let's get you out of this place. I'll drive you to the hospital, wait, and then take you to the house."

"I'll drive myself," Carolyn told Hank, wanting to distance herself from anyone who had a penis.

"I can't let you drive," he said. "You need medical attention. Besides, no one who's been through something like this should be out on the roadway. Why won't you let me take care of you?"

"If you want to do something for me," Carolyn said, "catch this rotten bastard before he rapes and kills again. If you don't, I'll hunt him down myself."

"You already tried that," the detective said quietly. "It didn't work out that well."

Carolyn cut her eyes to him. "Next time I'll be better prepared."

Mary Stevens arrived on the scene, rushing over and embracing Carolyn. "I'll take it from here," she told Hank, placing a blanket over Carolyn's shoulders. "Don't worry about your car, honey. Give me the keys, and I'll get someone from patrol to drive it to your house."

"I don't want my kids to know," Carolyn told her.

"No problem," Mary said. "I'll have them park it down the street. Then when I drop you off later, we can move it to the driveway."

After Carolyn handed Mary the keys, she turned to Hank and smiled. "At least one good thing came out of this."

"Really?" Hank said, the corners of his mouth barely lifting. "And what is that?"

"You don't have to worry about getting a search warrant. Now that it's a crime scene, you can rip that house apart."

CHAPTER 22

Carolyn sat through an hour-and-a-half examination. She had bruises where Holden had slugged her and slammed her head into the porch, but she figured she'd be able to conceal them with her hair and makeup. The doctor wanted her to spend the night to make certain she didn't have a concussion. She knew the warning signs, she told him, and would return to the hospital if she experienced anything disturbing.

A young blond nurse inspected every inch of her body for physical evidence. Even though Holden hadn't penetrated her, the nurse scraped her fingernails, combed her pubic hair, and searched for bodily fluids, such as blood, saliva, and pre-emission sperm.

Hank had assigned Mary Stevens to handle the paperwork. She waited outside the room as the SAAE nurse, Sexual Assault Abuse Examiner, did her job. Before females had entered the police force, a male officer had to be present during examinations of rape victims, adding another level of humiliation to an already degrading situation. Now female nurses were trained specifically for this purpose, although not every hospital had them. But women police officers were generally available.

Carrying a pair of jeans and a red shirt, Mary entered the room after taking possession of the evidence. "You ready to get out of this place? I brought you some clothes I had in my car."

"Isn't this your murder shirt?" Carolyn said, stepping into a pair of Mary's jeans, which were two sizes too large.

"Yeah, I figured the way you feel right now, it might be appropriate."

"You're right on that one," Carolyn said. "I'm not sure what's worse, the assault or the embarrassment of someone probing my private parts with a cotton swab."

Mary gave her a sympathetic look. "Bad, huh?"

"Holden was like a bull," Carolyn told her, buttoning up the red shirt. "I didn't stand a chance with him. I'm just lucky Hank picked up his cell phone and showed up when he did."

"I feel sorry for the next rapist you handle," the detective told her, leaning against the wall. "Bet you won't be buying their sob stories."

"Amen to that one. I'd personally be willing to castrate the bastard if the court doesn't put Holden away for life this time. The death penalty would be even more satisfying. Callous, huh? As a Christian, I'm supposed to forgive my enemies, turn the other cheek."

"I'm more of an eye-for-an-eye kind of girl," Mary said, rubbing the side of her face. "On that note, you want to get something to eat? You'll feel better with food in your stomach."

"No thanks, I want to get home to my kids."

Once they were on the road, Mary turned to her. "Can you talk about what happened with Holden, or would you rather wait until later?"

"We have to nail this guy, Mary," Carolyn said, wrapping her arms around her chest. "He's out there right now stalking his next victim. Trust me, he had no reservations whatsoever about killing me. I'm almost positive there are other victims we haven't found, some from before he killed Tracy Anderson. When I interviewed him, he practically confessed to it."

"I don't understand," Mary said. "We know Holden had four victims. What are you're trying to tell me, Carolyn?"

"He wasn't talking about the three other women he raped," she said. "He said specifically, 'When I put my fingers around *their necks.*' He didn't touch the rape victims' necks, only Anderson's. I tried to tell the DA's office he might have killed other women, but they refused to listen. As far as they were concerned, it was over. Now look at the nightmare we have on our hands."

After contemplating that fact for a few seconds, Mary said, "We hit a snag this morning in St. Louis."

"You mean Lisa Sheppard isn't our victim? I thought you said she had the same fracture to her leg."

"No, we're good on that," said the detective, pulling out of the hospital parking lot. "The X-rays should be here by tomorrow morning. They have to dig them out of archives, but at least they think they still have them. The problem is Lisa's grandmother, Eleanor Beckworth. The PD in St. Louis said she committed suicide around the same time her granddaughter was reported missing. She wrapped an electrical cord around her neck, then hung herself from the bedpost."

"How sad," Carolyn said, thinking how she would feel if either Rebecca or John disappeared. The waiting was the worst, not knowing if your child was alive or dead. The more she thought about it, the stranger Eleanor Beckworth's suicide seemed. The maternal instinct was one of the most powerful emotions a woman possessed.

"If the grandmother had died of a heart attack or something, it would make sense," she reasoned out loud. "But her granddaughter could have eventually surfaced. Why kill yourself before you know for sure your child or grandchild is dead? And what a terrible thing to do to them. Have the missing woman turn up safe only to learn that her grandmother killed herself." Carolyn thought of something else. "How long after Lisa's husband reported her missing did her grandmother commit suicide?"

"The next day. It didn't set right with me, either. Sounds almost convenient, doesn't it? Husband tells the police his wife moved back in with her mother, then the one person to substantiate his story dies a day later."

Carolyn placed a hand over her chest. "My God, the husband may have killed both of them."

"It's certainly a possibility," said Mary, slapping the steering wheel in frustration. "You realize this means not one, but two police agencies may have walked past a murder and just kept right on going. Damn, how much worse can it get in this stupid world?"

"You're asking me?" Carolyn tapped her chest with her fist. "A maniac just tried to rape me. I thought for sure Holden was our man, especially after what happened tonight. Do you think it's possible that Holden passed himself off as Matthew Sheppard and married Lisa, then killed her?"

"Maybe. St. Louis is sending me everything they have on the case. Don't think I'm making excuses for them if Beckworth's death turns out to be a homicide, but suicides among the elderly are fairly common. We handled a case last year where an old guy about to be placed in a nursing home used the same technique. You know, stringing themselves up on the bedposts. Like the situation in San Diego, Mrs. Beckworth's house has already been resold."

"What in the hell are we dealing with?" Carolyn asked, nervously scratching a place on her wrist where the duct tape had been. "This case was complex to begin with. Now I don't know what to think. If Sheppard murdered his wife in San Diego, he had to get on a plane and fly to St. Louis the next day to get rid of her grandmother. You not only have to catch Carl Holden, you've got to track down Matthew Sheppard."

Mary's eyes met hers. "Unless they're the same person."

The thought was not new. Carolyn realized that they now had to give it serious consideration. "Are either of these cases in Ventura's jurisdiction?"

"Good question," the detective said, passing Ventura College and turning down Day Road toward Carolyn's house on Bethel Drive. "If our Jane Doe is Lisa Sheppard, which seems to be the case, then we own the homicide. The rationale is that the murder occurred somewhere in Ventura because the body was dumped here. St. Louis is left holding the bag on the grandmother. Our only involvement there is how that crime ties into ours. Don't forget, Matthew Sheppard could also be a victim of Carl Holden. And the grandmother could have killed herself for reasons we may never discover. Once we take a look at the phone records, we'll get a clearer picture. It's possible that Eleanor Beckworth may not have known her granddaughter was missing."

Carolyn fell silent, her thoughts returning to the incident with Holden. She considered telling John and Rebecca the truth, but she could imagine their reaction. If she'd stayed in law school and managed to open up her own practice, her life would have been fairly simple. Simple was static, though, and static was boring.

Pulling up alongside Carolyn's white BMW, parked at the end of her street, Mary said, "I'm going to have to submit a formal report on the attempted rape, you realize. If you're not up to it tonight, we can do it tomorrow, maybe even handle it over the phone to make things easier."

"Tomorrow would be better." Carolyn pulled out her compact and dabbed makeup on the bruises on her forehead. "Keep me posted on what's going on. I've got to buckle down and get some work done. My cases are piling up like mad."

Mary leaned over and hugged her. "Are you sure you can drive?"

"I'm fine," Carolyn told her.

"Would you like me to come in for a while?"

"No, but thanks. Like I said earlier, I'm more pissed than anything. I don't mind being roughed up now and then if there's a chance of getting someone like Holden off the street. If I went through this for nothing, it'll be a shame. I had my gun drawn when I snooped around his place. I should have used it before he got his hands on me. But after what happened last year and all—"

The detective cut her off. "I've never shot anyone," she said, a pensive expression on her face. "I hope I never do. Sometimes it's either us or them. The guy you shot would have killed you, Carolyn. He deserved to die."

"Sounds good in principle," Carolyn agreed, "but once you pull the trigger, you have to live with the fact that you've taken a life." She stared out the window, then took hold of the door handle. "I have to get some rest if I want to be productive in the morning."

"I wish my dad was still alive," Mary told her. "Not only would he have liked you, he would have tried to recruit you. You go through a night of hell and all you're concerned about is your work. You're a real trooper."

"Thanks." Carolyn stepped out of the car and waved good-bye as Mary took off. As she walked up the sidewalk leading to the house, she glanced at the flowers lining the walkway and thought of watering them before she remembered they were artificial. She needed to plant more as they were somewhat sparse in areas. This time, she decided, she'd use the arrangement in her bedroom.

She found Rebecca in the kitchen, eating ice cream and staring at a sink full of dishes as if she expected them to clean themselves. "Hi, honey. How was your day?"

"Same as always. Kinda crappy." The girl glanced at her mother's apparel. "Wow, Mom, you don't look half bad. Turn around. To be really cool, though, your crack has to show."

"Cute," Carolyn said. "I had to go out to a crime scene, so one of the female detectives loaned me some of her clothes. Any calls for me?"

"Sorry, no hot guys called," said Rebecca, twirling a spoonful of ice cream. "Since I already screwed up my diet, I decided to pig out."

"Please, Rebecca, don't slop that stuff all over the floor. All I need is an army of ants crawling around here in the morning. And you have to clean up the kitchen before you go to bed. If you don't, I'll hold back your allowance."

"You mean my big ten bucks?" She wiggled her fingers in the air in mockery. "That barely buys lunch at McDonald's. Kids in grade school get more money."

"I give you lunch money every day," Carolyn said, letting her shoulders roll forward. "Why don't you baby-sit for Mrs. Robertson? There are other jobs you could do as well. You could get a paper route. It pays very well."

Rebecca looked at her as if she'd lost her mind, shoving the container of ice cream into the freezer and tossing her spoon into the sink. "Oh, the FedEx guy called to confirm our address," she shouted as she headed out of the room. "They've got a package for us."

Carolyn rushed over and grabbed her arm. "You didn't give out our address, did you?"

"Let go of my arm," Rebecca snapped. "How else do you expect him to deliver the package? I thought it was something important, maybe about one of John's scholarship applications."

"That wasn't a FedEx man," Carolyn said, her eyes flashing with concern. "Haven't I warned you to never give out our address? Where's your brother?"

"In his room. What's wrong, Mom?"

"Everything," she said, realizing Holden could have taken her gun as well as her cell phone. Now she had no way to defend herself. "Check the windows and lock the doors. Have John help you, I'm calling the police." When she picked up the phone, it was dead. "Get your cell phone! Hurry!"

Rebecca ran down the hallway. Carolyn looked out the kitchen window into the backyard. She felt fingers grip her neck and ragged fingernails dig into her skin.

"Hello, Carolyn," said Carl Holden.

CHAPTER 23

Wednesday, September 20—9:10 P.M.

The cold barrel of Carolyn's own weapon pressed against her temple. "You forgot this," Holden said. "Thanks. It's a lot harder to get a gun these days."

Carolyn struggled not to cry out, terrified Rebecca would come running into the room. She should have told her to dial 911. "What do you want?" she asked.

"You'll find out," he said, strained yet confident. "Get your daughter in here." He shook her neck, causing her head to rock. "Call her now, I said!"

"Rebecca," Carolyn said with her speaking voice.

"Louder."

"No," she said. "I won't let you hurt my daughter."

"Call her, bitch, or I'll kill both of you."

"Rebecca," she yelled, tears welling up in her eyes. The girl appeared in the doorway to the kitchen, her cell phone clasped in her right hand. When she spotted the man and her mother, she froze.

"Give me that phone," Holden barked. "If you don't, I'll splatter your mother's brains all over this nice white refrigerator. You wouldn't want that now, would you?"

"Mom?" Rebecca looked for her mother's approval.

Carolyn didn't respond. She tried shaking her head, but she couldn't. Rebecca put the phone on the floor and kicked it toward Holden. He released his fingers just long enough to shift his forearm to the front of her neck in a choke hold. Leaning sideways, he scooped up the phone with his free hand.

As the blood flow to her brain became restricted, Carolyn's knees began to tremble. She gasped for breath, determined not to pass out.

"Stop, you're hurting her!" Rebecca screamed. "She can't breathe."

Holden let up on the pressure. "Your daughter's a pretty girl, Carolyn," he said. "You've done good by yourself. She's not like you, though. She's more the killing type than the fucking type. You want to die, baby doll?"

"Let my mother go," Rebecca said, forcing her shoulders back and thrusting her chin forward in defiance. "We didn't do anything. When the police get you, you're the one who's going to die, not me."

"You're spunky, but ignorant," he said, checking the cell phone to make certain the line wasn't open, then pulling up the last number dialed. After noting that it displayed a girl's name, he slipped it into his pocket. "Youth is easily deceived because it's quick to hope. Your only hope is that your mother cooperates with me. Am I making myself clear?"

"I'm not scared of you," Rebecca said, shooting a black gaze at him. "I don't think you're gonna kill us. This isn't about us. You said you wanted my mom to cooperate. She can't cooperate if she's dead. Isn't that right, dickhead?"

Carolyn couldn't believe her little girl had become such a courageous young woman. She reflected that Rebecca's rebelliousness was more than likely because of her strength. Strong people didn't like others to tell them what to do.

The girl was trying to buy time, but why? Had she called the police before she came into the room? *Doubtful,* Carolyn decided. *She wouldn't have had time.* What scared her was that Rebecca might be waiting for John to intervene. The single-story home was built in a circular pattern. The formal living room couldn't be seen from Holden's present vantage point. Her son could come at him from behind by going through the back entrance to the kitchen off the dining room. Rebecca was standing in what they referred to as the TV room. Carolyn didn't keep a spare gun in the house because of the children. If John tried to jump Holden from behind, Holden might shoot all of them.

"You look thirsty," Rebecca said, moving toward the refrigerator one step at a time. "Would you like a drink of water or maybe some booze?"

"Don't test me. I'll shoot her."

"I'm not testing you," Rebecca said, taking another tentative step. "I'm just trying to be polite. What do you want my mother to do? Why don't you tell her so we can stop all this?"

"Do whatever he says," Carolyn pleaded. "The gun's loaded. He won't hesitate to use it. If he doesn't shoot me, he'll shoot you. He's killed before. I was late tonight because he tried to rape me. Please, honey, listen to me."

Rebecca swallowed hard but stood fast. "He's crazy, Mom."

"Crazy, my dear, is highly subjective," Holden told her, keeping a tight hold on her mother. "Many of the most brilliant people in history were considered insane. Did you ever think that maybe their path to higher understanding was a result of the fact that they didn't conform to society's exceptions? You could call me crazy. I consider myself highly enlightened."

"I'll pass on your type of enlightenment," Rebecca responded, her lips curled in contempt.

"You think this is a game, don't you?" Holden said, agitated. "I rape and kill girls like you."

Rebecca laughed, but it wasn't her normal laugh, more of a nervous jitter. She was afraid, trying to disguise her fear with false bravado. "You should have told me he was a rapist, Mom," she said, only a few feet away from them. "I read a book about freaks like you. You can't get it up without beating and degrading women. You should be ashamed of yourself."

Holden's demeanor changed. He dropped his head, appearing almost intimidated, as if Rebecca were scolding him like a mother. However, just because he appeared somewhat subdued now, Carolyn knew, didn't mean he wouldn't react violently if Rebecca continued to push him.

"Get back, bitch," he said, pointing the gun at her. "All you are is a miniature version of your mother. I've seen this act before, eight years ago. The difference is that now I have a gun."

Rebecca took several steps backward, although her rigid expression didn't change. "Go on, shoot me," she taunted. "I don't give a shit. Death has always fascinated me."

"Stop, Rebecca!" Carolyn shouted. "Please! I'll do whatever you want, Carl. She's just a kid. She doesn't know what she's saying."

Holden's face flushed. Carolyn could feel his muscles contracting. "I want the key," he told her, shifting his attention from Rebecca. "There's a safety deposit . . ." He stopped speaking. "It's just a key, okay? You have to go back and get it before the cops find it."

"I'm a probation officer, not a police officer," Carolyn said. "Your house is a crime scene now. The police won't let me carry evidence off the premises."

"It's taped on the wall behind the toilet," he continued. "Do what I say or I'll put a bullet right between your daughter's eyes. As soon as you come back with the key, I'll leave and no one will get hurt."

He was going to hold Rebecca hostage. He could rape her before she returned, and Carolyn wasn't even certain she could find the key he was talking about. What about John? Surely, he'd heard the noise by now and called the police. Everything was her fault. She should have never gone to Holden's house alone.

Carolyn saw Rebecca looking at something behind her. She had an overwhelming desire to try to see what it was, but she knew that if it was John, Holden could spin around and open fire before any of them could do anything. "I'll get the key for you if you promise you won't touch my daughter."

A sense of satisfaction filled Holden's face. "Karl Marx said, 'Nothing can have value without being an object of utility.' Congratulations, baby doll," he told Rebecca, waving the gun at her. "You're my object. Don't mouth off again and you'll be fine. Has she always been this difficult, Carolyn?"

"Yes," Carolyn answered, thinking she'd heard a footstep. "Release me so I can go."

Everything happened at once. Holden let go of Carolyn. Rebecca dropped to the floor in the TV room, then rolled behind the wall.

John plunged a pair of gardening sheers into Holden's back, causing the gun to discharge.

"What the . . ." Holden growled as he twisted his body around.

Terrified, John raced back into the dining room where he'd been hiding. Holden ran after him, squeezing off two more rounds. Carolyn tried to kick his feet out from under him. She caught his right heel, but then her hip crashed against the linoleum. Holden stumbled, yet continued after John.

"Were you hit, Rebecca? If you can, get out of the house now!" Carolyn shouted.

Another explosion of gunfire rang out.

Carolyn raced to the formal living room, Rebecca behind her. John was lying on the off-white carpet in a growing pool of blood. Holden stood over him, the garden shears in his bloodied left hand, the nine-millimeter clasped tightly in his right.

"What have you done?" Carolyn cried, dropping to her knees beside her son. The blood was coming from a gunshot wound in his leg. "Oh my God, what have you done?"

"Where the hell did he come from?" Holden said, panting. "He stabbed me. Is this your fucking son?"

John's eyes were open, his face a mask of pain. "My thigh," he said weakly. "I think he shot me in the thigh."

"I'm going to get you to the hospital, honey," Carolyn told him, ripping the tablecloth off the table so she could wad it up in a ball and apply pressure to the wound. "You'll never see that key, Holden," she said, hate darting from her eyes. "Not until my son receives proper medical attention."

"It doesn't work that way," he told her. "He lays here and bleeds until the key is in my hand."

"You can't do this to us," Carolyn said, tears streaming down her face. "I refuse to go. I'm not leaving my children with you."

Holden grabbed Rebecca, placing the gun at her temple. "I guess I'll have to kill one of them to prove my point. Which one, Carolyn? The daughter, the son, or the key. You choose."

"Go, Mom," Rebecca said, her face ashen. "I'll look after John until you get back. You have to do what he says now. Please!"

Carolyn kissed John on the forehead. "Hang in there, tough guy. I'll be back before you know it." She rushed to the front door and took a moment to glance back, wondering if she'd ever see her children alive again.

Holden had left Carolyn with no options. She couldn't call the police for fear he would kill John and Rebecca. Without her weapon, she couldn't defend herself. The last place the police would be looking for him would be at her house. She cranked the engine on the Infiniti and backed out of the garage, gripping the steering wheel with both hands.

John's injuries didn't appear life-threatening, Carolyn consoled herself. The bullet hadn't struck any major arteries. That didn't mean that he couldn't bleed to death, though, if he didn't get medical treatment within a reasonable amount of time. How long, she wasn't sure. At least Rebecca was there with him. She'd shown Carolyn that she wasn't afraid of fighting through difficult situations. This was reassuring and unsettling at the same time. Her daughter had been far too bold with Holden. If she tried to stand up to him again, he might shoot her. The engine raced as she pressed the gas pedal to the floorboard.

What did Holden want with the safety deposit key? From the look on his face, he hadn't intended to tell her what the key was for. Of course, he could have been lying when he said it was for a safety deposit box. The key could be for a car, some type of hideout, even a warehouse. He'd been in prison for eight years, and since he'd been holed up in his mother's dilapidated house, it was doubtful he possessed anything valuable. Maybe someone he'd met in prison had given him the key. If that was the case, perhaps they could contact the prison to find out who that person was. The key could belong to a former cellmate who had stashed his loot in a safety deposit box before he was arrested, then somehow managed to smuggle the key inside the prison.

But why would an inmate give Holden access to his money? Carolyn asked herself. Perhaps this other man was serving a life term. Having nothing to lose, lifers tended to brag about their exploits. Or the man could have traded the key for sexual favors from Holden.

A person couldn't use a safety deposit key without knowing the address of the bank and having appropriate identification. But Holden was smart. He could probably figure out how to obtain a fake ID.

She pulled up in front of the residence on Park Avenue. The clock on the dash read eleven-forty. There was only one police car protecting the crime scene, so she assumed CSI and the other units had already cleared. The front door was sealed with yellow police tape.

Formulating a plan, Carolyn knew she needed a flashlight. She'd taken the one she carried in the trunk of her car into the house when Holden attacked her, so that one was gone. Rummaging through the glove compartment, she finally located a small penlight, the kind you attach to your key ring. It didn't give off much light, but it would have to do. She got out and walked to the patrol unit, leaning in to speak to the officer. "Hi, Clark," she said, pleased to see a familiar face. He had been one of the first officers to arrive on the scene after the assault earlier.

"What are you doing back here, Carolyn?"

"There's additional evidence inside the house I need to get. Do you mind if I take a quick look around?"

"I'm not sure I can let you do that," he said, turning all business. "You could contaminate the scene. We tried to get the lights turned on so we could finish up tonight, but there's some kind of problem with the wiring."

"Contaminate it?" Carolyn shot out. "Half of the evidence in there is mine. I was already inside this place, remember?" She hit the top of the police unit with her open palm. John lay bleeding while she stood there arguing. She wanted to call Hank, but she knew as soon as the police showed up at her house, Holden might kill her kids. Or something else bad could happen. Not long ago, the LAPD had shot and killed a sixteen-month-old baby during a shoot-out with the child's father. Things could go terribly wrong in a hostage situation. She was certain the best way to proceed was to try to meet Holden's demands. She needed a gun, though, and gave thought to trying to grab Clark's gun when she was ready to take off. Then she realized that would bring the heat down on her for certain.

"I've had a really rotten night, Clark," she said. "Hank Sawyer gave me permission to go inside. You want to buck him, go right ahead."

She took off in the direction of the house, ripping the yellow tape from the door and stepping inside.

The officer got on the radio, alerting the dispatcher that he had a problem. He ran toward the house, yelling, "Carolyn, please, I can't let you rummage around in there."

"I'll just be a minute," she told him, the seconds ticking off inside her head. The officer didn't respond. Good, he wasn't going to bother her anymore.

Carolyn proceeded down the hallway and stopped. The tiny flashlight barely provided her with enough light to see, and a foreboding came over her. Horrible things had happened inside this house, she sensed, and not just what had occurred this afternoon. She was certain Holden had lied when he'd said there hadn't been a problem with his mother. The abuse he'd suffered was probably even worse than he'd indicated in that interview. Was that why he'd dropped out of school? Was that the reason he had become a rapist and murderer? Then again, what she sensed might be her own fear.

The door to the bathroom was open. She went to the toilet and fell to her knees. As she reached around the bowl, her face was inches from the urine-stained buckled flooring. Trying not to breathe, she ran her fingers across the key. She ripped the tape with the key off.

As she emerged from the hall, the beam of light from the officer's flashlight struck her. "You got the key?"

"I'm about through, Clark," she said, holding a hand up to shield her eyes. How did he know about the key? The only person who knew about the key was Holden. Holden! That was Holden with the flashlight! In an effort to escape its beam, she fell to the ground, but the circle of light found her.

"Give it to me, Carolyn."

Carolyn wasn't about to let Holden have the key or finish what he'd tried to do earlier. She ducked into the bedroom to her right, slipping the small penlight into the pocket of Mary's jeans. She could hear his footsteps moving toward her.

Holden entered the room on the other side of the hallway. Carolyn rushed to open a window. She pushed the screen out. It hit the porch and banged against the wood. She quickly hid in the closet.

"Shit," Holden said, looking out the window, believing Carolyn had escaped.

Carolyn sprinted behind him toward the front door. Like a wrestler, he went to his knees and lunged at her, trying to grab her foot. She stumbled, then picked herself up and blasted out of the front door. She stepped over the unconscious police officer lying in the driveway as she raced to the Infiniti.

She should have known Holden wouldn't remain at her house.

Looking back, Carolyn saw him running past her to a Hummer parked on the street. Holden might have John and Rebecca tied up inside. Or he might have already killed them. Were their dead bodies inside that car? As she got into her own car and cranked the ignition, she looked back at Clark, cursing herself for not stopping to pick up his gun. Fear and rage filled her as the engine engaged and she roared off.

If her children were dead, Carolyn had no desire to continue living. But right now she wouldn't think about that.

She drove toward the corner. About a mile down the street, Holden roared up beside her and rolled down his window. The intensity in his face was horrifying. "Pull over and give me the damn key."

CHAPTER 24

Wednesday, September 20—11:10 P.M.

En route to his home in Santa Rosa, Marcus decided to swing by Carolyn's house to make certain everything was all right. He'd called earlier as she'd requested, and a recording had said her phone was out of order. As he pulled the Bentley into the driveway, he saw light radiating from the windows and assumed Carolyn and her children were still awake.

He knocked on the door. "Who is it?" a male voice yelled.

"Marcus Wright," he said. "I'm a friend of your mother's."

"Help us, please!" Rebecca screamed. He heard the male voice gruffly telling her to shut up. "Don't, no . . ."

Marcus tried the knob. When it didn't turn, he raised his foot and kicked the door open, entering the house and seeing a man dart out the rear slider door.

"He shot my brother," Rebecca said, crying hysterically as she pressed the bloody tablecloth over her brother's wound. "Call an ambulance."

Marcus squatted next to John. He pulled the cloth away, ripped it with his teeth, and wrapped a long piece tightly around the boy's leg above the wound to stop the blood flow. "Christ, was that the man who did this? The one that just left? Where's Carolyn?"

"Don't let him get away," Rebecca shouted, pointing as she saw Holden running across the front lawn through the window. "He cut the phone lines. We couldn't call for help. My brother left his cell phone in his friend's car, and that man took mine."

Marcus reached into his pocket and flipped open his phone, dialed 911, and handed it to Rebecca while he raced outside to try to catch the assailant.

The man entered what appeared to be a black late-model Hummer. The massive car roared off, leaving Marcus standing in the middle of the street. Squinting, he tried to make out the plate. It was too dark, though, and the Hummer had already disappeared around the corner.

Returning to the house, he told Rebecca, "Your brother's lost a lot of blood. He's not going to die, but he needs to get to a hospital right away."

"Son," he addressed John, "can you hear me?"

"Where's . . . my . . . mom?" the boy mumbled, his face alarmingly pale.

"My God," Rebecca said, grabbing Marcus's sleeve. "He made Mom go to get some kind of key he left at his house. He told her to bring it back to him here. Now that you showed up, he might go there and kill her. You have to do something."

"Where is this place?" Marcus asked, his voice tense. "Do you know who this man is?"

"Mom said he was a rapist," the girl told him. "Th-that he was a killer. She told me I should do everything he said."

"Was his name Carl Holden? Someone your mother investigated in the past."

"I'm not sure."

"I need to get hold of her detective friend." Marcus pushed himself to his feet. "He works with your mother. Ventura PD, I think. You must have his number somewhere."

"Mom's backup phone book is in the kitchen," Rebecca told him. "It's taped under the cabinet above the phone. I think you're talking about Hank Sawyer."

When Marcus went over to the counter, he saw a file folder sitting next to the phone. The name on the tab was Carl Holden. He opened the folder and saw a Post-It note with an address on it. Carolyn had circled it and written, "Holden's mother's address." Perspiration dripped from his forehead and soaked the underarms of his shirt. He found Carolyn's address book and rushed over to Rebecca. "The police and paramedics will be here any minute, okay? I've got the address where your mother must have gone. I'll call Hank on the way. I need my phone. Lock all the doors. Don't answer unless you're certain it's the authorities. How did he get in?"

"I forgot to lock the back door when I took the trash out."

Marcus rushed out of the house and jumped behind the wheel of the Bentley. The sound of approaching sirens violated the peace of the once quiet neighborhood. He punched the address from the Holden file into his navigation system. It told him his destination was only twelve miles away.

With the Bentley's tires chirping on the concrete as he threw the gearshift into reverse and stepped on the gas, Marcus thought that now he would see how this luxury car handled when he pushed it to the limit. As he drove down the residential street at sixty-five miles per hour, an old couple on a walk stopped to watch the car zip by. "Turn right in one hundred feet," the automated voice said. As he turned the steering wheel, his body shifted against the door and the rear of the car fishtailed toward the curb on the opposite side of the street.

Carolyn made him feel alive again. Meeting her children, even in such a desperate situation, had given Marcus a glimpse of what his life could be like if things worked out between them. Sometimes when he drove through middle-class neighborhoods like Carolyn's, he longed to be an average person. Success had a tendency to isolate people, dull their senses, and rob them of one of the most enjoyable human experiences—anticipation. Putting money aside for that new car you'd always dreamed of owning, the vacation to Hawaii, even something as insignificant as a new pair of shoes. He imagined what it would be like to get up every morning and go to a regular job. No employees who depended on you, no heavy responsibilities. With Carolyn, he might find happiness. Everything would come to an end, however, if he didn't stop Holden from killing her.

Marcus found Hank's number and punched it into the phone.

After identifying himself and explaining the situation, he asked the detective, "This key Rebecca spoke of at the house, what's the significance? Why does Holden want it so bad?"

"Hold on," Hank said, "we have a unit in front of the Park Avenue address now. The bastard tried to rape Carolyn there earlier this evening."

Marcus's blood boiled as he waited for the detective to return to the line. This no-good piece of human garbage had not only shot Carolyn's son, he'd tried to rape her! Why hadn't she called him? His car swerved in the residential streets as he tried not to smash into parked cars.

"We have additional units responding to the scene," Hank told him. "Where are you now?"

Looking down at the navigation display, he saw he was only three blocks away. "I'm there in two minutes," Marcus barked into the phone. His eyes panned the horizon as he searched for the Hummer. The area was riddled with rundown houses and apartment buildings.

"Listen to me," Hank yelled. "This is no time to be a hero. This guy will open fire if you get close to him."

"Don't tell me what to do," Marcus said, enraged to the point of unreason. "I'm going to show this murdering scum what real justice is about. All you need to do is bring a body bag."

Seeing that Holden was alone in the car gave Carolyn the resolve to stand up to him. Her car accelerated, leaving Holden behind as the streetlights flew past. The Hummer caught her in no time, though, slamming into the rear bumper of the Infiniti like an army tank and making it shake violently. Holden tried to come up alongside her, but the narrow road and parked cars made it impossible. She swerved from one side to the other, the odometer reaching fifty.

Holden rammed her again. This time the impact tilted the suspension, and the Infiniti skidded to the right, then spun and careened into a retaining wall.

The impact knocked the wind out of Carolyn. Next she was jarred by the crashing of the front of the Hummer's massive black meld of metal into the passenger side of her car.

Reaching for the door handle, she realized her only exit was blocked by the wall. Holden's face appeared beyond the rubble. Training the gun on her, he shouted, "Don't mess with me, Carolyn. This game is over. Give me the key."

It was as if she'd entered a soundproof chamber. Time slowed, and she could hear her breath rushing in and out of her mouth. Her heart pounded like a giant drum inside her chest. "Are my children alive?" she yelled.

"Yes, for now," Holden said, shaking his left hand at her. "The key, bitch."

Carolyn closed her eyes, praying that he was telling the truth. If the children were safe, though, that meant there were two rounds left in her gun. "I lied about finding the key," she said, knowing he would kill her as soon as he got what he wanted. "It's back at the house. That cop was on my ass. Since you took care of him, why don't you go back and get it yourself? I'm not helping you anymore unless you prove to me that my children are safe."

Carolyn slithered out through the window, taking shelter behind the wall. She could hear the engine on the Hummer revving. He was going to try to drive through the wall, kill her, and take the key. Then, peeking over the top, she saw the headlights and distinctive grill of Marcus's Bentley moving in a straight path toward the Hummer.

The collision of the two large cars was deafening. When Carolyn climbed over the wall, she saw Marcus's airbag had deployed, and his face was buried in the tan material. She heard metal scraping on pavement as Holden's vehicle sped away. The momentum had caused his bumper to disengage and clunk to the ground in the middle of the roadway.

Hank Sawyer was standing on the sidewalk at the intersection of Prospect and Ventura Boulevard, staring at Carolyn's wrecked Infiniti jammed against the retaining wall. Several officers from patrol had cordoned off the area, but there was no sign of Holden, Carolyn, or her new boyfriend, Marcus Wright.

The detective answered his cell phone, seeing nothing but a string of zeros on his Caller ID. Instead of speaking, he merely listened, thinking Holden might be injured and be ready to bargain. "Where the hell are you?" he barked when he heard Carolyn's voice. "Your car's wrecked. I've been out of my mind trying to find out what happened out here. They took John to Community Memorial. Where's Holden and that jackass boyfriend of yours?"

"Calm down," Carolyn said. "I'm okay, Hank. I'm with Marcus. I just got off the phone with the hospital. We're pulling into the parking lot now." She went on to describe what had transpired. "Holden was driving a black Hummer."

"I'm aware of that," Hank said. "We have the bumper. The Hummer was reported stolen earlier this evening. Holden ditched it about five blocks away. We have no idea what he's driving now. No one has reported a stolen vehicle in the immediate vicinity. Because it's so late, we may not hear anything until morning. We're setting up checkpoints, though, on all the major roads leading out of Ventura. We have the helicopter up as well. I've also got my men canvassing the neighborhood."

"Holden could be in another state by morning," Carolyn told him, bordering on hysteria. "In the name of God, we have to find a way to stop this hideous man! He shot John! It wasn't enough for him to try to rape me. He came into my home, held my family hostage, and shot my son. I want this man to pay, understand?"

"I'll meet you at the hospital. I sent Mary over to be with Rebecca. She wasn't injured, just shaken up."

"Just get me Holden," Carolyn said. Then, "Wait." She asked Marcus for his cell phone number, which she rattled off to Hank. "We'll have to turn it off while we're inside the hospital. You can leave a message on Marcus's voice mail, or call the hospital and have them page me. Holden has both my cell phone and my gun. Unless he fired a round I'm not aware of, he should have two shots left in the chamber."

"Good to know."

"You have my Nextel cell phone number," she went on. "Do me a favor—have one of your people call and have them disconnect it. That's how Holden got my address. He called the house, told Rebecca he was with FedEx and needed our address to deliver a package."

"Since the phone was used in a crime, there's no problem having the service terminated," Hank responded. "You realize as long as the battery has juice, though, Holden will have access to all your information. Whose numbers are stored in that thing?"

"Everyone's," Carolyn said, holding the phone to her ear as she and Marcus jogged toward the emergency entrance to the hospital. "Neil's, my mother's, IP numbers for the computers at the agency, even your home number. You name it, it's in there. What should I do?"

"Hope he doesn't stop off at a Nextel store and buy a charger."

"Thanks, Hank," she said. "As if I couldn't have figured that one out for myself."

Marcus was looking back at her from several feet ahead. Carolyn started to say something else when she heard the dial tone.

Satisfied there was nothing more he could do in the field, Hank headed to the hospital, his thoughts returning to Carolyn. He hadn't even met Marcus Wright and he already despised him. Carolyn had gushed about how he'd rescued her from Holden by ramming his Bentley into the Hummer. What kind of pompous asshole would drive around in a Bentley? More important, why was a man with that kind of money involved with a divorced probation officer with two teenage kids? Something didn't add up.

Yeah, he had a thing for Carolyn. Everything he'd become within the last year was motivated by his fantasy of their one day being together. Above all, though, he couldn't stand the thought of her being hurt by some smooth-talking phony who wanted to spend a few nights in bed with her, then move on.

How could he not go to the hospital? Carolyn, John, and Rebecca were about as close as he came to having a family. He'd been divorced for years, and he and his former wife had elected not to have children. Now that he was getting older, he realized what a mistake that had been.

Ten minutes later Hank was walking down the stark white hall to the emergency room. After he flashed his badge to the admitting clerk, the automatic double doors opened to a sea of stretchers. Injured people lay under thin white blankets, IV bottles dangling beside them. Dodging the paramedics bringing in an Asian woman with a crushed leg, he approached the center desk. "Where's John Sullivan?"

"Hank, I almost didn't recognize you," a pretty dark-haired nurse said, smiling. "Long time no see. Atkin's diet, huh? To answer your question, they just took the Sullivan boy into surgery."

"How bad is he, Erica?"

"He was conscious, but he'd lost a lot of blood. The kid would be dead if the shooter had hit an artery. Other than that, the gunshot wound was fairly superficial. Once they dig the thing out, he should be back on his feet in no time. If you're looking for the family, they're on the seventh floor in the surgical waiting room. You'll see it when you get off the elevator."

"Thanks," Hank said, turning away.

"Anytime," said Erica, leaning over the top of the counter. "Stop by again when you're not in a hurry. Maybe we can grab a cup of coffee."

The detective was so engrossed in his thoughts he didn't realize the nurse had been flirting with him. He stepped into the open elevator and pushed the button for the seventh floor. When he found the waiting room, he saw Carolyn through the glass window with two men. He recognized Neil, so he assumed the man in the suit next to her was Marcus Wright.

Carolyn's brother was a tall, slender man with dark hair and expressive eyes. He wore a white shirt with the sleeves rolled up to his elbows, black jeans, and paint-splattered tennis shoes. When things were going well in his life, Neil was quite the character, cracking jokes and incessantly teasing his sister. He'd gone through some rough times the year before, primarily due to his involvement with a woman with some extremely bad habits. Hank had been pleased when Carolyn told him Neil had finally extricated himself from the relationship.

Hank saw Marcus stroking Carolyn's hand. *Sleazy bastard,* he thought, *trying to take advantage of a woman when her defenses are down.*

What was so special about this guy, anyway? Hank suspected he was pushing fifty. Carolyn's former infatuation with Brad Preston was understandable. Any woman would go nuts over a man that good-looking. And the fact that he raced cars made him even more appealing. Girls were turned on by men who did dangerous things. Being a cop used to do the trick, but it didn't seem to hold the status it did in the past, probably because women had finally realized how little police officers were paid.

Hank took a deep breath and released his fist, opening the door and stepping inside the waiting room. "Carolyn," he said, giving her a tense look. He turned to acknowledge her brother. "Hi, Neil." Then, "Any news on John?"

Carolyn got up and hugged the detective, whispering in his ear, "Thanks for coming. Between Holden and John, I'm a basket case."

Hank stared down at the floor. "I worry about you, you know," he said quietly. "Maybe if you'd use more caution, you wouldn't put yourself in these kinds of situations all the time." *Damn,* he thought, wincing. He'd said the wrong thing again. "Forget that, okay? Just tell me the status on John."

Carolyn glanced over her shoulder at Marcus, then turned back around. "The wound itself isn't that bad. What they're worried about is the amount of blood he lost. Once they remove the bullet, we'll know more. Anything on Holden?"

Hank sighed. "Not yet," he said. "He'll make a mistake eventually. I don't think he has much money. He'll have to pull a robbery or something so he can get out of town. He'd be a fool to stay here with this kind of heat. That's good because it will give us a chance to nail down a location on him."

Carolyn took a seat on a small sofa. "Unless he kills someone with my gun."

"Pleasant thought. Where're Rebecca and Mary?"

Carolyn chewed on a fingernail, then dropped her hand to her side. "Mary took Rebecca home to spend the night with her. Oh, this is Marcus Wright. Marcus, Hank Sawyer. He's the detective I told you about."

Hank gave the other man a bone-crushing handshake. "Didn't need that body bag, huh?"

"I missed the passenger's door and caught the back bumper," Marcus explained, massaging the hand Hank had shaken. "Next time I'll shoot him."

"You two know each other?" Carolyn asked, taken aback.

"We spoke on the phone before I took off to find you," Marcus told her. "Hank gave me some pearls of wisdom. Now I know why you think so highly of him."

"Oh, he's got a lot more where those came from," she said, digging into the pocket of Mary's borrowed jeans. "Here's the key Holden had hidden in the house. He said it was a safety deposit key. Can we find out where the box is?"

"Maybe," Hank said, slipping on a pair of rubber gloves. He figured he could get something to place it in from the nurses' station until it was booked into evidence. "Safety deposit boxes are a bitch. What do you think is in there?"

"I have no idea," Carolyn said, shrugging. "It could be souvenirs he took from his victims. Or maybe money. With the chances he took to get the key, it must be something valuable."

"Can I take a look at that?" Marcus asked, standing.

Hank held up a gloved hand. "What do you think these are for, pal?"

"It's evidence," Carolyn said, placing a hand on Marcus's forearm. "Someone's prints might be on it other than mine and Holden's."

"Turn it over," Marcus requested. When the detective did, Marcus said, "See these five numbers? They may tell you where the key was made and possibly the bank that issued it."

Hank was annoyed that Marcus would have the balls to tell him how to do his job. Besides, he didn't know what he was talking about. Locksmiths didn't put numbers on keys, and finding the company who manufactured it wouldn't tell them anything. He might be thinking of Medeco keys, which couldn't be duplicated, but the source code wasn't on them. The only way to track down a safety deposit box with nothing more than a key was to canvass banks. Even if a bank said it was their key, he'd have to get a court order. A judge would want to make certain you had the right box, or whatever was in there would stay in there. "We'll shake down Holden's former cellmates, Carolyn. There's also the chance that he's committed crimes other than rapes and homicides."

"That's what I was thinking," she agreed. "Have one of your people check all the unsolved robberies and burglaries, see if anything links back to Holden." She excused herself to go to the restroom, adding before she left, "He could have stashed his loot before he went to prison and hid the safety deposit key in his mother's house."

Neil followed his sister into the hallway, waiting for her outside the women's restroom. "I don't want to tell Mother over the phone," he said when she returned. "I'll drive over to Camarillo and tell her in person. We should wait until we're certain John is out of the woods, don't you think?"

"I agree."

Neil reached over and tugged on a strand of her hair. "Jesus, Carolyn, what were you thinking? Maybe that's why that man attacked you. Guys in prison have better haircuts."

Carolyn grasped his hand. "This isn't the time to critique my hair, Neil."

"Sorry." Diving right back in, he said, "What's the deal with this Marcus fellow? Why didn't you tell me you were seeing someone? Did he really save you, or was that just bullshit?"

"Yeah, he did," his sister said, a dreamy look in her eyes. "He really saved me. I barely know the man, Neil, and he risked his life for me. He's amazing."

"Let's not get carried away, sis," Neil told her, placing his hands in his pockets. "Maybe he just wanted to get his name in the paper. Is he an undertaker? Hanging around cops would be a good way to drum up business. No one wears a suit anymore in Los Angeles. If you don't believe me, drive downtown one day."

Carolyn's brows were knitted with concern. While he'd been talking, she'd been staring at the doors leading into the surgery unit, hoping the surgeon would come out and tell her John was okay. "Will you pray with me like we used to when we were kids?"

Neil began pacing, running his fingers through his already tousled hair. "That's not fair, Carolyn. You know how I feel about this religion stuff. I'm going to get an earful from Mom tomorrow. This saint does this, and that saint does that. By the time we get to the hospital, I'll have prayer cards sticking out of all my pockets. Knowing Mom, she'll probably pin one on my ass." He saw the water fountain behind them and filled up a paper cup, slugging it down.

Carolyn said, "People die in surgery, Neil."

"Okay, fine, I'll pray with you. Are we going to do it right here in the hall? You want me to get down on my knees?" He stepped aside as a nurse walked past them. "We could pray in the bathroom where no one would see us."

"You're mocking me," she said, blinking back tears. "I just wanted to go to the chapel and say a prayer for John."

He draped an arm around her shoulders. Carolyn snuggled under his armpit. "What are we standing here for?" he said, lifting her chin up with his forefinger and smiling. "Where's the damn chapel? Maybe I'll paint their ceiling in exchange for a meal in the cafeteria. That's probably more than Michelangelo got paid."

Hank took a seat beside Marcus in the waiting room, pulling out a toothpick. Staring at the small sliver of wood in his fingers, he wished it would magically transform itself into a cigarette. A toothpick wasn't much consolation when you were forced to act civil to your rival. "So, you met Carolyn in an accident?"

"Yeah," Marcus answered, tossing the magazine he'd been reading down on the table. "She ran a stop sign and broadsided me."

"Where's your gun? The one you're going to shoot Holden with."

"In my car," he said. "I have a permit, in case you're wondering."

"How did that come about?"

Marcus coughed. "I sometimes handle property that belongs to the government."

"Humph," Hank said, checking his cell phone to see if he had any messages. He wondered what was keeping Carolyn. He couldn't stay at the hospital much longer with his cell phone turned off. He didn't understand why they prohibited them. They claimed it interfered with their equipment, but he'd seen nurses communicating with each other by cell phone. "What kind of government property do you handle, if you don't mind me asking?"

"I don't mind you asking," Marcus told him. "I just can't tell you. My work is classified." Changing the subject, he added, "It took an odd set of circumstances to bring us together. Carolyn's a terrific woman, Hank, one in a million." He smiled. "Of course, I'm not telling you anything you don't already know, right?"

"True," Hank said, barely getting the word past his clenched teeth. The guy had seen right through him.

"Does Carolyn attract trouble or something?"

Hank leaned forward over his knees. "Maybe you're the one who's bad luck. She's only known you a short time, and she's been in two accidents."

"She ran into me the first time. I'd crash every car I have to meet someone like Carolyn. How bad was the Infiniti damaged? She just got it out of the shop yesterday."

"I don't think they'll be repairing it this time," Hank told him, still smarting over the "every car" remark. How many cars *did* he have? "Can't you give me a general idea of what you do for a living?"

"Computer software," Marcus said, shifting anxiously in his seat. He looked up when Carolyn returned, then stood. "Here, sit down next to Hank."

"Thanks." Carolyn had dark circles under her eyes, and her posture showed signs of exhaustion. Her shoulders were rolled forward, her arms hung limp at her side, and she walked as if in a daze. "Did you hear anything?"

"No," Hank said, standing. "I have to take off. I just wanted to stop by and check on John. Looks like you have plenty of support here, Carolyn. Try and get some rest. If you need anything, you know where to find me."

"How about Holden's head on a stick?"

"Working on it," Hank said, walking out the door to the waiting room.

Was it jealousy that made him dislike Marcus Wright, or was it something more sinister? Over the years he'd developed a talent. He could sniff out a rat, no matter how cleverly they disguised themselves. Then again, maybe Marcus was CIA. Guys from the Agency were trained not to blow their cover, even when subjected to torture. The problem was they would also use anyone necessary in order to complete their assignment.

Hank was in deep thought when he stepped into the elevator and pressed the button for the ground level. While in prison Holden could have hooked up with a terrorist, or become involved in something that had high-reaching ramifications, perhaps a plot to assassinate the president. His concern for Carolyn's safety heightened.

Why had he let Marcus examine the key to the safety deposit box? There was a number etched on it, and he might have been trying to verify it. Had Marcus been after the same thing as Holden—the key?

Holden had gone to extraordinary lengths to get the key back. By going to Carolyn's house and holding her family hostage, as well as assaulting a police officer, he'd put himself in a position to either be killed or returned to prison. Why would a man who'd just been granted his freedom do such a thing?

Stepping out of the elevator, Hank ran into the brunette nurse he'd seen earlier. "I was just coming up to find you," Erica said, flashing a seductive smile. "I'm off work. Want to come over to my place for a drink?"

Hank's ego shot up several notches. Maybe Carolyn wasn't for him. Sometimes a person wanted something they weren't meant to have. Before he'd left Martha Ferguson's lab, she'd handed him her home number and told him to call her. Since she'd pinched his ass, he doubted if she wanted to see him to discuss business. Martha wasn't so bad, now that he'd gotten to know her. She might be a hot number.

He decided to accept Erica's offer. As long as he left his cell phone on and the station could get in touch with him, there shouldn't be a problem. He'd already put in over seventy hours this week. "Sure," he told her. He recalled her remark about having a drink. "I'm a recovering alcoholic. I'll have to pass on the drink, but I wouldn't mind visiting with you, if that's okay."

"So am I," Erica told him, seemingly thrilled that they had something in common. "I've been sober for fifteen years. It doesn't bother me if someone else has a drink. I don't keep liquor at my house, though. I would have had to stop off at a liquor store on the way. My car's in the employee parking lot. I'll pull up in front of the hospital so you can follow me. I live about three blocks away."

Hank sucked in his stomach and thrust his shoulders back. Losing the weight had definitely been worth it. He watched Erica's hips sway as he walked behind her through the lobby and out of the hospital.

CHAPTER 25

Friday, September 22—5:23 P.M.

The hospital had just moved John out of the ICU. Finally, his vital signs had stabilized. Marcus had slept in the chair in the waiting room since John had been shot. He had left at five o'clock that morning to go home, freshen up, and then drive to his office in Los Angeles.

Carolyn had spent two nights on a rock-hard convertible bed next to her son. Monitors and machines hung from the ceiling, and warning sounds and blinking numbers on the screen had flashed, making it impossible to sleep for more than a few hours at a time. John's condition, as the nurses had told her, had been touch-and-go. His blood pressure had plummeted, causing the doctor to order another transfusion. Carolyn had felt helpless to do anything other than hold his hand and call the nurses when she saw changes on the monitors.

She not only blamed herself for what had occurred, but the criminal justice system in general. What had happened to her family was an everyday occurrence across America. Convicted criminals were released to wreak more havoc. This time it had hit the hardest for Carolyn. Getting shot or assaulted on the job was tragic, but it came with the territory. Holden had crossed a barrier that no mother could tolerate. He had shot her son. She would not let him get away with it. Once John was released, she would hunt down Holden herself. She'd done it before; she could do it again. At present, the bastard was free, and the police had no leads whatsoever.

John was sleeping. Now that his blood pressure was under control and there was no sign of infection, the doctor said he would probably be able to go home by Monday.

Carolyn listened to the woeful sound of an elderly man crying in the adjacent room. Her thoughts kept returning to Marcus. Risking his life to save her from certain death had made him her personal hero. He was a businessman, not a seasoned cop like Hank, trained to act in a crisis. He could easily be the man of her dreams—but they had met at a rough place in time. She had only two priorities right now, and neither her job nor Marcus were among them. Number one was her children, John in particular, and the second was making certain Carl Holden didn't destroy more lives. How could love possibly thrive when she was so consumed with hatred?

The golden boy, Brad Preston, suddenly filled up the room with his presence. Carolyn placed her finger over her mouth to let him know that John was sleeping.

"Coffee?" he whispered, pointing down the corridor.

Carolyn slipped out of the room, stopping off at the nurses' station to let them know John was alone in the room. They took the elevator to the basement, where the cafeteria was located. "Have you eaten?" Brad asked. "I just got off work."

"I can't stomach another bite of hospital food. You go ahead, though. We can talk while you eat."

"Actually," Brad said somewhat sheepishly, "I've got a prior commitment. It's been balls to the walls at work, or I would have been here sooner. How's he doing?"

Carolyn brought him up to date on John's condition as they went through the line and got their coffee. He paid the cashier, and they managed to find an empty table. The cafeteria was packed, most of the patrons being hospital personal. Relatives of patients didn't appear to be eager to eat hospital food for their Friday-night meal.

"I hear you're getting tight with this Marcus guy," Brad said, flipping his tie over his shoulder so he didn't spill coffee on it. "Is that true?"

Rumors traveled fast. Veronica had the biggest mouth in town, and she'd stopped by the hospital the other night while Marcus was there. "I don't know if I'd classify our relationship as tight," Carolyn told him. "With everything that's happened, we haven't had much time together outside of the hospital."

"You're not in love with this guy, I hope," Brad said, taking a sip of his coffee. "Hank said you went gaga over him because you think he saved John's and your life. What'd he do, call an ambulance? He was in the right place at the right time, that's all."

"You have a date tonight, don't you?" Carolyn said, annoyed by the way the men in her life were acting. "Well, I finally found someone I really like, even though I doubt if anything will come of it. And no, Brad, Marcus wasn't merely in the right place at the right time. He drove his car straight into Holden's stolen Hummer. Holden could have shot me if he hadn't done what he did, and Marcus could have been killed in the collision."

Brad had the smirk on his face that she despised. "A Bentley and a Hummer seem like a fair match to me. Your new sex machine wasn't driving a Mini, Carolyn. If he thought he was going to get hurt, he wouldn't have done it. He didn't do it to save you. He did it to impress you."

"Look at you," she erupted, waving a hand toward him. "You've probably slept with fifty women since we split up. What right do you have to—"

"Fifty women, huh?" he jumped in, grinning rakishly. "All in one night or on different occasions? According to you, I'm living like a sultan. What's a man like that doing working for the county for peanuts?"

"That's not what I'm getting at," Carolyn argued. "Why can't I fall in love with someone? And why can't you and Hank, people who profess to care about me, be happy for me? I'd be happy for you if you told me you'd found someone and wanted to get married."

"Shit, now you're going to marry the guy!"

"I'm just trying to make a point, Brad," Carolyn told him, bracing her head with her hand.

Brad fell serious. "Love is overrated, baby. It doesn't last. That's the big secret no one tells you. Those old couples you see together holding hands, they don't love each other anymore. Being with each other has become a habit, and habits are hard to break. What matters is finding a partner who stimulates you, makes you laugh, someone you share common interests with. What do you have in common with this guy, outside of this one incident?"

Good question, Carolyn thought. "We both have children."

"All right, that's one thing," Brad said. "How old are his kids? Do they live with him? Is he a good father? I know you're one hell of a mother. You've worked your buns off to give those kids of yours a good life. Damn, you're even selling your house to pay for John's college tuition. That's sacrifice. There are people driving BMWs, living in nice houses, wearing nice clothes. How many would sell their home and move into an apartment so their kid could go to a top-rated university?" He thumped the table with his fist. "You're the hero, Carolyn. Last year you drove a damn car off a cliff rather than take a chance a bomb would go off and kill people. I've seen you confront men who could kill you, and without a thought to your own safety, push them to the breaking point on the mere chance that you might be able to get something out of them that would aggravate their sentence. All I'm saying is, make sure this man is your equal, that he has at least a fraction of the outstanding qualities you possess. Don't be impressed because he drives a fancy car and has a few dollars in his bank account. Money doesn't mean shit."

People at the adjacent tables had been listening with rapt attention. Brad always drew an audience. Although Carolyn hated to admit it, most of what he'd said made sense. She remembered how it had been with Frank. Six months or so into the marriage, and the fluttering hearts and surging hormones had disappeared into a routine of mundane existence. Then a couple had to struggle and innovate just to bring about a few fleeting moments that mimicked how they'd felt in the beginning.

"That feeling you get when a relationship is new isn't love, Carolyn," Brad went on, vocalizing what she'd been thinking. "It's excitement, and excitement only exists when something is new."

The problem with love, Carolyn decided, was it wasn't always rational. And woman weren't the same as men. Regardless of how many times they'd been disappointed and hurt, they never lost hope that a great love would one day find them, a love so tender and beautiful that it could never be tainted. And Carolyn was no different. Suppose

Marcus was the person who could give her that love? She was willing to take that chance.

"Thanks for the coffee and the lecture, Brad," she told him, rising and walking behind his chair. She placed a hand on his shoulder. "I'll take it under consideration. Right now, I need to go upstairs and check on John."

"Wait," he said. "I came to tell you something before we took off on a tangent."

"What?" Carolyn asked, circling back around.

"You've been approved for a three-week leave of absence. With pay, of course. I had a meeting with the chief this evening. That's why I ran late. Put work out of your mind for the time being. Concentrate on John and Rebecca."

"But you don't have enough people as it is," Carolyn protested.

"I'm going to pick up the slack."

"That's ridiculous, Brad," she said, dropping back down in the chair. "You have to run the unit." His responsibilities extended beyond making case assignments. Every report had to be conferenced with him before a probation officer could submit a recommendation to the court. He had to agree that the sentence was justified, as well as go over all the terms to make certain they were computed accurately. Interpreting and applying the laws was a complex task. It was easy to make a mistake, even in something as simple as the math. Conferencing up to a hundred cases a month, along with his other duties, was time-consuming. "No," she said. "Really, Brad. All I need is maybe a week to get John back on his feet. Not that I don't appreciate—"

Brad interrupted with, "I'm going to work at home and on the weekends. I'll stay late and interview the defendants and victims. You need this time, Carolyn. You've been through a terrible ordeal. I'd rather you take time off now than to have you crater on me later."

Carolyn reached across the table and touched his hand. "You really are a wonderful friend, Brad. If you need me to do work at home, all you have to do is call me."

"Don't worry about anything. Leave the scumbags to me. Now get back to your son before he wakes up and finds out you're gone."

* * *

The winding roads leading down the coast were perfect for Dean Masters's burgundy Porsche 911 Carrera. Navigating the corners at high speeds was exhilarating. Each turn distanced him from his life with Kathleen. He should have never left the golf course. That's where he belonged. In college it was all fun and games. Today golf had become a reality-avoidance mechanism, his way to disappear from the world and try to heal the past. The future was much more unpredictable than it used to be. Dean would start a new life now, as he had done before, but this time, he had a loose end remaining: Kathleen.

She had somehow survived.

Dean pulled off the road into one of his favorite spots. The late-afternoon sun reflected on the water, turning it a shimmering shade of silver. The ocean looked as if it had turned into a sea of mercury. His thoughts brought him back fourteen years, to a time before people called him Dean Masters.

He heard his assistant, Kimberly, and was back in his office in Manhattan.

"Dr. Wright," she announced over the intercom, "your one-thirty is here."

His large executive suite was paneled with dark wood, the walls covered with certificates of accomplishment and framed photos of him with important people. He was a prominent psychiatrist, and his practice was flourishing. Why wouldn't it be? He was not only smart, he was good-looking and personable. Most of his clients were women, either depressed housewives or single career women who dressed and acted like men. They wondered why they had problems when the answer was blatantly obvious. The housewives were stupid or superficial, the businesswomen overbearing.

Dr. Wright would have given up his practice several years ago, but seeing patients was his entertainment. He was probably one of the few remaining psychiatrists in Manhattan who still believed he could help people without dispensing medication. Listening intently, he could hear how vulnerable they were, and he molded their minds with simple, clarifying discussion. Many times only a few well-placed words made all the difference.

His fee of $150 per hour was adequate. Instead of placing his money in blue-chip stocks, he'd gambled in the technology arena and pocketed a fortune. Now he saw patients on Monday, Wednesday, and Friday. The rest of the time he spent in Connecticut or upstate New York at country clubs, playing golf and chasing women.

Once Thomas Wright acquired something, whether it was a possession or a lover, he would not relinquish his hold on it until he no longer wanted it. When he decided he wanted to elevate his status in New York society, he realized that wealth alone wouldn't provide him with a ticket to mingle with the upper echelon. Having millions of dollars in Manhattan was like having a warm coat in Alaska. Marrying the daughter of a highly esteemed state senator, however, coupled with his professional accomplishments and polished appearance, would open doors that had previously been closed.

He met his fiancée at what he had thought was going to be another boring political fund-raiser for her father, state senator Clarence Simons. A thirty-two-year-old gorgeous brunette, April was a physical therapist. Like him, she didn't work for money. What she wanted was independence from her smothering father, and her job was a necessary outlet.

He had fallen in love with her, but the risk of love was that it masked the reality of the inevitable disaster. April would grow old and ugly, cheat on him, leave him, or die. He hadn't decided which of those alternatives was the worst.

"Leonard Steinberg is on the phone," Kimberly said, poking her head into his office.

As usual, he'd been daydreaming while the seventy-eight-year-old silver-haired matron sitting across from him blubbered, having spent the past nine months grieving over the death of her poodle, Bitsy. "As you can see, Kimberly," he said, annoyed, "I'm with a patient. Tell Steinberg I'll call him back."

"I told him that, Doctor, but he insists that you speak to him. He says it's urgent."

"I'm sorry, Ethel, can you excuse me?" he said in a placating tone. "If you don't mind waiting in the lobby, we'll resume in a few minutes. Kimberly, get Mrs. Mooney a soda. She doesn't drink caffeine, so make sure it's decaffeinated."

After the two women left, he walked over to his desk and snatched the phone off the cradle. "What's so important, Len?"

"We've got trouble," the attorney said. "Did you sign for a package yesterday afternoon?"

"I don't usually sign for things," he said, wondering what was going on. "Kimberly handles . . . Oh, wait, I did. Something came in while she was out to lunch. Why?"

"You signed for a summons to appear in court, Thomas, a ninety-page complaint filed by Harvey Goldberg on behalf of a woman named Nicole Pelter. You're being sued. Out of courtesy, her law firm sent a copy to my office. It's Brown, Franklin, and Weiss, the same firm that handled Sarah Briscoe's unfounded accusations against you last year. Is Pelter one of your patients? Did you have sex with this woman?"

The psychiatrist stood, placing his hand on his head. "This can't be happening again. She's lying. Nicole Pelter is a bitch. Believe me, she's a gold digger. Her last husband was in his eighties. She got tired of waiting for him to die, so she filed for divorce and took him to the cleaners."

"We're not talking about Sarah Briscoe," the attorney continued. "Need I remind you? This is one of the top medical malpractice firms in the country. We slid with Briscoe because she didn't get her facts straight, and Goldberg refused to make a fool of himself in the court-room when he learned we weren't going to settle. I guarantee you Brown, Franklin, and Weiss wouldn't have taken this case if they didn't think they could win. They're asking for two million."

"Ridiculous! This is blackmail!" Wright said, seething. "Yes, she's my patient. I didn't have sex with the woman. Christ, Len, I'm engaged to April Simons."

"Nicole Pelter has a different story," the attorney told him. "Did you ever treat her at her residence?"

"Yes, that's not a crime," Wright said, pacing behind his desk. "She lives four blocks from me, and she sounded like she was borderline psychotic when she called me at three in the morning. I was afraid I might have to commit her. When I got there, I gave her a sedative by injection and she calmed down. I've seen other patients at home. What's your point?"

"How many?"

"Two," he said, having had to rush out and sedate Ethel Mooney the night her dog died.

"That's not enough to make it seem usual or customary," Steinberg told him. "Unfortunately, it'll be your word against hers. Pelter claims you gave her some type of narcotic and she woke up an hour later with you on top of her. She didn't call the police right away because she passed out again from the drug." He paused, letting the weight of his words sink in. "I'll fight this thing for you, of course, but it doesn't look good. They also filed a formal complaint with the New York Office of Professional Medical Conduct. You could lose your license."

Wright sucked in a deep breath, then let it out in an audible whoosh. "So what do we do now?"

"Pay her off," Steinberg suggested. "Your insurance will cover it. The fact that another claim was brought against you won't help us, particularly with the medical board. Usually where's there's smoke, there's fire."

"I've never touched a patient," the psychiatrist yelled. "Nicole Pelter doesn't deserve a cent. Do you understand me? Not a penny. Tell them I'll see them in court. No one is going to extort money from me."

"Have it your way," Steinberg said. "Just remember, I warned you."

"Mom," John said. "Can I have a drink of water?"

"Sure." Carolyn helped him sit up by propping a pillow at the base of his back. "Comfortable?"

"Yes," he said, still pale and weak. "I need to talk to you about something."

"Okay . . . what is it, honey?"

"I've been doing a lot of thinking," he told her, taking a deep breath. "I don't think I should go to MIT."

"Didn't we have this conversation already? The doctors say they'll have you walking in a few weeks."

"It's not that," John said, lowering his head. "What Rebecca told you was true. I use pot. And I'm not talking about a hit here and there. I've used every day since I was twelve. Sometimes I just can't relax, Mom. Pot helps me to sleep at night. I usually smoke it in the backyard, or at Turner's house. That was the first time I smoked in Rebecca's room. I'm sorry I let you down."

Carolyn was shocked at his admission, even though she'd feared this possibility, after Rebecca's accusation. But under the circumstances, she had to be supportive. "Does Rebecca smoke?"

"No," John said. "She's really a cool kid, Mom. She's got a good head on her shoulders. Unlike me, I'm sure she'll do fine."

"It's okay," she said, moving her chair closer to the bed and stroking his thick hair back from his forehead. "Everyone makes mistakes, sweetheart."

"I feel so bad," John continued, choking up. "Pot started out as a way to escape. You and Dad were fighting all the time. It was right before the divorce. I couldn't believe my father was a drug addict. Then I thought, hey, what the heck, it's just a little grass. I know that's a cop-out, but I . . . I don't deserve to go to MIT or any other college for that matter. At least, not until I prove myself. In the meantime, I can just work at Giovanni's and try to save more money. It wouldn't be right for you to sell your house for a loser like me."

"Stop, John," Carolyn demanded. "I want you to go to MIT because of what you have up here," she said, pointing to her head. "You're going because you can, understand? You've been accepted. Losers don't get accepted to MIT, Harvard, or any of the other top schools. Of course I'm not happy about you smoking pot. At least it's not crack or heroin."

"I'll wait a few years," John said, his eyelids getting heavy from the medication. "I can always go later."

"Your success is my success," Carolyn told him, stroking his arm. "I wasn't as intellectually gifted as you, so I didn't have the same opportunities. My happiness comes from seeing you achieve things I wasn't able to do. I know you can stop using pot. It's not physically addictive. And now that it's out in the open, it should be easier."

He shook his head. "I'm not so sure about that, Mother. Pot isn't the same as it used to be. Today's stuff is pretty potent."

"You can do anything you want to do," Carolyn insisted. "Just think, you're going to be in an entirely new environment. The bad influences here at home will stay here." She was thinking of his friend

Turner. They'd been friends so long, it was hard to think he'd been a negative influence on her son. Now she knew. "Concentrating on your studies will help you put this behind you. I'm sure you wouldn't risk being thrown out of MIT because of drugs."

Both Carolyn and John stopped speaking when they saw Neil, Rebecca, and Carolyn's mother enter the room.

"There's my brilliant boy," Marie Sullivan exclaimed, rushing over and kissing him on the forehead. Petite like her daughter, she wore her short silver hair naturally curly. She was dressed in a pair of purple pants and a pink sweater. She handed John a box of See's candy. "Sometimes chocolate is better than medicine."

"Thanks," John said, smiling. "They told me I could go home Monday."

"Well, you're going to be staying at Neil's house," Mrs. Sullivan said, exchanging glances with her daughter. "That awful man knows where you live. There's no way you can go home until he's back in jail where he belongs." She saw Rebecca glaring at her. "And you're not going back home, either, young lady."

"Please, Mom," Rebecca said, turning to Carolyn. "I'm not afraid. If he comes back, I'll kick his butt. You know how far Neil's house is from my school. When John gets out of the hospital, we'll both have to sleep in the studio. Neil took the bed out of the guest room so he could store some of his paintings. What about all my clothes and things? His computer is an antique, and he doesn't even have Internet access. Even the pope knows how to use the Internet."

Carolyn placed a hand on her forehead. "John's going to be on crutches for a while," she said, looking over at her mother. "It'll be easier for him to get around at home. I appreciate the offer, Neil, but your studio is a long walk from the main house. I don't want him to slip and fall into the pool."

At the mention of the pool, her brother's face darkened and he looked away. A girl he'd planned on marrying had been murdered and dumped in his swimming pool the year before, sending him into a severe depression.

"You're talking like an idiot, Rebecca," John argued. "How are you going to kick Holden's butt? I don't mind staying at Neil's place. It'll be fun. At least I won't have to worry about someone shooting me again." He turned to his mother. "I'm not a baby. I'm not going to fall into the pool, Mom. Even if I do, I can swim."

Carolyn held up a palm. "We'll figure everything out tomorrow. Maybe by then the police will have arrested Holden. I'm too exhausted to think. You guys stay here with John. I'm going home to take a nap, shower, and change into some fresh clothes. I'll call Veronica and see if she can pick Mother up in a few hours and drive her back to Camarillo, Neil."

"What about me?" Rebecca said, flinging her arms out to the side. "I have to go to school tomorrow."

Carolyn's patience was wearing thin. She couldn't handle the bickering. "You need to stay here in case Holden comes around," she told her daughter. "You know, so you can kick his butt."

CHAPTER 26

Friday, September 22—8:15 P.M.

Carolyn ran into Marcus in the parking lot. "I bet you're beat," she said. "Did you get any rest today?"

"Don't worry about me," he told her. "I'm used to going without sleep. I know you don't have a car, so I thought I'd come by for a visit, then give you a lift home."

"My friend Veronica arranged to have a county car dropped off for me. I have the keys. Now all I have to do is find it."

"Those pool cars are rattletraps," Marcus said. "I have an extra car I can loan you."

Carolyn laughed. "You're right about the county cars. I was driving one a few years back, and the brakes went out on the freeway. I was lucky I didn't get hurt. But, really, I'll be fine. I'll turn the car in to-morrow and use John's Honda until I find out what the insurance company intends to do about the Infiniti."

"Come to my house. Then you can decide," Marcus said. "I'll feed you. You need a change of scenery. You haven't left the hospital in three days. Ride with me. You probably shouldn't be driving."

"Thanks, Marcus," she said, touching his arm. "I need to go home and freshen up, maybe catch a few hours sleep." She looked down at her clothes. Mary's red murder shirt was ripped in several places. "I feel like these clothes are glued to my body, and they're not even mine."

"You can take a shower at my house," he offered. "When you're ready to go back to the hospital, we'll swing by your place and you can pick up whatever you need."

Carolyn acquiesced, and they drove twenty minutes to get to Marcus's Spanish-style home on the outskirts of Ventura. Once inside, he gave her a quick tour. The house was charming, spacious but not pretentious. Marcus told her that he'd sold his condo in Los Angeles and turned one of his offices into a bedroom for whenever he needed to stay in town. He loved the unique privacy his new home afforded him. The house was surrounded by two acres of land, half planted in avocados and the other half in oranges.

"Makes me feel like a farmer," he joked, standing next to her on the back porch. "Of course, unless there's fruit on them, I can't tell one tree from another. In a few years, I'm going to subdivide it and build houses. If my business doesn't pick up, that's the only way I'll be able to afford the payments. My alimony and child-support payments are huge. My wife and kids don't have much use for me, but they have plenty of use for my money."

Although the main house had been recently renovated, the other buildings were not in good condition. The barn, where the previous owners kept their horses, needed paint and a new roof. "Would you like a glass of wine?" Marcus asked when they'd entered the kitchen.

"Sounds great," Carolyn told him.

"I have to go down to the cellar. Be right back."

Carolyn wandered into the living room. It was dark, so it was hard to make out the furnishings. She started to turn on a light when she heard Marcus calling to her from the other room.

"Here you go," he said, handing her a glass of merlot. "John's going to be fine, they'll catch Holden, and before you know it, I'll be whisking you away to Paris."

Carolyn had kids and responsibilities. She'd be lucky if she could find the time to go to Palm Springs, let alone Paris. It was a pleasant thought, though, and lately there hadn't been enough of those to go around. "I'll drink to that," she said, clicking the wineglass against his before she took a sip. "This is terrific," she added, the delightful aroma of the fine wine waking up her senses. She started to take another drink when he reached out and took her glass from her.

"First, we need to get some food into you. I don't want you passing out on me."

Carolyn smiled. "You cook?"

"Heavens, no," Marcus said, opening the refrigerator and removing a glass container. "My housekeeper is Italian. She tries to mother me, so she always makes three times more than I can eat. This is one of her specialties, lobster in white wine and capers over linguini. All I have to do is pop it in the microwave. If that doesn't sound good, I have a roast chicken from yesterday that I never got around to eating."

Carolyn smiled. "The lobster dish sounds delicious."

He leaned back against the counter while he waited for their food to cook. "Your friend Hank seems awfully intense. Is he always that way?"

"Hank and I've been having a lot of arguments lately."

"Not uncommon when you work with people," Marcus said, the microwave beeping behind him. He removed two plates from the cabinet and collected some silverware, carrying it to the table. "Disagreement can be good now and then. Lets off steam, gives people a chance to come up with new ideas, or improve on existing ones. I like my employees to voice their opinions."

"You own the company, then?" Carolyn said, surprised. "I was under the impression that you only worked there."

"It's not a big company," Marcus explained. "I'd be able to sleep better at night if I was just an employee. There's a lot of responsibility when you own your own business. Most of the defense contracts for software go to giants like Microsoft. I was fortunate in that I developed a unique program. There's better stuff out there now, and we're working ourselves to death trying to compete. The entire future of my company rests in the hands of a few brilliant geeks. I can't afford to pay a fortune, so I have to rely on new talent. Some of the smartest programmers around are coming out of the gaming field. I've got one kid working for me who just turned eighteen. His starting pay was over a hundred grand, and already other companies are trying to steal him."

Marcus set the wine bottle in the middle of the table, then

spooned their food onto their plates. "What have you and Hank been arguing about? You going to Holden's house without backup, I presume."

"That among other things." Carolyn took a seat beside him at the round mahogany table. She explained what had transpired between her and the detective at Lisa Sheppard's gravesite at the Alessandro Lagoon. "I was shocked Hank had forgotten the glove we found on the first victim. They were made by different companies, though, so it didn't take us anywhere."

"What significance does the glove have?"

"I believe the killer left it intentionally," she said. "Sort of like a calling card."

He pointed at her plate. "Eat your food before it gets cold."

Carolyn laughed. "Look who's acting like a mother hen." Falling serious, she said, "I shouldn't have criticized Hank in front of the other officers. Mary Stevens did the same thing. Neither one of us gave a lot of thought to what we were saying that day." She took a bite of her pasta, then washed it down with her wine.

"Who's Mary Stevens?"

"A homicide detective, and a good one, too," she told him. "She let Rebecca stay at her house the night John was shot. We're practically neighbors, but we seldom socialize outside the office."

'So the killer's a golfer?" Marcus asked, hungrily attacking his food.

"No," she said. "I doubt if Holden has ever played golf in his life, not even miniature golf. Leaving the glove was his way to taunt us. He's probably angry that we didn't notice the first glove, the one he left on Tracy Anderson's body. This isn't an ordinary murder case, Marcus. There's no telling how many women Holden has killed over the years."

He stopped eating and stared at her. "Why didn't he get the death penalty? How can they turn these murderers loose like that? The system stinks, Carolyn. I don't know how you put up with it. Just because some lab guy screwed up doesn't mean they have to release all these violent criminals."

"Not every case where Abernathy processed evidence was overturned, just the ones that couldn't be proven without DNA or some other type of forensic evidence. And the people who handle forensics these days aren't referred to as 'lab guys,' Marcus. They're experts, and their skills are vital to the system."

"They're not that highly trained," Marcus commented, dabbing at his lips with a napkin. "After I met you, I did some research. Only three states require DNA labs to be certified. They don't even have a Ph.D. program in forensic science. Yet these people are dealing with human lives."

He was an intelligent, thoughtful man. Carolyn became animated. "You're right, Marcus. Everything outside of forensic science, particularly DNA, is considered circumstantial, and juries today don't want to convict on circumstantial evidence. They want to sleep at night, leave the burden of deciding someone's fate to the experts. What they want is unimpeachable proof that the defendant is guilty. We've convinced them that forensic evidence is infallible. But it's only as good as the people who process it. And human beings make mistakes."

Finished with his food, Marcus leaned back in his chair. "You think Holden's turned into a serial killer?"

"It looks that way," Carolyn told him. The police hated to bring the FBI in on a case, but she knew it was something they should consider here. What difference did it make if someone stepped on your toes as long as they got the job done? Leaving the glove was a ritualistic gesture, typical behavior among many serial killers. It was also a way to attract media attention, something most of them desired.

"What makes you think Holden has killed other women?"

"Only a fraction of an offender's crimes ever come to light," she said. "If Holden killed women he'd never met, as was the case with Tracy Anderson, the chances of catching him decrease dramatically." She then filled him in on her original interview with Holden, when he had alluded to other victims.

"Well," Marcus said, "when they catch him this time, maybe the murdering bastard will end up on death row."

"From your mouth to God's ears." Carolyn pushed her plate aside. "There is something else about Hank you should know. According to Mary, he's infatuated with me. That's probably why he's not wild about you appearing on the scene."

Marcus scowled. "How many guys do I have to compete with? What's the deal with the race-car driver? He isn't still around, is he?"

If he only knew, Carolyn thought, standing and looking around. Brad had told her relationships were only exciting when they were new. When had she started to bore him? After a few weeks? A month? No wonder they'd been continually breaking up and getting back together. "I need to call and check on John."

"No problem," Marcus said. "Walk past the living room and turn right."

She wondered why he was sending her so far away when there was a phone sitting on the kitchen counter. "Go on," he told her, "you'll get a kick out of it. I had it installed as a way to protest the lack of privacy we have these days. Well, specifically, people forcing me to listen to their idiotic conversations in public places."

Carolyn followed his directions, laughing when she saw an old-fashioned red phone booth. The hallway was dark, but when she opened the folding door to the booth, a light came on. First, she called Veronica and made arrangements for her to pick up her mother and Rebecca at the hospital.

"I'll keep the brat over here tonight," her friend said. "Once everything settles down, you're going to have to set that girl straight. She could have got all of you killed the other night. What kind of a kid smarts off to a murderer holding a gun to her mother's head?"

"Rebecca and I are making some headway," Carolyn said, thinking of the night her daughter had fixed her hair. "And she was very brave to do what she did, even if it didn't work out that well. At least she tried to do something. Most kids her age would have been paralyzed with fear. "

"Where are you, by the way?" Veronica asked. "I tried to call you at home about fifteen minutes ago and no one answered. Were you asleep?"

"Not exactly," Carolyn said trailing her finger around the dial phone that Marcus had converted into a push-button. "I had dinner with a friend."

"What friend? You don't have any friends outside of me, unless you count Brad, Hank, and that detective, Mary Stevens."

"I'm with Marcus," Carolyn whispered, although she knew he couldn't hear her from inside the booth.

"The Bentley guy?"

"The nice guy. The extremely heroic and handsome guy, who just might turn out to be the best thing that ever happened to me."

"Whatever you say. I was around for the early Brad days, in case you've forgotten. You know—best lover you've ever had, gonna get married and live happily ever after, nothing could ever go wrong between you. You don't fall often, Carolyn, but when you do, you land right on that thick head of yours, and it knocks you silly."

When her friend started ranting, it was time to end the conversation. Carolyn called and spoke to John. He tried to talk his mother out of returning to the hospital until the next day. When she protested, he put Neil on the phone.

"You've been through hell, sis," Neil told her. "I brought some sketch pads in my van. I'm going to work while John sleeps. I'll be a better watch guard than you—I stay up until dawn all the time. That's when I do my best work."

"Call the police if you notice anything even slightly suspicious," his sister instructed. "Promise me, Neil."

"I promise, okay, but why would Holden come here? He's got to know you handed the key over to the police, and John certainly doesn't have anything he might want."

When Carolyn stepped out of the phone booth, it was pitch dark. She had an eerie feeling that someone was right beside her. Then she felt his warm breath on the back of her neck.

"Is everything okay?" Marcus asked, massaging the tense muscles between her shoulders.

Carolyn wasn't sure how to react. "Why don't you turn some lights on?"

"It's easier to relax when it's dark."

She closed her eyes and let out a long sigh. She had to put the events involving Holden out of her mind. She turned around and faced him. His fingers trembled on the buttons on her blouse. When he pulled her to him, she realized he wasn't wearing his shirt.

"I wanted to feel your skin against mine," he said. "I know it sounds strange, but I'm shy. I've always been shy around women. I'm sorry. This probably isn't the right time."

"Why?" she said. "I want you to touch me."

"I think I'm falling in love with you, Carolyn. I really wanted it dark because I didn't want to see the expression on your face when I told you. I was afraid you'd reject me."

"I feel the same way," she said, reaching behind and undoing her bra. For a long time, they just stood there, touching each other. Then the pent-up emotions of the past two days surfaced. Carolyn placed her head against his chest and sobbed. "I'm fine," she told him, sniffling.

"You cried that first night, on the beach," Marcus said, disturbed. "Is there something I'm doing wrong?" Now that their eyes were adjusted to the dark, they could see each other from the light coming from the bathroom at the other end of the hall. "Please, Carolyn, tell me. I don't want to make you unhappy."

"It just feels so good to be held, to know someone cares about you."

"I can do better than that," Marcus said, releasing her and taking her hand. He led her down the dark corridor into a large room with high ceilings. It took Carolyn a while before she realized it was his bedroom. Sitting on the edge of the bed, he kicked off his shoes, then reached out to her. "Don't worry," he said once she was stretched out on the bed. "I can wait to make love to you. Shut your eyes, get some sleep. No one will hurt you. I'll be right here beside you."

How did he know? Carolyn thought. Terrifying thoughts and images kept passing through her mind. Being trapped in that awful house with Holden, the disgusting feel of his rough hands groping her vagina, the gun pressed against her temple. Then the terrible moment when he'd started shooting, and she saw her son bleeding on the floor. She pressed her fingers against her eyes, willing the images to go away.

Marcus gently took her hand and brought it down to her side. Softly, he stroked her forehead, her nose, her cheeks, her eyelids. She remembered putting her children to sleep that way when they were babies. Her body relaxed, and she drifted off into a peaceful slumber.

CHAPTER 27

Carolyn awoke, refreshed and excited. She had no idea how long she'd been asleep, but it was dark in the room. She was curled up tightly, snuggled against Marcus's chest. Why did she feel so comfortable with this man, and how did he manage to extract her carefully controlled emotions? One of his arms was flung over her shoulder, his long fingers brushing against her bare breast. She pressed her nose against his arm and inhaled. The smell of his skin was intoxicating.

Images flashed in her mind—sandy beaches and suntan lotion, happy days from her past, her first boyfriend, Randy Ketchum. They used to park and neck for hours, thrashing around in the backseat of his father's station wagon. The big moment occurred when they took their shirts off and pressed their bare chests together, similar to what she'd done earlier with Marcus. There was something about Marcus, the way he'd courted her, the tentative way he touched her, that reminded her of that first experience with Randy. Marcus wasn't pushy like most men, nor did he make sexual innuendoes. Perhaps he really was shy, although most men who owned their own businesses didn't fit that image. But business wasn't intimacy, and Marcus seemed to know what most men failed to comprehend: making love was not something to take lightly.

A sliver of light entered the room from the bathroom. Carolyn rolled over, wanting to look at him. Sleep had transformed him. His face was a picture of contentment and innocence. She ran her hands lightly over his chest, marveling at the sinewy muscles and the smoothness of his skin. Careful not to wake him, she extricated herself and slipped out of bed, taking a shower in the spare bedroom.

When she crawled back in bed, she wiggled inch by inch until she was pressed flush against his body. Taking a deep breath, she reached down and unzipped his slacks. Even though his upper body was asleep, what rested inside his jockey shorts was awake and aroused. She grasped the edge of his undershorts and was about to tug them down when his eyes opened.

"Do you know what you're doing?" he asked, yawning.

"Yes," Carolyn said, smothering him with kisses. "I don't want to wait. The way things have been going, I could be dead tomorrow. Make love to me."

He did, and it was fantastic—tender, erotic, romantic, and completely satisfying. She discovered they had something in common. They were quiet lovers, moving into the moment without the need for words or sounds. No acrobatics were required, just spontaneously synchronized movements, sensuous kisses, coupled with considerate exploration of each other's bodies.

"So this is how it's supposed to be," Carolyn said, curling up next to him. His skin was slick with perspiration. She slid out of bed to go to the bathroom. When she saw the sun streaking in through the windows, she yelled at Marcus, "How can it be morning? I thought it was still night. I have to go to the hospital. Everyone's probably panicked that something has happened to me."

When Carolyn saw her almost forty-year-old body bathed in the harsh morning light, she darted back in the bedroom and tugged at the tangled mess of sheets. They didn't budge. She realized he was lying on top of them. She tried to find her clothes, but it was too dark.

"I have blackout drapes," he told her, thinking she was looking for a clock. "Don't worry, it's only six."

"Oh," she said, trying to figure out what to do. Finally she removed one of the pillowcases and wrapped it around her body. It didn't cover her completely, so she had to decide which part she wanted him to see, her top or her bottom. Since her breasts were small, she moved the pillowcase up. A moment later, she decided she didn't want him to see her bottom as he might think it was too large and moved the pillowcase down. He knew her breasts were small because he'd felt them. Men had an uncanny ability to determine a woman's dimensions by touch, some even to the exact bra size.

"It's okay," he said, laughing, "I won't look."

He went to the bathroom and turned on the water in the Jacuzzi. "I'll go scrounge up some breakfast for us while you soak."

"Great," she mumbled, turning sideways.

For someone who claimed to be shy, prancing around naked didn't seem to bother him. Of course, Carolyn thought, his confidence level must have skyrocketed. It wasn't fair, she thought. Guys looked the same when they went to bed as they did when they got up.

No reason to hide now, she told herself, leaning over to check the water temperature. Marcus gave her a pat on her buttocks, then bent down and planted a kiss in the small of her back. "You have the cutest ass I've ever seen."

"Yours isn't so bad, either," Carolyn told him, smiling as she submerged herself in the swirling water. "Did I tell you you're an amazing lover?"

"Not specifically," he said, his eyes dancing with happiness. "I could tell, though. Enjoy your Jacuzzi."

Carolyn lowered herself into the water, placing her chin on the edge of the tub so she could watch him walking down the hallway. A few days ago, her life had seemed dismal. She was selling her home. Holden had first tried to rape her, then held her hostage at gunpoint. John had been shot, a mother's nightmare. Later, he'd confessed to regular use of marijuana. Rebecca had driven her crazy.

Everything had shifted, and the glass was half full instead of half empty. They would apprehend Holden and either execute him or lock him up forever. John would stop using drugs, and Rebecca was just an exceptional teenager, whose independent spirit mimicked her own. Both children had suffered from the absence of a father figure. At last, she'd found a suitable prospect. There was no doubt about it, Carolyn decided.

Marcus was *the* guy!

* * *

"Who the fuck is this?" Carl Holden said, speaking from his room at the Econolodge in the San Fernando Valley. "It's three-thirty in the morning."

"This is your wake-up call, asshole," a man's voice said. "I might have something you want. That is, if you can get your lazy ass up to come and get it."

Holden blurted out, "The key?"

"Yeah . . . the key."

"You must be a cop," Holden said. "No one else knows about the safety deposit box key. Well, look what we got here . . . a dirty cop trying to cut a deal. I should have expected as much. How did you find me?"

Holden was playing right into his hands. He'd first seen him in the flesh the night he'd swung by Carolyn's house to check things out. A man darted across the street, jumping into a black Hummer and burning rubber. Deciding to follow him and see what was going on, he'd been only a half a block away when the accident had occurred. Knowing the police would arrive shortly, he'd chased after the Hummer to see if an opportunity might present itself to take out Holden. Staying a safe distance away, he'd watched as Holden had ditched the Hummer in a hospital parking lot. Since medical personnel were coming and going, he laid back and watched as Holden broke in and hot-wired a '95 white Cadillac Seville. After tailing him to the hotel, he saw the car parked in front of room 105. The man asked, "Want to make a trade for the key?"

Holden answered, "Depends on what you want."

"Fifty percent of the loot." He heard Holden exhale into the phone. "Half of something is better than half of nothing. What do you say?"

"There's personal stuff in the safe, not money. You know, things that belonged to my mother. I'm going to hang up if you don't tell me who you are."

"We both know that's not true, Holden. And it doesn't matter who I am. What's important is that you get the key back and stay out of prison. I could have a dozen cops on top of you in minutes. I'm waiting for an answer, and I'm not a patient man." The line went silent. Holden had no choice.

"I'll do it, but how do I know this isn't a setup?" Holden said. "You could have a swarm of police ready to arrest me when we get to the bank. I'll never make it to prison, not after what I did. The cops will shoot me on sight."

"You're probably right. You're certainly not the most popular person at the police station right now. Shooting Sullivan's son wasn't a very good idea, was it? And you could have found someone other than a probation officer to try to stick your dick in." Holden was accustomed to being the predator rather than the prey. The caller smiled, thinking how surprised Holden must have been when Carolyn had stumbled across his hiding place at his mother's house. Instead of knocking her unconscious and fleeing, as anyone with a brain would have done, the moron had tried to rape her, then driven to her house and terrorized her family. Smashing this cockroach would be good for society. "I don't have time to chit-chat about your problems, Holden," he said. "We'll meet somewhere that has a large open space. Where's your bank?"

"I'm not going to tell you over the phone."

"You're going to do exactly what I say. You're not calling the shots anymore, I am. Are we clear?" He pulled himself together, lowering his voice to a reasonable level. "Just tell me if the bank is in the Oxnard area."

"Pretty close," Holden said.

"Then get in that stolen white Caddy and drive yourself down to Olivas Park Golf Course in Oxnard. Take the 101 to the Victoria off-ramp, make a right on Olivas Park Road, and head toward the ocean. You'll find it."

"The bank doesn't open until nine," Holden told him. "Why do you want me to meet you now?"

"For your protection. First of all, you're a wanted man. Even a fool like you would limit his outside activities, especially in daylight. Everyone knows they don't schedule as many cops on the graveyard shift, and Oxnard isn't as familiar with your case as Ventura. Once you see I'm legitimate, we'll hook up later at the bank. How long will it take you to get to Oxnard?"

"About an hour," Holden told him. "How will I know it's you?"

"People don't play golf at three in the morning, idiot," the caller said, wondering how Holden had gotten away with so many crimes. "Don't try anything stupid." After disconnecting, he was satisfied that his plan was in motion. It was going to be a long night. He'd head out to Olivas after a quick stop for coffee at an all-night donut shop. He had to be there before Holden in order to get himself into position.

As he drove down the dark road, the fog floated listlessly around his car. He was anxious, yet exhilarated. His palms were sweating on the steering wheel, and a line of perspiration had popped out on his brow. After turning into the parking lot at the golf course, he parked his car behind an equipment shed. The stench of the nearby sewage plant permeated his nostrils. He'd picked this location because the parking lot wasn't landscaped. It was hard to see through trees and bushes; he wanted unobstructed vision. Here was only blacktop, stripes, and limited lighting.

Through the dense air he saw a set of headlights moving down the road toward him. Holden stopped and turned off the engine, leaving his headlights on. He got out and stood within the safety of his car door.

A voice called out, "Carl Holden?"

Holden turned around in a circle. "Where are you?"

"Hello, Carl," he said. "I'm over here. Can't you see me?"

"No, I can't." Holden stepped a few feet away from his car.

"Just a minute, Holden," he said, pressing the button on the walkie-talkie. Before Holden had arrived, he'd placed another walkie-talkie on the ground near the entrance to the parking lot, leaving the microphone open. "I'm here," he told him. "I'll come to you, but I need you to step farther away from the car. Do you have any weapons?"

"No," Holden said, squinting into the darkness.

Time to execute his plan. He listened to the quiet purring of his car engine. As if he were a warrior going into battle, he yelled at a deafening level into the walkie-talkie, then floored the accelerator. Holden was focused on the noise behind him. Opening his nylon parka, he pulled out his gun. By the time Holden's eyes locked on the oncoming car, it was too late. His face became stricken with fear. Then a look of resignation appeared. He knew he was about to suffer the death sentence he should have received eight years before.

CHAPTER 28

Monday, September 25—10:01 A.M.

"I don't know what you're talking about," said Daniel Thorn, general counsel for the county of Ventura. "Why would I ask you to send me records on Carl Holden? He's one of the defendants that were released due to the incompetence of Robert Abernathy. Abernathy is dead, and the rest's history. What's this other man's name again, the one who's supposed to be filing a lawsuit against the county?"

"Troy Anderson," Mary Stevens told him, thinking the attorney was either indifferent or brain-dead. "Holden murdered Anderson's wife eight years ago. Recently, he sexually assaulted and shot the son of a senior probation officer named Carolyn Sullivan. Don't you watch the news?"

"I'm not a criminal attorney, Ms. Stevens."

"Detective Stevens," she said.

"Fine, *detective,*" he continued. "My wife mentioned something about that. When I'm not working, I try to concentrate on my family."

Mary rested her chin on her fist. "Are you saying you don't remember calling me on Saturday, September sixteenth and asking me to fax you our records on Carl Holden?"

"Precisely," Thorn said. "Now, I'm sorry, but I have another call."

"Let them wait," Mary snapped, tired of his unconcerned attitude. "Whether you realize it or not, Thorn, this is a serious situation. A person using your name and credentials obtained confidential police information on a violent criminal. The least you could do is to help me get to the bottom of this. Check around your office and see if someone else may have made that call. You might also want to see if the reports arrived in your office."

Thorn sighed. "What number did you fax to?"

Mary pulled out the paperwork and read him the digits.

"That's not even one of our lines. Since you're the detective, I suggest you verify the next person's identity before you give out information."

After he hung up on her, Mary grumbled, "Prick." She immediately dialed the fax number and got a recording that said the line was no longer in service. Next she called the country operator to see if she could find out whose number it had been.

"The prefix sounds like a cell phone," a woman named Doreen told her. "Things aren't as easy as they were when I started on this job fifteen years ago. You probably faxed it to a computer or some kind of handheld device. All you need is a functional number these days and you can do just about anything."

"Call me as soon as you find out anything, Doreen."

"No problem."

Sure, Mary thought, disconnecting. *No problem, not a chance.* Her career was on the line, and problems were coming at her like bullets. She opened her calendar again and stared at the dates. Lisa Sheppard's body was found on Sunday. The call from the man posing as Thorn had come through on Saturday. Whoever had wanted the records on Holden had to have a reason, and since they'd impersonated a county attorney, she doubted it was legit.

She spread her hands across her face, thinking. What was this person looking for? The circumstances of Carl Holden's earlier crimes had been detailed in the press. What was in the file that wasn't public record? Names and addresses of the surviving rape victims, of course, but two of them had moved out of state. Angela Cummings still resided in Ventura, but she had remarried, and her new name and address weren't in the original documents.

Since Carolyn and her family had been attacked, the media's interest had intensified, so there was an outside chance the call had been made by a reporter. Newshounds would do anything to get a story. Today they had to have an unending stream of new information to keep people's attention.

Then there was Tracy Anderson's husband, Troy, the man Carolyn had encountered at lunch Saturday afternoon. Whoever had called Mary asking for Holden's records knew about Troy, as he'd used his name. The call had come in around four, and she assumed Carolyn's lunch at the Olive Garden had taken place somewhere closer to noon. The only thing that made sense was that Troy Anderson had made the call himself. The question was why?

The glove!

They had never revealed that they'd found a golf glove on top of Tracy Anderson's body, not even to her husband, as it had seemed inconsequential at the time. The discovery of the second glove, and the fact that Sheppard was buried in the same location as Anderson had made Holden an instant suspect. After reading about it in the file, could Troy Anderson have planted the glove to frame Holden? If so, he would have had to know that there was a body buried in the Alessandro Lagoon, and would have had to place the glove there before the body was discovered. In all likelihood the only one who would have known about the body was the killer.

Lord Jesus, Mary thought, her mind spinning. If Troy Anderson had killed Lisa Sheppard, it was a horrifying scenario. The results of the mtDNA tests on the minute hair fragment found at the grave, which hopefully belonged to the killer instead of the victim, hadn't come back yet. If they hadn't stumbled across the box in the attic in San Diego containing Lisa Sheppard's medical records, they wouldn't have been able to make a positive identification. They would have been forced to exhume Eleanor Beckworth so they could attempt to match her DNA with her granddaughter's. This was no longer necessary.

Carolyn had told her Troy Anderson wasn't aware Holden had been released when she spoke to him at the restaurant. But that could have been an act, concocted to throw them off-track. Lisa Sheppard being dead for approximately a year didn't completely rule out Troy Anderson, as Holden had been a free man for two years. How sick did a person have to be to murder an innocent woman in order to frame the man who'd killed his wife?

Another possibility flashed in her mind. Could Troy Anderson have killed his wife instead of Holden? Tracy Anderson hadn't been sexually assaulted like Holden's other victims. The DNA evidence that ultimately caused Holden's conviction to be overturned might have been mishandled and contaminated by Robert Abernathy, but it could also have belonged to another man. If the husband was guilty, though, he'd already gotten away with murder. Why kill someone else?

Holden being exonerated could have posed a threat, Mary decided, as someone might eventually expose the truth that he was innocent. Although Holden couldn't be prosecuted again for Tracy Anderson's death, her husband could. The PD hadn't reopened the case as they would normally have done under the circumstances because they were certain Holden had committed the crime. With this new information, the department might be forced to reinvestigate the murder of Tracy Anderson.

On the other hand, it wasn't all that far-fetched that Holden could have posed as a cowboy and created a new life in San Diego after he was released from prison. He wasn't on parole, so he didn't have to worry about someone snooping around. From what she knew of Holden, however, he didn't seem like the marrying type. Still, it wasn't entirely implausible that he'd cleaned up his act for a few months, then returned to his violent ways. What they now had to consider was whether Holden had been guilty of the rapes but innocent of the murder of Tracy Anderson. That would mean they had two murders to solve. If Eleanor Beckworth had also been murdered, the body count was three.

Mary picked up the phone and dialed the St. Louis PD, asking to speak to Detective Sheldon Parker. After identifying herself, she asked what new information they'd found regarding the Eleanor Beckworth case.

"Sure, there's a possibility it was a homicide," Parker told her. "But there were no signs of forced entry. That's one of the reasons Beckworth's death was ruled a suicide. The autopsy showed an injury to the victim's hip that appeared to be untreated, but nothing else that would indicate she was murdered. The wounds on her neck were caused by the cord to her telephone. The house was in fairly good order, except for some clothes and things on the floor. When people are about to kill themselves, they generally aren't that concerned with things being neat and tidy."

Mary didn't agree. She'd heard of numerous suicides where the person dressed in their best clothes and made certain their house and affairs were in perfect order. One woman had even worn diapers, knowing that at the time of death, the body expelled its waste. "Your partner said there was a handyman who had access to the house."

"Yeah," Parker said. "He was at home baby-sitting his children at the time of the death. His wife worked at an all-night diner."

"Couldn't he have left the children alone," Mary suggested, "murdered Beckworth, and then returned before his wife got off work?"

"Anything's possible, but we didn't find any evidence that would support such a premise."

Mary shook her head in frustration. "He could have scrubbed down the house, don't you see? His fingerprints or DNA not being there is suspicious in its own right. He must have been in the house on numerous occasions if he had a key and did repair work for Beckworth. That sounds like a suspect."

"Everything pointed to suicide," Parker continued. "The victim's age, the lack of relatives living nearby, even the injury to her hip. The handyman advised that Beckworth was living close to the bone. Her heater only worked part of the time, but she told him she didn't have the money to repair it. This isn't California, you know. It's cold as a bitch here in the winter, so the poor thing must have been freezing. Some of these old folks would rather die than lose their independence. Sad, but it happens all the time."

"Don't you think it's a coincidence that her granddaughter was murdered around the same time she committed suicide?" Mary asked. "We checked the phone records and there was a phone call from the Sheppard residence to Beckworth's the day before Lisa's husband reported her missing. He's unaccounted for as well. Can you see where I'm going with this?"

"I can see that you're reaching," the detective said. "Do you really believe that the same person who murdered the Sheppard woman in San Diego flew up here and killed her grandmother, then staged it to look like a suicide? A husband getting rid of his wife is fairly common. What reason would he have to kill her grandmother in another state? The woman wasn't a witness. Older women aren't normally much of a threat, Stevens."

"I don't know," Mary said, having arrived at the same reasoning. "Maybe the grandmother knew something incriminating about him. He could have beaten Lisa, and she was threatening to go to the police. Once he killed her, he had to get rid of the grandmother for fear she could testify against him if he was apprehended."

"Look," Parker said impatiently, "we'll cooperate any way we can. Right now, I just don't know what else we can do for you. The case is closed, the woman's buried, and the house where the crime took place has been sold."

"Who buried her? I know it wasn't the granddaughter, because she was dead."

"The handyman." He laughed. "I don't mean he went out and dug the grave—he paid for all the expenses. Mrs. Beckworth was good to him and his family. He told us he wanted her to have a decent funeral. And don't try to convince me he did it out of guilt, Stevens. Mitch Tidwell is a decent man. Dozens of people vouched for him. Seems he didn't charge for half the work he did, particularly with the seniors. As soon as Beckworth's estate is settled, he'll be reimbursed, but you have to admit it was a nice gesture." He paused, then added, "Are you still considering exhuming the body?"

"We don't need the grandmother's DNA after all. We were able to identify Sheppard from a leg fracture."

"Great," he said. "I hate to exhume bodies."

"Not as much as I hate to see homicides passed off as suicides," Mary told him, slamming the phone down.

Staring at the white ceiling in her hospital room, Kathleen Masters tried to remember the good times she and Dean had shared. Then her mind flashed in a different direction. Images of Dean standing over her with a knife. She tightened her fists and closed her eyes, trying to make the terrible visions go away. Her shrink said that her mind had intertwined her husband with the loathsome events that had occurred, more than likely due to misdirected anger, because the man who had attacked her was dead.

Her face, head, and abdomen were disfigured, and the doctor said her hair might not grow back in the spot where she'd been struck over the head with the bottle. She looked so awful, she'd ordered the hospital room to cover or remove all the mirrors. A plastic surgeon said he could improve things, but only after she'd fully recovered, both emotionally as well as physically. How could anyone recover from such an ordeal?

Arnold Layman had been a professional burglar until his last stint in prison. The police had studied his records all the way back to Juvenile Hall, and he'd never once committed an act of violence, nor was there any evidence that he belonged to any type of satanic cult. Sure, he'd been wearing a Charlie Manson T-shirt. He could have found it in the trash can.

Something wasn't right.

When she had first experienced the flashbacks, Kathleen discounted them as nightmares. As the hospital reduced her pain medication, however, they became even more vivid. Dean had disappeared shortly after the crime. The fact that the police weren't concerned was appalling. What kind of man would walk out on his wife when she was fighting for her life?

Kathleen didn't understand why their world had come crashing down on them. Everything seemed to be coming together. Dean had balked at first, then acted willing and even happy to accept her decision to travel with him. Not being apart all the time would have strengthened their relationship.

Her feelings of insecurity slapped her back to reality. In her career, she was strong and assertive. It had all been an act. The successful, confident real estate agent didn't exist. She was a fictional creation, an actor in a play written by Dean Masters.

At sixteen, Kathleen had fallen in love with George Dupont. He'd been almost twenty years older, but she didn't care. A handsome and charming man, he'd worn beautiful clothes and had possessed impeccable manners. His hands and skin had been so soft, and he'd touched her as she'd never been touched before. The boys she'd

dated previously had pawed her like animals, with their dirty fingernails and rough skin. Of course, she'd been influenced by George's
wealth. What girl wouldn't be? She was working as a waitress, trying
to support herself and find a way to complete her education.

George had used her up and then discarded her. Just like Dean.

Ruby Boyle, a stone-faced gray-haired nurse, came striding briskly
into her room. "How are you feeling today?"

"Terrible," Kathleen told her, scowling. "I need my pain shot."

"You know Dr. Blankenship discontinued the morphine," the nurse
told her, squeezing the blood pressure pump. "The chart says you
were given your pain meds only three hours ago, so you'll have to
wait at least another hour before I can give you any more." Changing
the subject, she asked, "Did you walk some this morning?"

"Yes, and it hurt like a bitch," Kathleen said. "I almost fainted.
How can they force me to walk so soon? I felt like my stomach was
going to pop open and my intestines fall out."

"You have to get out of bed, Kathleen, or you could develop com-
plications. Don't you want to get your strength back so you can go
home?" Boyle pulled down the covers and lifted Kathleen's gown.
"I'm going to change your dressings." She removed what looked like
a large Band-Aid and examined the incision on Kathleen's abdomen.
"You're very fortunate. They had to remove your left ovary, but otherwise none of your organs were perforated."

"Then why did I have to be rushed back into surgery six hours
after the first operation?" she asked, wishing she could just jump off
a bridge. *Go home?* she thought bitterly. *To what?*

"Well," the nurse said, ripping open a package containing the new
bandages, "your husband informed the surgeon that you'd ingested
a large quantity of Valium a short time before you were admitted.
They stopped the bleeding and then had to wait until you could be
safely sedated to complete the operation."

"But I didn't take a lot of Valium," Kathleen protested. "I only took
half of one pill. My husband was lying. He's the one who did this to
me. That's why he's not around. He hasn't even called me."

Boyle sighed, dropping her hands to her side. "That poor man,"
she said. "Don't you know his mother passed away? He called and
spoke to me on several occasions. He was very distraught. This terri-

ble thing happened to you, and then the very next day he lost his mother." The nurse started to leave, then stopped. "I remember putting several calls from him through to you. You must have been too heavily medicated to remember."

Not long after he'd built her up, Kathleen remembered, struggling to get comfortable, Dean had used emotional warfare to stay in control of their relationship. When he doted on her, she was blissfully happy. Then it was as if the sun had darted behind a cloud, and she was left for weeks alone in their cavernous house. She became so starved for his attention, she reached the point where she was prepared to accept that he might be unfaithful.

Dean was the type of man who thrived on adoration. He must have been having affairs all long. More women meant more adoration. Why hadn't she realized it before? The expression on his face when she'd told him that she wanted to go on the road with him was unmistakable. He was furious, enough to lash out at her in a public place. Then when she confronted him about Andrea seeing him with a woman in Ventura, his rage had intensified.

Had he been enraged enough to kill?

Before Dean disappeared, he'd come to see her in the recovery room. Although she had been barely conscious, he'd told her that he loved her and kissed her forehead. Her eyes had flickered open. His face had been blurred and distorted. What she remembered wasn't what she'd seen, but what she had smelled. Her husband had the stench of the dead burglar, Arnold Layman. The noxious odor was forever sealed in her memory, a mixture of urine, body odor, and alcohol.

She remembered awakening when a coarse fabric had touched her skin, probably seconds before the blow to her head. The worst, though, was the picture in her mind of Dean's twisted face as he held the knife high in his hands.

Now that her mind was becoming clearer, Kathleen was growing more convinced that Layman may have been innocent, somehow used by Dean as a pawn.

She depressed the call button pinned to the bed. When another nurse came in, she told her she needed to call the police. "Is something wrong?"

"Yeah," Kathleen said. "My husband tried to kill me."

CHAPTER 29

Wednesday, October 18—4:15 P.M.

Dean sat in a white wicker chair on the terrace at Geoffrey's Restaurant in Malibu, the ocean stretching out beneath him. The vistas were nowhere near as spectacular as they were on the Monterrey Peninsula, but he would never be able to enjoy those again.

He whipped his head around as a tanned young blonde brushed past him on the arm of a man who had to be in his sixties, her perfume drifting to his nostrils. The women here were beautiful, perhaps not as rich, but far younger and more lithesome than the majority of women in Carmel. This time he wanted someone attractive yet simple, with decent values and a job that kept her busy so she wouldn't pry into his affairs. A ready-made family, with older children, would be perfect on several levels. He'd come to suspect that his narcissistic supply could never be filled by one woman. Older children whom he could manipulate into loving and needing him might be the answer. Then those children would one day have children, additionally expanding his sources. The past had robbed him of any thought of marrying a woman who wanted a baby, so his options were limited.

Younger women were there for the taking, Dean thought, his eyes zooming in on the blonde two tables over. With his wealth and persuasive personality, he could have any woman he wanted. The problem was that most girls wanted children.

Tossing down his gin and tonic, Dean waved the waiter over to order another. He would never be able to be around a baby without remembering that terrible day Iris's carriage had gone over the embankment. In reality, Carmel had been a poor hunting ground, something he'd only recently realized. What's more, the picturesque shoreline that everyone found so breathtaking was too similar to the terrain near his childhood home in Tarrytown, New York.

He stiffened in his chair, hearing Iris shrieking as the stroller crashed against the boulders and landed upside down in the Hudson River. No one had ever told him if she'd died instantly or remained alive and terrified inside the stroller as the river swept her away.

Dean rushed to the men's room and splashed water on his face. He heard a shrill sound and pressed his hands over his ears. He felt as if his body were boiling inside, about to explode in a fireball of misery. Adjusting his jacket on his shoulders, he got control of himself and returned to his table. As he walked past the entrance, he heard the shrill sound again and realized it was only cars applying their brakes as they drove down the steep driveway to the restaurant. He'd been spending too much time alone. When he was alone, the past surrounded him.

Back at the table, Dean clutched the cold cocktail glass in his hand, reliving the events that had brought him to this place in time—where he judged his future companions primarily on his attempt to predict whether he would one day develop a compulsion to kill them.

Fourteen years dissolved, and he was back in his office in Manhattan, defending himself against the lies of a conniving and money-hungry woman.

Every aspect of his practice was scrutinized. The OPMC dragged him in front of committees and board members, interrogating him about his personal and professional life. They had a zero tolerance for what they classified as moral unfitness.

How could they believe Nicole Pelter when everything she said was total bullshit? She was the one who should be questioned about moral unfitness. Pelter was an actress in real life as well as on stage—a pathological liar. Part of her psychosis centered around preying on well-to-do men. As things progressed he became so enraged, he thought of killing her.

Halfway through the process, he knew that he no longer wanted to see patients. It was true that abuse of patients by psychologists and psychiatrists was far too common, but professionals in his field were also targets of unscrupulous, predatory, and mentally disturbed people, primarily women. Nicole Pelter's developing a fixation on him was understandable. Most women were attracted to him. He simply couldn't place himself in such a vulnerable position again.

The attorneys hired by his insurance company advised him that he was on the verge of losing the lawsuit. He could tell by the looks on the jurors' faces that they were convinced he was guilty. Nicole had given a command performance, probably better than anything she'd ever done on the stage.

The attorneys agreed on a settlement. The board had already yanked his license, and now the greatest hurdle was in front of him— picking up the threads of his life.

April was slipping away from him. If he didn't focus on what was left of their relationship, he would lose her, an outcome he refused to accept. She'd moved out of his brownstone a few weeks earlier to an apartment on the Upper East Side. Despite his numerous messages, she hadn't returned his calls. He knew the address, and in desperation, he decided to go to her.

The twenty-story building was protected by an overweight, elderly doorman. Dressed sharply in his charcoal-striped shirt and cufflinks, Dr. Thomas Wright fell in behind a group of businessmen, following them to the bank of elevators. One of the men pressed the floor button, then resumed his conversation with his friends. Thomas stared down at the stone design on the elevator floor until the doors opened and the men stepped out. Glancing at the paper with April's apartment number on it, he headed to the eighteenth floor.

By the time he reached her place, his nerves were frazzled. A noise was coming from inside. Placing his ear close to the door, he heard a male voice. His body shook in outrage. His fiancée had another man in her apartment. This was his April, the woman he'd planned to marry. He heard footsteps approaching the door, and scurried down the hall, ducking into the rubbish-disposal room.

Peering through the circular glass portal in the door, Thomas saw a Latin man with long, curly hair and strong features. His body became limp as he watched them embrace and kiss. Rejection seized him. If he'd acted swiftly, paying off Pelter under the table, instead of insisting on establishing his innocence in a court of law, he might have saved not only his practice but his fiancée.

April escorted the man to the elevator. As soon as the elevator door closed, Thomas stepped into the hallway and impulsively called to her: "April."

"What are you doing here?" she said, spinning around in surprise.

"You didn't return my phone calls," he said. "I need to talk to you."

April glanced up and down the hallway. "Don't make a scene, Thomas. I just moved in here. We'll talk in my apartment."

They went into the living room, and she took a seat on the green sofa. He stood stiffly in front of her. "Who was that man?"

"I'm sorry you had to see that, but you shouldn't be spying on me," April told him. "He's someone I work with. We started dating when I moved out. It's over, Thomas. I thought you understood."

"You can't give up on us," he pleaded. "We've been through too much."

"We had good times, but things have changed. You're not the same anymore, and neither am I."

"What do you mean?" he said, walking around in a circle. "I'm exactly the same. The mess with Nicole Pelter didn't change me. Anyway, we settled it today. It's finished. We can move on with our lives now."

"You paid her off?" April exclaimed, her jaw dropping. "That means you're guilty. You drugged this woman and tried to have sex with her. How could you? You know how frightening it is to find out you don't even know the man you're planning to marry?"

He knelt down in front of her. She turned her head away. "April, look at me. I didn't do anything with that woman. It was her word against mine. There was no factual basis for her claim. The malpractice attorneys forced me to settle. They don't care if I'm innocent or not. All they're concerned about is putting out the least amount of money. I love you. Please, you have to believe me. Why would I drug a patient and force her to have sex with me? We have a wonderful sex life."

"I don't know," April said, shrugging. "That's a question you should be asking yourself."

"If you'd agreed to testify, maybe things would have turned out differently."

"Don't lay a guilt trip on me," she snapped. "You dug your own grave. Besides, my father wouldn't let me get involved. What did you expect? He's a senator. He's campaigning for reelection."

"Remember our plans?" he said. "We were going to buy a house in the country. We can still have a great life together. I'm giving up my practice. We can travel now."

"You think it's about the money?" She shook her head. "Money can't buy the important things in life . . . honesty, integrity, love. As far as I'm concerned, you and my father can keep your filthy money." She stood and forced her way past him. "You wanted to talk. We talked. Now it's time for you to leave."

"Wait," he said. "We could go to therapy, work through this. I could arrange for someone to see us tomorrow."

"You're just afraid of being alone," April snarled. "One of your shrink buddies told me you're a narcissist. You think the whole world revolves around you, that you can control everyone you meet, that you're the most brilliant man in the universe. No one else would have had the balls to sink all that money into a company that didn't have an established track record. Isn't that what you told me? That you know things nobody else does. Like a god."

His face was ashen. "April, stop, I . . ."

"Don't worry, you'll find someone else," she continued. "You brag all the time about how all the women are crazy about you, that your patients always fall in love with you. You've probably slept with half of them."

"I treated you like a queen, and this is how you repay me." Thomas exploded. "You think you're special because your father's a senator. I could buy and sell him. You're nothing, understand? You're ignorant. You say stupid things and embarrass me in front of my friends. I tolerated it because I loved you. You'll never find another man like me. You deserve to live in a shack with a loser like that greaseball you were with tonight."

April gritted her teeth. She headed to the door and was about to open it, when he rushed over and placed his hand on the knob. She slapped his face. Grabbing her by the shoulders, he hurled her to the ground. She sprang to her feet and ran to the kitchen, pulling a nine-inch carving knife out of a rack on the counter.

"What are you planning to do with that?" he asked, his body surging on adrenaline. "Are you going to cut me? I've already been stabbed in the back by Nicole Pelter." He moved toward her until the tip of the knife was only an inch from his chest. "You don't have the guts to do it. You're just a spoiled rich girl who thinks she's redeeming herself by holding down a job. Who do you think you're fooling, April? Who's paying the rent on this apartment? Whenever something goes wrong, you run back to Daddy."

"I'll do it, Thomas," she said, raising the knife. "I'm warning you. Leave this minute."

He grabbed her wrist, turning it down until the blade sliced across his right forearm. Her fingers involuntarily opened, and the knife fell to the floor. A streak of blood bubbled up through the torn fabric of his starched shirt. "Go ahead, call the police," he said. "I'll tell them you tried to kill me. I got cut when I threw my hands over my head to defend myself." He stopped and gulped air, his chest heaving. "After you spend some time in jail, maybe you'll understand what it feels like to be falsely accused. Or even better, maybe I should snap your neck. Self-defense, love. Don't you realize I can kill you right now and get away with it?"

Dean felt a chill, and heard people chattering around him, jolting him back to the present. The popular restaurant was crowded now. He gestured for the waiter to bring the check. *It must be happy hour,* he decided as he made his way out of the restaurant and waited for the valet to bring his car around.

While he was waiting, he gazed out at the ocean, remembering how he'd stood on the rooftop of April's building so long ago. He had come close to committing suicide that night. As he was about to plunge to his death, his purpose in life was revealed and stopped him from jumping. If he killed himself, April and Nicole Pelter would have destroyed him. Living gave him a chance to establish a new life, one where he could have and do anything he wanted. That night, he had stepped over the line and found he liked it better on the other side.

Mysteriously, even the injury to his arm hadn't hurt once he'd made his decision. As a psychiatrist, he'd often wondered what it would feel like to be psychotic. Some of his patients had told him they preferred madness to reality. He wasn't certain if he'd experienced a genuine psychotic break or had merely reacted in a blind rage. Things had become brighter, though, more intense and enthralling, even something as minor as the cold night air brushing against his face was deeply pleasurable.

Overall, though, it had been the feeling of omnipotence that had been so seductive, knowing he could have taken a life and escaped punishment.

He'd always known his intelligence and quick thinking made him far superior to the average person. But he'd never faced a situation remotely similar to what had occurred with April. The vulnerability he'd experienced over Nicole Pelter's false accusations had been washed away the moment he'd forced the knife down on his arm, gaining control of the volatile and demeaning situation with his former fiancée.

In retrospect, killing her would have been more exciting than marrying her.

After he had left April's apartment that night, he'd made a vow. Every money-hungry, lying, back-stabbing, cheating woman he met would pay him back, and he would accomplish his task by the same traits that had caused his ruin—his looks, charm, wealth, as well as his knowledge of the female psyche. Just as unscrupulous women had preyed on him, so he would turn the tables and become their predator. He would stalk them, uncover their desires, and take advantage of their weaknesses.

After his sister's death, his mother had developed a serious drinking problem. His father had asked her to move out when he was eleven. She'd never returned, not even to visit him. Years later, he'd seen her walking down the street, and he took off in the opposite direction.

From the day his mother left, he'd been determined to be the brightest and most popular boy in his school, regardless of how much his father hated him. At thirteen, he'd had sex with his first girlfriend, a sixteen-year-old. His craving for female affection had followed him throughout adulthood. He'd taught himself how to please a woman sexually, which made him even more desirable. Women loved doctors, so he'd pleaded with his father to allow him to enroll in medical school. When he had barely passed his boards, he'd decided to specialize in psychiatry. Many of his classmates whose academic performance fell below standard had done the same. He'd built his practice around women, women who paid to spend time with him and who hung on his every word.

His attorney, Leonard Steinberg, had assisted him in setting up his assets so they were readily available whenever and wherever he needed them. After that, the former psychiatrist Dr. Thomas Wright had disappeared.

Establishing a new identity, he'd found himself playing the ultimate game. Taking whatever woman he wanted, he disposed of her when she no longer pleased him. He would never be abandoned or rejected again.

His father was dead. Too bad, he thought, as he would have enjoyed telling him what kind of monster he'd created by blaming an unintentional act on a frightened five-year-old boy with sensitive ears. Even baby Iris, with her delightful giggle and soft skin, would have forgiven him if she'd lived.

Handing the valet a ten-dollar tip, Dean settled into the soft leather seat, staring at his image in the rearview mirror before he placed the gearshift in drive and took off. There was one person his father had loved, and he'd left the boy who could do no wrong what was rightfully Thomas's. Once he destroyed his rival, the doors to his tortured childhood might finally close.

Kathleen opened up the front door to her home. The stale smell of an unoccupied house greeted her. She crumpled to her knees, with the emotions that assailed her. Rising unsteadily, she was about to return to the taxi when she saw its taillights disappear from the circular driveway.

She collected herself and walked to the kitchen in the faint light provided from the entryway. The darkened living room made her feel as if someone or something was lurking in the shadows, watching her every move. Flipping on the kitchen light, she picked up the phone, retrieved Detective Irving's card, and dialed his number. "I need to see you right away," she said, after identifying herself. "I was released this afternoon." When she'd mentioned her suspicions to the detective before, he'd done nothing, but now she could tell him, "I found new evidence here at my house."

"You know how many people have been out there, Kathleen?" Brian Irving said, an annoyed tinge to his voice. "Our forensic people were there for days, then your husband hired Ackerman's Crime Scene Cleaner Service. I can assure you there's nothing left to be found." He turned and said something to his partner, then added, "The first few days back are difficult. I sympathize with you. Didn't your sister fly out to be with you?"

Kathleen looked around the vacant house, knowing he was right and she should have accepted Connie's offer to fly out and take care of her. Her sister had three children, though, and had already spent two weeks with her while she was in the hospital. Even she refused to listen when Kathleen tried to convince her that Dean had been involved. But what could Connie do? It was the detective she had to get to take her seriously. "I demand to speak to you," she said, raising her voice. "I know Dean told you I was hooked on Valium, or that I drank too much. I'm a victim, Brian, something you and your police buddies seem to forget. Get your ass over here or I'll call the chief. Or maybe I should call the mayor instead. I sold his house last year and made him close to a million dollars. I have his home number on my speed dialer."

"Give me thirty," Irving said, sighing audibly.

CHAPTER 30

Wednesday, October 18—4:30 P.M.

Carolyn felt a tap on her shoulder as she was typing the report due the following morning. She swiveled around to see Veronica Campbell, standing with her arms wrapped around her chest. "I have to tell you something," Veronica said. "I'd rather we don't talk here." She seemed on the verge of hysteria.

"Want to go to an interview room?" Carolyn suggested.

"No," Veronica said. "I need to get out of this place. Can we take a walk or something?"

"Sure," Carolyn agreed, even though she didn't have a moment to spare. After her leave of absence, she'd returned to an avalanche of work. The time off had helped her and the children get beyond their terrible ordeal. John still favored his injured leg, but was otherwise recovering well. He'd been forced to give up waiting tables at Giovanni's, though, and was now interviewing for other jobs.

She followed Veronica down the stairs and out the front door of the building. "We can talk over by the fountain."

"Not there," Veronica told her, buttoning up her white sweater. "There're too many people around. Let's go to my car."

"Is something going on between you and Drew?" Carolyn asked as they made their way through the parking lot. When Veronica didn't act as if she'd heard her, she decided to keep her mouth shut and wait. Whatever was going on was obviously serious.

Her friend unlocked her blue Ford Explorer, tossing baby bottles and toys in the backseat so Carolyn would have room to sit.

"Now will you tell me? You're scaring me."

"Do the police have any new leads on who killed Robert Abernathy? I know you're tight with the police. I figured if anyone would know, you would."

"I've been out of the loop since John was shot." The time Carolyn didn't spend with John and Rebecca now went to Marcus. The only cases she'd been following while she was out were the ones involving Carl Holden, and as yet the police still had no leads on his whereabouts. She hadn't been keeping tabs on any of her friends, just checking in routinely with Brad. "You probably know as much as I do about the Abernathy homicide. The last thing I remember Hank telling me was that the partial print they lifted from the gate to his front yard was no good because whoever touched it had some kind of oil on his hands. They aren't even sure if it was the killer's print. Why are you so interested in Abernathy? You were ready to hang the guy."

"Maybe I did." Veronica let her words hang in the air. Finally she resumed speaking. "Remember Billy Bell, the child mutilation?" She placed her hand at her throat as if she was having trouble breathing, then dropped it beside her on the seat. "You've got teenagers. My kids are young, Carolyn. Well, at least the last three. I've seen my share of autopsy pictures. God knows, we all have . . . seeing Billy Bell's severed limbs . . ." She stared out the front window. "One of his feet was still attached to his shoe. It was the same brand of shoes I buy for my kids. Lester McAllen used a chain saw to dismember him. It was . . . so . . . terrible."

"What happened with the case?" Carolyn asked. "The last time we talked, you said it was up on appeal."

"Lester McAllen was killed yesterday," Veronica told her, her eyes widening. "He was shot in an ally behind an elementary school. His conviction had been overturned because of Abernathy. The ruling came down while you were out. Cases are falling apart all over the place. This is the second murderer who's walked, and that's just on my caseload. The other guy beat a man to death with a hammer."

Carolyn recalled how she'd felt when she had heard the news

about Abernathy's murder. It was amazing how one person's mistakes could impact so many lives and generate such an intensity of animosity. But hate was like poison. You had to find a way to rid yourself of it or it would destroy you. "Do they know who shot McAllen?"

Veronica shook her head, her lips compressed.

"Listen, sweetie," Carolyn said, reaching over and placing her hand on the other woman's shoulder. "I know what you're going through. It seems sick to be happy when you hear someone's been murdered. It goes against everything we do. We spend every day working with the aftereffects of violence, trying to protect society, making every effort to be fair and impartial." She rubbed her eyes, bringing forth images of that awful night with Holden. Sometimes she woke up in a cold sweat, seeing his loathsome face looming over her in his mother's dilapidated house. "I wouldn't shed a tear if someone shot Carl Holden. Like him, McAllen was nothing more than human garbage. A bullet's too good for a man who butchers children."

Veronica's shoulders shook as she sobbed. "You don't understand. I can't do this anymore. I've already told Drew I'm going to turn in my resignation."

"But why? This isn't you, Veronica. You're been at this job longer than me, and I've never known you to let things upset you to the point where you want to quit. Who's going to replace you, huh? Some kid off the street that'll put in his eight hours and take years before he can even begin to comprehend the complexities of the law. Not many people are willing to carry this kind of responsibility. A situation like the one with Abernathy will probably never happen again, at least not in this county. Forget about McAllen and Abernathy. Get back on the horse."

"I know who killed them," Veronica said, the wild-eyed look returning. "I should have gone to the police when Abernathy was killed. I caused it to happen, don't you see? Because of me, a father who's already lost his wife and son may end up in prison. He might even face the death penalty. There's no doubt that his actions were premeditated, and he's killed two people now."

The picture was coming clear. Carolyn said, "The boy's father, right?"

"Yes," Veronica choked out. "Tyler Bell might never have known about Abernathy if I hadn't called and told him. How could I have been so stupid, Carolyn? The man had nothing to lose, don't you see? He buried his son in pieces. A month later, he found his wife with her wrists slit in a bathtub full of blood. He lost his business, his home. He didn't need to know about Abernathy."

"Don't be so hard on yourself. Bell would have found out eventually."

Veronica slapped the seat. "You're not listening. You're just trying to placate me. I called and told Tyler about Abernathy while everything around him was collapsing. Maybe he would have moved away or something and never found out that McAllen was turned loose. Even if he'd found out about McAllen, he would have had more time to recover."

No matter how she had tried to play it down, Carolyn knew that her friend was in trouble. A law enforcement officer who had information about a crime and failed to report it could be prosecuted. Now she was in the same boat as Veronica. "But you don't know for a fact that Tyler Bell killed Abernathy and McAllen. Is that true?"

"Tyler was in the Marines," Veronica said, relieved now that she'd gotten it off her chest. "When I interviewed him, he mentioned that he was a sharpshooter. I'm certain he would have killed McAllen back then had he not been in jail under protective custody. Both Abernathy and McAllen were killed by a single shot between the eyes. Not only that, Tyler was a house painter. He had something slick on his hands the day I interviewed him. He apologized after we shook hands, telling me that his skin was too sensitive to use turpentine, so he cleaned them with some kind of oil-based solvent. That's probably the substance the police found on Abernathy's gate that distorted the killer's fingerprints."

It was after five now, and people were streaming past them on the way to their cars. The temperature during the day still remained somewhere near seventy, one of the reasons California real estate was so high. At night, though, it dropped down into the high fifties, except when the Santa Ana winds blew in and warmed the air enough that people could go for a swim. Everyone was wearing coats and jackets now.

Carolyn's house hadn't sold, and she had no idea how she was going to pay John's tuition. Her little family was just now beginning to surface from the nightmare they had experienced at the hands of Carl Holden, and she was developing what could end up being a lifelong relationship with Marcus. Now she had this problem regarding Abernathy's death to contend with.

"Everything you've told me is supposition," she said. "The same person may not have killed both Abernathy and McAllen. There's no telling how many people wanted Abernathy dead. That's also the case with McAllen. Didn't he serve a prison term for sodomizing a boy around the same age as the Bell child?"

"Yes," Veronica said. "He should have never been paroled the first time, or Billy would still be alive. He was sixty-five when he got out. I guess the parole board thought he was rehabilitated. Won't those people ever learn that there's no such thing as rehabilitating a pedophile?"

"Even prison inmates hate child killers," Carolyn said, running through all the possibilities. "McAllen might have sodomized an inmate and the guy was waiting for him on the outside. And there could easily have been other child victims. Some parents don't go to the authorities because they don't want to expose their kid to the trauma of a trial, particularly if the child is male. Since they'd be adults by now, one of them could have heard that McAllen was out and killed him. There was something in the paper the other day about a guy in prison who kept a detailed diary. The prison officials got their hands on it and discovered a list of over a thousand boys this man had molested in the course of his lifetime. Don't you think some of those victims might want revenge?"

"Sure," Veronica said. "But there's too many—"

"Look at me," Carolyn said, taking hold of the other women's chin and turning her face so they were eye to eye. "Do you really know who killed Abernathy and McAllen? Aren't you just like the millions of people who watch the news and shows like Court TV, then make unsubstantiated speculations?"

"I guess you could put it like that," Veronica said, resting her head against the seat cushion once Carolyn released her.

"If you want to go to the police, that's fine. Only you can make that decision. Sometimes a higher justice steps in and takes care of things that we just can't seem to make right. When that happens, who are we to ask questions?"

Veronica clasped Carolyn's hand. "I knew you could help me make sense of this. You're like a sister to me. When we were kids, I never dreamed we'd be working together. You were so smart. I was sure you'd be a doctor, a lawyer, a congresswoman, or someone else important. And me, I was going to be a prima ballerina, remember? Silly, wasn't it?" She smiled weakly. "Of course, I didn't know then that I'd end up with tree trunks for thighs."

Carolyn reached for the door handle, then stopped. "If something definitive surfaces that links Bell to these killings, you'll have to go to the police. For the time being, sit tight and see what happens."

"Okay," Veronica said, sniffling into a tissue.

"This is just a temporary fix. We can't let a man who's murdered two people go free, regardless of whether the people he killed deserved it. If Tyler Bell is responsible for these crimes, he may be insane enough to kill someone else."

"Who would he kill?"

"Other criminals, people like child molesters or rapists. This man may have turned into a vigilante under the delusion that he's doing society a favor. If that's the case, we would have a moral obligation to stop him."

"I don't know," Veronica said. "Maybe we do need people like that."

"That's the last thing we need," Carolyn said firmly as she opened the car door, preparing to return to the office. "People who take the law into their own hands make mistakes and kill innocent people. That's why we have courts and trials. If something comes up, let me know."

When Carolyn arrived home at six-thirty that evening, she heard the phone ringing, dropped her purse and briefcase by the door, and raced to the kitchen to answer it. "I have good news for you, Carolyn," Margaret Overton told her. "Your house sold. The money's already in escrow, so you can pick up a check tomorrow."

John walked in and opened the refrigerator. "Are you going to cook, or are we going to go out to dinner?"

"I'm on the phone," Carolyn said, waving him away. "I don't understand," she told the real estate agent. "How could you sell my house without contacting me?"

"Well," Margaret said, excited, "the buyer paid the full asking price. He paid cash, Carolyn. That means you don't even have to wait for the check to clear. I thought you'd be elated."

"But don't I have to sign the papers? I can't just move out of my house on a moment's notice. I have to rent an apartment, hire a moving van, pack everything up. When do these people want to move in?"

"You're a lucky lady," Margaret said cheerfully. "The man who bought your house insisted the title be left in your name. He even paid off the existing mortgage. The house is yours. He said it was a gift."

Carolyn was so flabbergasted that she told the agent she would call her back later. For a while, she just stared out the kitchen window. Her eyes drifted over the chipped tiles on the countertop, the white refrigerator that was on its last legs, the cabinets so desperately in need of refinishing. Without a house payment, she could not only pay John's tuition, she could make some long overdue repairs. A short time later, she slumped against the counter, knowing she couldn't accept such an enormous gift even if she and Marcus were engaged. He'd talked about the possibility of getting married, but it was far too soon. In reality, they hadn't even been able to see each other that often. He was working long hours at his business, and Carolyn had wanted to spend as much time as possible with her children.

In a daze, Carolyn went down the hall to change her clothes and decide what they were going to do for dinner. She stopped in the door to Rebecca's room. A canvas was on the easel, and her daughter was holding a palette in her left hand, her head tilted to one side as she studied her work. Neil was sprawled out on her bed, flipping through a fashion magazine and sipping a soda.

"What do you think?" Rebecca said, craning her neck around.

Neil peered out over the top of the magazine. "The skin tone is too white. Add some more pink, then paint over what you just did."

"Why can't I just paint flowers?" the girl whined, setting the palette down and searching through the tubes of oils on top of her bureau.

"Because flowers are boring," her uncle told her. Seeing Carolyn in the doorway, he said, "When are you going to feed us kids? I'm starving."

A minor miracle had occurred. Neil had a tendency to be obsessive-compulsive, particularly when it came to his surroundings. It was odd seeing him in the midst of Rebecca's girlish clutter, relaxed and happy. When the kids had first moved into his house after the shooting, he'd run around picking up after them and swearing he was going to have a nervous breakdown if they didn't go home immediately. Then one day it had all just stopped. Carolyn had come over and found dirty dishes in his sink, dirt on his normally pristine-perfect marble floors, and unmade beds piled high with clothes and schoolbooks. When she'd looked for Neil, she'd found him in his studio furiously painting. And since she'd brought the kids home, she couldn't get rid of him. He spent the afternoons tutoring Rebecca, then wolfed down Carolyn's home-cooked meals and after dinner lay around watching movies with John. He didn't leave the house until the kids went to bed. At his own place, he worked through the night.

"Why don't you cook tonight, Neil?" Carolyn said.

"Don't be cruel," her brother said, adjusting the pillow behind his neck. "Can't you see I'm working with Rebecca? It would break her heart if I had to cut her lesson short. Isn't that right, angel?"

"Not really," the girl said, tossing her paintbrush down. "Get up off your ass, Neil, and help me mix the flesh tone. I don't know what I did wrong, but it looks yellow now."

Neil uncurled his lanky frame and walked over, placing his hands on her shoulders. "You're doing great, honey. If you're going to become a painter, you need to get used to frustration." Once he'd shown her which colors to mix, he flopped down on his stomach on Rebecca's bed again, hugging her ruffled pillow to his chest. "Make meatloaf and mashed potatoes. No, I changed my mind. Whip up some of that lasagna you made last week. Oh, and don't forget the garlic bread. Call me before John gets to the table or there won't be anything left to eat."

"I'm not your mother, Neil," Carolyn told him. "Marcus—"

"I thought you weren't seeing lover boy until tomorrow night."

Rebecca snickered, but continued painting. "I'm not," Carolyn answered, running her hands through her hair. "I just need to talk to him. You know, uninterrupted. There're some steaks defrosted in the refrigerator. All you have to do is turn on the grill and cook them. Rebecca, make some baked potatoes in the microwave, and I've got some fresh asparagus. If you don't want the asparagus, you can make a salad."

Neil and Rebecca exchanged almost identical sneers. Carolyn felt as if she now had three teenagers instead of two. She went to her bedroom, closed the door, and called Marcus.

"How's my girl?" he said.

"Are you still at work?" Carolyn said, sitting on the edge of the bed.

"Yes, but I can talk. What's going on?"

"What you did was wonderful, Marcus. Never in a million years would I have thought anyone would do something like that for me. You have the biggest heart in the world. But the bottom line is I can't let you pay off my house."

"I don't know what you're talking about. Did you really say someone paid off your house?"

Carolyn had suspected it was going to be this way. "I know it was you, Marcus, so don't play games with me. Just call the Realtor and arrange to get your money back."

"I swear it wasn't me. You know I'm struggling right now with my business. I'd love to help you out, Carolyn, but I just don't have a lot of extra cash lying around. Now if you and the kids want to move into my Santa Rosa place . . . "

"It's too soon," she said. "We've already discussed it. The kids are just getting to know you. Besides, I wouldn't live with a man unless we were married."

"Then we'll get married."

Carolyn felt like crying. This wasn't a valid proposal, nor was it romantic. Marcus was merely trying to accommodate her. "Just so you'll know, I'm going to reject the offer on the house. And there's no reason to deny that it was you because I'll find out the truth tomorrow when I go to the escrow company. I appreciate the gesture,

Marcus, I just can't accept it. Please try and understand. I want things to be right between us. I don't want to take things from you."

The line fell silent. Carolyn waited, knowing he was thinking. He was the type of person who weighed every word before speaking.

"When you find out who did this," he finally said, "I'd really like to know. It must be one of your other admirers. I'm not sure if I should thank him or beat the shit out of him. How can I compete with someone like that? Buy you a hotel or something?"

What an act, Carolyn thought, smiling. "Am I going to see you tomorrow?"

"Doubtful," Marcus said, yawning. "If I can break away, I'll give you a call."

Brian Irving's partner, Quentin Starr, was a twenty-nine-year-old black detective. He was fit, and moved with the power and grace of an athlete. Even though Irving was only forty-three, Starr made him feel like a clumsy old man.

"I can't believe you told Kathleen Masters we'd respond now," Starr said, sitting behind the wheel of an unmarked police unit. "My shift is over in fifteen minutes. You're not in Modesto anymore, my man. These rich people think they can order us around like their house servants. I tell them to go fuck themselves."

"She knows the chief," Irving explained, fidgeting in his seat. "I haven't been with the department that long. My wife and kids like it here. You're lucky you were on vacation when this went down." Starr steered the car onto the freeway. "The lady went through a horrible ordeal, Quent. Anyone would be a little crazy after going through something like that. If we can placate her and she calms down, you'll be home in an hour and I won't have to face the chief in the morning, mad because an irate woman called him at home to report two of his officers."

"We'll see," Quentin said. "Do you think there's a shot in hell Arnie Layman is innocent?"

"There's always a chance," Irving told him. "Several things didn't set well with me. The problem is that Chief Riggs wants this case closed. Public attention is a good thing when you've closed a case, not when you have to reopen one. Anyway, the evidence is stacked on Layman. It's a slam dunk."

"Now that I think about it, it was strange that he took off."

"Turn right here," Irving said, seeing the shrubs in front of Kathleen's driveway. "You mean Dean Masters?"

"Yeah, what's the deal with that?"

"When I spoke to him, Masters told me he'd been having problems with the wife even before the assault. She has a history of alcohol and prescription-drug abuse."

"Her and just about everyone else who lives in this town. Even a rich drug addict has an advantage. They don't have to go out on the street to score their dope, worrying they may get busted, or that some dealer cut their coke with rat poison. They get it from their doctors."

"Masters couldn't stand it anymore and was planning on asking her for a divorce." Irving looked up at the sprawling house as his partner threw the gearshift into park. "What bothers me about this case is why someone living in a place like this would own a bottle of Old Crow whisky. I seriously doubt Layman brought his own bottle into the house and then smashed it over Kathleen Masters's head. With a drunk, especially one who lived on the street like Layman, most of the crimes they commit are either to steal booze or the money to buy it. Guess Layman was more than your average drunk."

"Unfortunately, he's not around to answer that question. It's hard to imagine that this Masters guy wouldn't have at least waited until his wife got out of the hospital before he took off. Pretty heartless, don't you think?"

"That doesn't mean he tried to kill her." Irving opened the car door. "Forget about it for now. Let's find out what's got Kathleen on a rampage this time."

They knocked on the door, then waited until Kathleen answered and waved them inside. "Follow me," she said, leading them upstairs. "Look around, then tell me if you notice anything out of the ordinary. I didn't notice it at first, either."

"No, not now or the dozens of other times I've been here," Irving said, glancing into the library and master bedroom, more to placate her than with any thought that he might find anything. "What's this about, Kathleen?"

"Dean took all the photographs of us together," she said, sweeping her hand toward a grouping of ornate frames sitting on top of a long narrow table. "Those people are models. The stores put pictures like that in empty frames to help them sell. I usually don't take the time to throw them away, and just put my own photos on top of them."

"Isn't it possible these are new frames you bought before the crime?"

"I'm not an idiot, Irving," said Kathleen, giving him a steely gaze. "Tell me . . . if my husband hated me enough to leave me, why would he want to steal the few photos we had of us together? He'd only do that if he was planning to murder his wife. Did you find any fingerprints or DNA evidence that would link back to my husband?"

"Not your husband," Irving answered, "but enough to make an airtight case against Arnold Layman."

"Just so you'll know," Starr said, "murderers usually take off before the police show up, not after. My partner saw your husband. From what I heard, he saved your life by calling the doctor who lives next door. Why would he try to kill you, then save you?"

"You didn't answer my question," Kathleen said, glaring at Irving. "In this extensive investigation you did, wouldn't you expect to find evidence of my husband? He lived here, you know. He bathed here, slept here, shit here, had sex here."

Irving started to lose his cool, then decided the harder he pushed, the harder she would push back. All he wanted was to put as much distance between him and Kathleen Masters as possible. "Let me explain," he said in hushed tones. "Your husband wasn't a suspect, so we had no reason to take a DNA sample from him. Since Layman had been in prison, his DNA was on file." He raised his right hand to keep her from interrupting. "It wouldn't have helped us in the case, so why go to the trouble to take a sample from your husband? We knew he lived here. We had our perpetrator. Does that make things clearer?"

"It makes one thing clear," Kathleen said, blowing an annoying hair off her forehead. "What about fingerprints?"

"The same applies to prints. We always find unidentified prints at crime scenes . . . you know, such as yours, your housekeeper's, your husband's, maybe some of your friends'. Once we got a match on Layman, like I keep telling you, there was no reason to do anything else. I gave thought to the possibility that your husband could have something to do with what happened, but there wasn't a shred of evidence to substantiate it."

"My husband didn't leave any DNA or prints," Kathleen said. "He cleaned the house, don't you see? You were so focused on finding evidence to convict Layman, you failed to notice the lack of evidence that would make my husband a suspect."

Detective Irving shrugged. "We did our job, Kathleen. Arnie Layman is the guilty party. Since he's dead, the case is closed unless some kind of substantial new evidence comes to light. A few missing pictures and speculation that there were no prints or DNA belonging to your husband doesn't fall into that category. And since we didn't check, we can't even verify what you're saying is true."

"We need to get going, Brian," Starr said, trying to edge things along. "We have to get to that robbery."

"It is what is it, sorry to say," Irving added. "The best thing you can do, Kathleen, is learn how to accept it."

She raised her arms and then let them drop to her side before heading down the stairs, leaving the detectives to follow. When they reached the family room, she spun around and faced them. "Sit down," she instructed, pointing to the sofa. "Your department has plenty of other officers they can send to that robbery. That is, Detective Starr, if it wasn't just a ploy so you could leave." She paused and cleared her throat. "Like it or not, you're going to listen to me. Dean devised a plan to kill me and pin the murder on Layman. He wore the drunk's jacket to make me think it wasn't him. He stood right over me. I saw his face. It wasn't Layman, it was my husband. I don't understand why you people won't believe me. You're going to let him get away with it, aren't you?"

"Try to calm down and think rationally," Irving said, brushing his finger under his nose. "You're home now. You can pick up the pieces of your life and go on. You survived. The man who attacked you is dead. Thousands of crimes victims would like to be in your shoes right now."

"Think rationally?" she shouted. "How else do you think I'd feel? When Dean visited me in the hospital before his disappearing act, I smelled the same stench that was on Layman. When was the last time you spoke to my husband? Do you know where I can find him?"

"I spoke to your husband at length the morning after the incident and then on several other occasions by phone," Irving said, both he and Starr standing. "After he answered all my questions, he told me you two were having relationship problems. He later called me and expressed his desire to move to Europe to play golf. I told him we had no problem with that since Layman was dead and the case was closed."

"Relationship problems, that's an understatement. I threatened to divorce him. This is my house, so I told him to leave. Dean's a control freak. He flew into a rage."

"Can you give us a second?" Irving said, moving into the entryway. "Quent, maybe we should give her the benefit of the doubt. She may have a point here. I even remember smelling something on her husband the night of the crime. I just thought it was body odor."

"Great, sure," Quentin said, pissed. "I tell you, we're wasting our time."

The two men went back into the living room and sat back down on the sofa. "Did you or your husband drink Old Crow whiskey?" Irving asked, leaning forward over his knees. "Maybe use it for cooking?"

"Absolutely not. I prefer vodka, and Dean drank cognac. I've never known anyone in my life that drank Old Crow whiskey, and can't imagine why anyone would use disgusting rotgut like that to cook. Why? What does this have to do with anything?"

"The lab determined that a bottle of Old Crow was what caused the damage to your face," Irving said, figuring he was making a mistake by telling her this but deciding to get everything out in the open. "To be honest, there were other things that didn't add up. How did Layman get here? Your house is a long way from town, and a person would have to hike up some pretty steep hills. It's dark at night, and a guy like him would stand out like a sore thumb. It's not like you live next to a shopping mall or a building where he might have found shelter. Also, we didn't find any of your property in his possession. I'm not sure what his motivation was to attack you. Had you ever seen Layman before that night?"

"Never," she answered, her expression softening. "So what's the next step?"

Irving looked over at Quentin, whose sour face stared back at him. "I'll start making some inquires." He paused and took a breath. "You have to keep this quiet, though. If we can't come up with something solid, we never had this conversation. But if we stumble onto something that looks promising, I'll take it to the chief. We really need to take off now. Can I call you in the morning?"

"Yes," Kathleen said, staying on the sofa while they walked toward the door. "Help me to bring my husband to justice and it'll be one of the most satisfying things you've ever done."

"Quentin and I will do all we can, Kathleen."

"Good," she said, "because if I find Dean first, there won't be much left for you to do." She gave a fake smile and a flick of her wrist, looking past Detective Starr as if he weren't there. "Talk to you tomorrow, Brian."

Outside in the car, Starr threw out, "Did she just threaten Dean Masters's life?"

"Sounds that way to me," Irving said as they pulled out of the driveway. "We better get in touch with him right away."

"You're crazy," Starr said, knowing exactly what Irving meant. "What happened to the stuff you told me earlier? You know, the wife likes it here, you've got to protect your job, Kathleen Masters is a pill-popping nutcase. I'm telling you, if Chief Riggs gets wind of this, you'll be the first one he gives the boot. While you're sitting in the dirt, don't expect me to bail you out."

CHAPTER 31

Mary smelled food and saw a large man in a brown sports jacket, carrying two boxes from Pizza Hut. Her stomach was rumbling, but she didn't have time to go out for lunch. She jumped up and darted into Duffy Crenshaw's cubicle a few doors down. "Are you going to eat both of those pies, Duffy? I'm hungry enough to eat wood."

"You're my kind of woman," Crenshaw said, an older detective scheduled to retire in three months. "No one eats this shit anymore, especially the ladies." He tore off two large slices and handed them to her on a paper plate. "Here, save me from a heart attack."

Mary returned to her office, chomping on the pizza while she stared at her computer screen. The search for information on Matthew Sheppard had led to a dead end. For all practical purposes, the man didn't exist.

The phone rang. "Detective Stevens," she said, answering it.

"This is Detective Fisher from San Diego," the voice said. "I neglected to give you a few e-mails that didn't make their way into the Sheppard file. One of them you may be interested in."

"I'd be interested in how you made detective."

He ignored her jab and continued, "When Matthew Sheppard called me and told me his wife had disappeared, he claimed he didn't have any recent pictures of her. I thought it was a domestic case from the start, so I just assumed the wife ran off with the photo albums. We used her DMV photo for the report and on our Web site. This morning, we came across another picture. One of the neighbors sent it in, advising us it was taken at a block party on Labor Day."

Was this his exciting lead? Why had he bothered to call? "What good is a picture of Lisa Sheppard now? We've already identified her."

"You don't understand," he insisted. "Matthew Sheppard is standing beside her."

Mary's pulse rate jumped. "Why didn't you tell me this before?"

"I forgot, okay?" Fisher told her, defensive. "I don't even think I saw the damn thing. The tech who handles our Web site had it stored in his computer. He heard about some of the things that have been going on there in Ventura and e-mailed it to me this morning."

"Get it over to me," Mary said. "Right now, damn it! We need it so we can issue a warrant. Sheppard could easily be our murderer, and as of now we have nothing whatsoever on him."

After giving him her e-mail address, Mary tapped her fingernails on the desktop until the New Mail icon appeared. She opened the attachment, and a large digital photo filled her screen. Right-mouse clicking, she reduced the size. In the foreground were a middle-aged man and woman. Behind them was a grainy image of an attractive blond female she recognized as Lisa Sheppard. Although she already knew what Lisa looked like, seeing pictures from a victim's past was sometimes more gut-wrenching than autopsy photos. They were usually taken during happy times in their lives, when they were surrounded by friends and loved ones. It was even sadder in this case. The way things were shaping up, the man Lisa Sheppard thought loved her may have brought her to her grave.

So this was their mystery man, Matthew Sheppard.

Clearly, it wasn't Carl Holden.

Sheppard was wearing a black cowboy hat pulled down low on his forehead. She could tell he was tall, as he towered over his wife. He was dressed in Wrangler jeans, and the sleeves were rolled up on his white cotton shirt. On his feet were brown western boots. He looked as if he'd just finished riding a bull in a rodeo.

Sheppard had clear, unmarked skin. He either had a dark complexion or spent a lot of time in the sun. It was a difficult call as to his age, but she estimated late thirties or early forties. The shape of his face seemed to be oval, and a dark brown or black mustache obscured his upper lip. His most distinctive feature was his cleft chin. Some people jokingly referred to it as a "butt chin." Sheppard's dimpled chin wasn't at all unsightly. If he wasn't a suspect in a murder, she'd classify him as handsome, the kind of man who wouldn't have a problem finding a woman.

Having two criminals to apprehend, Mary thought, wasn't as easy as pinning the murders on Holden. In addition, they had to rule out the idea that Troy Anderson was somehow involved. The multiple jurisdictions posed another enormous problem.

Tracy Anderson's body had been discovered in Ventura, so they held jurisdiction unless it was discovered that Anderson had been murdered in San Diego and only buried in Ventura. Mary would have gone to the chief in San Diego if she'd thought there was anything to be gained. How could she have known there was a photo of Matthew Sheppard floating around?

Eleanor Beckworth was a different matter. If the coroner ruled Eleanor Beckworth's death a suicide, there was nothing Ventura could do unless new information surfaced to prove that she'd been murdered. Even then, St. Louis would still be the investigating agency, as the crime occurred in that city.

What had originally been a single case of murder had turned into an extremely complicated series of interlocking crimes. Mary generally tried to keep her hours to a reasonable level, but the department had recently lost two investigators. One had retired, and the other had been transferred. They just didn't have the necessary manpower, and she could envision racking up hours of overtime until the crimes were resolved. It would take a minimum of an hour just to explain to Hank what she'd learned that morning.

Now that they had ruled out the chance that Holden was Matthew Sheppard, they were back to first base. Believing Troy Anderson was responsible for two homicides that occurred eight years apart in two different cities was too much of a stretch.

She sent the photograph to the color printer and picked it up on the way to Hank's office. When she walked in, his face was twisting. He'd just consumed a foamy green substance out of what had once been his coffee cup.

"I just started a detox this week," he said, taking another sip. "Blue-green algae, wheat grass, and all kinds of other good stuff. You should try it. You'll be jumping over tall buildings in a single bound."

"Sounds delish, but I'll pass." Mary placed the picture on his cluttered desk, holding it in place with her hand until he picked it up and looked at it.

"Am I supposed to know this person?"

"You're looking at Matthew Sheppard."

"How did you get this?" Hank asked, staring at the enhanced computer image. "Are you certain it's Sheppard?"

"It fits the description the neighbors gave us perfectly. The detective in San Diego was sitting on it—you know, Fisher, that piss-poor excuse for a cop I told you about. Bastard never even wrote a report when Lisa went missing. Nice of him, huh? He sent me the picture about ten minutes ago. We should get this out immediately, don't you think? No one has seen Matthew Sheppard since his wife disappeared."

Hank's gaze was riveted on the photo. "Will you look at that? He has a chin just like Carolyn's new boyfriend. Even the shape of their noses is the same. Have you met this guy?"

"No," Mary said. "Don't you think you're taking this thing with Carolyn a little too far? No disrespect, boss, but it might be time to give it up. " He looked up and scowled. She quickly threw up a palm. "Before you bite my head off, hear me out. Keep heading down this road, and you're going to get yourself in a world of trouble. The poor woman has been through hell, and you're trying to turn her new boyfriend into a murderer. Hey, I'm sorry things haven't worked out. You gotta get over it."

"I'm seeing several women right now," Hank said, a look of pride on his face. "This has nothing to do with my feelings for Carolyn. This guy's a dead ringer for Marcus Wright. I met him at the hospital the night John was shot. Weren't you there with Carolyn's daughter?"

"I took Rebecca home with me from Carolyn's house," Mary told him, rubbing her chin. "I think we can rule out Holden, do you agree? The lab didn't match his DNA from anything found inside the box of clothes from San Diego, and this picture doesn't look anything like him. Holden's got some kind back problem that causes him to stoop forward. This guy looks as if he's in great shape."

"Can you get into your photo-editing program and take off this moustache, lighten his hair, and zoom in on his face?"

"First," she said. "Promise me you won't go on a witch hunt involving Carolyn's boyfriend unless you have something concrete. She finally met a nice man. That's all she needs is for you to scare him off with your false accusations."

"I'm investigating a murder," Hank told her. "You got a problem with that?"

"Maybe. You're Carolyn's best friend, Hank. No one wants to screw up their relationship with their best friend. Things don't work out, the friendship is ruined. Personally, I'd choose a friend over a lover any day of the week. Friends stay together forever, lovers come and go." She reached over and grabbed a half-empty water bottle off his desk, removing the top and taking a slug. Slamming it back down with a thud, she said, "Can we get back to work now? Troy Anderson may have murdered his wife instead of Holden, and I'm almost certain Eleanor Beckworth didn't commit suicide."

Hank acted as if he hadn't heard a word she'd said. "Whoever this man is, he looked exactly like Marcus Wright. I want you to run Wright every way possible."

"How am I going to do that, pray tell?" Mary asked, flailing her arms around. "You got a DOB, SOC, DMV? What you got, huh? You ain't got nothing, that's what."

"I've got better instincts than you," Hank said, smiling. "Come on, you're a genius at this stuff. You're bound to be able to come up with something. Marcus Wright is forty-five, give or take a few years, six one, maybe one ninety. Jesus, you got his damn picture." When she winced, he added, "Hey, at least we know we can find the sucker. That's got to count for something."

Every once in a while Hank really got to her, with his puppy-dog eyes and playful smile. He had sort of a rugged look. Thank God he'd stopped smoking. All he had now was a serious toothpick addiction. Since he'd dropped the weight and bought himself some decent threads, Mary had placed him on what she called the "just might" list. Age didn't matter, especially now that they'd come up with a chemical rocket booster for men. And older guys were sometimes hotter lovers. "I'll work on the photo and see what I can find out on Wright," she said. "But only if you finish the report on that stabbing we worked last night."

"Now we're negotiating? I'm a lieutenant. You're a detective. Write your own damn report."

"We got a deal or what?"

"All right, you win," Hank said, waving her away. "Get a move on it."

Kathleen was about to embark on the next chapter of her life. The players were the same, but the game had changed. The stakes were at the highest possible level.

His life or hers.

She sat down at the computer in her home office. In her real estate business, she used the Internet only when it was necessary. Real estate was a people business, not bits and bytes floating around in a digital cesspool. Pulling up the Web browser, she typed in "Dean Masters." When the results came back with nothing relating to her husband, she typed in "professional golf tour," and *www.pgatour.com* appeared on the screen. She remembered his talking about the Nationwide Tour. She looked under the player profiles. Dean's name wasn't listed. Strange, she thought, but maybe she'd entered something wrong. One way to find out was to drive to Pebble Beach and ask around. She poured out two Percodans, swallowed them with a glass of water and took off.

Twenty minutes later, she strolled into the pro shop. "Hello," she said, reaching forward to shake a man's hand. "I'm Kathleen Masters, Dean's wife."

"Nice to see you," he said, with a smile that only someone being paid would give. "I'm Jake Bartley. What can I help you with today? Do you want to take a golf cart to the driving range, or are you going to putt a little?"

She looked around at other people in the shop. "Can we talk in private?"

"Sure," Jake said. "Let's go into my office."

"You know my husband, of course?" she said, waiting until he removed a box of golf balls from the chair so she could sit down.

"I've heard the name, but I can't place his face."

"Dean Masters," Kathleen repeated, wondering if the man was new. "He's a professional golfer on the tour. You know, six one and somewhere around one eighty, unless he's dropped some weight recently."

"I think I know who you're talking about," Jake told her, staring at a spot over her head, "but he's not a professional golfer. The guy I'm thinking of has a low handicap, though. Let me think. Yeah, he drives a red Porsche 911. Is that your husband?"

"Burgundy," Kathleen said, thinking he had to be mistaken. The people who played at Pebble Beach all drove luxury cars. "Do you have a picture of him for his membership card?"

"Let me check the computer," he said, dropping down in his chair and clicking on the keyboard. "Here we go, but wait, there's no picture. That's not the way it's supposed to be. There's always a picture with our member's information. If you don't mind me asking, what's this about?"

"My husband has disappeared," Kathleen told him. "His mother is critically ill. We haven't heard from Dean in weeks. I filed a missing person's report, and the useless police haven't done a thing. Please, can you help me?"

"All I can do is tell him you're trying to contact him," he answered, cautious now. "That is, if he comes out to play. I don't think he's been around for a month or so."

"There was a caddy," Kathleen said. "Shorty, I think. Does he still work here?"

"Yeah," he answered. "Shorty Montgomery. He's out with a loop right now. Should be finished with his client, I'd say, in about ten minutes. You're welcome to wait."

"Thank you," she said, as the man left his office. It was obvious Dean had lied to her about being a professional golfer. Then how was he filling his time? The travel—why was he flying all over the place in a fancy jet? Maybe the people at the airport could answer that question. Extracting information from them might be tricky. Wealthy people didn't want their business made public. Confidentiality was probably a high priority at Jet USA.

Her patience running thin, Kathleen walked back into the pro shop. "He's right there, Ms. Masters," Jake said, pointing at a caddy through the window.

She pushed open the door again, seeing a small, slightly built, olive-skinned man wearing dark sunglasses. "Shorty," she called out. "Do you remember me? I'm Kathleen Masters. I met you a few months back. You went on the tour with my husband, the one who has the jet service."

"Just a minute, Ma'am," he responded, taking a hundred-dollar bill from the golfer he'd been caddying for and stuffing it into the pocket of his white smock.

She didn't want to waste time with small talk. "I know you were my husband's regular caddy. Have you seen him lately?"

"Sorry, Ma'am, I haven't. Been quite some time now. Does he need me to caddy for him?"

"No," Kathleen said, using her hand to shield her face from the sun. She was wearing a shoulder-length blond wig to help cover the scars she'd sustained from the assault. Since the left side of her face was where most of the damage had occurred, she pulled the artificial hair forward to conceal it. "Was he a good golfer?"

"Sure, Mr. Masters could hit the ball," Shorty said, stretching his back as if it was bothering him. "Low seventies type of guy."

"But he wasn't a professional golfer?" Kathleen said, stunned at what she was hearing. Her entire marriage had been a fraud. She pulled a hundred-dollar bill out of her purse, holding it in front of her for the caddy to see.

He laughed. "Dean Masters is a long way from a professional golfer. That's a fact."

"I need you to tell me everything you can remember about him," Kathleen said, steering him to a quiet corner so they could talk privately. "He's intentionally disappeared, and I need to find him."

"I'll do my best," Shorty said, reaching toward the money. "Is this for me?"

She released the bill, then grabbed his arm. "Do you remember Dean talking about anything that seemed out of the ordinary? You flew on the plane with him. Where the hell did you go if he's not on a professional golf tour?"

"I'm not sure what you mean," the caddy hedged, looking anxious. "I don't think he had another woman on the side, if that's what you're asking. I try not to get into the personal lives of my clients, Ma'am."

Kathleen's eyes narrowed. *Whore,* she thought, reaching into her purse and pulling out another hundred. "If you want this, start talking. I'm not here to waste my time. If you tell me something worthwhile, there's more where this came from. Lots more, understand?"

"We spoke mainly about golf," he told her. "The time you picked him up at the airport, we'd spent three days in San Diego. His favorite course is Torrey Pines South. He told me he played there at least twice a month. Is something wrong, Mrs. Masters?" he added, tilting his head. "You look like you're not feeling well."

"How would you feel if you . . . ?"

"I'm sorry," Shorty said, indicating a loud-talking group of men walking past them. "I didn't hear you."

"Forget it." Kathleen started to walk away, more confused and frustrated than before. She stopped and glanced back over her shoulder. "Did he leave his clubs here?"

"I'm not sure, but I'll check," Shorty told her, rushing around the corner.

She wasn't recovered enough to run all over the state of California. She'd have to hire a private investigator, someone who specialized in finding missing persons.

"Here you go, Ma'am," the caddy said, placing a smallish golf bag upright in front of her. "This isn't his regular bag, just one he used as a backup."

Kathleen knelt down and started searching the bag. Shorty stood by, looking around to see if anyone was watching. She stuck her hand in the first pocket, finding nothing but balls. In the second, she found a sealed Baggie that contained a white Titleist golf glove, tees, and several circular ball markers. As she ripped into the plastic bag, several items slipped out of her hand onto the pavement.

Shorty picked up one. "See? I told you he loved this place," he said, extending his hand to show her that the writing on the ball marker read Torrey Pines. "If you want to find him, that's the place to look."

"Thanks." Kathleen turned to leave.

"Wait, you didn't check one of the pockets." He unzipped a pocket at the top of the bag and retrieved several business cards. "Here you go."

There were four identical business cards that read "Matthew Sheppard" with a San Diego phone number. She assumed it was someone Dean played golf with at Torrey Pines. "Thanks, Shorty," she said, more optimistic now.

He shuffled his feet, peering up at her over the rims of his sunglasses. "Normally, I wouldn't let a wife dig around in her husband's bag, know what I mean?"

Was there no decent man left on the planet? "I know exactly what you mean," Kathleen said, pasting a phony smile on her face. "How much money did I give you? You've been so nice, I'd like to double it."

"You gave me two hundred," he said, reaching into his pocket and pulling the bills out to prove it.

Kathleen reached over and snatched the money out of his hand. "Doesn't anyone ever do anything these days just to be nice? You think Dean Masters is a super guy, huh?" She yanked the wig off, showing the jagged scar on her scalp and the slash marks on her cheek. "This is what he did to me, okay! Still worried about protecting his privacy?"

CHAPTER 32

·

Thursday, October 19—1:30 P.M.

On her way back to the government center after interviewing a five-year-old child-molestation victim, Carolyn retrieved her voice mails on her cell phone, finding one from Hank. His voice was urgent, asking her to come to the police department right away. Not able to reach the detective on the phone, she transferred to Mary. "What's going on?"

"I'll explain everything when you get here. It concerns both the Holden and Sheppard murders. Hank thinks it might involve you."

"Of course I'm involved," Carolyn replied, thinking Mary had lost her mind. "Why can't you tell me over the phone? Preston's got me working my tail off. Don't tell me you tracked down Holden and then lost him."

"Something else has come up. Where are you?"

"On the freeway. I'm about to exit on Victoria."

"Hold on," Mary said, and the phone went silent for a few seconds. "That was Hank. We came up with a picture of Matthew Sheppard. Hank thinks he looks like Marcus. I've got to go. I'll see you in his office when you get here."

Holden and Sheppard somehow connected to Marcus? This was the most absurd thing Carolyn had ever heard. When she arrived at the police department on Dowell Drive, she walked past the front desk and followed a detective through the security door. The desk officer jumped to his feet and caught her on the other side. When he recognized her, he said, "You can't come barging in here, Sullivan. You have to sign in like everyone else."

"Not today," she said, continuing briskly down the corridor. She entered the detective bay and kept walking until she reached Hank's office, pushing past a detective who stepped out of his partitioned office to speak to her. "Would one of you please tell me what's going on?"

"It may be nothing, Carolyn," Hank said. "We've got a picture of Matthew Sheppard. Mary, why don't you show her?"

"This first picture is one that I altered to remove the moustache and add hair where there was once a cowboy hat." Mary placed the photo down on Hank's desk. "This is the original shot." She set the other photo beside it." Ignore the people in the front. Look at the couple in the back. That's Lisa and Matthew Sheppard."

What Carolyn saw was terrifying. The altered photograph bore a striking resemblance to Marcus. "You made this look like Marcus. It's obvious this isn't the original picture. What are you trying to do to me?"

"It's not about you, Carolyn," Hank explained. "Even without Mary's changes, the features are almost identical." He stood and came around the desk. "Look at his chin. A cleft chin like that isn't all that common. And the nose, even the forehead. Don't tell me you don't see it."

"My God, Hank," Carolyn told him, "you've only seen Marcus one time."

Mary and Hank exchanged tense glances. "What do *you* think?" Mary asked her. "If anyone should know, it would be you." She waited for Carolyn to respond. When she just stared at her, she continued, "I created this computer composite because Wright is too common a name for a DMV search. If you can provide us with his DOB, his driver's license number, or even some type of physical evidence, we might be able to eliminate him. Can you do that, Carolyn?"

Carolyn fell silent, locking her hands on the arms of the chair. She'd brought a person into her life that she knew nothing about. She was even engaging in sex with him. Her eyes drifted to the floor as she played back their first night together. The old-fashioned phone booth, the way he had snuck up on her in the dark hallway, already partially unclothed. Why did he live in such a remote location when his business was located in Los Angeles? And there was the accident. He'd been adamant about not getting the police involved.

Most people would sue you if you ran a stop sign and crashed into their car, not offer to pay your repair bill and ask you to lunch. She hadn't had time to call the escrow office, but why would he pay for her house? Was he buying her off in some way, making certain that if anything came to light, she wouldn't cooperate with the police? Danger signals had been flashing all around her, and she'd been oblivious.

On second thought, everyone was a stranger when you met them. In today's world, with the trend in computer dating, Carolyn had been less reckless than the majority of women. Hank and Mary were making her paranoid, tainting her reasoning. Marcus had stayed in the hospital by her side for two nights after John was shot. What kind of killer would do that? Considering him a suspect based on a computer-generated image of a man who may have had nothing whatsoever to do with his wife's death was the epitome of speculation. Mary knew it, she could tell. Hank may have convinced himself there was something to this, but subconsciously, she was certain he was trying to push Marcus out of her life.

Hank coughed to get her attention.

"What proof do you have that Matthew Sheppard killed his wife?" Carolyn asked them. "Maybe he's dead, killed by the same person who murdered Lisa. You're badgering me because I'm dating someone who looks like a man you aren't certain even committed a crime."

"Well," Mary said, settling into her seat, "we know it's not Holden."

Lisa Sheppard's body had been found in the same place as Tracy Anderson's. Carolyn had been certain Holden had killed her. "Just because Holden's DNA wasn't in the box of the Sheppards's old clothes doesn't mean anything. He's a sweeper, just like the press has dubbed him. Meticulous about cleaning up after his crimes. To be honest, I'd be surprised if you found anything. Holden spent eight years in the joint. These guys watch *CSI, Law and Order*, and all those other crime shows. He's a smart man. He's studied the Greek philosophers. He probably had a stack of forensic books in his cell."

"She may have a point," Mary said, looking at Hank. "Carolyn, that doesn't mean we're not going to follow through on this."

"Maybe Lisa Sheppard was having an affair with another man and left her husband to be with him." Carolyn said. "Since you found out the name of the computer company she did consulting for, why didn't you find out if they had access to her files? Most people who do that kind of work from their home use the company's computer systems."

"She disappeared over a year ago," Mary reminded her. "The independent consulting firm she worked for went out of business. We've been trying to track down the principals through their business license, but as far as we can tell, they didn't have one. Some of these people work under the radar, selling bootlegged programs to a handpicked group of customers. Major players such as Microsoft are attempting to put a stop to it, causing many of these types of operations to fold."

"Marcus is a gentle man," Carolyn said, feeling perspiration pop out on her upper lip. "He's not a murderer. He's a successful businessman."

"Have you ever called him at work?" Hank interjected.

"Once," Carolyn said. "Usually we communicate over his cell phone."

"Do you know the name of the business?"

"No," she said. "When I called him, he answered the phone. I heard people talking in the background, though, so I'm certain it was a business. What about the safety deposit key? Have you tracked down the bank yet?"

"We're working on it," Mary said, reaching over and touching her arm. "I didn't think there was anything to this, either, Carolyn. But wouldn't you rather be safe than sorry? Just because a person has money doesn't mean they aren't a criminal. Even serial killers have been known to have decent jobs, a nice car, even a family. Look at the BTK killer from Wichita. The man murdered ten people and was elected president of his church council. Do you want something like this on your conscience if Hank's suspicions turn out to be true? Please, Carolyn, tell us what you know about Marcus Wright."

Carolyn attempted to detail her various contacts with Marcus. The only thing she held back was the intimate details of their sex life. After drilling criminals for years, she suddenly knew how they felt. "I would have found out more about him," she said, flicking the ends of her fingernails, "but we met just before everything went down with Holden. There was too much going on. I was occupied trying to take care of John, as well as terrified that Holden would come back. Besides, Marcus isn't a talkative person."

As she spoke, the memory of the feeling of well-being she had when she was with Marcus returned. "Everyone always praises me for my ability to get inside the head of a criminal," she said. "You don't think I'd know if I was dating a murderer?"

Hank said forcefully, "Look at the picture, Carolyn."

Her eyes drifted toward the piece of paper, then her head jerked back up. "You know how many people look alike? Think of all the witnesses who identify the wrong suspect. Before I became a probation officer, a ten-year-old kid up the street was killed by a hit-and-run driver. One of the witnesses helped the police put together a composite of the suspect. When I saw it, I was certain it was one of my neighbors. I was shocked when they caught the right person. The man they arrested didn't look anything like the composite."

"Lisa Sheppard was a computer programmer," Mary threw out, seeing Carolyn reaching for her purse. "Maybe Marcus met her in school or at a convention. It's not out of the realm of possibility."

"His company develops software for the military," Carolyn countered. "Marcus and Lisa Sheppard weren't in the same league. All she did was tech support. Your premise doesn't hold water."

"You don't know that," Mary said. "All you know is what this man has told you."

"I have to go back to work."

"We need Marcus's address, Carolyn."

Carolyn started to hold back, but this was too serious. She'd committed his address in Santa Rosa to memory. She pulled a piece of paper out of her purse and scribbled it down, handing it to Mary.

"Can you get us a DNA sample?" Hank asked. "If it doesn't match the San Diego samples, Marcus will be in the clear. Then we can all rest easier."

"A DNA sample," Carolyn said, her face muscles twitching. They didn't have enough to substantiate a request for an arrest warrant, or even to pick Marcus up for questioning. Hank was using her to feed his own fantasies. She didn't mind stepping to the line under reasonable conditions, but this wasn't one of them. "How in the hell am I going to do that?" she said, fuming. "You must not take your own premise seriously, Hank, if you want me to sleep with him to get a DNA sample. This is ridiculous. I can't believe you wasted my time."

Hank looked away in embarrassment. "There's other ways to get a person's DNA, Carolyn."

"Maybe I should leave so you two can talk privately," Mary said, half out of her chair.

"Stay where you are," Carolyn commanded. Turning to Hank, she said, "If you persist in trying to discredit Marcus, our friendship will be over."

Hank was somewhat taken aback, but he refused to back down. "You're a professional, Carolyn. Just cut me some slack and bring us a DNA sample."

"I'll think about it," she tossed over her shoulder, storming out of his office.

Kathleen dialed the number on the business card she'd found in Dean's golf bag, her frustrations escalating when a recording said the number was no longer in service. She tossed the phone to the floorboard of the rented Cadillac Escalade. "Dead ends, nothing but dead ends," she yelled, speeding on the 101 freeway toward the Monterey Peninsula Airport. Picking up the card and holding it in front of her as she drove, she noticed a San Diego address, fax number, and e-mail. Maybe she could still reach this person.

The company name was Premier Farm Equipment. This man must have known her husband well. Why else would Dean carry more than one of his cards? *Farm equipment,* she thought, baffled. It was just so odd. Even if the guy was a golfer, it was hard to picture her husband hanging around with a farm-equipment salesman. If all else failed, she'd have to go to San Diego and pay this man a visit.

Arriving at the airport, Kathleen passed several signs before she spotted the red and white letters of Jet USA. She made a sharp right into the driveway. Slamming on the breaks, she flung open the door, adjusted her jacket collar, and checked her blond wig in the mirror.

"Can I help you?" a professional-looking man in a white shirt and dark slacks asked, seeming to be more interested in her legs than in being helpful.

"I don't know," Kathleen said. "That all depends on what you have to offer? Are you a pilot?"

"That's what I do," he said, smiling. "Why don't you come in the office?" He raised his arm, directing her to go up the small flight of stairs.

Dean had not only tried to kill her, he had taken her self-esteem. Maybe if she acted like an attractive woman, she would be perceived as one. Most men didn't focus on a woman's face, as had just been proven by the pilot. At least she didn't have to worry about extra weight. She'd lost all interest in food. She walked past the man and slowly climbed the stairs, letting her hips sway. "What's your name?"

"Ralph Hayward," he said. "I'm fairly new here. They just trans-ferred me in from North Carolina. I'm sorry. I don't know all the cus-tomers. And you are . . . ?"

"Kathleen . . ." she said, stalling while she considered if she should use her real name or a phony one. "Sheppard," she continued, re-membering the name on the business cards. Using "Masters" at the golf course had only hurt her chances of finding her husband. It was time to go undercover and see if she could make some real progress. "My boss, Dean Masters, asked me to come down and get a printout of his recent flights. You know, he likes to watch the expenses."

"I know what you're talking about," Hayward said. "Luxury and convenience come with a price. Would you like something to drink?"

Looking at two jets outside the small window, Kathleen noticed the water dispenser. "Water," she said. "I can get it myself. You go ahead and get me that information. I have to be back at the office as soon as possible. I'm the one who holds the fort down, you know."

"Right." He went behind the small desk and tapped on the com-puter. Kathleen's back was turned. When she bent over to fill the cup, the typing stopped. The pilot was sufficiently distracted. The few attributes she still possessed were a pair of great legs and a nice ass. She could ask this guy for his wallet and he'd probably give it to her.

"Nice airplanes," she said. "Are those the ones my boss travels on?"

"Be with you in a minute," said Hayward, sending the document to the printer and then picking it up and walking over to stand next to her. "Looks as if Mr. Sheppard takes the smaller jet, like the one over there on the left. He must travel alone or in smaller groups."

She turned around and snatched the papers out of his hand, seeing the name Matthew Sheppard on the header. What kind of farm-equipment salesman flew around on a private jet? Multiple trips were detailed to Las Vegas, New York, Santa Barbara, San Francisco, and San Diego. "Got you," she said, just loud enough to be heard.

"Excuse me? Is there a problem?"

Collecting her composure, Kathleen folded the report in half. The last thing she wanted was for Dean to find out she was on to him. Several important elements of her husband's existence were at Hayward's fingertips. "Nothing, just that this report you gave me is for my husband, not Dean Masters. I might as well take his, too, since you've already printed it. You can save a stamp that way."

"Oh, so sorry," said Hayward. "Sure. No problem. You know, I have to work a lot of hours and sometimes I have trouble focusing. Give me a minute and I'll have the other one for you."

"And you say you're a pilot?" Kathleen teased, trying to cover her excitement at getting just the information she wanted. She was supposed to be home recuperating. But lying around the house feeling sorry for herself would accomplish nothing. She'd lain around enough in the hospital. Going after Dean kept her mind off the pain. What remained she controlled with Percodan.

"Well, I'm focused when I'm in the air. So you need Masters, too?"

"Please," Kathleen told him, leaning on the edge of his desk as she peered down at the computer screen. His eyes followed her finger as she pressed the Enter key. Reaching up behind his head she stroked his hair. "You've done good, Ralph." Grabbing the additional pages, she walked out the door and down the steps.

Once inside the Cadillac, she hit the automatic door locks, backing up and speeding a mile down the street before she pulled off and parked to look at the paperwork. On the first page of the Dean account, the payment column jumped out at her. It read, "Payment by Check KDM Real Property."

This was Kathleen's corporation!

Dean had been paying for this absurd extravagance with her money.

She looked at the total on the third page and gasped. The amount for the year read $623,497! Her husband was not only a murderer, he was a thief.

She retrieved her cell phone from the floorboard and called her business manager. "I'm sorry, Mr. Cohen isn't in the office right now."

"I want his cell phone number," she demanded. "This is Kathleen Masters."

"Okay, Ms. Masters," the woman said. "Can you hold on for a minute?"

After a few seconds, she came back to the phone. "He just walked in. I'll transfer you to him now."

"Alec Cohen here."

"Good," Kathleen said. "I'm coming to see you. I need an explanation of why you were paying Jet USA for my husband's traveling expenses. This is unacceptable. What were you thinking?"

"You sent me a letter approving my disbursement of those funds," Cohen told her. "Don't you remember?"

"No, I don't," she said, furious. "Dean hustled me. How many more of his expenses are you paying?"

"We should talk about this in person, Kathleen," Cohen said. "Take some deep breaths, and your mind will clear. I'm sure we'll work through this problem. You've been through a terrible ordeal."

"My mind is clear, very clear," Kathleen shouted. "Are you getting a kickback from Dean?"

"There must be some kind of misunderstanding. Everything's going to be fine. You still have plenty of money in your accounts. When will you be here?"

"A 'misunderstanding' is an understatement. You've paid out over six hundred thousand dollars to Jet USA. God knows how much more of my money you've squandered. My husband is gone, Alec. He tried to kill me, and you're paying his bills."

"I'm sure there's a logical explanation for all of this," Cohen said, his voice cracking. "We'll figure this out when you come in. Please try not to be hysterical when you show up at my office. You'll upset my employees and clients."

Kathleen ended the call without saying good-bye. Her husband had been draining her dry and all Alec was concerned about were his employees and clients. She placed her hand over her stomach, resting her head on the steering wheel, fighting against the pain. She fumbled with the clasp to her purse, found the bottle of Percodan, and tossed the pills into her mouth, washing them down with the Coke she'd been drinking. Dean might have stolen millions from her. What did Alec mean when he said there was still money left in the accounts? How much money? She'd broken her back selling real estate for years while Dean was jetting around the country on her dime. She felt like smashing her fist through the windshield, but she had enough scars already.

How could she have been so stupid, allowing this hideous man to snake his way into her life?

Kathleen started the car, but her body was shaking so much that it was impossible to drive. Her attention returned to the reports she'd left lying side by side on the center console. She wasn't sure if her eyes were deceiving her. The papers were very similar. Both Dean Masters and Matthew Sheppard had made trips to San Francisco, New York, Santa Barbara, and San Diego on numerous occasions. The only difference was where the trips had departed and who'd paid the bills.

Main Street Corporation was the payee on the Matthew Sheppard bill. Kathleen wondered if she could trace it through the Department of Corporations. How many other women was Dean stealing from? Suddenly everything slammed together like a freight train.

Dean was Matthew Sheppard!

Since Brian Irving had never even called her back, she knew it was up to her to stop Dean. She knew he wouldn't give up the luxury and status of flying on his private jet, particularly since he probably thought she was still picking up the tab. Now she understood why he'd tried to kill her. He couldn't allow her to file for a divorce, knowing the truth would surface. As soon as Dean found out she'd been asking questions, which he would eventually, he would come back to finish what he'd started. The only way she could keep that from happening was to get to him first.

It was time to buy a gun.

CHAPTER 33

Thursday, October 19—3:45 P.M.

Marcus steered his dark green Range Rover to the Ventura branch of the Bank of America. Grabbing his briefcase from the passenger seat, he went inside. "I need to get into my safety deposit box," he said, smiling at the girl at the counter.

"How are you, Mr. Wright?" Tammy Deerfield said, her eyes lighting up as she handed him a form to sign. "I'll take you in now." She took him into the vault, located his box on the row next to the bottom, and inserted her key into one of the two locks. Their heads were almost touching as Marcus bent over to put his key in the other.

"You smell great," he said, receiving a shy smile in return. He carried the metal box to one of the private rooms and closed the door. Lifting the lid, he removed the neatly organized stacks of bills and placed them on top of the counter, exposing multiple CDs that were labeled with codes and dates. Underneath was a black steel container with a combination lock. Sorting through it until he found the CDs he was seeking, he then deposited them in his briefcase and locked it. Before closing the safety deposit box, he took a stack of hundreds and slipped the bills into his jacket pocket. Finished with his business, he left the room and handed the box back to the clerk. "How is it going with your boyfriend?"

"Not too good, we broke up last weekend," Tammy told him.

Marcus followed her out of the vault. "I'm sure there's dozens of guys looking for a pretty girl like you."

"I'm not so sure about that," she replied, downcast. "I'm just disappointed, you know. I thought everything was going so good."

"It's hard to know people these days," Marcus said, slipping his key back into his pocket and walking out of the secured area into the lobby of the bank.

"Marcus Wright," a male voice called out.

Hank Sawyer was sitting in a chair, a toothpick sticking out of his mouth. Surprised to see the detective, Marcus said, "What brings you here? Opening a new account?"

"I'm a public servant," Hank said, pushing himself to his feet. "We don't make that much money. Anyhow, I like to stick to one account. Keeps things simple."

"Simple is good," Marcus said. "Did you catch Holden?"

"No, he's still on the loose," Hank told him, a stern look on his face. "Right now, I'm more concerned about you than Holden."

"What does that mean?" Marcus said, watching as the detective slid his hand inside his jacket. *He must be wearing a shoulder holster,* he thought. *Is he reaching for his gun? And how did he know I would be at the bank? He must be following me.* Cop or not, Hank's infatuation with Carolyn could have reached an irrational state, Marcus figured. Determined to protect the contents of his briefcase, he pressed an autodial button on his cell phone that was programmed to alert his personal security service.

Hank moved toward him. "Mr. Wright, we have preliminary information that tells me that you may be dangerous."

"Incredible," Marcus said, shaking his head in dismay. "Have you lost your mind, Hank? Does Carolyn know that you're following me around and harassing me?"

Hank spit the toothpick clenched between his teeth out into a trash can. "She knows what I know."

Tammy was pretending to do work at her desk, but it was obvious that she was listening more than working. "If you're going to cause a scene," Marcus told him, glancing over at the teller, "we should go outside."

Not waiting for Hank, Marcus strode toward the door. When he stepped outside into the sunlight, he saw the black Suburban already parked at the curb. "I'm not sure what's going on inside that thick head of yours," he told the detective as the two burly men in dark suits stood by sullenly, waiting for his signal, "but you don't have any idea who you're dealing with."

"You're right." Hank put on his mirrored sunglasses. "That's going to change, though. Watch your back, Wright. I'll be right behind you."

"Then you might as well join me for lunch," Marcus told him, hoping to turn things around.

"No thanks," Hank said. "I don't eat with suspects."

"Now I'm a suspect?" Marcus exploded. "What am I suspected of doing, stealing your girlfriend? Forget lunch. We probably wouldn't enjoy each other's company."

"What makes you think I'm interested in living the high life?" Hank asked. "I uphold the law, and to some people that's mighty important. We don't have anything in common. In my mind, that's a positive, not a negative."

"You don't have Carolyn," Marcus said, getting in the detective's face. "And if I have anything to do with it, you never will. Back off, Hank. You're out of line here. What will your supervisors think if they find out you're using your badge for personal reasons?"

The detective's expression told it all. His face became red, and his hand clenched into a ball. "I won't let you hurt her."

"Who says I'm going to hurt her?" Marcus said, fed up. "I don't know who's feeding you this bullshit about me being dangerous, or if you're just manufacturing it. Find the guy who assaulted Carolyn and shot her son." He continued toward his car.

"Not so fast," Hank said, latching onto his arm. The two large men rushed up and intervened, breaking his grip and pushing him aside. Hank kept his balance and flipped open his jacket to pull out his gun. A moment later, he came to his senses and placed it back in the shoulder holster.

"Don't do anything stupid," Marcus told him. "Shoot me, and you'll be the one who goes to prison. If you want to arrest me for a crime, then handcuff me and read me my rights." He held his wrists in front of him. "Go ahead." When Hank didn't respond, he smirked. "That's what I thought. Leave me alone, all right? I'd hate to see something happen to you, mainly because it would break Carolyn's heart. Unlike you, I really care about her."

"Are you threatening me, asshole?" Hank barked. "I'm a police officer. I can do anything I damn well please."

Marcus surged forward into his face. "I've never been afraid of anyone, and I'm not going to change now. Do whatever you have to do. Talk to my friends, follow me around. I don't break the law, and I don't run around accusing innocent people."

He proceeded to his car and opened the door, driving off and leaving Hank standing on the curb.

The detective returned to the bank, approached Tammy Deerfield, and flashed his badge. "I see you know Marcus Wright?"

The girl looked around. "Yes," she said. "He's a nice man. Did he do something wrong?"

"What would make you think he did something wrong?" Hank said, leaning against the counter.

"I heard you arguing with him," she told him. "I didn't know you were a police officer."

Hank reached into his pocket and pulled out a small evidence packet containing the safety deposit key Carolyn had removed from Holden's house. "Does this look like one of your safety deposit keys?"

Tammy stared at the key, then looked up. "I can't really tell," she said. "It looks like all the other safety deposit keys I've ever seen. You really can't tell one from the other. There's no box number on it."

"Then how do you find it?"

"We follow a specific procedure," she explained. "The customer comes in, fills out a form with his name and box number, then we verify his signature and the teller initials it before we take him into the vault. It takes two keys to open the box. No one else is allowed to enter the box without a court order unless the customer has left us with specific instructions in case of his death. Without the customer's key, we can't even open the box." When he just stared at her, she continued, "Is there anything else I can help you with?"

"No," Hank said. "I think you've told me everything." He would have to get a court order, and Marcus could have ten safety deposit boxes scattered throughout Los Angeles. It was days like this that he wished he'd never gone into police work.

*   *   *

Back in her office, Carolyn booted her computer and typed up the interview she'd taken this morning. There were twelve victims, and since they were all young boys, she'd scheduled the appointments at their homes. Doing it this way could take almost triple the time, but she decided the victims had already spent enough time away from their homes during the trial. Sometimes the legal process could do more damage than the crime. The boys needed to forget what had happened to them, not memorize every detail and suffer the embarrassment of having to discuss it repeatedly with strangers.

After a half hour she realized that all she was doing was staring at her monitor. How could she think, after what she'd heard from Mary and Hank? She had slept with Marcus only a few days ago, even told him that she loved him. Even if he wasn't involved in anything, why had she moved so fast? She'd only known him a short time. Was it because of what had happened with Holden? Most women wouldn't have wanted to be with any man after such a terrifying experience. But her son had also been shot, and Carolyn had needed to be comforted.

Although the photograph of Matthew Sheppard bore a shocking resemblance to Marcus, she couldn't imagine him wearing a cowboy hat. It wasn't his style. If he was the man in the picture, he would be a chameleon, changing his looks and personality to whatever suited his needs. For all she knew, the cars and the expensive home in Santa Rosa might not even belong to him.

The house! Carolyn remembered. She called the escrow officer. "The person who purchased the home, Ms. Sullivan," a woman named Sue Atwater told her, "left strict instructions that you not be informed of their identity."

"I'm sorry, Sue," Carolyn told her, "but this isn't a reality TV show. Why would a corporation purchase my home, pay off the existing mortgage, and give it back to me. I don't want the money, okay? Tell them the deal is off."

"You can't do that," the woman said, agitated. "All the paperwork has already been signed and the deed sent off to be recorded. This was a very complicated deal, Ms. Sullivan. Everyone involved worked long hours to put it together this fast. If you'd like, I can mail you your check. It's for $432,000. If I were you, I'd be ecstatic. Someone loves you very much."

Carolyn gulped and swallowed. She could send both the kids to college, make some badly needed repairs on the house, replace the appliances, buy *real* flowers, maybe even hire a gardener after John left for college. No, she thought, a gardener was too extravagant. But she would have a savings account for the first time since her divorce. "Who signed off on all of this?"

"The person who holds your power of attorney," Atwater advised. "Don't you know who that is, Ms. Sullivan? We verified the papers were legitimate with your attorney."

Suddenly Carolyn knew. "His name was Neil Sullivan, right?"

"Well, since you already know . . ."

She thanked the woman, hung up, and immediately called her brother. "You stinkpot," she said when he answered. "I just got off the phone with the escrow company. I love you more than life itself, but I can't let you give me almost half a million dollars. Jesus Christ, Neil, what were you thinking?"

"I knew that old biddy at the escrow office couldn't keep her mouth shut," Neil said, laughing. "It doesn't matter. I was going to tell you anyway. You think I was going to let Marcus take credit for it? No way, man, not when I can get home-cooked meals out of you. Not all the time, of course. I never realized that you can really cook."

"Neil . . ."

"I'm doing fabulous, Carolyn," he said, bursting with enthusiasm. "Everything I did while the kids were here has sold, and for huge amounts, way over my normal prices. If you'd read the paper, you might know about it. Four galleries in New York have asked to give me a show. I've got several million in paintings in my storage shed. I have more money than I could spend in three lifetimes in my bank and investment accounts. You have no idea how much I have because I've been hoarding it."

"I still can't . . ."

"Listen to me," Neil continued. "I've been living in this controlled environment for half my life. I'm free, don't you see? Messy rooms, clutter, even dirt doesn't bother me. You and the kids did this for me. I see so much more *life* everywhere now. I don't have to date only the models who pose for me. I can go out in the world now. Maybe I'll find a nice girl, someone I can marry. I'm even thinking about having kids for the first time. I can travel. What you've given me is priceless."

"What if it doesn't last?" Carolyn asked. "It might be a fluke, sweetie. If you get stressed out—"

"No," her brother told her. "I've already seen my psychiatrist. It's a breakthrough. Once you go through that wall, you've made it. You don't think I've been under stress after the things that happened to you and the kids." His voice became firm. "You're taking that money, Carolyn. Don't take away my joy. I would have helped you before if you hadn't been so hardheaded. That's what families do, they help each other. Are we square now? Promise me you're not going to mess this up."

Carolyn's breath caught in her throat. She had fought hard to maintain her independence, to never lean on anyone. But she could sense how much this meant to her brother. "I promise," she told him. "You're the greatest brother in the world."

"Now that," Neil said, "that's exactly what I wanted to hear. Are you still bringing the kids over tonight? Rebecca has real talent. We may have another artist in the family. Isn't that exciting?"

"Yes," she said, her thoughts turning back to Marcus. "We'll talk more tonight."

Carolyn went to the bathroom, then returned to her desk. There was no proof as yet that Matthew Sheppard had murdered his wife. Maybe the man had moved away from San Diego after Lisa disappeared, developing a new identity because he feared becoming the subject of a police investigation. People who weren't killers still had skeletons in their closet. An unknown assailant could have kidnapped Lisa while she was out somewhere and killed her. But then, why would her husband tell Detective Fisher that she'd gone to St. Louis to live with her grandmother? Since the woman was dead as well, they couldn't confirm that Lisa hadn't spent time in St. Louis before she moved on with her life.

No matter how she spun it, Matthew Sheppard was the most likely suspect in the death of his wife.

Carolyn needed to talk to someone. She thought of Veronica, but her friend had enough problems on her hands. She hadn't had a chance to ask Hank if he knew anything about the death of Lester McAllen. Camarillo was out of his jurisdiction, but he could make some inquiries for her with the sheriff's department. What she was interested in were the ballistics reports, so they could determine if the same gun had been used in both crimes.

She knew the only person she could lean on for objective advice was Brad. It took only a few steps before she entered his office. "I need to talk to you about something," she said, closing the door. "You'll need to keep it off the record. You got a few minutes?"

"Off the record, huh?" he said, loosening his tie. "I've got all the time in the world for that kind of talk."

"Never mind," Carolyn said, turning to leave. "This was a bad idea."

"Get back here," Brad said, smiling. "You can't hold a carrot over my head, then walk away. You know curiosity is my only weakness."

"Right," Carolyn said. "You have so many weaknesses, it would take a year to remember them all."

"Come on, don't be mean to me. I'll spend all day trying to figure it out." He became serious. "Sit down, Carolyn. I guess you're not in a joking mood after what happened to John. How is he?"

"He's doing fine," she told him.

"Well, at least we put the insanity issue to rest on Carter," he said. "The prelim is scheduled for next week. You said in your report that she's claiming some guy murdered her girlfriend. Think there's any truth to that?"

"She seemed sincere," Carolyn told him. "But then again, Helen is a highly proficient liar. I assume she told the same story to the police and they didn't buy it. Maybe more will come to light at the prelim."

"What did you want to talk about?"

"Marcus," she said, taking a seat in a chair in front of his desk.

"Humph," Brad said, walking around and perching on the edge of his desk. "What's going on?"

"You know the San Diego woman who was buried in the Alessandro Lagoon? We thought Holden killed her, but his DNA doesn't match. Then the PD got a picture of the husband of Lisa Sheppard, who disappeared about the time his wife was murdered. Hank thinks the photo of Matthew Sheppard looks like Marcus, the man I've been seeing."

"What? Wait a second," Brad said, throwing his hands in the air. "This Marcus guy is a suspect in a homicide? I knew your judgment in men was no good. Next time you need a guy, let me know, and I'll find one for you."

Couldn't he be serious for more than five minutes? "I guess you must be right, Brad," Carolyn said, "I dated you, didn't I? We both know that was a mistake."

"You made your point, okay? The world is coming to an end, and I'm an insensitive oaf for not believing you. Everything's going to work out. You're a strong woman. So, you hit a bump in the road."

"More like a land mine," Carolyn grumbled.

"What happened to you and John was terrible," Brad went on. "Shit happens. Have you forgotten what I went through last year? That maniac Raphael Moreno attacked me. The little shit broke my back. I could have been paralyzed for life. You warned me not to come down hard on him, but I refused to listen. I didn't let it bring me down, though. My back healed, and I went on with my life. The good news is that you and John are all right." He paused, fiddling with his right ear as he thought. "As to your boyfriend, don't jump the gun. See how things play out. It may not amount to anything. Until you know for sure, there's no reason to panic."

"There's more that I haven't told you," Carolyn said with a sharp intake of oxygen. "A day after I met Marcus, Lisa Sheppard's remains showed up in the lagoon. When Marcus and I had lunch on Saturday, Tracy Anderson's husband came up to me in the restaurant, enraged over Holden's release. He thought I had something to do with it. I was upset, so I started running off at the mouth about Holden."

Now she had his full attention. "What exactly did you tell him?"

"Practically everything." She nervously scratched her arm. "I told him Holden buried Tracy Anderson in the lagoon. Don't you see? What if Hank is right, and Marcus really is Matthew Sheppard? He could have used the information I gave him to dispose of his wife's body so it looked like Holden killed her. I feel terrible, Brad. I know better than to discuss my work. The case was ten years old, though, and I didn't think it mattered."

"You only screwed up if Hank's assumptions are accurate." Brad told her, returning to the other side of his desk and picking up the phone. "What does he have on your boyfriend outside of the physical similarities?"

"Who are you calling?"

"Hank. I want to find out what else he knows."

"Please don't," Carolyn said, her brows furrowing. "I didn't ask you to get involved. I only asked you to listen because you're my friend. Hank and I have enough problems getting along without you stirring everything up."

"Whatever." Brad put the phone back in the cradle. "Here's what I suggest. Don't let Marcus know that you suspect anything. Ask leading questions. You're the best at this stuff. Listen, and watch his reactions. If he isn't telling the truth, you'll be able to tell. Trick him, catch him in a lie. I don't know . . . just do what you do."

"Okay," Carolyn said, satisfied with his advice.

Brad continued, "Hank is probably being overprotective with his favorite probation officer. That doesn't mean that you shouldn't be careful. Cut and run if you get any bad feelings from this guy. Rely on your instincts. They've always paid off for you in the past."

"Thanks, Brad." She stood and started to leave when he walked over and pulled her into his arms. Looking up at him, she said, "Sometimes I feel sad that things didn't work out between us. I'll always care about you, Brad. You know that, don't you?"

"If you need me, you know where to find me."

It was an awkward moment. Carolyn pulled away and headed toward the door. He was a good man, except in certain areas. In time he might set aside the fast cars, young girls, and other bad habits he'd acquired. It was hard to imagine him any other way, though. Carolyn kept her head down as she made her way back to her desk. If what they said about Marcus was true, Brad would seem like a choir boy.

Mary was waiting for Carolyn inside her cubicle. "I need to go over the procedure for collecting evidence with you," she said, holding up a paper sack.

"I know how to collect evidence," Carolyn told her, annoyed that Mary was pressuring her. "I started out in supervision."

"Urine samples aren't the same. And I doubt if you're going to be able to control the situation like you do with a probationer."

"I haven't agreed to do this."

"Don't you want to be prepared if you do?"

In answer, Carolyn directed her friend to an interview room. The two women took seats at the small table. Once Mary had given her several evidence bags and rubber gloves, she told Carolyn to place her hands on the table. Brandishing a small pair of scissors, the detective clipped a chunk out of the nail on Carolyn's right thumb.

"Why did you do that?" Carolyn exclaimed, jerking her hand back. "Do you want *my* DNA now?"

"No," Mary said, "what we need is Marcus's blood. I wanted to make certain you wouldn't have a problem scratching him."

Carolyn stared at the jagged nail. "I could have just stabbed him with my toenails. I haven't gotten around to trimming them lately."

Mary did a double-take. "Gross," she said. "And you've been having an affair with this guy?"

"You mean the murderer?" she said bitterly. "He likes to have sex in the dark." She leaned forward. "Do you have any idea what it's like to have a maniac try to rape you and then shoot your son? My beauty needs haven't been a high priority these days. Now what am I going to do after I claw Marcus for you?"

"You're going to cut off the rest of the nail and put it in an evidence bag. If it doesn't look like enough blood is on your nail, then you need to collect a hair sample. Don't use a brush. What we need is a hair with a root. That way, we can get the DNA results back overnight."

Carolyn's mouth fell open. "You want me to yank hair out of his head?"

"Just a few strands. You can act like it got snagged. Wear something with a zipper—jeans or a jacket. I don't want you to actually snag it. I want you to pull it when he isn't looking."

Carolyn asked which detective had investigated the Grace Findley homicide.

"Duffy Crenshaw. The case hasn't even got past the prelim. What do you have to do with it?"

"The DA charged Helen Carter with violating a restraining order. I guess they thought she was going to plead insanity, so they wanted me to talk to her. She swears she's innocent."

"Don't they all. You've got enough problems, Carolyn. Why waste your time with scum like Carter? I hear she's got a record a mile long and has been working the system since she was a teenager. The case has some holes in it because Carter had previously lived with the victim on the premises. The DA's office wouldn't have filed, though, if they didn't think they could bring in a conviction."

Carolyn knew Duffy Crenshaw. A man only a few months away from retirement, he might not have given the case the attention it deserved. Something Helen Carter had said kept darting around inside her head. "You asked me to do you a favor regarding Marcus," she said. "Now I want you to do something for me. Send over everything you've got on the Findley homicide. Don't say anything to Hank or Duffy. I just want to check a few things out."

"No problem," Mary told her. "I'll call Records now. The file should be on your computer by the time you get back to your desk."

CHAPTER 34

Thursday, October 19—6:05 P.M.

She needed a gun, and this looked like the place to buy one.
Kathleen had spoken to a few private detectives, deciding they couldn't find their way out of a paper bag, let alone track down a man as deceptive and shrewd as her husband. What she really needed was an assassin, but she didn't have the necessary contacts. Her home was a horror chamber to her now, so she dumped the Darvocet her doctor had prescribed in her purse and took off to San Diego. The Percodan was gone, and she couldn't get it refilled. She was experiencing a few withdrawal symptoms, so she doubled up on the Darvocet.

Kathleen exited the 101 freeway to avoid rush-hour traffic, getting lost and ending up in a seedy area of Oxnard, a city a few miles from Ventura. California law prohibited her from walking in and buying a handgun off the shelf. A clerk at the first gun shop she'd visited had given her an application to fill out and told her to come back in a few weeks for gun training. What the hell did she need gun training for? She'd been married to a Dupont. His ancestors had made their fortune in munitions and gunpowder. Not only was George a member of the NRA, he had an extensive gun collection and had insisted that his wife become proficient in the use of firearms. Once the instructor at the pistol range began calling Kathleen "Deadeye," George got jealous and stopped taking her with him.

Kathleen found another store and attempted to bribe the owner.

Suspecting she might be an undercover cop, he asked her to leave. Since her intent was to shoot her husband, she decided gun control had its merits.

Nothing was going to stop her, though.

Once she made a decision to do something, Kathleen never backed down. As a child, she'd suffered from acute asthma. Her brother had run track, and she'd sat in the bleachers and watched him, clinging to her inhaler and wishing she could be normal. By the time she was thirteen, without her mother's knowledge, she started running laps after school on the track at the junior college behind her house. Her asthma improved considerably, and before she knew it, she was running upwards of an hour without stopping.

She went on to run high school track, winning the league championship in the half mile. Her trophies were still lined up on a shelf in her home in Carmel. When she became overwhelmed with the frustrations of the real estate business, she would go look at the trophies and remind herself what she'd overcome to obtain them.

Kathleen stopped to get gas, waiting at the pump for the attendant. "Isn't anyone going to help me?" she yelled out the window to a man with a Mobil Oil emblem on his shirt.

He pointed to a sign. "Self-service, lady."

She hadn't pumped gas in years. At least the Cadillac Escalade she'd rented while her Mercedes was being repaired had a large fuel tank. She liked the feeling of sitting high off the ground, looking down at the smaller cars and knowing she was protected inside the large mass of steel. A vehicle large enough to carry a body might also come in handy.

Grappling with the hose, she finally managed to get the nozzle into the gas tank, and then broke off her fingernail trying to hold down the lever.

Oxnard had originally been a farming community and had fields where migrant workers labored all day in the hot sun. The pungent odor of insecticide and fertilizer brushed past her nostrils. The wind whipped through her hair, and with her free hand, she held the blond wig in place. She couldn't wear the strap inside the wig as she still suffered from headaches as a result of her head injury. Dean had not only disfigured her, he'd seriously impeded her chances of re-establishing her lucrative career as a Realtor. People who purchased multimillion-dollar estates didn't want to be reminded that a locale of exquisite natural beauty such as Carmel could be infiltrated by violent criminals.

After filling the gas tank, Kathleen used the station's bathroom to wash the smell of gasoline off her hands. If it was so hard to get a handgun, she thought, why did all the criminals have them? Ah, she realized, they obviously stole them, and they must steal them from upstanding citizens who'd purchased the guns for their own protection. How idiotic. The crooks didn't have to fill out paperwork, go for gun training, or foot the bill. They just burgled someone's home and walked off with a legally registered handgun. If the owners caused them any trouble, they could shoot them with their own guns. The good thing about stealing a gun from a regular person was it had probably never been used in the commission of a crime.

Kathleen's earlier regard for gun control disappeared.

The sun was setting, and a faint glow of orange and blue stretched across the horizon. Several blocks down, she saw a group of Hispanic males who appeared to be baby gang-bangers. They were wearing black beanies pulled down to their eyebrows, baggy pants, and long T-shirts. Rolling down the passenger window of the Cadillac, she gestured for one of them to come over. His pants were so low, he walked like a toddler with a full load in his diaper. "Do you know where I can buy a handgun?"

"Nice ride, lady," the boy said, looking no older than fourteen. He turned around and yelled to one of his friends, "Look what we got here, José. A brand-new red Caddy. Bet she got a TV and DVD player in this thing."

José sneered. "She ain't letting you watch it, Pablo."

"I really need some help," Kathleen said, digging into her wallet and pulling out a wad of hundred-dollar bills. "Are you sure you don't know anyone who has a gun? Can't you steal one from your older brother, maybe your father?"

"We got guns, man," Pablo said, posturing. "My bro and my father are in prison. I got my homeboys. They my family now. How much money you got?"

"Five hundred," Kathleen said. "Bring me the gun and it'll be yours."

"*Nada,*" the boy said, rubbing his fingers together. "No *dinero,* no gun."

"How long will it take you to get it?"

He extended his hand. "Give me the money and you'll find out."

Sure, Kathleen thought, not about to let some pint-sized street punk scam her. She pointed at an even smaller boy. "You," she said, "get in the car. You stay with me until your buddy gets my gun."

The boy's eyes widened, and he took several steps backward, looking around as if he didn't know what was going on. "It's cool, Berto," Pablo told him. "You're just taking a ride in the nice lady's fancy car." He patted his friend on the back, then made eye contact with Kathleen. "You givin' me the cash or what?"

"Not until he gets into the car," she insisted. As soon as the boy opened the door and slid into the seat, she hit the button for the automatic locks. "Here." She handed the money to Pablo through the open window.

"Take a drive. Cops see you here, and they think something's going down." The money disappeared into the pocket of Pablo's jeans. "Be back here in thirty minutes," he said, walking away with a grin on his face and a bounce in his step.

"How old are you?" Kathleen asked Berto.

"Eighteen," he said in a raspy voice.

"Yeah, you're eighteen all right," she said. "More like thirteen or fourteen. What are you doing hanging out on the street with these wannabe thugs? Why don't you make something of your life?"

Berto gave her a blank look. He coughed several times, and then wiped his runny nose with the back of his hand.

"Do you have a cold, or are you snorting drugs?"

"Cold," he answered.

Great, Kathleen thought, handing him a tissue from her purse. All she needed was a germ-laden kid in her car. "Did you drop out of school?"

"I liked school, but I got jumped last year. I was hurt pretty bad, so I stopped going."

"Who jumped you?"

"Uh . . . Pablo and José."

"Well, that sounds brilliant, Berto," Kathleen said. "These guys beat you up, so you decide to throw your future away and start hanging out with them. Good move. The way you're going, you might not live to turn fifteen."

A look of sadness appeared in his eyes. "You don't understand."

"I understand more than you think," she told him, glancing at her watch. After making three passes, she saw Pablo leaning against the wall with his hands behind his back. As soon as she pulled to the curb, he walked over and handed her a brown paper bag. She looked inside and saw an older-model revolver, along with a box of bullets. "Does this thing work?"

"What you think?" Pablo said. "My uncle popped it just last week."

Kathleen arched an eyebrow. "He didn't kill someone, I hope?"

"Nah," Pablo said. "He gets drunk and shoots at tin cans."

Berto reached for the door handle to get out. Kathleen threw her hand over his chest, holding him in place. "I'm an undercover police officer," she said to Pablo. "I'm not going to arrest you and your little friends for illegally selling firearms if you swear you won't ever hurt Berto again. Don't even talk to him, okay? If I hear you're harassing him in anyway whatsoever, I'll haul both your asses to jail. Am I making myself clear? Now give me my five hundred dollars back."

"Bitch," Pablo said, sprinting off down the street.

"What are you going to do to me?" Berto said, frightened.

"Take you home to your momma, where you belong," Kathleen told him. "You do have a mother, don't you?"

"Yeah."

Kathleen's fingers closed on the cold steel of the revolver in her lap. A feeling of satisfaction filled her. Maybe if she did something right, it would make up for what she intended to do to Dean when she found him. In her eyes, though, she had every right to exact revenge, particularly since the police weren't going to help her. "Where do you live, Berto?"

He mumbled, "About ten blocks from here. Go straight, and I'll tell you where to turn."

She dialed Alec Cohen. "Tell him I won't be coming," she told his assistant. "I'm taking care of everything on my own."

"Just a second," the woman said. "I can connect you to Mr. Cohen right now."

"I don't have any desire to talk to him. Just give him a message. Tell him he's fired. As of this moment, he's no longer authorized to handle my business affairs. I'll send someone over to pick up my records later."

"Hang on," the woman said, "I'm sure he wants to speak to you."

"He can talk to my lawyer," Kathleen said, flipping the phone closed. Before she placed it back in her purse, she stared at the Verizon insignia imprinted on the cover. An idea came to her. She dialed 611 and got the company's operator. "My name is Kathleen Masters," she said. "My husband wants to reactivate his number."

"You can't reactivate a number. Is your husband there?"

"Yes, but he's driving."

"Did he put the phone on vacation?"

"Yes," Kathleen said, taking a wild guess. She remembered doing this when she and Dean had gone to Europe the year before.

"Give me his phone number and the last four digits of his social security number," the man said. "Let me pull up your account." After she gave him the information, the line went silent for a minute. "You're in luck. The ninety days hasn't expired. But I have to get authorization from Mr. Masters before we can continue."

Kathleen handed the phone to Berto and whispered, "Just listen and say yes to everything they ask you."

Berto said, "Yes" a few times, then passed the phone back to her. "Can you set up the call-forwarding feature so that my husband can get his calls at this number? We just got back from vacation, and he doesn't have his phone with him."

"Not a problem. I'll take care of that now."

"Thank you," Kathleen said, satisfied that she'd beat the system not only once today, but twice.

"This is where I live," Berto said, pointing at a run-down apartment building.

"I'm going in with you," she said, grabbing her purse as they both got out of the car. "I have a gift for you and your mother."

They went up the stairs and entered an apartment not much

larger than Kathleen's walk-in closet. Immediately she felt claustrophobic. The drapes were drawn, the lights dim, and an odd assortment of furniture was crammed into the small room. Crosses and religious pictures covered the walls. Spicy cooking smells drifted out from the kitchen. A tiny woman with a weather-worn face appeared, startled by the tall stranger with the blond hair. "This is my mother," Berto said, dropping his head.

"I'm with the county youth intervention program," Kathleen lied. "I'm sorry, I didn't get your name."

"Rosaria Gonzales," the woman answered with a thick Spanish accent. "Is my son in trouble?"

"Actually, no," she said, smiling at Berto. "We have a special award that we give out for promising young men. Your son has won a thousand dollars to be applied to after-school private tutoring."

"Holy mother of God," the small woman said, making the sign of the cross. Rushing over to Berto, she hugged him and kissed his cheek.

Dean wasn't aware of it, but Kathleen had donated money to needy families for years. She didn't trust traditional charities, as she believed the majority of what they collected went to pay inflated salaries to administrators and fund-raisers. She'd connected with a social worker years before, when she was married to George, and the woman had continued to supply her with the names of families like Berto's. Unlike most of her wealthy friends, who only donated money to charities so they could attend elaborate parties and wear their latest designer evening gowns, Kathleen visited the families she helped on a regular basis, attempting to tailor her financial contributions to their specific needs. She didn't tell anyone, because they had no reason to know.

Kathleen sat down on the sofa and removed her wallet, counting out ten one-hundred-dollar bills. "There are conditions, Mrs. Gonzales. Berto must attend school every day. As soon as school is out, he must come straight home and begin his work with the tutor. I'm sure the school can provide you with the names of people who do that type of thing." She stopped and looked hard at the boy. "If he's found hanging around on the street or associating with Pablo or José, the boys I found him with today, call me immediately at this number."

She jotted her cell phone number on the edge of a newspaper. The money might end up going toward the family's living expenses, but either way, she had helped.

She glanced over at Berto, his youthful face in a state of bewilderment. "You have an opportunity now," she told him, reaching up and removing the wig. "If you don't do what I say, you could end up looking like me. I was also stabbed in the stomach. A bullet can do far more damage."

Repositioning the wig back on her head, Kathleen stepped through the doorway and left. She'd helped these people out of the goodness of her heart. But there had also been another reason. She wanted to make certain that if the police ever traced the gun, at least Berto might keep his mouth shut about the woman in the red Cadillac.

CHAPTER 35

Thursday, October 19—7:12 P.M.

Carolyn waited until John and Rebecca left the room before she embraced her brother, clad in his customary white shirt and black jeans, and thanking him again for what he'd done. She didn't want to spoil Neil's happiness, but she'd decided that she simply could not accept such a large sum of money. Once things settled down, she would refinance the house and insist on paying him back. If he wished, though, she would let him contribute to John and Rebecca's education.

"Instead of working with Rebecca on her painting," she told him now, leaning against the granite counter in his kitchen, "why don't you take the kids out for dinner and a movie?"

"Sure," Neil said. "Don't they have school tomorrow, though?"

Carolyn smiled. "Don't tell me you're worried about them getting to bed on time? They're Sullivans, remember? Who sleeps in this family outside of Mother?" She noticed the morning paper strewn haphazardly across the table. In the past, her brother would have read it and folded every page precisely. Still, she couldn't be sure that Neil's obsessive-compulsive behavior had been cured. It might well surface again somewhere in the future.

"What are you going to do?" Neil asked. "You could go with us."

"Marcus is coming over."

"I thought he had to work."

"He was able to get away after all." Carolyn had received a phone call from Marcus just before she'd left her office. She removed a glass from the cabinet, turning her back so her brother couldn't see the concern on her face. She glanced down at her jagged fingernail, wishing she could just tell Marcus the truth. Removing a can of Diet Coke from the refrigerator, she poured it into the glass while Neil went to the other room to plan his outing with John and Rebecca.

She and the children had camped out at Neil's to make certain they were safe from Holden. Now the man Hank suspected was a killer would be pulling into her brother's driveway any minute.

When Marcus arrived, the computer-generated image flashed in Carolyn's mind, and she couldn't stop herself from staring at him. Her feelings were filtered through the things she'd heard that morning from Hank and Mary.

John chatted with Marcus in the living room. Cornering her mother in the kitchen while she poured him a glass of wine, Rebecca asked, "How many cars does Marcus have? Wasn't he driving a Rolls Royce the other night?"

"A Bentley. They look similar." *Right,* she told herself, *just like people.* Marcus must not have had any meetings today as he wasn't dressed in his customary suit and tie. Instead, he was wearing a pair of black slacks and a black shirt with some kind of design on it. It reminded her of what he was wearing the day she'd first met him.

"He drove up in a Jag tonight," Rebecca said, excited. "He's really rich, isn't he?"

"I don't think so," her mother said, wiping her hands on a towel. "He just likes cars."

After Neil and the kids left, Marcus asked for a tour. Carolyn showed him the way to Neil's studio, located behind the pool.

"Do people really buy this stuff?" Marcus said. "It's boring. I like contemporary art. I wasn't aware anyone was still painting like this. What does he do, copy the old masters?"

Marcus was a computer expert. It wasn't a shock that he had no appreciation for classical art. He was probably a right-brain person. "Neil has a large following," Carolyn told him. "His paintings sell in the range of fifty thousand and up. Recently, they've been bringing in even higher prices. Walk around to the other side. You should see some paintings that may be more to your liking."

"Now we're talking," Marcus said, laughing. "Does he use live models? These girls are beautiful."

"Yes," she said, joining him. "The majority of them are college students. He pays them to sit here hours on end, bare to the bones. I think he lures them by complimenting them on their natural beauty, along with convincing them that working with him will beef up their résumé."

"I wouldn't mind getting into the art business. He's got a pretty good gig going here. Can you see me with a French hat, glass of wine, sitting on a stool, my paintbrush dangling in the air between my index finger and thumb, and a gorgeous girl waiting for me to recreate her beauty on canvas?"

"Don't be silly," Carolyn said flatly. "You'd look ridiculous. Seriously, have you ever tried painting?"

"No, but that doesn't matter. As long as I could surround myself with naked women, I could learn how to paint. Of course, between eating hand-fed grapes and having massages, my production would be limited. I'd have to raise my prices. It's all about supply and demand, baby."

Carolyn was put off by his crude remarks. She knew he was trying to be humorous, but he seemed so different. She could see another side of him and it frightened her. Then again, perhaps Hank's accusations were making her paranoid. "It's not as easy as you think," she said. "It took my brother a lifetime to learn how paint the human form. Look at the shadows in her face. You can almost see her personality. Neil's extremely talented."

"Sorry, I didn't notice. Haven't gotten past the body yet. If you ask me, she's the one with the talent."

Carolyn shook her head in dismay. "Let's talk about something other than art. I thought you had to work late tonight."

"How could I stay away from you?" Marcus said, coming over and embracing her. He held her tightly against his body, nuzzling her hair.

Carolyn's thoughts returned to the times they'd made love and how good it had felt to be with him. "The other night was great."

"Tonight will be even better. Do you think your brother would mind if we used his couch?"

"What? Right here? Have sex?" Carolyn backed away from him and locked her arms across her chest.

"Is there a problem with me wanting you?" Marcus said, walking over and plopping down on the fluffy cushions.

"Yes, there is. I don't make it a habit to have sex in my brother's house. What happens if they come home early and walk in on us? I won't expose my children to that. Would you want to find your mother thrashing around with a man?"

"I didn't have a mother," Marcus said, a dark look clouding his eyes. "It's not like Rebecca doesn't know about sex. When did you tell her about the birds and the bees—yesterday? Don't worry about it. Everything will be fine. Let's have some fun. It'll make you feel better." He went over and pulled her toward the sofa.

"I'm sorry," she said, breaking loose and moving to the other side of the room. "I'm not going to have sex here. We could go to your house."

Ignoring her, he picked up a white cotton sheet Neil used to drape over his subject's chair and spread it out on the sofa. His arrogance filled the room. "What's wrong with this? We should be fairly comfortable."

"You're taking an awful lot for granted," Carolyn exploded. "If you want a slut who will sleep with you whenever you get the urge, then maybe you should leave. It's early, so you have time to pick up some broad at a bar and have your way with her before the night is over."

Marcus sat down, leaning his head back and stretching his legs out in front of him. "You're overreacting, Carolyn. You just look so fabulous tonight I can't contain myself. Is that so bad?" He patted the cushion next to him. "Come over here and relax. We'll just talk, I promise."

She hesitated, then took a seat beside him. "I'm not a prude, you know. But my family is very important to me. I've already made enough mistakes. I can't afford to make any more."

"I hear you loud and clear. Why are you so tense? Did you have a bad day at the office?"

Carolyn looked down, not wanting to make eye contact. How could she desire this man when there was even a remote possibility that he was a murderer? *Time to go to work,* she decided. But she would have to be subtle. "It's scary to think that Holden is still outstanding. He's probably trying to figure out how to get the key back." She reached over and stroked his hand. "What you did was wonderful, Marcus. I don't know what would have happened if you hadn't shown up when you did. John could have bled to death." She looked away. "I can only imagine what Holden might have done to Rebecca. You were very brave."

"It was nothing," Marcus said, shifting so their legs were touching. "I did what any person would do under the circumstances. As far as Holden, I wouldn't worry about him. I'm sure they'll either catch him or he'll catch himself."

"What do you mean?"

"He's an ignorant, common criminal."

She didn't agree that Holden was ignorant, but maybe Marcus was right. She'd been naive eight years ago. Just because someone read a few books on philosophy didn't mean they were intelligent. "Maybe someone will put a bullet in his head."

"That'd do the trick," Marcus said, draping his arm over her shoulder.

She contemplated her next statement before speaking. "We should get away for a weekend now that John's recovered. You know, spend time together, just you and me."

"Sounds great. I'd have to check my schedule. So, we'd be kid free?"

"No, they'll be sleeping in the bed next to us," Carolyn told him, smiling. "Of course we'll be alone. What do you think about going to San Diego?" She watched closely as he rubbed his forehead. "We could stay in a place on the ocean." Silence was powerful. Carolyn had full control of it. If she spoke, she'd be giving him a way out.

"San Diego's fine, but I know a better place. It's much more romantic."

"Oh? Where?"

"Santa Barbara. The Bacara Resort overlooks the ocean and the Sand Piper golf course. The spa is sensational."

"I didn't know you liked to play golf," Carolyn said, feeling a sinking sensation.

"I used to. I don't anymore. It takes up too much time if you want to consistently shoot under par."

The hairs on the back of her neck prickled. The seemingly obvious connections to the murders of Lisa Sheppard and Tracy Anderson could be strictly coincidental. Nonetheless, they were frightening. He played golf and shied away from vacationing in San Diego. Made sense, if he was the murderer. The last place he would want to go would be San Diego, for fear someone might recognize him. "Santa Barbara sounds great," she told him, forcing a smile. "I'll be back in a minute. I need to freshen up.

"Don't leave me here too long," Marcus said, chuckling. "Patience isn't one of my finer virtues."

When she stepped into the bathroom, she pulled out the picture Mary had given her. Closing her eyes, she brought forth Marcus's face. Then she stared at the image in her hands. She sucked in a quick breath, startled at what she saw. Placing the picture back in her purse, she flushed the toilet, washed her hands, and returned to the studio. She would get the DNA sample another time. She knew she was stalling, but she didn't care.

Carolyn placed her hand on her head and grimaced. "I have a headache. The last few days have been hell. I don't want to be rude, but it's probably better if you go so I can get some rest. Tomorrow we can have dinner together. I promise we'll make it a full evening."

"I'm not sure I'll be able to see you tomorrow," Marcus said, pinching his lips together. "Fine. I need to go to Europe on business, anyway. If you don't want to see me anymore, I'll leave tomorrow."

"Go then," Carolyn said, pointing to the white door on the other side of the room. "I just told you I didn't feel well, and you're trying to manipulate me."

He closed the distance between them, grabbing her arm with the pointing finger and pushing it down. "Don't be like this, Carolyn. I've been looking forward to being with you all day. I understand about your kids. Why are we arguing? I know it's too late to go to my house in Santa Rosa. I have a solution that will make both of us happy. We could go to a hotel. There's a Ramada Inn not far from here. I'm sorry I acted like a jerk."

The stark reality of her situation struck home. If she ended it with

Marcus tonight, she'd never know the truth. More important, she might be letting a murderer slip through her fingers. She'd fought too hard over the years to put violent offenders behind bars. Hank had been right. The only way to know the truth was to get the sample. She couldn't simply walk over and pluck a hair out of his head or draw blood with her fingernail. She'd have to be in close contact with him. Also, she didn't know how he'd react. As she'd told him, Neil and the kids could come back to the house for some reason. "I'll take a couple of Advil. By the time we get to the hotel, my headache should be gone."

Marcus pulled her against his chest. "Great," he said, smiling. "I'll wait for you in the car."

In her job Carolyn had repeatedly placed herself at risk. In order to extract information, she would wear a short skirt and flirt with a vicious criminal. She did it for one reason—for the victims. And now, if she had to sleep with a killer, so be it.

Lisa Sheppard deserved justice.

Marcus's good looks and charisma may have seduced her, but his guilt or innocence could never be proven without scientific fact. *Just collect the sample, she told herself. Just do it, and get back to the people you love.*

She insisted they take separate cars. At first Marcus resisted, but later he gave in. She argued that if an emergency occurred, she didn't want to wait for someone else to drive her.

The hotel room was cold and dark. It had a lingering smell of cigarette smoke, mixed with a sickening room deodorizer that reminded her of a public restroom. Marcus went to the bathroom and deposited his gym bag on the counter next to the one-cup coffeemaker. Did he have a gun in there, Carolyn wondered, swallowing hard. Probably not, as there was no evidence the person who'd killed Tracy Anderson and Eleanor Beckworth had used a firearm. He could have a rope or cord to strangle her, though. Her eyes panned the room, looking for something she could use to defend herself with. Brad had written her a requisition for a new gun, but she'd just submitted it Monday.

Carolyn resisted the urge to leave. Without the sample, the police would have nothing more than they'd had that morning.

Marcus walked over and pushed her down on the bed. "I've got you all to myself finally," he said, climbing on top of her. His lower body pressed into hers, and she could feel his erection.

"Stop," Carolyn said, wiggling out from under him. His face registered surprise, then disappointment.

"I'm sticky and disgusting," she explained. "I need to take a shower."

When she sat up, Marcus wrestled her back down on the bed, saying, "You're fine." He unbuttoned her pants and shoved his hand inside. This was the perfect moment, she decided, his actions reminding her of what Carl Holden had done the night he'd tried to rape her. She dug the jagged nail into the soft flesh at the back of his arm.

"What the hell!" Marcus exclaimed, rolling off her. "I think a damn bug bit me." He pulled his left arm forward but wasn't able to see the spot where Carolyn had cut him.

"I'm going to jump in the shower," Carolyn said, scooping up her purse with her other hand as she raced into the bathroom before he could stop her.

She closed the door and locked it, then removed the nail clipper Mary had given her, seeing a small quantity of blood under what was left of her fingernail. She opened one of the plastic evidence bags first, then clipped the nail and let it fall into it. Once it was sealed and safely in her purse, she turned on the shower and began searching Marcus's gym bag. Inside she found a small hairbrush. Pulling a pair of tweezers out of a sealed paper package, she carefully fished out several strands of hair and placed it into the first bag, then did the same with the other. If the hairs didn't have roots, they would have to resort to mtDNA typing, but she wanted to have a backup in case something was wrong with the blood sample.

"Carolyn," Marcus said, pounding on the door, "you have a phone call."

She must have left her cell on the dresser with her car keys. "Is it one of the kids?" she said, surprised that he would answer her phone.

"No," he yelled, "it's Hank. He says it's important."

"Tell him to hold on." She couldn't walk out in her clothes, Carolyn thought, pulling her sweater over her head and yanking down her slacks. Removing her bra and panties, she tossed them on the floor and wrapped a towel around her naked body. Splashing some water on herself, she darted out of the room, snatching the phone from his hands.

"We found Holden," Hank said, his voice more strained than usual. "Are you with Marcus?"

"Right," Carolyn said, her eyes tracking him as he entered the bathroom and turned off the shower. "Thank God you caught him. Was there a problem? Did anyone get hurt?"

"You could say that," Hank answered. "Holden's dead. Looks like someone killed him and propped his body up against the fence at the Alessandro Lagoon. He had a piece of paper attached to his chest. I don't want to tell you what it said over the phone. Just get your butt down here."

Once Hank had disconnected, she rushed into the bathroom to get dressed. "Aren't you going to tell me what happened?" Marcus asked, following her.

"Someone killed Holden."

"What's the rush, then?" he said, tugging on the edge of her towel. "The guy's dead. Let the cops handle it. I already paid for the room."

Carolyn looked at him. "Holden tried to rape me and almost killed my kids. I want to dance on his grave, understand?"

"I'll go with you."

"No," she said, shoving him in the chest and turning quickly toward the bathroom. She slammed the door in his face. Hurrying into her clothes, she grabbed her purse containing the samples. When she opened the door, she said, "This is official police business, Marcus. It's confidential, kind of like your work. Rather than drive to Santa Rosa, why don't you spend the night here?"

"I'm going home," he said, frowning. "This night was a disaster. You weren't in the mood, anyway. See you around."

Carolyn ignored his theatrics and left. "Not in the mood" was an understatement. Marcus could pat himself on the back for being astute. *What a good turn of events,* she thought, wondering whom she had to thank for Holden's death. The first person that came to mind was Troy Anderson.

CHAPTER 36

Thursday, October 19—9:45 P.M.

Floodlights lit up the Alessandro Lagoon. Police cars and unmarked detective units lined the narrow roadway. The sound of traffic hummed on the 101 freeway less than twenty feet away from where Holden's body had been found.

The crime appeared to have occurred somewhere else, as there was no blood or physical evidence outside the parameters of the body. The killer had evidently transported the body and placed it in an upright, seated position near the opening in the fence, only a short distance from where Lisa Sheppard and Tracy Anderson had been buried.

Holden's face was bloated and bloody. A large abrasion was visible on his forehead. His head was tilted backward at an unnatural angle, and a pattern of distinctive marks was visible on his neck. His left leg was partially severed above the knee, and the only clothing on his body was a ripped shirt and a pair of white undershorts, both stained with dried blood.

Mary was dressed in one of her red murder shirts. "The cases have to be connected now," she told Hank. "This makes four homicides, if we don't buy the suicide ruling on Eleanor Beckworth. We can't afford to make any mistakes. Don't you think it's time to call in the FBI?"

"Hell no," Hank barked. "You know how I feel about those tight-assed pricks."

"If we have an interstate serial killer, the FBI could really help. They're experts in these kinds of crimes, and they have fifty times more manpower. The Behavioral Science Unit at Quantico could profile him for us. Not only that, they could knock some sense into those goofballs I've been dealing with in St. Louis and San Diego."

"Don't go throwing around the words 'serial killer,'" Hank told her. "The press will descend on us like a swarm of locusts. They just stopped printing articles about the 'Sweeper.' Frankly, I'm not sure that's what we've got right now."

Mary stared at the piece of paper safety-pinned to Holden's shirt. "This guy wants attention, don't you see? We could have been wrong about Holden all along. I'm not saying he didn't rape those women, just that he might not be our man in the Sheppard and Anderson homicides."

"He must have rolled him up in a plastic tarp or something," Hank said, preoccupied with trying to figure out how the crime went down. "If he dragged him from the car without some type of protective covering, there'd be blood in the street. What do you think, Charley?"

"I agree." Charley Young was kneeling near the corpse. He removed the note and safety pin, handing them to a CSI tech, who placed them in an evidence bag. "See the striae on the neck?" the pathologist said. "These stretch marks are caused by violent bending with subsequent massive fracture to the cervical vertebrae. This man was struck by a car traveling at a high rate of speed."

"His neck was broken, right?" Mary said. "I saw this once in a hit-and-run accident. Holden must have been facing the vehicle. Those abrasions on his forehead look like road rash from when he flew over the top of the car and hit the pavement. That's why his pants are gone. They must have connected with the front of the car and were pulled off."

"That about sums it up," Charley said, pushing himself to his feet. "From the state of decomposition, I estimate time of death between two to three weeks, maybe as long as a month. As Hank was saying, the killer had to move him in something fairly sturdy and waterproof. The leg injury would have caused massive bleeding. I doubt if there's much blood left in this body."

Hank saw Carolyn talking to one of the men guarding the scene. He waved, and the officer let her pass. "This should be a pleasant sight to behold," he said, "at least for some of us. Holden certainly didn't enjoy it, but I know you will."

Carolyn gazed intently at Holden's broken and rotting body. "I might be damned for saying this," she said, "but I hope he burns in hell. Who do you think killed him?"

"Where's your boyfriend?" Hank said, chomping on a toothpick.

"Don't tell me it was Matthew Sheppard," she said, glancing over at Mary. "Let's say Marcus is Sheppard, what possible reason would Sheppard have to kill Holden?"

"If Sheppard and Marcus are the same person," the detective said, "then this isn't the first time he tried to kill Holden. Not only that, the circumstances are similar. He tried to run over him with his Bentley, didn't he? Maybe Holden was his patsy. Ever think of that?"

Carolyn shot out, "What about Troy Anderson? He had every reason to want Holden dead. And the key. Maybe whoever the safety deposit key belonged to thought Holden ran off with his goods and decided to kill him."

"I have some good news," Mary interjected. "After you gave us Marcus's address, I was able to obtain basic information on him through the tax rolls. Then I ran him through all the databases. He's got a high-level security clearance with the government, no prior criminal history, and he owns the property in Santa Rosa. His corporation, MRW Software Solutions, also looks completely legit."

Carolyn breathed a sigh of relief. "I told you—"

Hank cut her off, "Just because he's legit doesn't mean anything. Guys who have everything get bored. So instead of playing the stock market, he starts killing people."

"Where's the note you said you found?"

Mary cleared her throat. "The actual note is already booked into evidence, Carolyn. It was typed, so there's no way to compare handwriting. Here's what it said, 'You picked the wrong woman this time.'"

"I assume *you're* the woman, Carolyn," Hank said, convinced she knew the answers to his questions and was holding out on him. "Is there something you want to tell us? We know you wanted Holden dead. Where were you last night?"

Carolyn flew off the handle. "Now you think I killed him? First Marcus, and now me! You're insane, Hank, totally whacked out of your skull." Her eyes darted to Mary. "Do you think I killed him, too?"

"No," Mary said. "You have a point about Troy Anderson. The note may have been an attempt to throw us off-track. We'll find Anderson and bring him in for questioning."

Charley waited a few moments before he interrupted. "If you kids are through fighting, one of my guys found something that might be interesting." They took a few steps, and he pointed at the sharp edges of the fence. "There's a small quantity of blood here, and I don't believe it came from the victim. The killer may have originally intended to bury the body in the lagoon, possibly in the same spot where we exhumed the Sheppard remains. Then he decided it was too much trouble, or, since he left a note, he wanted to make sure someone would find it. I've already checked Holden's body for puncture wounds on the upper torso and didn't see anything that matches the diameter of the fence wire. The sample looks good. I'll be able to tell you something in the morning. Who knows? This may be your man from San Diego."

Hank turned around and addressed Carolyn, "Were you able to get what we asked for from Marcus?"

"Yes," Carolyn said, removing the evidence bags from her purse.

"Good." Hank was wondering, *How could Carolyn get this involved with a stranger?* She knew too much about what was out there to use such poor judgment. "It's time to hunker down and solve these crimes instead of standing around and talking about them. Where's Belinda Connors?"

"She's already cleared," Charley advised, referring to the county's new chief forensic scientist. "Everything's pretty much done, Hank, and Belinda's swamped back at the lab."

"We need her to run DNA on the samples Carolyn has. It's vital that we get the results before our suspect skips town."

"Which suspect?" the pathologist said. "Carolyn, where did these samples come from? And what procedure did you use to collect them?"

Mary stepped in. "Its okay, Charley. I went over everything with Carolyn. I'll log this in right now, so we won't have a problem with chain of evidence. Carolyn's accustomed to collecting samples." She took the blood and the hair from Carolyn, labeled them with the case number and other particulars, and handed them to the pathologist. "There's a possibility—a slim possibility—that what she collected may contain the DNA of Matthew Sheppard. Just compare it to the DNA you found on the clothes from San Diego."

"Leon," Charley said to a young man standing beside him, "take these to the lab and have Sanders start running the DNA on them as well as the blood from the fence. I'll give him more particulars when I get in."

"Right on it," Leon said, heading toward one of the coroner's vans.

"Sanders works fast," Charley said, removing his gloves. "I'm going to give permission to transport the body now. Call me tomorrow morning for a status report."

Hank had a long night ahead of him. Charley had done his job, but Hank's was only beginning. Once again, he would see the sun come up over Alessandro Lagoon. He turned his collar up, rubbing his hands and blowing on them. The difference was it was October now and a lot cooler than it had been before.

Mary went to talk to one of the officers, leaving Hank standing alone next to Carolyn. He took a chance and draped his arm around her shoulder, hoping she wouldn't pull away. "Let's look on the bright side," he told her. "In a few hours, we should be closer to knowing the truth. If it turns out your guy isn't involved in this mess, I'll eat crow for the next year."

"Your odds may be better than you think," Carolyn said, turning and walking off.

When she got to the office Wednesday morning, Carolyn checked her voice mail, finding a message from Marcus. She wondered why she hadn't heard the call when it came in, and then noticed that the time coincided with her arrival at the lagoon. With all the noise, she must not have heard her phone ringing. Playing it back, she was stunned by what she heard.

"I'm sorry I didn't call you earlier," Marcus's voice said on the recoding. "We ran into another problem with that new program we're developing. I'm going to crash here at the office. I miss you, darling. I'll catch up to you in the morning."

Carolyn rechecked the time, then compared it to her watch to make certain there wasn't something wrong with the clock on the phone. If he'd called her earlier in the day, maybe around three or so, it might make sense. She was with Marcus when the call came in.

She placed her head in her hands. Did he have another girlfriend, and had dialed her number by mistake? Maybe when he'd told her that he had to work late, he'd been planning to be with this other woman. Then, at the last moment, he decided to see her instead. For security reasons, she had programmed her new cell phone to answer with the number instead of a greeting in her own voice. Even if Marcus wasn't a murderer, he was an asshole. She should have expected as much. All along, she'd thought he was too good to be true.

Mary called her. "We got the lab reports back," she said, panting as if she'd been running. "I'm sorry, Carolyn, but we should have listened to Hank. The blood you obtained from Marcus matches the samples from San Diego. It also matches the DNA from the blood found on the fence at the lagoon. Hank wants you to come down here right away."

Carolyn felt as if she'd been struck by a bolt of lightning. Thinking Marcus had another woman was bad enough. That he'd been linked to two homicides was horrifying. A scream tried to funnel its way up from the pit of her stomach. She refused to break down. "Hank's got what he wants," she said, still reeling from what she'd heard. "What does he need me for?"

"We picked up Marcus this morning at his business," the detective told her. "Hank wants you to be present during the interview. Because of your involvement, he thinks we may get more out of him if you're here."

"I don't want to be there," Carolyn cried. What would she tell her children? Her mother? Neil? For the sake of her family, she had to do everything in her power to remain on the sidelines. "Tell Hank I'm not coming. I got you what you needed. The rest is up to you."

"I know how you must feel," Mary told her. "But think of the victims, Carolyn. You're one of the best interrogators in the county. Not only that, you know this man well enough to trip him up. Merely seeing you will rattle him. His house of cards has finally collapsed. If we work this right, we might get a confession."

Carolyn didn't believe a man as devious as Marcus would confess, not unless someone attached electrodes to his scrotum. He'd spun such an interlocking web of lies, she doubted if they'd ever know the whole truth. The worst was that she was involved by virtue of her romantic entanglement, as well as the information she had provided him regarding the Anderson murder. She was an unknowing accomplice to a homicide. Marcus wouldn't have disposed of Lisa Sheppard's body in the lagoon if she hadn't told him where Holden had buried Tracy Anderson. She must have even told him about the glove. And there was Lisa's grandmother, Eleanor Beckworth. Holden's death had been such a relief, and now the worst thing she could ever imagine had happened. The kind of criminal she'd devoted her life to bringing to justice had ended up in her bed. She picked up a stack of file folders from her desk and hurled them at the wall, watching as the papers fluttered through the air.

"Carolyn," Mary said. "Are you all right?"

"No, I'm not all right," she said, pushing her chair back and listening to the file folders crunch and tear beneath her feet.

"Are you coming?"

"I'm leaving now," Carolyn said, knowing she had to see this through to the end.

Carolyn stood next to Mary, staring at Marcus through the one-way glass in Ventura PD's interrogation room. This wasn't the confident, well-dressed man she had known. Marcus's shoulders were slumped, his face etched with fear. He hadn't shaved, his hair was disheveled, and his white shirt was wrinkled. Mary had told her that they'd picked him up at five o'clock that morning, so she assumed he'd slept in his clothes.

She watched as Hank exited the room. When he walked through the door of the observation booth, he thanked Carolyn for coming. "Did he say he was with me last night?" she asked, her eyes shifting between the detective and the glass.

"No," Hank said. "He said he was at his office from eleven yesterday until we arrested him this morning. We spoke to some of his employees. Three programmers said they were with him until nine last evening. When they left, he was still working. They claim he's the only one who can figure certain things out. Makes sense since he owns the business."

"That's a lie," Carolyn said. "He told me he was going to work late. Then he called and said he would meet me at Neil's around seven. Everyone saw him . . . John, Rebecca, Neil. When I refused to have sex with him at my brother's place, he insisted we go to the Ramada Inn. That's where I got the blood and hair samples. I left him at the hotel when you called and said you'd found Holden's body." Seeing the expression on Hank's face, she added, "No, I didn't sleep with him. He went to the hotel with that intent, but all I wanted was to get his DNA. He said he was going home, but maybe he changed his mind and went to the office." She stopped to think. "Christ, why would he kill Holden? Isn't the premise that Holden was his fall guy on the Sheppard murder, that once I told Marcus where he'd buried Tracy Anderson's body, he dumped Lisa Sheppard's remains there so we would assume Holden killed her?"

"Marcus may have felt certain that we'd catch Holden," Mary told her, "and the case would be closed. Things didn't work out as he planned. You found Holden hiding out at his mother's house. Then he stirred everything up over the safety deposit key. Not many business-men would take off after an armed suspect, Carolyn. That's when I think Marcus decided he had to get rid of Holden."

"He could have paid Holden to bury Lisa Sheppard in the same place he buried Anderson," Hank added. "Maybe Marcus gave him some money up front and told him the rest was in a safety deposit box in his name. I saw Marcus at the bank yesterday. Guess where he'd been?"

"Safety deposit box?" Mary asked.

"Exactly," Hank said. "Holden became a liability, so Marcus killed him. Even the manner of death fits. He wasn't killed at close range. This wasn't a strangling, stabbing, or shooting. He just ran the guy over with his car. Marcus didn't have to worry about blood on his clothes, or any of those nasty little details that go hand and hand with murder. As to the safety deposit box, we'll have to get a court order."

"He still had to move the body," Carolyn reminded him, not as yet convinced. "If Marcus's credentials checked out, how could he be Matthew Sheppard? Sheppard had a wife and lived in San Diego. I saw the house where the Sheppards lived and it was a shack. Why would a successful man like Marcus want to live like that? And who was running his business while he was playing cowboy?"

"Are you implying he was set up?" Hank asked, pulling out a toothpick. "We have DNA, Carolyn. His attorney's going to be here within the hour. You slept with the guy, so we might as well get some mileage out if it."

"Don't tell me we're going to start this again," Carolyn said, her lips compressing.

"The way things have turned out," Hank said, "I'm thrilled that you slept with the bastard. Mary and I can't interrogate him outside the presence of his attorney. You, however, have a valid reason to talk to him. When you go in there, don't confront him with the things we've told you. Act confused and outraged. Pretend you're on his side. Whatever you do, don't mention the DNA."

"Shit," Carolyn said, arriving at a sudden understanding. "The DNA evidence is inadmissible. This whole case could fall apart." She turned to Mary. "If you knew it was going to be illegally obtained evidence, why did you make such a fuss about how I collected it?"

"Because I didn't want it contaminated," Mary explained. "We wanted the test to be valid."

"We filed a request for a search warrant this morning," Hank explained. "I used the photograph of Matthew Sheppard and a photo we shot when we brought Marcus in for questioning. Once the judge signs it, we'll search his home and collect new DNA samples. Then we can arrest him and start building our case." He tilted his head toward the interrogation room. "Marcus Wright, or whoever he is, may have killed an untold number of people. This man used you, Carolyn, which I know is a terrible thing. I'm sorry that you have to go through this, and Mary feels the same. There's not an investigator in the country, though, who wouldn't jump through hoops of fire to have a confidante with your skills that might be able to crack their subject and make certain a violent predator gets what he deserves."

Carolyn was standing as still as a statue, her chest rising and falling with emotion.

"There's a murderer in that room," Hank said, his voice laced with conviction. "He used you as a source of information. He had human remains he needed to dispose of, and he needed someone to take the fall for him. I don't know if he staged that accident when you first met, or if he just seized the opportunity. All I know is you can either run home and cry about this, or turn this into your finest hour."

CHAPTER 37

Carolyn sat in a chair across the table from Marcus. She was upset enough to look the part of the distraught lover. All that was history now—DNA didn't lie. "I don't understand why you're here," she said, forcing herself to relax and appear sympathetic. She had to use the tactics she used with violent offenders. Her task was far more difficult, as she'd never been personally involved with a killer. "How could they possibly think you killed these people?"

"I have no idea," Marcus said wearily.

"When you stopped by Neil's last night, I—"

"I wasn't with you last night," Marcus said, snapping to attention. "I was working at my office in Los Angeles."

"We were together," Carolyn said adamantly. "That's why I don't understand the message I got on my voice mail after I left you at the hotel."

"Did you sleep with this man?" he asked, his face turning unnaturally pale. "Please, don't tell me you had sex with him."

"Him?" Carolyn asked, genuinely confused now. Was he truly psychotic? If so, how could she have not noticed? "What are you talking about? Since I was with you, you should know if we had sex or not."

"Answer me!" Marcus demanded, slamming his fist down on the table. "Did you sleep with this man you thought was me?"

"No," she said. "You're talking crazy. If it wasn't you, who was it?"

"I should have told you," he said, lowering his voice. "I have a brother, an identical twin. I knew he was in the area because of the accident. You crashed into his car, not mine."

"You can't be serious," Carolyn said, placing a hand over her chest.

"When I met you at the Holiday Inn," Marcus continued, "it was primarily out of curiosity. You mentioned a murder when you called me, and I was frightened Thomas might have had something to do with it. Then after I spent time with you, I was certain you'd never see me again if I told you the truth. I wouldn't have lied to you about my ex-wife and children. I guess I should have walked away, but there was something between us . . . you felt it. I'd never experienced anything like that before with a woman, especially one I'd just met."

Carolyn's jaw dropped. "You're trying to tell me you're a twin, that the man I was with last night was your brother. Jesus Christ, Marcus, if you thought your brother was involved in a murder, why didn't you go to the police?"

"After we talked, I decided Thomas was just fooling around with me again. You were certain Holden was the killer, so I didn't think there was anything to be concerned about. I've always been shy. Thomas is an extrovert. He used to set me up with girls all the time when we were younger."

Carolyn stood and began pacing. She shot a wide-eyed glance toward the two-way mirror, wanting Hank and Mary to bail her out before she lost it. Marcus could be a sociopath. Since people like that believed their own lies, they could even pass lie detector tests.

She reclaimed her composure, determined not to let her emotions sabotage her. "Why would you even suspect your brother might be involved with a murder? Did he have a history of violence?"

"Thomas was a narcissist," Marcus explained. "He was used to getting what he wanted. Something terrible happened when we were kids. We grew up in Tarrytown, New York. Our house was on a cliff overlooking the Hudson River. I'm sure it was an accident, but all I know is what my father told me. He said Thomas pushed my six-month-old sister, Iris, off the cliff and killed her."

"How old was he?"

"Five," he said, moving his head from side to side. "Our mother felt responsible because she'd left Iris in the stroller alone. She moved out, and we never saw her again. I got over it somehow, but Thomas never did. He developed a rejection complex with women. If a girl broke up with him, he smeared her reputation at school." He stopped, taking a sip out of the glass of water on the table. "Later, when his fiancée dumped him, she said he'd threatened to kill her and boasted that he could get away with it."

"How?" Carolyn asked. "By blaming it on you?"

He ignored her question, his story spilling out as if he hadn't heard her. "Thomas was under a great deal of stress at the time. One of his patients had accused him of drugging her and forcing her to have sex with him. He settled out of court, but the board yanked his license to practice psychiatry."

"Your twin was a psychiatrist?" Carolyn said, his story beginning to have a ring of authenticity. Marcus looked straight at her without blinking. His statements seemed spontaneous, and there was no degree of hesitation or variations. He seemed anxious over his predicament, but fairly calm when talking about his brother. She had to remind herself that the person he was so confidently describing could be himself.

"Yes," Marcus said. "He swore he was innocent, but the attorneys for his malpractice insurance didn't want to take a chance they might lose if the case went to trial. Another woman had accused him of misconduct the year before. I'd already relocated to California when this was going on, so I heard most of this from Thomas. How much of it is true, I can't tell you. After that, he disappeared. I was afraid something had happened to him. To be honest, I was somewhat relieved when he surfaced in Ventura."

"Do you know where he is?"

"He was with you last night," Marcus said, his eyes sparking with anger. "There's no telling where he is now. I haven't talked to him in fourteen years. I have no idea where his permanent residence is, or if he even has one. He's like a shadow. I know he's around when he pulls stunts like he did with you. Trying to find him would have been a waste of time. Thomas hates me. The last time I talked to him, we fought over money."

At this point, Carolyn didn't know what to believe. Hank and Mary must think he was lying through his teeth. But they didn't know what she knew. The man she'd been with last night had been crude and aggressive, nothing at all like the person sitting at the table only a few feet away. Now that she thought about it, even the voice inflections were different, and Marcus's hair was slightly longer. When a person looked exactly the same, your mind tricked you and insignificant details frequently went unnoticed. "How does Thomas support himself? You say he's been banned from practicing psychiatry?"

"I don't know," he told her, staring down at the table. "Everything went to worms between us when our father died. He was a wealthy man, and my brother anticipated inheriting half of the estate. It didn't work out way, and Thomas was furious. I got the bulk of the estate, outside of the money my father earmarked for various charities. Dad had another reason for doing what he did, besides what happened with Iris, although I personally think he carried it to an extreme."

"How's that?" Carolyn asked.

"Thomas was smart, but he was also wild, always getting into trouble," Marcus told her. "While he was attending medical school, he spent weekends gambling in Atlantic City. We were amazed when he graduated and passed the boards. I was certain he'd found a way to cheat, or had someone else take the exams for him." He paused and took a breath. "That's not the point. He stole about twenty grand from my father. By the time my father realized what had happened, Thomas had lost all the money at the tables." He let out a long sigh. "Dad left my brother twenty thousand in his will, the same amount he'd stolen. I might have evened the score, but my father had drafted specific language that prevented me from doing so. If I gave a dime to Thomas, I forfeited my share of the estate. Needless to say, it was a bitter pill for my brother to swallow. Later, I heard he made a killing in the stock market investing in tech stocks." He smiled weakly. "Sometimes the right gamble pays off."

The door opened, and Hank escorted a distinguished-looking middle-aged man in a dark suit into the room. The man walked over and plunked his briefcase down on the table, then took a seat beside his client. "Fred Cusack, attorney at law," he said, glancing up Carolyn. "Are you a detective, too?"

"No," she said, introducing herself. "I'm a probation officer, but

I'm not here in an official capacity. Marcus and I have been seeing each other. Would you like me to leave now?"

"No," Marcus said, glancing over at Cusack. "She knows the truth. I want her to stay."

Mary burst into the room, a computer printout in her hand. She looked over at Hank and shook her head. The detective asked, "Do you have a twin brother, Mr. Wright?"

"You don't have to answer that," Cusack advised him.

"I have nothing to hide," Marcus told him. "Yes, I do. I assume you were eavesdropping on my conversation with Carolyn. That's a one-way glass, isn't it?"

Mary checked the paper in her hand, then asked, "Mr. Wright, were you born at St. Andrew's Hospital in Manhattan on August 11, 1960?"

"That's correct," Marcus said, relieved.

"According to the Bureau of Vital Statistics, you don't have a twin brother. The only birth recorded to a Mr. and Mrs. Thomas Wright was you. You're Marcus Raymond Wright, aren't you? That's the name on your driver's license."

"There has to be a mistake," Marcus said, leaping to his feet. "I swear I have a twin. I'm not making this up, for God's sake. Ask Carolyn, she met him. She was with him on at least two occasions when he passed himself off as me."

All eyes turned to Carolyn. "I'm not certain," she said, clasping and unclasping her sweaty hands. "I did notice different personality traits. One instance was last evening, and another the first day I met him." How could she keep Marcus from seeing how devastated she was? She wanted desperately to believe him, but if he had a twin brother, the birth would have been recorded. Even in the midst of the present chaos, she couldn't help but feel sorry for him. For the first time in her career, she felt compassion for a man who apparently was a murderer. There was such a sensitive, forthright look in his eyes. She cupped her hand over her mouth, her eyes darting to Mary, then to Hank. The two detectives were watching her composure disintegrate. "I have to get some air," she said, the small room closing in on her.

"Please," Marcus said. "Don't leave, Carolyn. You know these people. You understand how the system works. Outside of a few traffic tickets, I've never had any contact with the police."

Mary and Hank remained silent. Carolyn wasn't certain if they thought she was putting on an act or they were simply using her. If they were, what they were doing was cruel. Then again, Lisa Sheppard and her grandmother were dead. Their subject was responding to only one person. She slowly lowered herself into a chair. "Isn't there anyone who can substantiate your brother's existence?"

"I have no other siblings," Marcus said. "For all I know, my mother may be dead. Before he died, Dad told me she'd remarried, but since I had no desire to see her, he didn't tell me anything else. Either find my mother or call my brother's former fiancée. Her name is April Simons. Her father was the state senator of New York at one time. I read that he passed away recently, but you should be able to track down his daughter."

"Cut the bullshit," Hank said, placing his palms on the table and leaning close to Marcus's face. "Did you really think you could put something over on us? What's in that safety deposit box at the bank? And who were those goons who were protecting you?"

"I told you, my company is a subcontractor for the military," Marcus said, a line of perspiration appearing on his forehead. "We write software. As a precaution, the codes we're not actively working on are kept in the vault at the bank. We do this in case someone manages to hack into our system or burglarizes our office. During transport, my security team is always nearby. I can't divulge the details of my work. All I can tell you is it's a matter of national security that it's kept out of the wrong hands."

"Do you know why you're sitting here?" Hank said, his shoulder twitching with nervous energy. "It's not because of codes or whatever you do for a living. You killed Lisa Sheppard, then flew to St. Louis and murdered her grandmother, making it look like a suicide. You tried to make us believe Carl Holden was responsible. When he got out of hand, you ran him down with your car. Why don't you come clean? If you cooperate, we may be able to talk the DA into cutting a deal for life in prison. If not, you're looking at the death penalty."

"My client refuses to answer any more questions," Cusack said, standing and placing his hand on Marcus's shoulder. "Are you prepared to arrest him, detectives?"

Hank and Mary exchanged tense glances.

"That's what I thought," Cusack said, picking up his briefcase and turning to Marcus. "You're free to leave."

CHAPTER 38

Friday, October 20—4:35 P.M.

Kathleen had checked into Embassy Suites Hotel in Los Angeles on her way to San Diego, her new gun tucked inside her pink lizard tote. After four drinks in the bar, she'd gone upstairs to her room and promptly passed out. She was awakened by a call on her cell phone. Not recognizing the caller's number, she thought it might be a call for Dean. Lowering her voice to sound like him, she said, "Hello."

"Matthew, dude. This is Resare. I didn't think you had this number anymore. I take you off the map, then you hang me out to dry. We're not done. We've got to settle up on the last project I did for you."

Kathleen bolted upright. Turning on the light, she realized this might be the call she'd been waiting for. "Hi, this is Matthew Sheppard's accountant. I handle all his affairs when he's traveling. Can I help you?"

"I haven't heard of you before. Are you really his accountant? You write the checks, huh? I thought you were Matthew."

"Do you have an outstanding invoice with Mr. Sheppard?"

"Yeah," Resare said, "but I should probably talk to the man himself. It's kind of personal, know what I mean? We usually communicate electronically, but he hasn't been responding to my e-mails."

"I see," Kathleen said. "Mr. Sheppard has another number for his personal business. Do you have it?"

"What is it?"

"I'm not authorized to tell you. I can only confirm if you have the right number."

"Cloak and dagger," Resare said, laughing. "That's the man I love. Let me give it to you."

Kathleen grabbed a pen and jotted down the number on a hotel notepad. "Can you repeat that, please? You may have been calling the wrong number." Once she was certain she had it, she said, "I'm sorry, I was mistaken. The number you have is correct after all. All I can tell you is to keep calling, unless you want me to take care of it for you. For budgeting purposes, how much does he owe you?"

"Your man owes me fifty grand," he said, a sharper edge in his voice. "Tell him if he doesn't get in touch with me, he's going to run into some major problems. I've called that number and no one answers."

"He should be calling in any time now," Kathleen said. "Maybe it would be better if you give me your number. That way, I can make certain he calls you."

The man rattled off a number, then told her, "Giving the runaround to Resare is not a smart thing to do. I'll give Matthew twenty-four hours before I cut off his credit cards. In another twenty-four, I'll start selling off his assets."

Kathleen hung up and immediately dialed the number Resare had given her. When she heard Dean's voice, she slid off the side of the bed. "Hello, sweetheart, do you know who this is?"

"Kathleen!" he said. "How did you get this number?"

A fiery rage coursed through her veins. If she started screaming at him, though, he would hang up and she would have accomplished nothing. She was already on the floor, she decided, so she might as well grovel. It was the only way to get to Dean. "I'm surviving. It's been hard without you. I know I was wrong now, honey. I should have never accused you of having an affair. Isn't there some way we can save our marriage?"

She heard a long sigh on the other end of the line. "Anything is possible."

"I want to see you. Where are you?"

"Southern California," Dean said. "Are you at home?"

"No," Kathleen said. "I'm visiting a friend in LA. By the way, Resare called and said if you don't pay him fifty thousand dollars, he's going to start selling off your assets."

When several moments passed without a response, she knew he'd taken the bait. "Are you there, Dean?" she said. "This man sounded dangerous. He told me all these crazy things about you. How you lived in San Diego under the name of Matthew Sheppard. Why don't we meet somewhere so you can tell me all about it. It sounds fascinating."

"Ah, Resare," Dean said. "Maybe we should talk, Kathleen. I have a place in Santa Rosa, on the outskirts of Ventura. Call me when you get close, and I'll give you directions."

Kathleen reached into her bag and cradled the cold steel of the revolver. Was he luring her somewhere so he could finish what he'd started in Carmel? Her father had served in Vietnam. He'd taught her that surprise was the best way to defeat your enemy. "All you have to do is give me the address, darling. I used to be a Realtor before that horrible man broke into our house and tried to kill me. I can find anything."

Kathleen had no intention of waltzing up to the front door and confronting Dean. Both of them knew the cordial phone conversation was only a front for their true intentions. He wanted to finish what he'd started; she wanted him dead.

By the time she'd battled rush-hour traffic and reached Santa Rosa, it was after seven. She found the street, then a wooden mailbox with the address Dean had given her. About a mile down, she parked the car and got out, zipping up her jacket.

The sweet smell of oranges filled the air, and she could hear insects chirping as she walked into a dense orchard. Dean had picked an idyllic place to establish his new life. Kathleen wondered if her money had paid for it. Even if he hadn't tried to kill her, and she was certain he had, he deserved to die for stealing from her and leaving her alone after suffering such a horrendous ordeal.

Dean's perfect world was about to be shattered by a bullet.

Moving branches aside, Kathleen stumbled on the uneven ground and fell. Dusting herself off, she got back on her feet and continued toward the large, lighted house in the distance.

When she made it to the spot where the orchard stopped and the yard began, she was able to make out the silhouette of a person inside one of the windows. Recognizing Dean's profile, she reached into her pocket and pulled out the revolver. Then she put the gun back. Her chances of landing a long-distance fatal shot through a glass window were too small. There had to be a better way. Also, killing him without seeing his face when she pulled the trigger wouldn't be satisfying enough.

Retrieving her phone from the other pocket of her jacket, she hit Redial. "Dean, I'm outside your house."

"Did you ring the doorbell?" he asked. "I didn't hear anything. Is something wrong?"

"I don't feel comfortable," Kathleen responded in a soft voice. "Why don't we meet somewhere else?"

"It's okay, baby," Dean told her. "If you want, I can come outside and we can take a walk. It's a beautiful night. You came through the orchard, didn't you? When you drove by, did you see two men in a parked car?"

"Yes," she responded. "I thought they were neighbors or something."

"They're my private security," he told her. "I wouldn't hurt you with two witnesses around. They're armed, though, and they might panic if they see someone sneaking up to my house."

She didn't like the way things were shaping up. "Why don't you just call them and tell them you have a visitor?"

"You set the stage, Kathleen," Dean said. "My visitors don't normally come through the orchard. Why don't you go back to your car and drive to the front of the house?"

"I don't want to do that," she said. "Maybe those men are cops, and you told them I'm stalking you."

"If you want to see me, you'll have to come to the front like everyone else. Otherwise, go back where you came from."

Things had suddenly become more challenging. It was too late to give up. She'd lived through the injuries he'd brutally inflicted and was enduring excruciating pain. Now was the time to destroy him.

"Come on, Dean," Kathleen said. "You know I'm scared after what happened in Carmel. I drove all the way here to see you. I don't want your people to accidentally shoot me. I'm just so confused right now. I guess I could go to the police in San Diego and ask them what they know about Matthew Sheppard. This man, Resare, seemed more than willing to talk to me. Maybe—"

"I need to throw on some clothes," he said. "I'll meet you out back in ten minutes."

She had him.

Without saying good-bye, Kathleen ended the conversation. Had it been too easy to get him out of the house? What did he have planned? Shuffling back into the trees, she knew showing her face first would be suicide.

Kneeling down, she had a direct view of the back door. The porch light was on, but dim. As if Dean was blind to her intentions, he casually stepped out of the house. He looked to the right and then to the left. She saw his hands, relieved that he didn't appear to be holding anything. She moved out of the shadows.

He turned to see the barrel of the revolver pointing at his face. "Turn around and put your hands over your head," she said. When he turned, Kathleen saw something protruding out of the back waistband of his pants. "You fucking bastard," she snarled, snatching the gun and hurling it into the orchard. "You were going to kill me, weren't you?"

"Why are you here? Where's my brother?"

"What are you talking about?" Kathleen said, circling around to his side and pressing the revolver flush against his left temple. "We're going to take a walk. Move!"

"Please, don't do this," he pleaded, following her orders and cautiously moving forward. "I got a call from my twin brother, telling me he was waiting for me in the backyard. He set us up, don't you understand? My name is Marcus Wright. His real name is Thomas, but he's using another name. He must be the man you know as Matthew Sheppard."

Kathleen repositioned the gun into the small of his back. "That's a good one," she said. "I know you've been going under the name of Matthew Sheppard. You're going to die, Dean, and you're still trying to lie your way out of it. You smashed a bottle over my head, stabbed me, and left me for dead. I swore that you were going down if I survived. Well, I survived."

"You're making a terrible mistake."

Kathleen poked the gun hard into his spine. He yelped, bending forward. She jabbed him again, "Stand up and move, asshole! I'm going to teach you what real pain feels like."

They reached an opening amongst the trees. The farther away she got from his security officers, the better. A gunshot could echo through the hills and confuse them. They wouldn't know which direction the shot came from. She stopped and faced him. "Maybe a bullet will help you to cough up the truth," she told him, the fury of a thousand abused women rushing through her veins. Her hands were shaking. When he started stepping backwards she pulled the trigger.

The explosion was deafening.

He fell to the ground, rolling over and crying out in pain. Blood gushed out of a bullet wound in his left shoulder.

"Damn, I missed," Kathleen said, having aimed for his heart. It was okay. It was a shitty gun. She didn't want him to die that fast, anyway. First he had to suffer, but how could she make him suffer to the extent she had? Her eyes zeroed in on his crotch. He was grimacing in pain, pressing his hand over the bullet wound in an attempt to stop the bleeding. "Start talking, Dean. I've got five more bullets. Next time, I'm going to shoot your balls off."

"I'm not my brother," he said. "If you kill me, you'll go to prison for murder."

"My God, you're still lying," she said, incredulous. She heard the sound of a car engine in the distance. She'd waited so long for this moment, she hated to rush. She had no choice, the clock was ticking. "Since I haven't killed you yet, tell me why you did it. Was your life with me that terrible?"

"Please, believe me," he said. "I didn't do anything to you. I may be able to help you find the man who hurt you. Jesus, don't shoot me again."

A sliver of doubt passed through her mind. The man in front of her looked exactly like her husband. Could he possibly be telling the truth, and she'd shot the wrong man? Dean had never mentioned having a twin brother. She couldn't be taken in by another of his elaborate deceptions. If he was willing to go this far, no wonder she hadn't figured out he was stealing from her.

Kathleen heard something on the right. A second later, a gunshot whizzed past her. Jerking her head around, she instinctively fired, then dropped to the ground. She heard a person yell and knew she'd found her target. Glancing over her shoulder she saw that Dean had escaped. Then she heard the sound of running footsteps and picked herself up to give chase.

As soon as she saw the back of a man darting through the orange trees, Kathleen took aim and fired. She saw him go down face first and ran toward him.

Standing over him, she caught her breath, certain he was dead. Using her foot to roll him over onto his back, she stared into Dean's terrified eyes. "What the hell?" she said, wondering how he'd moved so fast. "You had another gun stashed out here, didn't you? You've just got to die, you rotten bastard!"

"Wait," he said, saliva dripping down his chin, "I can explain."

"I don't think so," Kathleen said, taking direct aim at his face and firing. She took a step away, then returned and kept pulling the trigger. She placed three shots in close proximity in the area of his heart. When she heard the gun clicking on empty, she took off toward the orchard.

CHAPTER 39

Under the circumstances, Carolyn felt it was better that John and Rebecca spend another night with her brother.

"You can't do this to me," Neil said, whispering to her in a corner at the back of his studio. Rebecca was dipping her brush into a palette of oils and carefully applying strokes on a canvas. John was in the main house watching television. "It's Friday night, damn it. They're your kids. I'm an artist, not a nanny. I told Olga to come over at ten. I haven't got laid in almost a month."

The old Neil was returning, Carolyn thought. She'd known his fascination with domesticity would be short-lived. Her eyes went to the sofa, thinking of the man who'd tried to coerce her into having sex there last night. Was it Marcus the murderer, or Thomas the seemingly nonexistent twin?

"Oh no," Rebecca said, dropping her brush to the side and pouting. "I've ruined it now. Neil . . ."

"I'll be there in a minute, sweetie-pie," Neil called out. "Whatever you did, we can fix it. It's art, remember? Sometimes when you make a mistake, it turns out even better."

"You want me to tell sweetie-pie that you don't want to be with her?" said Carolyn. "Don't you remember what I told you on the phone? The man I've been dating may be a murderer. Please, I promise I'll pick them up first thing in the morning."

"You win," Neil said, running his hands through his dark hair.

"Olga is beginning to bore me, anyway. The least she could do is learn how to speak English. This is America."

Carolyn smiled, leaning over and kissing him on the cheek. "I love you, guy."

On the drive home, she experienced a pang of guilt for not staying at Neil's with the children, but it was hard to feel guilty when Rebecca, at least, appeared to be having such a good time. Not only did she need time alone to gather her senses, she was concerned for John and Rebecca's safety. The police had a unit stationed in front of Neil's house on the chance that Marcus might decide to use the children as leverage to get out of town. The department was stretched so thin, they couldn't spare another officer. Carolyn had to look out for herself.

Once she reached the house, she stripped off her clothes, then flopped on her bed in her bra and panties, the new nine-millimeter she'd picked up that afternoon clutched in her hand. She was still in a state of shock over the day's events. She'd come to the realization that she would probably have to spend the rest of her life alone. Brad hadn't grown up yet, and the way she'd been butting heads with Hank lately, she certainly couldn't envision being with him.

She was better off remaining single.

When it came to relationships, nothing had ever worked out for her. Frank had chosen drugs over his wife and children. Paul, the physics professor she'd been involved with the previous year, had a penchant for having sex with his students. Even if Marcus somehow turned out to be innocent, she didn't know if she could continue seeing him. What good had come of it? From the day they'd met, it had been one disaster after another.

The phone rang. She almost didn't answer it, afraid it was Marcus and not knowing what to say to him. Then she saw "Ventura PD" on the Caller ID, and placed her gun on the nightstand.

"Marcus was telling the truth!" Mary said, shouting over the roar of her police unit. "I spoke to his former fiancée, April Simons, about fifteen minutes ago. She confirmed the Wrights were identical twins. Thomas has a scar on his right forearm. Do you remember seeing a scar on Marcus's arm?"

"No," Carolyn said, searching her memory. "But he usually wears long sleeves, and whenever we made love, it was always dark. So . . . at least what he told us about having a twin brother was true. We have to find him to see if he has a scar or not."

Some time passed before the detective answered. "I'm sorry Carolyn. I'm en route to Marcus's house now. There's been a shooting. We haven't confirmed the identity of the victim yet, but we had a surveillance unit watching the house. They say he's deceased."

"Is it Marcus?" Carolyn asked, tears pooling in her eyes.

"We don't know."

"If it happened at Marcus's house, it's got to be Marcus."

"Don't jump to conclusions," Mary told her. "The shooter was a woman. Brace yourself, Carolyn. She claims to be the victim's wife. She insists the man she killed was Dean Masters. First we have Matthew Sheppard, now we have Dean Masters. I ran the Masters name through the system, and a woman named Kathleen Masters was the victim of an attempted murder in Carmel about three months ago. I haven't been able to talk to the police agency who handed the investigation yet, but this isn't going to be resolved right away. The man was shot in the face."

"I'm leaving now," Carolyn said, carrying the portable phone to her closet to get dressed.

"Stay at home," the detective said. "You're too close to this thing."

"That's why I'm coming."

Tossing on a sweatshirt and a pair of jeans, Carolyn rushed out the front door of her house. As she was backing the county car out of the driveway, she saw a man covered with blood and dirt stagger across the lawn. Recognizing Marcus's face, she didn't know if she should stop and help him or go for her gun. For all she knew, it could be his brother. She followed her first instincts, jumping out and helping him to the porch. "Sit down here on the steps," she said, seeing his bloodstained shirt. "Have you been shot? I'll call an ambulance."

"Don't call anyone," the man said, his face pale and haggard. "The police are trying to arrest me. Thomas and this crazy woman are trying to kill me. You're the only one who believes me. That's why I came to you. I swear, I've never hurt anyone in my life. I never even got into a fight. Once I got into computers, I hardly ever went outside. That's why I hired a private security company."

"Where were they tonight?"

"They don't work on weekends."

Was this the man the police thought was dead? Carolyn reached over and grabbed his right arm, shoving up the sleeve.

Marcus jerked away.

"This is for your sake as well as mine," she told him. When she didn't see a scar, she checked his other arm to make certain. She placed a palm on her forehead, feeling as if her head were about to burst. The porch light was bright enough to see clearly. But did not having a scar clear him?

In her mind, absolutely.

A rush of emotion engulfed her. Hank had been wrong. She'd known all along that there were two distinct personalities. The man who'd been with her the night before at Neil's house had repulsed her. The person sitting in front of her was the man she'd been on the verge of falling in love with. She reached over and tenderly stroked his face, then opened his shirt to check the wound. "Stay here," she told him. "I'm going inside to call an ambulance. You need medical treatment. I promise they won't arrest you."

After dialing 911, Carolyn washed her hands and picked up some clean towels from the laundry room, then went back to wait with Marcus. "I'm sure you're in pain," she told him, "but it doesn't look that serious. The bullet appears to have nicked your shoulder." She probed the wound with her fingers. "It's not embedded, so I doubt if you'll need surgery." Sitting down next to him, she placed her arm around him, holding the towels over the wound. "I told the dispatcher that you fell off a ladder. That way, the police won't respond. We'll have some leeway to set things straight. I told them not to roll code."

Marcus gave her a dazed look. "What code? They can't access my files. They're all encrypted. Besides, I don't keep anything classified at my house."

"No sirens," Carolyn said, kicking a snail off the sidewalk. "That means they may take longer to get here. I thought leaving the police out of the picture would keep you from panicking. If you panic, your body's going to pump out more blood." She checked the fresh towel she'd just applied. "The bleeding has almost stopped."

Marcus's head slumped toward her. She cradled him like a child. She'd also wanted time to tell him what he had to be told. "Before you got here, I got a call from Mary Stevens. A man was shot and killed on your property. Was your brother there?"

He lifted his head. "Thomas called me. He said he wanted to talk. I was going to call the police. After today I decided I had to take care of my own problems. When I went out back to meet him, a woman I've never seen before accused me of trying to kill her. Then she shot me." He stopped and gulped air, his eyes wide with fear. "More gunshots came from the orchard. While the lady's head was turned, I managed to get away, but I saw Thomas."

"Maybe you shouldn't talk," Carolyn said, seeing how he was struggling.

"Please," he said, "I want you to know what happened. I heard four, maybe five more gunshots. I didn't look back, I just kept on running. I made it to the road and stole that car." He pointed to a red Escalade with one tire over the curb, parked facing the wrong side of the street. "The doors were unlocked, and the keys were in the ignition. God, are they going to charge me with stealing a car now?"

Carolyn smiled. "They aren't going to charge you with anything," she told him, her strength returning. "Not if I have anything to do with it. All we have to do now is get you patched up. Everything else will fall into place."

"Thomas is dead, isn't he?" His voice dropped to a low pitch. "Even though we haven't seen each other in years, I know he's gone. I can feel that something is missing. No matter what he did, he was my brother. I should have given him more money. What my father did wasn't fair. Maybe he wouldn't have done these things if—"

"I'm sure it was more than money," Carolyn said. "I've worked with criminals a long time. Trust me, people all over the world have disputes over money and they don't go on killing sprees."

"I'm sorry for the misery I've caused you," Marcus said. "I should have told you about Thomas from the beginning. I deceived you because I wanted you from the moment I saw you. Not many people understand me. I even thought if things worked out, you might be able to help me repair my relationship with my children. Can you ever forgive me?"

"I already have," she said, reaching over and clasping his clammy hand. "You saved both me and my son. Thomas must have killed Carl Holden to set you up to take the fall, just like he tried to pin Lisa Sheppard's death on Holden by burying her in the lagoon. You may not realize it, but you served as bait to bring him in. If you hadn't been brave enough to confront your brother tonight, we might never have caught him." Her thoughts turned to Tracy Anderson and Lisa Sheppard. Thomas might have been a failure as a psychiatrist, but he'd been an expert at murder. The label the papers gave him of "The Sweeper" was fitting. The lack of evidence left behind, the state of Lisa's skeletal remains, how he'd soaked up the information she'd given him about the Anderson murder and Carl Holden's release from prison, then used them to his advantage, all proved Thomas Wright possessed a diabolically cunning mind.

Lisa's grandmother in St. Louis either knew something incriminating, or she was simply a loose end. They would probably never know the truth about Eleanor Beckworth, but Carolyn felt certain Thomas had staged her murder to look as if she'd committed suicide.

She didn't want to tell Marcus, but she felt certain that his brother had risked contacting him in order to frame him for the murders—or in order to kill him.

Something else had caused Thomas to unravel. What had happened at Marcus's house was only seen in the stage of a killer's career that law enforcement officers referred to as the end game. Carolyn assumed it was his failure to kill the woman in Carmel that had caused the unraveling. How many other women had he brutalized?

"The main reason I work so hard is to obtain justice for the victims," Carolyn told him. "I'm usually good at my job. This time I was outsmarted." With a steely look, she added, "It won't happen again."

"You were deceived," Marcus said.

Suddenly realizing she was being insensitive by talking about herself when he had lost his brother, she said, "I'm sorry about Thomas."

"Don't be. I was prepared to do whatever needed to be done. If that woman hadn't shown up, I would have killed him myself."

"There's another factor that you should be aware of," Carolyn told him. "Thomas knew that by virtue of being an identical twin, he had an opportunity to commit any crime he wanted. Since your DNA is identical, there would have been no definitive proof as to which one of you committed these crimes. They couldn't send you both to prison. Juries today don't convict on circumstantial evidence. Your brother would have more than likely gone free."

The emergency vehicles arrived. Carolyn stood by as they placed Marcus on a stretcher and started an IV. "I'll see you at the hospital," she said, leaning down and kissing him. "It's over now. When you've had time to recover, I may take you up on that offer to take me to Paris."

"Now I have something to live for," Marcus told her, managing a weak smile.

"So do I," Carolyn said, "even if you don't take me to Paris."

Carolyn darted into the house and called Mary. "Did the man who was killed have a scar on his right arm?"

"Yeah," Mary said. "Kathleen Masters claims her husband had a scar in the same place. We're fairly certain the victim is Thomas Wright. Charley would like to do a fingerprint comparison, though. The problem is there were no prints left at any of the crime scenes, not even the house he lived at in Carmel." She stopped and barked orders at someone, then continued, "There's a clear pattern here, Carolyn. Looks like Wright marries women from various walks of life, then when he gets bored with them or something goes wrong, he kills them and finds a way to make it look like someone else was responsible. That way, the authorities clear the case and he's free to do it again. Mrs. Masters was lucky to survive. He really did a number on her."

"I know where we can get prints," Carolyn told her. "Thomas was at Neil's last night. He drank a glass of tea. I put it in the dishwasher."

"Your brother probably washed it already," the detective said.

"I doubt it," she told her, thinking that would have been true in the past. "I left John and Rebecca with him tonight, so he probably hasn't had time to do any cleaning. I'm sure Thomas touched other things as well. Send a CSI team over there. I'll call Neil and tell him they're coming."

"Your brother's house isn't a crime scene, Carolyn."

"You have three people who saw Marcus at his office yesterday until nine at night. Thomas showed up at Neil's around seven. Besides, I have another lead."

"Wait," Mary said, "Marcus was involved in this, Carolyn. Kathleen Masters said she shot him thinking he was her husband. We don't know what happened to him. He isn't here. At least he's not dead. Dead bodies don't walk away."

"He's on his way to the hospital. The bullet wound isn't life-threatening. I need to go. I'll call you later."

Carolyn booted up her laptop. Something had been bothering her since she'd reviewed the reports on the Helen Carter case, one of the reasons she'd decided to have John and Rebecca stay with Neil another night. Opening the Grace Findley file, she picked up the phone and punched in the number for the victim's parents. After telling Mr. Findley who she was and apologizing for waking him, she asked if she could stop by.

Grabbing her briefcase, she raced to her car and headed for the Findley house. They lived in Santa Paula, a city not far from Ventura. Something Carter had said to her now seemed important, especially in light of what she'd learned tonight. There was also the similarity in names. Criminals such as Thomas who used aliases were known to occasionally pick similar names. Part of Thomas's psychosis seemed to revolve around his desire to take over his brother's life. Marcus had not only inherited the family fortune, he had maintained their father's respect.

The mystery man Helen Carter had mentioned was named Martin.

Another factor was that the man had asked Grace Findley to marry him after only a short period of time. All the pieces were coming together. Thomas had married Lisa Sheppard, or at least had lived with her as husband and wife. He could have hired someone to pose as a minister, tricking her into believing they were legally married, even filled out phony paperwork and told her it was a marriage license. With money, a person could do anything. There was also Kathleen Masters from Carmel, the woman who claimed the man she'd killed was her husband. Not only had Thomas been a murderer, he appeared to have been a polygamist as well.

Pulling up in front of a modest stucco home, Carolyn parked and jogged to the front of the house. A haggard-looking man in his bath-robe answered. "What's this about?" he asked, leading her down the hall to the kitchen. "My wife's asleep. She's been on tranquillizers since Grace was killed, and I don't want to wake her."

Carolyn handed him the two pictures of Matthew Sheppard, the one where he wore a cowboy hat and was standing next to Lisa and the computer-enhanced image Mary had prepared. "Have you ever seen this man before, Mr. Findley?"

The man slipped on his reading glasses to study the images as he and Carolyn sat at the kitchen table. "Well, yes," he said. "This is Martin Knight. He asked my daughter to marry him. I mean, it wasn't official or anything. Her mother and I were thrilled. Martin was a swell fellow. He was brokenhearted when that awful woman killed our precious Grace. We haven't talked to him in a long time, though. He sold pharmaceuticals. When the papers implied that Grace had been involved with a lesbian, he . . ." He paused and dabbed at a tear in his left eye. "I'm sorry. All we wanted was for Grace to have a nor-mal life. Can you blame us for that? If she'd stayed with that woman, she would have never had children."

"The police will be in contact with you, Mr. Findley," Carolyn said, thinking the best thing for Grace would have been for her to do whatever made her happy. "Do you happen to have any pictures of Martin?"

"No, no," he said, walking her to the door. "We tried to take some snapshots of him and Grace one day. He said he was camera-shy. I wish we had. It would have been something nice to remember."

"Do you recall if he had a scar on his right arm?"

Mr. Findley adjusted the sash on his robe. "Now that you mention it, he did. He said he was robbed. The thug cut him with a knife."

All they needed now, Carolyn thought, cranking the engine on her car, was to compare the unidentified prints found in Grace Findley's apartment with those of Thomas Wright. Even the most meticulous killers were occasionally sloppy. What had Grace found out that caused him to kill her? There were dozens of questions that would never be answered. Grace Findley, Lisa Sheppard, and Eleanor Beckworth had taken them to their grave.

Carolyn rolled down the window. The air seemed fresher and

more fragrant, as if someone had finally thrown out a trash can full of rotting garbage. She felt revitalized, able to take on the world again. She didn't know where things would go with Marcus, but she could once again trust her judgment. More important, this had been the day she'd been waiting for. As soon as she checked on Marcus, she would drive to the jail and tell Helen Carter the news.

She had saved a life, maybe not a spectacular life, but nonetheless a life.

EPILOGUE

Monday, October 23—4:45 P.M.

Carolyn, Hank, Mary, two FBI agents, and two attorneys from the DA's office, and DA Kevin Thompson were assembled around the large table in the conference room at the police department.

Hank was interrogating a man named Freddy Olson, a thirty-two-year-old hacker who went by the name of Resare, Eraser spelled backwards. He was wanted in seven states, and had cut a deal with the Feds in exchange for information on other crimes. The FBI was extremely interested in finding out how he'd managed to crack their system. Olson would still go to prison for four years. If he'd refused to cooperate, his sentence would have been considerably longer.

The body found on Marcus's property was positively identified as Thomas Wright. Charley Young had located a scar on his right forearm, and the same DNA recovered from the crimes scenes. When his fingerprints came back as a match to those found in the apartment of Helen Carter's lover, Grace Findley, they knew Thomas Wright had been a serial killer.

Hank asked, "When did you first start doing business for Thomas Wright?"

"Maybe fourteen years ago," Olson said, smacking a wad of gum. "He wanted me to establish a variety of fictitious identities for him. He paid well. I had no complaints until recently when he tried to stiff me for fifty thou."

"Precisely what did you do for him on this particular occasion that was worth this kind of money?"

"I hacked into the Bureau of Vital Statistics and erased all records of his birth," Olsen answered, tipping his chair back on its hind legs. "That was a bitch, let me tell you. Not as difficult as DMV, though. New York has a pretty tight security system. It took me about three months to get into that baby."

"Do you know of any other names Dr. Wright used outside of Dean Masters and Matthew Sheppard?"

"Yeah," he said, slapping the chair back onto the floor. "Morris England, Tad Summerset, Burt Wasserman, Harold Carmichael. Shit, there's so many, even I don't remember them and I invented them."

"Do you know what addresses he lived at when he used these aliases?"

"Nah," Olsen told him. "I don't even know the states. He was an elusive guy, man. You saw all the different pictures, didn't you? He was good at making himself look like someone else. The cowboy gig was pretty funny. I mean, he used to be a shrink. He was a sophisticated dude. I was curious so I asked him about it. He said he liked to sample different lifestyles. I guess that's how he got his kicks."

"He got his kicks by murdering women," Mary said, standing and slamming her chair back to the table. "You're lucky the FBI needed information, Olson. If it'd been left to me, I would have made certain you were prosecuted to the full extent of the law."

She gestured for Carolyn, and the two women stepped out into the corridor.

"Think there are other victims?" Carolyn asked.

"I hope not," Mary said, resting her back against the wall. "Now the FBI will have to check on all these other identities. Didn't that prick in there know what kind of man he was dealing with? Law abiding citizens don't use dozens of different names. We also don't know if Wright used another hacker and there are even more identities to track down. This case is going to take years to resolve. To be honest, I don't think we'll ever know all the crimes Wright committed."

"Hank said you found something out about the key."

"Yeah," Mary said. "We discovered some of Holden's things inside a car he'd stolen. There was a bunch of letters his mother had written to him in prison. She kept asking him to forgive her for the way she'd treated him as a child, and told him she was saving money for him when he got out of prison. She must have been living like an animal inside that old house. The water and power had been turned off for years. When we got a court order to open the safety deposit box at Washington Mutual, we found close to twenty grand in cash. The money will be distributed to Holden's surviving victims and their families."

Carolyn said, "Ventura is out of it, right?"

"Yeah," Mary told her, "unless we come up with another body."

"What's going to happen to Kathleen Masters?"

"Self-defense," the detective said. "There's not a jury in the world that would put that poor woman in prison. She's been through enough pain to last a lifetime. Kevin Thomas is even dropping the gun charges. She's back in the hospital. They say she's suffering from exhaustion and some kind of infection. I spoke to the doctor last night. He said she'll be all right. She was supposed to be home recuperating, not running all over the place chasing after her bastard husband."

"Just out of curiosity," Carolyn said, thinking of her conversation with Veronica, "has any new evidence turned up in the Abernathy killing?"

"Nope," Mary said, somewhat disinterested. "From what I heard, it's already on the back burner. No witnesses, no fingerprints, no DNA. Whoever killed him seems to have gotten away with it."

"What about Lester McAllen?"

Mary brushed her hair behind one ear. "Well, that's the Sheriff's case, and as far as I know, there are no leads there, either. I do know one thing."

"What?" Carolyn said, hoping it had nothing to do with Tyler Bell.

"Guy butchers a little kid like that," the detective told her, "I doubt if anyone's busting their chops to find the person who killed him. Know what I mean?" She smiled. "Everything must be going right for you in the romance department. Turn around. Looks like you've got company."

Marcus was striding toward her, dressed in jeans and a pale blue sweater. Carolyn's face lit up and she rushed over to embrace him. Together, they walked back over to where Mary was standing. The

detective extended her hand. "No hard feelings, I hope," she said. "Guess you were the right Wright brother after all, no pun intended. How's your shoulder?"

"Almost well," Marcus said, glancing over at Carolyn. "I had a great nurse."

"You got that right," the detective told him. "Take good care of our lady. Treat her wrong and you'll have Hank back on your ass."

Marcus put his hand on his head. "Oh, no," he said, joking. "Trust me, Carolyn is in good hands. Seriously, though, I know Hank's a good man, but I don't think he cares much for competition."

"You don't have to worry about that anymore," Mary said. "You won't believe who he's all hot and heavy with . . . Martha Ferguson, of all people."

For a minute, Carolyn drew a blank. "You mean Dr. Martha Ferguson? I thought he couldn't stand her."

"Things change."

Marcus said, "Did you tell Mary about our trip, sweetheart?"

"We're going to Paris," Carolyn said, a sly smile on her face.

"Wow," the detective exclaimed. "I should be so lucky. When are you leaving?"

"Next weekend," she told her. "We're staying at the Paris Hotel in Las Vegas. Who wants to fly all the way to Europe? You spend half your vacation just getting there and back. I just got back from a leave of absence and Marcus has a business to run, so this fits our schedule."

"Are you guys eloping or something?"

Carolyn laughed. "Not exactly," she said, locking eyes with Marcus. "But we're going to have two days to ourselves without kids."

"Humph," Mary said, arching an eyebrow. "Why is it I don't need to ask what you're going to be doing? Now that's the kind of vacation I need. You wouldn't happen to know any available men, would you, Marcus? Black, yellow, brown, I'll take whatever I can get as long as they're decent."

"Dozens," he said. "I'll start asking around and let you know."

Carolyn linked arms with Marcus and they took off down the corridor. Before they disappeared around the corner, she glanced back at Mary and waved.